ABOVE THE TRUTHS

COMPLICATED TRUTHS DUET

CHATHAM HILLS
BOOK 2

SARA TALLARY

ABOVE THE TRUTHS

complicated truths duet

SARA TALLARY

AUTHOR'S NOTE

Above the Truths is Book Two in the Complicated Truths Duet and Chatham Hills series/world.

Above the Truths is a full-length new adult, college romance with hints of underground fighting, binge-worthy family betrayals + secrets, and slow burn angst. It is the **second and FINAL book in the Complicated Truths Duet** and finishes with a HEA. <u>You *must* read the first book, Beneath the Lies, first to understand Colson & Violet's full story.</u> Recommended for 18+.

TW: *Death/grief, drug use, sexually explicit scenes, anxiety/panic attacks, strong language, violence.*

Enjoy your visit back to Chatham Hills!
  Xoxo, Sara

PLAYLIST

"Dangerous State of Mind" – Chri$tian Gate$
"Iris" – MOD SUN
"Empty" – Letdown.
"Bones" – MOD SUN
"TELL ME ABOUT TOMORROW" – jxdn
"Salt" – Sueco
"If Only" – Elle Mitchell
"Dear Agony" – Breaking Benjamin
"Death In My Pocket" – mgk
"I Found" – Amber Run
"@ my worst" – blackbear
"Shelter" – MOD SUN, Avril Lavigne
"it is what it is" – Abe Parker
"Waste Love" – mgk ft. Madison Love
"Holding On and Letting Go" – Ross Copperman

You can listen to the playlist here:
spoti.fi/3A3ZuvP

To Colson & Violet,

Thank you for reminding me that it's okay to be flawed. That love hurts but also heals. That we aren't a product of where we came from, but of who we choose to be in each and every moment. And that our weakest moments are just that - seconds of time where we feel stuck but don't need to stay.

ONE

VIOLET

SHE DIDN'T MAKE IT.

My pulse pounds wildly, and I know, without a doubt, it's nothing compared to the sledgehammer pulverizing Colson's heart. I'm squished between him and Sebastian in the back of a sleek SUV that the valet fetched for us when we sprinted out of the fundraiser with his aunt and uncle.

I want to lean into him and offer the reminder that I'm here, but his gaze remains fixed on the scenery on the other side of the window. A blur of trees and buildings and the nudge of life whenever we pass someone walking by.

My heart leaps into the back of my throat as I push my worries aside and reach out to rest my hand on his leg. I've never lost someone in my life. As much as I want to be here for him, I'm worried that I'll mess it up, that I won't know what to say to make this just a little bit easier.

A breath passes before his gorgeous blue eyes turn to me. It's when he speaks that I realize the devastation in his gaze doesn't hold a candle to the destruction evident in his voice.

"She's been on the brink of overdosing before and has

always made it back. You saw how she looked on Thanksgiving. She's fine." He declares it more for himself than me. It's clear he's turning to denial for comfort, but I hear the doubt underneath it. Even more so when he murmurs, "She has to be."

She looked as though life was ready to float out of her body and become one with the breeze on the other side of the living room wall that night. I remember how it twisted my insides up, how it made me worry for her well-being enough to momentarily question Colson, only to learn that he was right. She *was* fine.

But that was different.

His uncle wasn't there saying how she didn't make it.

I don't want to remind him of that, but I also know it's crucial that he doesn't take this lightly. His mom is gone, and he doesn't believe it's true. Getting stuck in a vicious turn-around of denial will only make it worse.

I swallow and my heart drops back down into my chest cavity. "Colson, I—"

"She could still be okay," he says in one solid breath. I don't miss the way his voice wavers at the end of his sentence as he tries to convince us that his mom is still a living, breathing human.

"Right?" Colson's one-worded question is a whisper on his lips and draws me from my thoughts. It reaches out into the air between us and tries to latch on to the one thing that's keeping us afloat: hope.

And because I don't know how to navigate this without crushing him all over again, I ignore the horrible feeling inside of me and offer a tiny nod before repeating his words back to him. "She could still be okay."

His fingers twine between mine, tightening until there's

no space between our palms. He needs someone, and he wants that someone to be me. Him leaning on me is everything, but I can't ignore the knot in my stomach that accompanies it. The one that confirms I don't know what I'm doing. The one that tells me Colson is only delaying the inevitable pain that lies ahead.

He looks back out the window as we merge onto the 401 to cross the Sycamore Memorial Bridge. Sebastian clears his throat on the other side of me, and I reach my other hand out to him, resting my open palm on his knee. He doesn't think twice before wrapping one hand around it and holding it in his lap.

I meet his gaze, desperate for the usual joy in the depths of his eyes. Sebastian, who's always in a likable mood with a smile tipping the corner of his lips upward, has apprehension written in the perimeters of his hazel irises. So much that if I were standing, it'd make me waver. Like standing in a moving car that suddenly brakes.

His focus flicks to Colson before it's back on me. Nausea takes over my stomach as I lean my head back onto the headrest.

The denial fueling Colson's hope will vanish when we get to the hospital. Everything he has ever known will become a series of questions he'll overanalyze. Answers to things he was never prepared to hear will be voiced. And there's this grand possibility that I'll have no idea how to help him out of the grief that will indefinitely consume his soul and try to darken every light corner he's ever known.

THE SUV ROLLS up to the emergency entrance at Harrison General Hospital. Sebastian thanks the driver and flings the door open. His large body blocks our view of the outside world when he steps out. I take it as an opportunity to scoot back and shift in Colson's direction.

I run my palm up his cheek, stretching my thumb to smooth the indent between his eyebrows. "I know you want to get in there," I tell him, swallowing down the sadness that threatens to come up. "But promise me that you'll remember that you can lean on my shoulder whenever you need it."

His blue eyes flit to the open door. He wants out of this car as much as I wish I could turn back time and create a second chance for his mom.

I wrap my hand around the back of his neck and pull his face closer until our foreheads are one. He pulls back slightly, flinching at our close proximity, antsy to flee. Like a caged animal being struck by a current of electricity, he can't get away fast enough.

Fear grips my chest and bubbles inside of me. Fear for so many reasons it's hard to think straight. Over him breaking down the second we get in there. Over all these feelings zipping through my body. How one palm pressed against his skin exaggerates every single one of them. Over him retreating and turning into the version of himself who tried pushing me away Thanksgiving night.

"Please, Colson." My eyes fall shut as his warm breath fans out between our faces. "All I'm asking is that whatever we're about to walk into, you don't shut me out."

His hand moves to my side, sliding up the fabric of my dress before moving back down to settle at my waist. He presses a gentle kiss to my mouth, and I hang on for dear life, dragging it out for one more measly second that he cuts in half.

The truth is…I'm worried for him, but I'm worried for me, too. I didn't expect Colson to come into my life the way he did. I didn't plan to lean on him as my confidant. Nor was I looking for someone new so soon after ending my relationship with Webber.

Colson fell into my lap, and the connection we share is unlike anything I've ever had with anyone else. It's everything I never knew I needed and more. The thought of him about to walk into a scenario that might bring him to his knees has me terrified over what our future together might look like.

I feel guilty for even thinking about us and our relationship at a moment like this.

"I know you are," he breathes out after pulling away from my mouth. His words barely soothe the ache that's taken over my body.

"Do you?" I murmur as trepidation laces in those two simple words. "Because I'm worried you might forget."

He blows out a heavy breath, and I back away. His expression softens but does nothing to calm me. His tongue darts out and glides over his bottom lip. "I could never forget about you, Vi."

I run a hand over his suit jacket and nod. "We should get in there then."

"Yeah, we should."

I twist, scooting over to where Sebastian has his hand held out for me so I don't trip over my dress. He helps me out of the vehicle, and I realize I've never been more grateful for him in my life than now. For being here. For not batting an eye back at the fundraiser but rather gracefully getting to his feet with that look in his eye that said he'd do anything for those he loves.

The reassuring squeeze he gives my hand before he lets

go tells me he's there for me, too. I offer him a small smile and walk the few steps to the side so I'm not blocking Colson in. Sebastian pats his shoulder and tightens his hold for a breath before slamming the SUV door shut.

Bess and Thad lead us into the emergency department, where they ask the check-in nurse for details about Janie Moore. Colson falls in step beside his aunt and listens intently, his shoulders pushed back and tense.

Bright fluorescent lighting shines down on us and instantly creates a soreness that settles in behind my eyes. The bulbs are almost blinding with the way they cast light over us. The distinct hospital smell that everyone knows but can't seem to describe fills the air, making it worse. My stomach tightens when the nurse points to the hall beside her desk and asks we wait in one of the family rooms.

"I'll page her doctor, and he'll be in to fill you in on the details," she says, devoid of the overwhelming emotion that consumes us. Then again, she does this on a daily basis, and because I can't fathom how hard that must be, I give her a pass.

Thad nods and expresses his thanks as he guides his wife in the direction of the hall. Poor Bess. She looks like she saw a ghost. The complete opposite of the lively woman I met at the fundraiser. She's drawn back, her eyes downcast, as her husband leads the way.

Colson walks with them without glancing back to see if Sebastian and I are following. I try not to take it to heart. This moment isn't about me, and I can accept that.

The thought of sitting with them while we wait for the doctor to come in and tell us what happened makes my stomach heave with sadness and dread. I want to be back there with them, but I'm not sure I should be. I'm not a Moore or a Rodriguez. What's the purpose of me sitting in there when I've never had a conversation with Janie? Or when it seems like Colson might not need me at all?

I was Colson's date for the fundraiser, and we might be together, but suddenly, this seems like a situation he and his family should handle together. Alone. Without outsiders. Without a girlfriend who's on the verge of her own break-down over a reason entirely separate from the one they're facing.

I reach out for Sebastian's forearm. He seems to be the only one who isn't falling apart at the seams in some way or another. Well, him and his dad, but Thad's too devoted to Bess to care about himself.

"Sebastian, wait." I glance at his family who are a good fifteen feet ahead of us.

His hand comes up to my elbow when he stops. Concern washes over his face. "What is it, Violet?"

I shake my head—back and forth, back and forth—like a bobble head. "I don't…I don't think I should go back there."

"Don't be ridiculous," he chides.

My face drops, my gaze settling on his ultra-shiny Armani dress shoes. "I'm serious."

He steps into my space and tilts my head up so I'm looking at him. The sorrow that came over me back in the car magnifies, and my eyes fill with tears. I hate that I'm not being stronger for Colson. That this all is starting to feel like a lot. That my heart is *breaking* for him and me at the same time.

His eyes dart between mine. "You've been there for him more than she *ever* fucking has. You *belong* in that room with him for that reason alone."

"He thinks she's still alive, Sebastian. He doesn't know how much his world is about to flip upside down."

"He's going to need you there when it does."

"What if he doesn't want that? What if I don't know how to be there? Jesus, I've never lost anyone before. How am I supposed to help him through something I've never experienced?"

"You don't need to have lost someone to love a person and take care of them. There's no one else he wants more than you when vulnerability has him by the balls. Now, we're going back there, both of us. When that doctor comes in and tells us whatever the fuck he has to say, we'll listen, and in the moments when Colson falls and can't get back up, you'll take one shoulder and I'll take the other. Together, we'll hoist his ass back to his feet."

He has a point.

I blow out a big breath.

I *can* do this.

My ability to be there for Colson has nothing to do with what I've survived in the past but everything to do with how much I care about him now.

"Okay, yeah," I nod in agreement despite my stomach being queasy with uncertainty. "You're right. I need to pull myself together. I'm sorry."

"Don't apologize for being empathetic. It just proves how good you are for him." He holds a hand out for me to take. "Whenever you're ready."

Moments after we settle into seats in the family room, a man stands at the threshold and taps his knuckle on the solid wooden door frame. A white doctor's coat hangs off his shoulders, but he swings it back and clamps his palms on his waist. "Is this the Moore family?"

Colson lifts his gaze from the floor.

Bess immediately looks at him. "Yes," she confirms through swiping a tear off her face. "We're here for Janie."

He softly clicks the door shut behind him before

motioning for Bess to sit again. He takes one of the chairs across from us and introduces himself. "I'm Dr. Elsher. I work here in the emergency department at Harrison General Hospital." He rests his elbows on the arm of the chair and clasps his hands together. The early stages of fine lines trace his light green eyes, and aside from his thinning hair, he looks like a man who deeply cares about his patients.

I scoot to the edge of my seat. I'm not the only one. Colson rests most of his weight on his legs, his hands fisted together like the doctors. Bess sits forward, Thad's hand a permanent fixture running circles over her back. It's so painfully silent as we wait for the doctor's next words that all of our heartbeats become one, racing toward the news he's about to give.

"I assume you were aware that Janie was an inmate at Harrison Heights County Jail." His eyes play a round of Frogger, jumping between the five of us. "She was found unconscious on a work assignment by the guards on shift. She was unresponsive with a shallow heartbeat. Medical personnel worked on her until an ambulance transport brought her here. The guards found an empty syringe next to her body."

Bess blinks multiple times. "A syringe?"

"Afraid so."

"Do they know what was inside of it or how she got it?"

"I don't have an answer to your second question. Cases like these usually go under investigation within the corrections system, but given Ms. Moore's history with drug abuse and some of the symptoms she presented with, we treated appropriately as we would with anyone who is having obvious signs of an overdose."

Bess brings her hand to her throat, and her eyes overflow with more tears. "Yes, that's, uh," she clears her throat, "that's what they told me on the phone when they called."

The doctor gives a sympathetic nod. "We also took blood for a drug panel."

Colson bypasses the doctor's words. "How's she doing now? Can we see her?"

The doctor's eyes linger on him for a moment before he asks, "You're her son, I take it?" Colson gives a terse dip of his chin. "We attempted to treat your mom with naloxone, a drug that often reverses the side effects of an opioid overdose. I'm sorrow-stricken to say that its effects were temporary. It's likely that years of drug use had impacted her system far too greatly. Her heart gave out shortly after we anticipated we were in the clear. There was nothing more we could do."

The weight of Dr. Elsher's words steals the air from the room, including the breath in our lungs. Like one of those food vacuum sealers, the hall sucks every bit of oxygen out, leaving us with nothing.

A high-pitched sob leaves Bess's mouth, and she buries her head into Thad's shoulder. I have a hard time getting a deep enough breath in myself. The more I try, the sharper it stings. A figurative needle pinches into my lung cavity, and *oh my God*, if I'm feeling this way, what is going through Colson's head?

His shoulders harden, and the muscles in his forearms turn to stone. He swallows, the ripple at his throat the only indication that he's connecting the doctor's admission with Thad's words from earlier.

Sebastian's large palm moves to the back of Colson's neck, and he kneads the muscles. It's his way of saying he's sorry. That his condolences are with him.

The corners of my eyes prick with the familiar sting of tears. When one slips past my eyelashes, I mentally log the sensation before it stops at my jawline.

Colson deserves more than losing his mom to her addiction on the same night we were celebrating people who have worked so hard to overcome theirs. She could've been among the many who stood on the stage at Willaker Hall and told their stories. Yet she was locked up in county jail and succumbed to the devil's whispered pleas for attention.

"I'll leave you to process the weight of the news. Please know that someone will have to claim the body, or the county will proceed with burial proceedings since she was incarcerated at the time of the overdose. When you're ready, let the triage nurse know, and someone will take you back." He rubs his hands over the material of his blue scrubs and stands. "My deepest condolences for your loss."

Sebastian is the first to his feet when the doctor leaves. He paces the length of the small space and runs his hands down over his face. I scoot closer to Colson, holding onto his bicep as I bring my hand to his lap.

"I'm so sorry," I tell him in a choked whisper.

He flinches, and his jaw tenses. As if he hates hearing those words come out of my mouth. For the life of me, I can't get a read on him. I can't tell if he's ready to storm out of the room, tear down the walls, or scream to the heavens above.

He hangs his head between his shoulders, and when I entwine my fingers between his, he fails to grip mine back. It's as if he's lifeless, unable to move under the realness of his new life. One where his mom is gone, and there's nothing he can do to bring her back.

"You don't deserve this," I croak. "She didn't, either."

He shakes my hand from his before standing along with Sebastian. The fact that he doesn't acknowledge my words or sympathy is a punch to the gut, but I push it away, knowing that today is about him more than me. It's not lost on me how it's the second time I'm reminding myself of this. He just found out his mom is dead. He's allowed to feel what he needs in order to get through this.

I sit back in my chair. I'm unsure of what to do with my hands, so I grip the armrests, hoping like hell it'll keep the room from spinning. It does about as much as holding onto the bar of a roller coaster cart.

Colson makes it halfway to the door before Sebastian palms his chest and stops him. "Where are you going? You shouldn't be alone right now."

Colson rips his cousin's hand away at the same moment Bess and Thad look in their direction. She wipes away the grief dripping down her cheeks as Colson lashes out. "Get the hell out of my way."

"If you're leaving, then I'm going with you," Sebastian tells him.

"No, you're not."

Sebastian challenges him by raising his brow and lowering his voice. "You're processing a lot, and it's going to sucker punch you in the side of the head when you least expect it. Let someone be there for when that happens."

"I don't need anybody," Colson claims in that stubborn voice of his.

"Colson, I think Sebastian is right," Bess offers quietly. "It's imperative we lean on each other right now."

The image of him punching through drywall suddenly hits me. She may be right, but the best thing for her nephew is for him to be alone, for him to have space. I see it in the way he's carrying himself that if he doesn't get distance soon, every-thing around him will suffer the consequences of his outburst.

"Let him go," I murmur, though it pains me to say it.

My eyes move to Colson's back and the way his suit jacket clings to his broad shoulders. I swear I see the faintest amount of tension lift from them. His head moves the slightest bit to the side and dips down. Like he's grateful for my input. More than he was a minute ago, anyway.

I don't want to watch him walk away but force the words out despite the turmoil swirling in circles inside of me. "Give him space to breathe and think."

Sebastian reluctantly steps out of Colson's way. He's gone a second later.

TWO

COLSON

I BREAK out of the family room and hook a left. When I initially got up from that cushy, sorrow-ridden chair, my plan was to stop by the front desk so the nurse could call whoever the fuck was available to guide me back to Mom's room.

I don't know if she has one of those, if her body is hidden behind a flimsy curtain on hooks, or if they've already taken her down to the morgue or somewhere else entirely.

I've been trying not to think about it ever since Dr. Elsher dropped the bomb a few minutes ago, but it's difficult when I keep repeating the same seven words in my head.

There was nothing more we could do.

On the drive over, I thought it'd only be a matter of time until I'd see Mom's face, alive and well.

People overdose all the time and come back to life. Get a second chance. Some people get more than two. Down to the marrow of my bones, I hoped the doctors knew what they were doing enough to help her through whatever shitstorm she got herself in.

But her heart wasn't in it. Dr. Elsher said so himself.

After years of continuous drug use, her heart was shot and

wanted out. The opioid antagonist medication that has existed for years wasn't enough to bring it—*her*—back.

I swallow the scratchiness at the back of my throat. It's as dry as sand and just as rough. I find the men's bathroom down the hall and push into it. I slam the door and twist the lock, not giving a damn if anyone needs to take a piss. I need a fucking minute. Time to wrap my head around what's happening. A moment to acknowledge what will come next.

My dress shoes squeak against the tile floors, and I duck to check for feet in the two stalls. When I find both empty, I let out a staggering breath and press my fingers to my eyes before my fists fall to the sink. My head reels, and the doctor's words chisel into my memory, never to be forgotten. I brace the walls of my mind, trying like hell to fight against them. Against my heart breaking more than it already has.

No one knows the hell I've been through with Mom. They don't know what I've endured, what I've given up for her. How I've tried so goddamn hard to take care of her and get people off her back so she could get back to a better place.

"It isn't supposed to be like this." I glance up at the ceiling as if there aren't endless floors of patients above me. I speak to Mom, wherever she is now. "You were supposed to get clean in there. What the fuck happened?"

I want to know how she got that syringe.

My head spins trying to figure it out, but it's hard when I'm being torn in multiple directions. I try to recount everything I know as if it'll help me get through the days ahead.

Aunt Bess said she got picked up for possession and intent to deliver. While I was paying off Finn, she was making deals with someone. So, who, then? Did she run to Clyde behind Finn's back? Was it that guy that Violet said she saw at the house on Thanksgiving? Or was it someone none of us knows?

I know things are murky in the corrections system, but there's no way in hell she should've gotten ahold of what she did. The guards should've kept a closer eye on her, knowing that she was a flight risk when it came to drugs.

Why didn't they give more of a damn?

The only explanation I come up with is that someone snuck shit in, and that's how she got it. That thought doesn't sit well. Unless she was getting her hands on the stuff the minute she got there, she'd have gone through withdrawal symptoms by now. She would have been on the other side of it already.

And yet, she wasn't.

I press back into my foot and stretch my leg out. I tap my shoe off the floor before slamming my fist down on the acrylic countertop surrounding the sink.

Pain icicles its way through my hand. I barely feel it. "Fuck!"

I twist around and look down at my hands. They're shaking and lack the calmness I've spent so many years perfecting. Mom pulled up the worst feelings imaginable in me over the years. I learned how to move through them, but now, as I'm minutes away from claiming her body, my control is spiraling, my resolve weakening.

My chest is heavy.

My head runs rampant with questions.

My lungs beg to expand so I can let it all out, but the restlessness in my legs begs me to run like I did when I was a teenager who didn't know what the hell to do.

I can't bring myself to do it. To leave. Even though Aunt Bess, Uncle Thad, Sebastian, and—*Jesus Christ*—Violet are here, I'm really the only one Mom had in her last days before ending up in jail. I have no choice but to lift my head, square my shoulders, and walk out there to face one of my biggest fears since I was a child.

No matter how much I don't want to do it, I can't let anyone else verify she's Janie Moore.

The only person who should do it is me, and as I stare back at myself in the bathroom mirror, I can't shake how that fact grips my stomach in its fist, squeezing until all of its contents come barreling up the back of my throat.

When I make it out of the bathroom, I find the others waiting for me outside of the family room. They're grouped in the hall, looking as hopeless and devastated as I am inside. Even Violet, who stands arm-to-arm with Sebastian looks as though she's been through a great loss.

If he weren't my cousin and we were in any other scenario, I'd walk down this hall and pull her to my side. Remind the fucking world that she's mine. That I don't intend on giving her up so goddamn easily.

But this is Sebastian she's tapping strength from, the boy who scoffed at my delinquent ideas of stealing whiskey out of his parents' stash, and the same person who told me not to fuck it up when I decided to jump all in with the girl beside him.

There's no one better in the world to be by her side right now.

He looks down at Violet like a big protective brother would. Like he'd never say no to offering his shoulder. And I'm fucking grateful for it, because ever since Aunt Bess stumbled to our table with bad news written in her features, I haven't known what to say to the girl I'm absolutely crazy about.

The reluctance that nearly had me pushing her away before clamps down on me, and I don't know how to get rid of it. Not when there are more important things to do. I decide to ignore it until I have no choice but to face it.

Violet deserves affection, communication, and explanations. Not this bullshit life of mine. Not the secrets I've kept from her about Mom's addiction. Shame fills me just thinking about her finding out how much I've lied to my family.

Lied about Finn.

Lied about Mom relapsing.

Lied about the money and drugs.

Aunt Bess is the first to break away from the rest of them. In the time I was gone, she's managed to pull herself together. Tears don't stain her cheeks, and her lips are set back in the firm line they were in earlier this evening at the fundraiser. She walks up to me and lifts her hands to the lapels of my jacket.

"Oh, Colson. We'll get through this," she promises. Just like that, the strength that resides in the woman who I grew up secretly wishing at times was my mom is back. She tugs on my suit jacket, and it's so damn hard looking down into her soft eyes that I almost don't. They look too much like Mom's.

I flick my gaze over her head, ignoring the glimmer of Violet's dress in the corner of my eye. God, she looks so fucking good. Pretty in a way I can't possibly describe, but now her dress is tainted with the news of my mother's passing. I fix my sight on a vending machine nearby. Far enough away from my girl that her dress doesn't push into my line of sight and cause a revolving door of guilt to trip me up.

I clear my throat and tell my aunt, "Mom's been alone long enough."

"I know." She looks down and shakes her head. "I don't want to do this anymore than you, but we'll get through this together. We'll figure out funeral details after."

It's so fucking hard to look at her, especially when all I see are the features she shares with the woman we're here for. "She wouldn't want that."

"She needs to be laid to rest properly, but we'll worry about that later. The triage nurse called the doctor again. We're just waiting for someone to come out and show us the way."

A minute later, a woman in scrubs greets us. She leads us back through the emergency department and stops when we reach the far back corner where there's an enclosed room.

The lullaby-like beeping coming from the nurse's station behind us fades. The woman points to a few chairs outside of the room. Sebastian moves to sit in one, and I hate that Violet follows. Hate it even more that I don't speak up and tell her how much I fucking appreciate her being here despite not being able to show it in this moment.

On the outside, I'm a rock-hard shell of the man she's gotten to know. On the inside, I'm liquid goo and slipping between my own fingertips with each step I take.

I try my damnedest to reach for any words I can find. Something to make me feel like my world isn't caving in around me as my vision narrows and a buzzing takes over my senses. I squeeze my hands into fists, hoping it'll relieve me of the tingling sensation that spreads through them. My heart hammers in my chest, thumping like the beat of a drum. Over and over and over until it covers the buzzing, and it's all there is.

My eyes lock on the door, the barrier between having a mom who's alive and one who has fallen victim to her addiction. I've imagined this moment more times than I care to admit; walking into a room and finding Mom lifeless.

I don't want to step through that door. I don't want to see her frail body void of life. I'd rather spear a knife into my gut than drag my feet inside. There's so much I'd *rather* do. So many other places I'd rather be. In some weird way, I'm still the little boy who watched his mother's greedy habit enslave her.

It makes me want to retch, but I swallow down the foul taste that creeps up the back of my throat and spreads over my tongue. My heartbeat creeps up the back of my throat and into my head. It's what I focus on so the nausea swimming deep in my stomach doesn't overpower my senses and take over.

"Colson?" Aunt Bess's voice seeps in, and I snap my gaze in her direction. She looks at me as if she didn't mean to startle me. "Did you hear what I said?"

"Sorry, what?"

"We think it's best if you go in first. You can find your peace without anyone being in your space."

Yeah, something tells me I won't be finding that for a while. Still, I nod and look toward the door. It's the most daunting thing I've ever stared down.

"Unless you'd like me to go in with you?" Aunt Bess suggests.

"No."

"Okay. Take all the time you need."

I take one step in front of the other, my eyes settling on Violet's golden-brown orbs. Sadness, so much of it, fills in the edges of them that it floods my chest with an insurmountable pressure.

I stop directly in front of her and kneel to my haunches. I don't miss the surprise in her expression. I've been aloof with her since the fundraiser, barely offering much in return. I've been too in my head to give her what she needs in such an awkward situation as this one, but I can't go in there without giving her one last piece of the person she knew before.

Before the overdose.

Before that car ride.

Before claiming Mom's body.

The Colson she knew before his mother sailed into the horizon without so much as a goodbye.

I'm also doing it for myself. There's so much integrity within Violet, so much strength she doesn't even realize she has, that I want a sliver of it before I face Mom's lifeless body.

My palms stretch over the material of her dress atop her thighs. I grip softly, getting the response I'm hoping for. She reaches out, holds my face, and looks down at me. Her bottom lip trembles, just barely, and like all the times we've done in the past, I look into her eyes and tell her without words just how much I fucking need her to be here when I come out.

She leans forward, and when her lips brush mine, this intense urge consumes me. The kind that always seems to push in unannounced when I'm with her. Always at the perfect moment. Always breathing life into my lungs when I can't gasp damn near deep enough.

I reach up and grip the back of her neck as I lick the seam of her lips and ask—no, *beg*—for all the strength she's willing to pour into me. When she pulls away on a strained breath, I roll my forehead against hers twice. Her eyes, lighter than they were a second ago, bore into mine. And while she silently tells me I'm going to be okay, I don't quite believe I will be.

THREE

COLSON

THERE'S a blanket over Mom's body. The air in my lungs pushes out, and for the life of me, I can't pull more back in. I glance away from the stark white cloth and take in my surroundings. Counters with drawers holding various medical supplies line both sides of the room. A quiet monitor, the kind that usually beeps with a patient's heart rate and blood pressure, stands at the head of the bed, a bright orange hazardous trash bin sitting not far from it.

My hands tingle all over again, and my vision goes hazy. I twist and drop my head on the wall next to the door, my back to my dead mother.

My.

Dead.

Mother.

What's left of my family sits directly on the other side of the wall, along with the girl I'm hopelessly in love with. So close yet so oblivious to the emotional war happening a wall away.

I lick my lips and bring my fingers up to trace the bottom one. A minute ago, I had them pressed to Violet's. I'd give anything to take this day back, to restart it, to find a way to solve Mom's problem and avoid ending up here. The love that consumes me when I curl into Violet's backside in the early morning hours before we're both up and at it for the day is ten million times better than what threatens to take me down in this room.

My palm spreads out over the wall. It keeps me anchored in place. The ache in my chest expands toward my extremities. As often as the thought of Mom overdosing came up over the years, I never thought it'd actually happen. For so long, I lived in denial, thinking that all it'd take is for her to get back into rehab for our problems to be solved. Hell, even up until I walked into this hospital, I thought she still had time.

I see now that this was always meant to be the outcome.

But I'm not ready to say goodbye. I'm not ready to bury my fucking Mom.

The realness of death grips me by the throat and forces my head off the wall. I tamp down my feelings because now isn't the time. When things are sorted, I'll have all the time in the world to feel empty.

Breathing in the deepest sigh I can muster, I pivot and yank my suit jacket off. I toss it on the counter to my left as I slowly make my way closer to the bed, my knuckles trailing the thin sheet covering her until it bumps into what I know is her hand. Emotion clogs my eyes when the chill in it brushes against my palm.

Using my foot, I drag a nearby chair closer and drop into it, my body too heavy to hold up on my own. I curl my hand around hers, and not for the first time since I was a preteen, I sob over Mom's choices and wish things were different.

And just like then, I know they never will be.

FOUR

VIOLET

Violet: Colson's mom died.
Everleigh: You're lying.
Violet: We're at the hospital right now.
Everleigh: How's Colson holding up?
Violet: Not good.
Everleigh: And what about you?
Violet: Also not good.

I THOUGHT there'd be more privacy back here, but as it turns out, the room Colson's in is surrounded by other emergency hubs where hospital staff are constantly coming and going. The nurse and doctor stations take up the middle section of the area, and from where we sit, we have a full view of them taking care of those who are still pumping blood through their bodies.

My eyes flit to a blonde-haired RN who I've seen shimmy

by too many times to count. From what I've learned by watching, she's assisting with a difficult patient at the other end of the ER. We've heard the patient shout and holler in discomfort, but my mind can't focus on much more than the man in the room behind me.

We passed the hour mark about ten minutes ago. I think the only reason the doctors haven't come by to remind us of that is because they're too busy with other patients to care.

But it's only a matter of time before one of them comes along and cuts his time short.

Time with his mother that he'll never get again.

Bess keeps checking the time on her watch. It's interesting to see how devoted she is to her nephew, but I guess that's what happens when you're there to pick up the slack of a sister more consumed with narcotics than her only son. Thad is similar, glancing at the door occasionally, but he's quieter and more reserved in his ways. Less noticeable. He doesn't check his watch or complain about how long we've waited. He just curls his hand into his wife's in an attempt to soothe away the terrible grief of a lost sister.

"You doing okay?" Sebastian asks, pulling me from my people-watching. His voice is low but no less kind than it always is. When Colson dropped in front of me and pressed his lips to mine, I damn near broke down. Sebastian took my hand gently after, and in a way, it was like he was saying, *see, I told you he needs you.*

That single moment has been my only comfort.

"Yeah, you think he's okay in there? It's been a while."

"If you were in his shoes, would you be okay?"

"No," I swallow. "I'd be losing my shit."

Sebastian presses his lips together. "Exactly."

I nod toward the hospital staff. "How long do you think until they kick us out?"

"No clue, but it seems like their hands are too full to care right now."

"Yeah it d—"

A bang comes from beside me, the reverberation of a door flying open and slamming against a wall. It moves through the floor and up my legs. When I look over to see what's going on, a flash of black blurs past me. Colson rushes by in haste.

I'm the first on my feet, yelling his name as I run for him. "Colson!"

He doesn't bother answering, but I grab the bottom of my dress, lifting it to ensure I don't trip over it, and race after him. My shoulder bumps into something hard, and my mind barely registers the haze of red hair when I twist and look over my shoulder. I offer a muffled apology as I breeze past and catch Sebastian's deep voice from behind. He's just as concerned over Colson's sudden departure as I am and catches up quickly. I pick up speed when Colson exits through a door leading back out to the main waiting area.

He can't just bail.

He can't *leave*.

No matter how hard it gets, he needs to be surrounded by people who care about him. People who will help him through. People who will risk being pushed under water so he can have a minute to clear his lungs and breathe the fresh air.

I push through the door after him, frantically searching for his black suit. I catch it as he leaves through the automatic emergency entrance and rush after him. I get two steps before arms shroud my shoulders and drag me back, pulling me to a stop and putting more distance between me and Colson.

"No," I wail, a sob threatening to wrack through me. "Let me go."

Sebastian is in my ear, trying to calm me. "Stop, Violet."

It doesn't work. I try to yank away from his grasp, jostling my shoulders. I'm not strong or quick enough. "*Stop it.*" He hisses it quietly, like it'll change me wanting to go after the man who's walking away with my heart. Who I'm so, so fearful has dropped it on the dirty sidewalk as an afterthought.

"Sebastian, get *off* me."

"No." He twists me around and firmly places his hands on my shoulders. He dips down into my line of sight. I look toward the entrance. Colson gets smaller and smaller. Sebastian grabs my chin and moves my gaze back to him. "He just spent a fucking hour in a room by himself with his dead mother. Let him go. He needs space. You said so yourself."

I bring my fists up and beat them against his chest as hard as I can. "Yeah, well, I take it back. He needs...he needs *us*, Sebastian."

"No," he breathes out a heavy breath and lets me pound my fists against his body like it's nothing. "This isn't what that looks like."

The last thing I want is to leave Colson on his own to fight all the thoughts and emotions that are hitting him. He's used to walking through life without someone by his side, but he doesn't have to do it this time. Janie may not have been there for him when he needed it, but I'm here, and I wish he'd see that. I wish Sebastian would let me go so I could show him how serious I am about not leaving his side.

My chest heaves out a breath, rising and falling from chasing after him. "I won't do that, Sebastian. I won't leave him to fend for himself when he doesn't need to. I can't..." My words cut off in my throat, heavy emotion slicing them in half. I dip my chin, my gaze resting on the floor before I press my eyes shut. "I won't let him do this alone. Whenever I've needed him, he's been there for me." I look back up. "And now that he needs me, I'm going to be there, and there's nothing you can do that's going to stop that."

"Jesus, I'm not saying *not* to be there for him, Violet. I'm just saying to give him a minute to catch his breath. If he wanted to be around us, don't you think he would've stayed? Do you honestly think if he wanted support right now that he would have walked the fuck out?"

I consider that, and no. He wouldn't have. Maybe Sebastian is right and Colson really does need space but...

Sebastian's voice lowers, and the edge of irritation that's there dissipates. "This is a hard fucking day, Vi. It's hard as hell for all of us. I know you care about him." I look away, but he tips my chin right back toward him. "That you love him and would do anything for the guy, and I fucking love that for the two of you, but let him simmer down before the fire inside of him burns everything around him to the ground. You don't want to get caught up in that."

I nod, finally relenting because at the end of the day, if I were in Colson's shoes, maybe I would do the same. Walk out of this place and not look back. Because looking back would mean it's real.

"Do you think he'll come back? Someone has to claim his mom's body."

He nods back in the direction of the emergency room. "Mom will take care of it. As much shit as Janie has caused, there's no way in hell she'd ever let the state take her."

"Of all days," I shake my head, "it had to happen today? On the night of your mom's fundraiser?"

"I know. That's life sometimes; fucks you up the rear when you least expect it."

FIVE

VIOLET

Violet: Where are you?

Violet: Please let me be there for you. We don't even have to talk.

Violet: I'm heading back to Spring Meadows. At least tell me you're okay?

I WATCH as the streetlights pass by in a blur. After spending another hour with Sebastian and his parents with no signs of Colson, I decided it was time for me to go home. Thad called one of the cars to the front, and Sebastian walked me out, promising to message me with updates.

It was too uncomfortable standing around while Bess and Thad were saying their goodbyes. It was too intimate, and mostly, I just want to be with Colson and make sure he's okay. To offer my shoulder if he needs one to lean on. To give my strength because I know he's bracing himself, waiting for the other shoe to drop.

I watched as his control crumbled to the ground on Thanksgiving. The way his fist cracked through the drywall wasn't just a shock but a sign that as much as he can hold himself together, he too has his limits. I'm afraid this is one of them, and without someone there to talk him down, he'll succumb to urges he doesn't typically respond to.

It's a constant thought as we drive over the Sycamore River and follow the 401 back to Chatham Hills. I rest my head on the window and take in the beautiful Renaissance design of the buildings, their rigid symmetry beautiful all on its own and the darkness of the night casting them with an eeriness that adds to their charm. It's one of the reasons I love this college town so much. Everywhere you look, there's beauty to be found.

Although, right now, I'm not as pressed to pick out the little details I've done thousands of times before. I'm too distracted, especially since I've sent Colson multiple texts and have gotten zero replies.

He's out there, who knows where and doing God knows what. *Alone.*

My stomach dips at the thought, and again I brighten my phone's screen to check if there's an unread message I didn't hear come through. There isn't. The only thing starting back at me are my own string of desperate pleas.

I reprimand myself over my last text.

At least tell me you're okay.

Of course he's not okay.

It's crazy how in seconds an entire life can change. One tiny little action can rip apart a person's world and have them teetering on the edge of facing their truths or pushing them away.

The driver flicks on the turn signal. It click, click, clicks in the silence then stops when he makes the left turn into Spring Meadows's parking lot. He drives up to the entrance and puts the car in park. "We've arrived, Ms. Adams."

"Just Violet is fine," I tell him as I dim my phone and shove it into the clutch I brought with me for the night. "Thank you for the ride."

"Of course. I'll wait until I see you're inside and safe."

As I slide out of the back seat, I murmur, "Have a good rest of your night."

I barely hear his, "You as well," as I shut the door, heft up my dress so I don't step on it as I climb the curb, and swipe my keycard. I make sure the entrance door is shut tight and glance over my shoulder at the SUV blanketed by the darkness. It's late, nearing midnight, and my feet ache from being on and off them all evening. Dressing up always makes me feel like a thousand bucks, but with the way my toes are on the brink of bleeding and blistering, I'm ready to toss my heels in the nearest trash can so I never have to wear them again. I settle for leaning against the wall as I wait for the elevator and unclasp them.

I sigh in relief the second they're off, and I can wiggle my toes. When the elevator dings open, I trail inside barefoot and press the button for my floor. I ruffle through my clutch for my key. It falls to the ground just as the doors slide open. I grab it then turn out of the cab, my eyes following the long hall toward my apartment.

My movement short circuits, every muscle in my body screeching to a halt at the glob of black further down the corridor.

Colson.

Sitting with his back against the wall and his knee drawn up, he appears calm. Like the shit didn't hit the fan a couple of hours ago. Like he didn't walk out of the hospital. Like he hasn't ignored my messages for the better part of the last hour.

Ever so slowly, because I don't want to spook him, I make my way closer. My breaths are tame, but my chest still quivers under each breath. His shoulders stiffen, and I know it's because he knows I'm here.

I drop my heels to the ground in front of the door and lower to my knees, my hands moving to grasp his arm stretched out over his leg. "You don't know how relieved I am to see you."

He looks at me then, his eyes replicating one hell of a tropical cyclone. I've never seen the color in them so dark, the brightness in them swept aside. "I'm fine."

I do a quick assessment of his face, appreciating that there isn't harm done. He looks the same as he did when I last saw him, and his suit is still as pristine as it was when he picked me up, though now there's this heaviness that clings to it in the form of a sporadic wrinkle here and there.

"How long have you been waiting?"

"Don't know."

It couldn't have been that long considering I left the hospital soon after he bailed. Which makes me wonder how he made it over the Sycamore Memorial Bridge. He couldn't have walked that far.

"How'd you get here?"

"Grabbed an Uber."

I rub my palm over his forearm, my heart pinching from the sadness on his face. "Why don't we go in? It can't be comfortable sitting on the floor."

He stands in response. I unlock the door and toss my heels off to the side before locking up behind me.

Quietly, we make it down the hall and into the privacy of

my bedroom. When I close the door with the heel of my foot, I sense how off the energy is between us. It's frail and distressing. Brittle. Like this connection between us will reduce to nothing if I take an unsteady step or say the wrong thing.

I'm torn between not knowing what to say and wanting to hold him in my arms while offering him every word of comfort I have in my arsenal. The only problem is…I don't know what he wants. I don't know what will help or what will break him more, so I choose walking on eggshells, thinking it might be what he needs most even though it makes my calves cramp.

I head over to my dresser, walking around him without brushing against him. I'm careful with my distance, and it's so unlike what I'm used to. I've grown accustomed to his affection when he's near. To him giving me every ounce of his attention. I can tell he doesn't want to talk. That he doesn't have much to say and is still processing one of the biggest changes a person can experience. So, for now, I'll give him his space. At least until I figure out how to be there for him.

It could always be worse, I remind myself. He could have gone somewhere else. Instead, he showed up at my apartment which speaks louder than any word he's spoken since leaving the fundraiser.

I tug open a drawer and take out a pair of cotton shorts along with its matching shirt. I don't miss the sardonic joke in the smiley graphic printed on the front. Long gone are grins and laughs and happiness.

A chill runs down my spine, and when my skin pebbles with the familiar pimples of goosebumps, I rub my hands over my arms to chase them away. My palms aren't what makes them scatter. It's the warm breath that slips down over my shoulder when pressure presses into the center of my back where the zipper of my gown is located.

I take in Colson's presence behind me as he gently drags the zipper down to the small of my back. When his finger slips under one of the straps, and he drags it off my shoulder, my stomach bursts with a familiar sensation of desire. When he does the same thing to the other, I close my eyes and hold onto my clothes a little tighter.

Is it crazy that with all the emotion trying to steal us away from each other that I might possibly want this man more than ever? When I pressed my lips to his the first time in Lucy's, I had no idea it would lead to this moment, but now that I'm here there's nowhere else I want to be.

"Colson," I breathe out softly.

He presses a tight circle of kisses on my left shoulder then trails the tip of his tongue to the side of my neck where he nips my skin with his teeth. He gives me a soothing, "Shhh," then peppers three kisses to my earlobe. My stomach tightens. My thighs clench for what's to come. He'll never *not* be able to do this to me, to drive me completely mad and make me crave him so desperately.

But as much as I want him to take over and give me all of him, I need to know *he's* okay with this. "Are you sure this is what we should be doing right now?" I ask carefully.

His voice is a low grumble. "There's nothing else I want."

His hand slips down inside my dress and glides down my side, his palm curving against my ribs and waist. My dress pools at my feet and leaves me standing in nothing but the thong I slipped on so underwear lines wouldn't be visible through the material.

He continues kissing me.

My shoulders.

My neck.

My back.

"Maybe we should talk," I suggest as fireworks light my skin wherever he touches.

"No talking," is his curt reply.

"It's been a hard day." I cringe when it comes out, because I don't need to remind him. His palm smooths over my ass before he pulls the string at my hip and lets it snap back at my skin. It leaves a sting that adds to the pressure between my legs, and as much as I want to say it doesn't make me hotter—because, *hello*, he just found out his mom died—I can't. Every way Colson touches me makes me fall for him a little more, and while I want to get to the bottom of how he's feeling after being told Janie overdosed and having to say goodbye to her, I want more of this. More of him. More of us.

"You're sure?" I ask again because I realize how messed up this is.

His voice hardens, and it reminds me of when his car broke down and he wanted nothing to do with the help I offered. "Goddamnit, Violet. All I want is *you*. I'm not asking for a conversation. I don't need you to try and decipher how I'm feeling right now." He pauses as if he's reeling in his emotions. "I don't need a fucking therapist. I need my girl-friend. Is that too much to ask?"

I swallow the lump in my throat and twist around. Standing toe-to-toe with him, I notice the slight flush in his cheeks. "I'm sorry. I don't know how to be here for you right now. I wish you'd tell me what you need. You don't have to carry it alone."

His bottom lip trembles. He silences the wavering by clamping his teeth down on it. "I just told you what I need." His eyes flick between mine, and it takes everything in me not to rip my heart out of my chest and hand it over to replace his broken one. To wipe that look of heartbreak off his face and fill the void in his eyes.

"You already have me," I whisper. "You always will."

He grips the back of my neck and drags my mouth to his. His kiss is rough and desperate and so different from what he's given me in the past. He kisses me like it's the only thing he has to cling to, like it's his oxygen. I let him take it. I let him breathe in every ounce of air I can give, and when he lowers to suck on my breasts, swirling his tongue around my hardened nipples over and over again, I hold his head there and appreciate the way he makes my body come to life.

"I need more of you," I murmur, loving the way he clamps his teeth down on me before my nipple pops out of his mouth.

He rises to his full height and grips my chin. "On the bed. Ass in the air."

Hearing him tell me he wants me in his favorite position has my panties dripping wet. When I go to slip out of them, he grunts, "No. Keep them on."

I pad over to the bed and prop myself on all fours. His suit jacket finds a spot next to my dress but that's as far as he strips. He unclasps his belt and pulls his zipper down while he stares at my ass. He licks his bottom lip, and I know for a fact it's the reason he's rock hard when he shifts his pants and boxers down enough to let himself spring free.

He spits into his hand and palms himself with a slow, lazy twist. Then he climbs behind me and grips the string of my thong nestled between my butt cheeks. Yanking it to the side, he exposes my slick seam and wastes no time running his thumb over it to spread me.

I moan in delight. In the way his touch always lets off an array of sparks that start deep in my belly and make my core come alive. I imagine his words of praise, the kindness he always gives me when he sees me bare but doesn't come now.

His thumb circles me slowly. Lazily. I drop my forehead to the comforter and breathe through the delicious pull in my abdomen before I hear the rip of a condom foil. His tip nudges my entrance seconds later, and I'm so ready for him to fill me that I arch my back and press back into him.

His hand moves to my hip and bites into my flesh. "Don't move," he grunts.

Those two words tell me he wants full control. I don't blame him. It's the one thing he hasn't had all day, and if it takes me giving him a semblance of normalcy, then I will.

I position my forearms on the mattress more comfortably and hold myself up. When he finally sinks into me, my walls wrapping tightly around him, a moan works itself up my throat. I don't move. I don't dare shift my hips or push back into him the way I want. In the way he enjoys when he's turned on.

I follow his orders, including spreading my legs a tiny bit wider to allow him better access. It only opens up space for more pleasure.

"Yes," I whimper. "Harder, Colson."

I expect him to groan at my request or give me some kind of sign that he likes what he hears. He doesn't. The way we normally communicate when we have sex isn't present. His throaty groans are nowhere to be found, and my neediness for more catches in my throat each time I want to voice it.

He fucks me raw.

Like the entire world is out to get him, but instead of taking it out on them, he takes it out on me, ramming into me harder, deeper, faster. I ignore the burn of my thong's fabric cutting into my hip as he rocks into me and takes what he wants. It's almost like I'm the only person he's comfortable enough to lose himself to. Which is the very reason I give myself to him, aside from being irrevocably turned on, of course, because it's *him* that's filling me.

I'm partly ashamed at how impure this is—giving myself to him so he can selfishly forget about his grief, but I'm one hundred percent okay being the person he lets go with. It makes my heart beat erratically, the blood in my body pump faster, and my clit throb uncontrollably when he fucks me fiercely and reaches around to rub my sensitive bud. My vision eventually wanes, and all that's left is the sensation of falling over the edge.

I forget to breathe through my orgasm and focus on the way my body convulses around his thickness. His palm slides up my back and grips the back of my neck. His body forms a cocoon around mine, his weight pressing into my back, and an animalistic groan rips through the room at a decibel I've never heard from him before.

His body stills, but like mine, a set of tremors work through him before he peels himself off me. The mattress dips, and he pushes up to his feet.

An ache settles into my lower back as I roll over. I shift my thong back into place and lift up on my elbows. He pulls the condom off, ties it and wraps it in a tissue, then drops it into a small wastebasket I have beside the bed.

I watch as he tucks himself back into his pants and zips them.

I clear my throat, not caring if my breasts aren't covered. I've never hidden myself from him before. I don't want to start now. "I can start the shower, and we can wash the day off before we crawl into bed."

He doesn't meet my gaze. "Gonna pass on that."

My heart hiccups.

He never says no to showering together.

Ever.

A ripple of hurt moves through me as he grabs his suit jacket off the floor without looking at me. He swipes his hand over the material like the fabric wrinkled in the few minutes it was mindlessly discarded. "You're going to pass?"

"That's what I said."

"So that's it?" I push up and sit tall, this new feeling of irritation claiming me. "You're going to fuck me then just *leave*?"

A nasty sting—one much worse than when my thong slashed into my skin—settles behind my eyes. I pretend it doesn't exist. As much as I was okay offering my body as comfort, I figured he'd at least stay. That it would help us clear the fog surrounding our connection and let us get back to normal. Or as close to it as humanly possible considering the circumstances.

"I can't be here," he tells me, pushing his hands through the arms of the jacket. He doesn't bother to fix the lopsided lapels. Just checks his back pocket to make sure his wallet is there. The one he got the condom from.

"You *can* be here," I insist, scooting to the edge of the bed.

"Don't look at me like that."

"Like what?"

"Like you're fucking disappointed."

"Then don't give me something to be disappointed about, Colson." His jaw tenses—it's been doing a lot of that tonight —and I take in the way the muscle ripples from my abrasive-ness. "We've always had each other. Don't push me away because things are hard right now. We can weather the storm together."

He scoffs. "Things aren't *hard*, Violet. They're royally

fucked, and they have been since before you walked into my life and forced your way into my fucking head."

"Forced?" A hurt-filled laugh leaves me. "Wow. Here I thought this was a mutual thing. That you wanted this as much as I did."

He cocks his head to the side and dips his fists into his pockets. "I warned you," he says, walking over to stand in front of me. He grips my chin. "I told you that the shit in my life would ingrain itself in you. That it'd follow you wherever you went. Surprise, Violet, it's now a part of your shadow."

"What does that have to do with this moment?"

"What does it have to do with now?" He shakes his head, looks away, then drops his hand from my face. "Every-fuck-ing-thing. Your eyes don't lie to me, Vi. I see how much hurt is in them. How badly you wish you could wipe away what I'm going through. That you wish you could turn back time and give me a different life. A different mom."

"Yeah, because I care about you," I choke out, somehow holding back the sob that wants to rip free.

"Those feelings will follow you everywhere. They'll never be easy to shake. I did that to you. Gave you hope when I shouldn't have. Let my walls down when I should've secured them like a goddamn naval base."

"I don't care if they follow me. Let them."

"I fucking care. That's why I'm leaving."

He says it so effortlessly, but I hear the depth in what's to come.

He's leaving.

My heart nearly cracks in half. This insurmountable pain fills me and as much as I want to let the emotional sting take over the corner of my eyes, I don't let my tears fall. There's still time for us to talk about this and work through it.

"Don't do this," I plead, reaching out for him and missing

when he steps back. "You told me you weren't going to let life take things from you anymore. That you were going to take what you wanted. What happened to that person?"

"He's gone."

"Please stay. We'll sleep then talk in the morning after we've had a good night of rest."

"There's nothing to talk about. What's done is done. I'll cherish what we had, but it's time for me to move on."

"You know that's not how this is supposed to go."

"My mom wasn't supposed to overdose while she was a fucking inmate, but that still happened."

"Colson."

He gives me one last glance before rounding the foot of the bed. I stand and watch him go. Each step wreaks havoc on my heart. When he twists the handle and opens my bedroom door without hesitating or looking back at me, it fully shatters.

Because I knew this would happen.

I knew life would catch up to us.

I just didn't think it'd happen this fast.

SIX

VIOLET

MY HEARTBEAT IS a mere pitter-patter in my chest as my back lies parallel to the floor. My earbuds are fastened in my ears, the volume so high I had to bypass the warning on my phone to listen. Music swirls in my ears, an array of tempos vibrating through me.

I keep my eyes closed, using my sense of hearing more than anything. Lyrics to a song I haven't heard before enter my head, but all I can seem to focus on is the piano music in the background and how it pairs perfectly with the bass. Words string into lines that mean nothing and everything.

The truth is, every syllable pecks me raw, making me simultaneously numb and responsive to the agonizing pain that comes in waves with every breath. I breathe in, and it's there. Right under the surface in the most infuriating way. Like it isn't even ashamed. And then I breathe out, and it lingers in my bloodstream, curling around my heart and rushing through my veins like they're a roller coaster track.

It rockets through my system. I'm taken on a whiplash-inducing thrill ride. I'd beg the operator to let me off, except she's me. *I'm* the one who hits that button that starts the ride all over again without lifting the bars to exit.

It's the worst kind of nightmare.

If I just opened my eyes, I know it'd lessen the emotion smothering me. But then I'd feel the aftermath on my cheeks. Streams of tears and the burden of itchy, swollen eyes after crying one too many minutes, and I don't want that, either.

I want none of this, but I've been subjected to it, anyway.

Something warm flits over my hand, and I have no choice but to crack my eyes and let in light. My surroundings come back in a flash. The white ceiling of the apartment building's gym, particularly the yoga room I use regularly. The wall of mirrors is off to my right, and I don't dare look at them. I don't want to see what it looks like to have had my heart thrown back at me. I'm too scared my wobbly hands will drop it on the dirty ground. As it stands, I'm the one holding it in pieces, wondering when someone is going to come along with the glue to fasten it back together.

I blink against the bright lights and find Everleigh kneeled at my side. Sebastian stands next to her, his lips contorted into a frown. Everleigh's expression doesn't look much better. One glance at both of them, and I can see the worry present.

Worry for me.

For where my head and heart might be.

Because the man I'm hopelessly in love with left.

He broke up with me...and *walked out.*

I pull a bud out of my ear and pause the music. "Hey."

"It's getting late," Everleigh says.

My brows furrow in response to her statement. "What time is it?"

"After one," Sebastian answers, tucking his hands into a pair of sweats. I look back over at Ev and realize she's in her pajamas, too. I check the time on my phone to confirm that minutes have faded into the early morning hours.

"I didn't realize." I lift into a seated position.

"You've been down here for hours," Everleigh says, nibbling at her lower lip like there's more she wants to say but isn't sure if she should.

When Colson left me last night—or well, two nights ago —they were the first people to know. And while they've been trying to give me space to work through it, they've also been making sure I take care of myself.

Sebastian drops down to his knees next to Everleigh and reaches for my shoulder. His fingers curl around it and squeeze gently. "You're strong." *I don't feel it.* "You'll get through this." *Will I?* "You both will and will be better because of it. Even if it feels like shit right now."

"Shitty isn't really the word to describe what's going on in my body," I murmur, looking at my friend. My voice cracks when one little word falls out of my mouth. One that has circled my mind for hours now. "Why?"

Why did he do this to me?

"I don't know, Vi," Sebastian answers with a look on his face that tells me how much he hates that I'm sad. "He's going through a lot. He probably doesn't even understand the weight of the decisions he's making. You shouldn't overthink it. I'm one hundred percent positive that him breaking up with you had nothing to do with you and every-fucking-thing to do with him."

"Sebastian is right, Violet," Everleigh adds, tucking a strand of her brown hair behind her ear. She reaches out and takes my hand in hers. "He'll realize how much of a mistake he made."

"I don't think he will," I mumble. I saw the look in Colson's eyes right before he left. They didn't. They didn't see the devastation outlined in his irises. How it flooded the blue in them and darkened them to a color I never even knew they were capable of. He was a completely different person. One washed out from hopelessness.

"Then he's making one of the biggest mistakes of his fucking life," Sebastian asserts, gripping my shoulder tight again. Only one emotion stirs inside of me as he gently turns my gaze to his—visceral heartbreak. "I know you love the hell out of him, but don't fall victim to the same pain he's suffering."

"Easier said than done."

"Faith," he says. "It takes you knowing that one day he'll pull his head of out his ass and grovel like no fucking tomorrow to get another chance with you."

I swallow the emotion filling my throat as Sebastian's unwavering gaze barrels into me.

"I know he loves you. You know he loves you."

"There's no other valid reason for him doing what he did," Everleigh adds.

I shake my head. "This can't be love. Love doesn't feel like *this*." Like I weigh a thousand pounds and nothing at the same time. Like each of my extremities are in a vise and all of them are slowly ripping me apart. Like nothing is worth getting out of bed for.

"Love is as big as the heartbreak it causes," murmurs Sebastian, lifting to his feet. "Now, let's go. You're not staying down here half the night by yourself."

"Says who?" I rasp in an attempt to lighten the load on my chest. It doesn't really help.

"Both of us," Everleigh says firmly, crossing her arms as she matches Sebastian's stance. "He'll take your legs, and I'll take your arms. We'll carry your ass back upstairs if we need to."

"You do know I can just hoist her over my shoulder, right?" he says with a smirk as he glances down at Everleigh.

"Shut up." She nudges him in the side. "I was trying to add to your point. That there's no way in hell we're letting her stay down here on her own." She holds out a hand to me. Sebastian does the same. Reluctantly, I pocket my phone and ear buds and grasp each of their palms. They hoist me to my feet, and then I'm tugged forward in a group hug, two sets of arms circling and squeezing me.

We stand there for a minute before I pull away and follow them out and to the elevator. We ride it up to our floor, and when the doors slide open, Sebastian ruffles my hair before promising to reach out tomorrow. Ev and I wave our good-byes and make it inside our quiet apartment.

We toe off our shoes and end up in the kitchen. Because I skipped dinner, I grab an apple out of the fruit basket and rinse it under the faucet. Everleigh pours a glass of orange juice in silence before a raised voice travels out from the bedrooms.

I snap my gaze to hers because Sylvia is the only other person who would be here. And we haven't exactly spent a lot of time with her. She's been too busy doing her own thing, and honestly, I'm surprised she's home. There are some nights she doesn't return at all, or is out super late.

"She wasn't home when I left," Everleigh tells me in a muted voice. "Is someone with her?"

I crane my neck and focus on what I'm hearing. I can't make out the words Sylvia says, but can definitely tell it's her. No other voice joins in when she quiets for half a minute. "I don't think so. She must be on the phone."

Everleigh's eyes go wide as she creeps to the other end of the kitchen near the hallway. She's there all of a second before Sylvia's door rips open, and she stomps toward us. She doesn't see us at first, her sights set on her phone. But then she raises her chin and catches us already looking at her.

Everleigh does a good job acting as if she wasn't just trying to eavesdrop on her conversation. "Hey, Sylvia. Everything okay?"

Sylvia gives her a dirty look, her phone still clutched in her hand like it's a lifeline. "You break up with Tristan, and now you suddenly care about what's going on around you?" She rolls her eyes. "Typical."

A flash of hurt crosses Everleigh's features. "That's not true. I cared about you while I was with him as well."

"Whatever," Sylvia huffs out. She grabs something from the junk drawer at the edge of the kitchen. A charger by the looks of it. "You don't need to feel bad pushing everyone but Tristan to the side now that you two are over."

"Sylvia, that's not what this is." The tone in Everleigh's voice tells me she's taking offense to Sylvia's harshness.

A spark of defense flickers in me. "She was just trying to be nice," I tell Sylvia. "You don't need to bite her head off."

Sylvia purses her lips and turns on me. "Please, I don't need you up my ass, too. Tell me, has that piece of shit boyfriend of yours set you free yet? You look fucking awful."

You don't even know.

She squints at me, and it's like she can read my mind. "Oh, my God. He dumped your ass, didn't he?" She throws her head back and laughs. "And here I thought *my* night was turning to shit."

Shame builds in me until it traces along my body, outlining me from head to toe. I don't know why. I'm not the one whose character is in question. Still, I don't want anyone questioning Colson's, either. A handful of excuses rests on my tongue, ready to come to his defense despite how he has treated me.

"You're better off without him. Just like you were better off without Webber," Sylvia remarks like she has the right.

I don't miss how she doesn't ask if I'm okay. If I need a shoulder to cry on or an ear to listen to me. There's no dedication on her part, no assurance she's there for me and no promise of making his life a living hell for causing me pain.

I hold my excuses back, not giving her a single ounce of my attention. She wouldn't understand, anyway. It's clear who my real friends are—Sebastian and Everleigh.

I square my shoulders with my apple in hand and shove past the girl who I was close enough at one point to want to live with. As I make my way down the hallway, I hear Everleigh say, "You know, you don't have to always be so mean. We're not your enemies."

I slam my bedroom door closed after that and attempt to sleep.

SEVEN

COLSON

Sebastian: Dude, where the fuck are you?
Sebastian: You can't just disappear off the face of the earth.
Sebastian: And totally uncool what you did to Violet.
Sebastian: She didn't deserve that and you know it.

MY PHONE VIBRATES on the bedside table, waking me from my slumber. It buzzes and rings simultaneously. It rotates in one full circle, Mom's lamp next to it causing a glare and making it difficult to see who's trying to contact me.

Who the hell is it this time?

After seeing the look of disappointment in Violet's eyes, I

walked out of her apartment without looking back and returned to Harrison Heights. It's where I belong.

Fact is, someone out there will love her better than me, and when she meets that person, she'll understand why I left. Why I couldn't drag her down. She's not destined to be my support system. I can't let myself think she is; otherwise, I might actually start believing it. And if there's one thing I've always been adamant about, it's not wanting to hurt her.

My phone rings again.

I sit up and lean against the wall, finally lifting a hand to retrieve it. An exasperated groan forms inside of me but falls away just as quickly. My body is a vessel of weakness at this point. I haven't eaten since I got here, and judging by the time on my phone, that was nearly forty hours ago.

Give or take.

I don't really fucking know.

All I know is that it's Sunday, according to the date on my phone, and there's no part of me ready to get up and deal with the world.

I'd rather lie in this bed for another few days in solace. Stare at the bottle of Jack I set on the dresser across from the bed and see how close I get to twisting off the cap and guzzling the amber liquid.

I've come close a few times.

Mostly when my chest is so goddamn heavy from grief that it feels like my ribcage is about to crack. In those moments, I get up, sit at the edge of the bed, and waffle my options.

Do I drink, or do I suffer?

It'd be easy to pop the cap off and succumb to the depression and kickstart an addiction of my own. There're also other options. Like picking up the bottle and smashing it against the wall out of the anger and resentment that chokes me. I can pour the fucker down the drain and find better ways to bargain with my pain. Or I can continue down my current path, which is sitting on Mom's bed, replaying memories and wondering if there's anything I could've done differently.

I always come to the same conclusion. I spent too much time worrying about Finn when I should've taken better care of her. Maybe I should've been more stern with him instead of letting him run my life these last few months. But there's another side of that, like how I shouldn't have let my head get caught up with a girl, and instead, should have focused on helping the one person in my life who needed it most.

It's a vicious cycle, the regret, and because of it, I haven't gotten much sleep. I've deprived myself of the bare necessities. Perhaps from lack of willpower, motivation, or maybe I'm just punishing myself for having to see Mom's dead body on that hospital bed, a thin sheet covering her sunken cheeks and pale skin.

My stomach twists with sickness as I remember how cold her body was, how lifeless.

I press the heels of my hands into my eyes. It doesn't stop the burn that stings them or the wetness that coats my cheeks seconds later. This is the ride I'm on. I break down when I least expect it. When the memories are too much. When it's as if one more breath could destroy me.

My phone stops ringing for all of five seconds before it goes off a third time. I wipe the dampness from my face with the back of my hand and look closer at my phone. Violet's name takes up a quarter of the screen. Below is my favorite picture of her. She's sitting on her bed in nothing but purple silk sleep bottoms and a bra, putting socks on. I had just roused her from sleep before heading to the bathroom across the hall, so her hair is messy, but her face is fresh. When I walked back into the room, I couldn't help but snap a picture because she looked so fucking beautiful. She glanced up to see me with my phone in my hand and closed her eyes, shaking her head over how ridiculous it was, a gorgeous grin breaking out on her face.

The call ends and goes to voicemail, effectively stealing Violet from the forefront of my mind. Lucky for me, my inbox is full. I have a notification at the top of my screen that tells me so. I have no desire to empty it or listen to the messages that have been left. I don't want to hear her voice. I don't want to cave to what I feel for her, not when I'm at my ugliest, and it's only going to get worse.

I've had this nagging in my gut—call it intuition or paranoia from my lack of sleep—that keeps telling me that this isn't the main event. I don't want Violet to be around when more shit hits the fan.

I place my phone back on the nightstand and pick up the cup of water sitting next to random shit Mom has on her nightstand. Tissues, incense, two lighters, a pile of papers with random words scribbled on them. I grab one of the papers and run my finger over her handwriting. It's a mess and clear that she scrawled it down in a haste. I can't make out what it says, but it doesn't matter. Just seeing it makes my heart swell with something I can't quite name. Love? Emptiness? Despair?

All of it is too fucking debilitating.

Who the hell knew she'd send me on a whirlwind when she finally decided to kick the bucket.

I toss the paper back with the rest of them. A moment later, a ruckus sounds from somewhere else in the house. I can't pinpoint where it comes from but know it's not normal. I'm pissed I have to get up to figure out what it is.

My body is a bag of bricks as I pad across Mom's bedroom floor, the carpet long since worn and offering zero comfort to the heels of my feet. The morning sun is nearly blinding in the kitchen, streaming in through the window above the sink and the one in the living room.

A fist pounds against the front door. It steals my attention immediately. Without looking out the window to see who the hell is bothering me, I swing open the door. One of the last people I want to see stares back at me.

Sebastian.

I slam it closed and turn on my heel, my head already back in bed playing tug of war with the bottle of Jack Daniel's that I dropped nearly fifty bucks on.

Much to my chagrin, the door opens behind me a second later.

"Go home," is what I call out over my shoulder as I enter the kitchen. I open one of the cabinets and find a pack of crackers. It's not paired with its box, so I have no idea if they're expired. I rip the plastic away and reluctantly pop one into my mouth. It's stale. I toss the rest of the pack on the counter, knowing I won't be eating another.

Sebastian stands at the opening of the kitchen, his expression pulled taut. One glance at him, and I drop my gaze. I don't want to see the pity in his eyes.

"People are trying to get ahold of you."

"I don't want to be contacted."

He plants his hands on his hips, and it's fucking weird. Mostly because I can't remember a time he's been in this house. When we were kids, he was never allowed inside.

"You can't hole yourself up here," he tells me, but oh, I can. I have since I fucked Violet for the last time and left her. "I know what you're going through is fucking hard—"

"No, Seb, you don't *know*. You've been sheltered your whole goddamn life. Given whatever you've wanted and needed. Had the support people would literally kill for. You don't get to walk in here and tell me anything about what *I'm* going through."

He rolls his lips into his mouth. His jaw ticks. "All I have to do is look at your face and see you're not okay. Jesus Christ, when was the last time you showered? I can smell you from across the room."

I cross my arms over my chest and square my shoulders. "No one asked you to come."

"That's where you're wrong."

I look out the kitchen window. I don't need this bullshit. I don't need Sebastian storming in here like a fairy fucking godmother with the promise of having the magic potion to heal all.

"Mom sent me."

"Yeah, well, tell Aunt Bess you didn't see me," I tell him.

"Do you hear yourself? I'm not gonna do that."

"Then don't. But you still need to go."

"I'd be a piece of shit if I left right now."

I lift my chin and stare him down. "Who says you're not one already?"

It's a low blow, one I feel in my stomach as hurt crosses my cousin's face. He doesn't deserve this. Doesn't deserve how awful I'm being. This is part of the reason I'm pushing Violet into the past. Because I know how much of an asshole I can be, and I don't need her seeing that. I don't want to be the one responsible for ripping her heart out of her chest and stomping on it like a pile of dead leaves on fire.

"I'm sorry she's gone, man. But you don't need to take a thousand steps back because of it. You don't have to be that angry teenager again."

Yes, I do, I want to scream.

I've been obliterated by Mom's departure. Her death coils into more of me the farther I get away from saying goodbye.

The complete opposite of the "time heals all wounds" phrase people cling to.

I'm pissed at the world.

At myself.

Every single person in my path.

And all the circumstances I couldn't change.

At having a mother who was too goddamn selfish to care.

I stare at him until I can't take it then head for her bedroom. If he doesn't want to leave, whatever, but I'm not going to listen to his Dr. Phil bullshit.

I fall back onto Mom's mattress and kick my feet up on her comforter. It still smells like her and the cheap brand of cigarettes she smoked like a chimney. I'm a breath away from scooting to the edge and yanking the cap off good ole Jack when Sebastian shows his face again.

Why can't he take a hint?

I'm beginning to welcome the burn of the liquid coating my throat and the way it'll blanket everything else I'm feeling, including the images of Mom that keep flashing through my head. I know she's not here, but I've seen her in different parts of the house. Like the last time I saw her stepping out of the bathroom and trailing down the short hall. She had her toothbrush in one hand and a ciggy in the other and kept going back and forth between the two. I don't think she cared that smoking while she was brushing her teeth totally defeated the purpose.

It's dumb shit like that keeping me on my toes. That has me getting closer and closer to the edge of *I-don't-give-a-fuck*. The biggest thing that holds me back is the nagging thought of addiction running rampant in the family. Grandpa Moore was an alcoholic. Mom, well, she was addicted to anything she could get her hands on. That's two generations of enslavement. I don't want to make it a third.

"Is this what you've been doing?" Sebastian asks, a hint of disgust in his tone that rarely comes through. I know it's because he's bothered by my reaction and doesn't know what to do to get me out of my head. We're not kids anymore, and this is a lot heavier than anything else we've ever faced.

I don't have it in me to fight. I spewed what I could in the kitchen. Now, I just want to be left alone. It's why I haven't answered anyone's phone calls.

He walks into the room, ignoring the trash lying around and plucks the bottle of Jack off the dresser. He twists it in his hold, eyeing the way the see-through liquid swishes and bubbles. I pay close attention to make sure he doesn't leave with it.

He lifts it higher and looks at me. "Is this why you look like shit? You've been drinking?"

I glare at him. "You want to stay, Seb? Fine, but I didn't sign up to get my ass chewed out. You don't like what I'm doing then fucking bail. No one is making you stay and witness what you don't want to."

He sets the bottle back on the dresser, the label facing away instead of staring me head-on the way I like. He walks around the bed and paces.

"They moved Janie to a funeral home. Mom mentioned you saying that you didn't want a funeral, but they can't keep waiting. She doesn't want to make any decisions without you. There's also shit that has to be handled with the life insurance policy. Money that will go to the state if it isn't claimed, and from what I hear, it's a pretty penny, man. Enough for you to start fresh, but you need your birth certificate and social security number. Info that proves your identity so it can be passed down to you."

Doesn't he see that I'm neck-deep in grief? That there isn't room for anything else. Not even a boatload of money.

Sebastian doesn't say anything else, but he does sit down on the other side of the bed. He mirrors me, lifting his feet up on the comforter and relaxing back against the wall. For the next hour, he keeps me company. I'm grateful as hell when he takes the high road and shuts up.

Sometime later, an alarm on his phone goes off, and he wordlessly leaves the room. My breath staggers when I hear the front door shut.

It's just Jack and me again.

Alone at last.

EIGHT

VIOLET

Violet: What did you tell her?

Olive: That you haven't budged. I know things are screwed up right now, but you can't spend the holiday alone.

Violet: I'll be fine.

Olive: I won't allow it.

Violet: Who are you? The Christmas police?

Olive: No, but maybe I should be if it means you'll spend it with your favorite sister.

Violet: I'd never ignore you on your most favorite day of the year, Olive Garden.

Olive: Deep down, I know that, but you can't ignore our parents forever, Vi.

CLASSES ARE DEMANDING as ever with finals and holiday break around the corner. Olive has messaged me countless times asking what my plans are for break, but I've been telling her that I don't know, and it's the truth. My brain swings between exams, working at the daycare, and Colson. I haven't had the energy to figure out the dysfunctional shit that's going on with my parents. Not when I'm trying to keep my grades above average, so I have a better chance at securing a solid teaching position after graduation.

While I may understand it a teensy more than I did back at Thanksgiving, I'm still not equipped to handle my dad's cheating full on or the obtuse understanding my mom has regarding it. Not when my heart is in shambles. Not when my boyfriend just lost his mom and is spiraling so far that he broke up with me and walked out. He also isn't answering anyone's phone calls.

It's been days since the Second Chances fundraiser. Some moments it feels like it was yesterday. I barely knew Janie, only what Colson shared and the glimpses I saw when I stayed with him in Harrison Heights, but I'm grieving her death for her son's sake, flipping back and forth between sadness and desperation. Denial and acceptance.

I'm so unbelievably broken-hearted for Colson, but I'm also scaling a mountain of my own.

I've called his cell every morning, and it's the last thing I do before I close my eyes at the end of the day. My phone stopped giving me the option to leave a voicemail two nights ago. The automated voice that tells me his inbox is full is like a fist around my heart, squeezing tight enough to convince me not to call again.

I shouldn't, considering we're no longer a couple, but I can't help myself.

It only makes it seem as if what we had was nothing. In some moments, I want to hate him for it, but I realize that's the selfish, desperate part of me talking. I know I'm only feeling this way for one reason, though I'm not sure I have the right to with what he's going through. His grief blows mine out of the water.

I pull my jacket tighter around my torso and wait for Sebastian near the Mathematics and Statistics building. We've been in lectures all day but happen to have the same forty-five minute break in the afternoon. He agreed to meet up with me and brief me on what went down when he saw Colson this morning.

I know he's hiding away at the house in Harrison Heights because Sebastian crossed the river in search of the one place he was pretty sure he'd be the other day.

My friend pushes out of the building with his backpack hanging off one shoulder and held close to his chest. There's a piece of paper in his mouth that he shoves inside of it once he gets a zipper open. He spots me and smiles. I give him the best one I can muster back.

He jogs down the set of steps and pulls me into a hug. They're no longer as quick as they used to be. Like when we were at Fletcher's party and he pulled back quickly with a lovable smile spread across his handsome face and a teasing tone in his voice.

He watched me falter at the hospital then break down when Colson left. He and Everleigh have talked more sense into me these last few days than ever. It's reassuring to have them there, especially when there was a lot more distance between us all at the start of the semester.

"It's like a fucking freezer out here," he complains, referring to the way the cold has snuck up on us. "Have you been waiting long?"

I shiver against Georgia's cooler winter temps. "No, actually. I had to walk over from the Education building and just got here."

He pulls away and leans down into my line of sight to get a better look at my face. "You doing okay today?"

I lift my hand, motioning so-so as I step back, then start in the direction of the coffee spot on campus we agreed on earlier this morning. "Yes and no."

The quad is just as busy as it is any other morning. At this time of year, students chat amongst themselves while lingering by park benches rather than the grassy areas. We skirt around an artistic bunch who have their easels out and paints scattered across the large wooden slats of the bench like it's a worktable. A guy's shout ricochets off the thick tree trunks, pulling my gaze up from the pavement as we walk.

"You want to elaborate on that?"

I shrug a shoulder, trying to make it seem like it isn't all that big of a deal, but we both know better. "I miss him, Sebastian. So much that it feels like it's slowly killing me."

"I know, Vi. It fucking sucks. I hate seeing him like this and knowing that he has pulled away so much in such a short amount of time. It's like he's back to the same angry kid he was when we were teenagers."

As I listen to him, my gaze catches on a familiar head of blonde hair swishing in the breeze farther up the quad. I settle on the broad shoulders of Fletcher and Nelson on either side of the girl whose hair has a mind of its own. Even from behind, it's not hard to point out two of the most popular football players at Chatham U. Since Sylvia has been spending a lot of time with them, I've noticed them around more than usual.

I squint, bothered that, even from afar, she looks as if she's pushing herself too hard. Like she's not sleeping enough and running her body into the ground. And not from studying, no, but from partying and keeping up with the football team. And then I see another familiar face.

"Is that Tristan?" I ask Sebastian, interrupting our conversation about Colson.

"Huh?"

I point to where Sylvia and the guys stand on a grassy patch underneath a tree. One of the guys launches a football above his head, sending it into the perfect spiral before it falls back into his hands. "Over there. Sylvia is with them."

"Oh, yeah. Look at that," he remarks, taking in the scene around them before verifying what my eyes see. "Yeah, I guess that is him. He's always been big on hanging out with the football guys. You know that."

"Yeah, but since when are those guys Fletcher and Nelson?"

Sebastian scratches the back of his neck as a student whizzes past on a skateboard. "Honestly, Everleigh breaking up with him is kinda hitting him hard. Whenever I try to get the guys together as of late, he's too busy or doesn't answer my texts. Webber can even tell you he's being kind of douchey."

"She had every right to end things with him," I mutter under my breath.

Sebastian's hand smooths over my elbow. "Vi, you don't need to convince me how messed up he treated her. Only a dumbass would look at her and turn the other direction. I don't know what's been going through his head lately but if that's what he wants to do with his time...if that's what *they*," he reiterates, including Sylvia, "want to do, then we have to let them. Sometimes you have to let go even when you don't want to."

I take one last look at them and realize that I don't have it in me to deal with that, anyhow. Sebastian is right. They should do whatever makes them happy, and I'm going to do the same, which is why I turn back to him and ask, "Tell me how he was when you saw him this morning?"

"Mostly the same as every other morning I've been there," he offers, but I hear the reluctance in his tone.

"Did he say anything?"

"You know the deal. I show up and we sit in silence. I think that's what he needs most right now. We can't relate to him, and he knows that, so naturally, he doesn't want to listen to a word anyone says."

"Did he…" The question is on the tip of my tongue, and I know I shouldn't ask, but my heart can't help itself. "Did he mention me?"

"I wish I had a better answer for you," Sebastian says. "Give him time, and he'll come around. His head is too fogged up to see how much he's fucking up. You're going to be the first person he wants when he's ready to let someone in."

Two weeks ago, I would've believed that, and as much as I know deep down that Colson and I share this unexplainable connection, the heartbreak I'm facing tells me differently. My biggest fear is that my time with him has already come to an end, that he *won't* come to his senses, and if I chase after him, he'll continue to push me out of the way until I have nothing left in me.

No energy to keep fighting.

I don't relay my thoughts to Sebastian.

We follow the trail to the campus's most loved coffee spot and change to a lighter subject. All the while I wish I were with Colson. I wish Janie was still alive. And most importantly, I wish my heart didn't feel as though it was going through a meat grinder on the slowest setting possible.

"SCREW THIS."

I can't take it anymore and slam my textbook closed. Focusing on my study notes for my upcoming exam on early childhood teaching methods is impossible. As soon as the information hits my brain, it floats away as if I never read it. Nothing is sticking, and it's all because my mind is focused on one thing.

Seeing Colson.

Getting updates from Sebastian isn't enough, and I know it'd be best if I stay away, but it has been days, and I won't do it any longer.

I can't.

I tug on a pair of black leggings and a loose shirt before slipping my jacket on. I pull my hair back in a ponytail, and I don't even care about the pimple that's on my chin or the smeared mascara under my lashes. I rush down the hallway, glad not to run into anyone until I make it to the kitchen for a bottle of water and spot Everleigh. She's been home a lot more since she broke up with Tristan, and honestly, I'm still getting used to it.

Her eyebrows stretch up her forehead as she pops a chip into her mouth. She has a clipped stack of papers on the counter next to her and her favorite editing pen with a frilly feather on the end of it. "Where are you going dressed like an assassin in the night?"

I glance down at my attire, noticing that I am, indeed, dressed in all black. Whatever. It doesn't make a difference. My pulse beats wildly regardless of the color of my clothes.

Clearing my throat and trying to sound as confident as possible, I announce, "I'm going to see him."

Concern flashes over her features. "This late? And are you sure that's a good idea?"

"Good idea or not, I need to see him, Ev."

She wipes the chip crumbs off on her leg. "I thought space was good right now."

I throw my arms up in the air out of exasperation. "He doesn't have anybody, Everleigh! Everyone is *leaving him alone.* Respecting his want for space when he needs someone there the most. And I know I originally agreed with that, but I was okay with it for, like, an hour. Not days."

"I hear you, and I say, if it feels right then go make sure he knows you're there for him, but also…be careful."

"Colson would never hurt me," I assure her.

"That's not why I said it." She moves toward the foyer and digs a can of Mace out of her bag before slapping it into my palm. "You're going to Harrison Heights at nearly ten o'clock at night. You don't know what you'll bump into there."

I nod and take it, grateful she's not trying to convince me to stay. "Thank you. For the Mace and being there for me when you'd probably rather be editing whatever manuscript you're working on now."

"That's what friends are for, Violet. Besides, I needed a little bit of a break. Let me know how it goes?"

"I will," I promise, then I'm out our apartment door, riding the elevator down and hopping into my car. I use my memory to navigate over the river and onto his mom's street. It takes me three times, but I finally get it and pull up to the curb with a heaving chest.

The house is darker than what I'm used to, which isn't much since I've only been here one other time. I came all this way, and it'd feel wrong to give up without at least going in to see if he's home. Besides, where else would he be?

I try his cell again before I get out of the car, hoping he'll answer and make this a lot easier. He doesn't, so I slip out and sprint to the front door. I realize I haven't thought my plan through when I twist the doorknob and find it locked.

I look back out at the street and take in the streetlights barely brightening the night.

Why did I think I could just walk right in?

Because I'm too in my head, that's why.

I just assumed that since his mom had the door unlocked in the past that he'd leave it the same way.

I think for a moment and find myself skipping down the front stoop to walk around the house. I try the back door—no luck—then resort to checking the windows with determination. The ones within reach, that is. The living room window is first but also locked. Then another window around the side. It doesn't budge. I move around the corner of the house to try the next. For a second it seems like it's going to budge but then catches on something. Probably rust. My best guess is that these windows haven't been open since the house was built.

There's only one left, but I already know my fate. I'm not getting into this house. Not tonight. I won't be seeing Colson or have the chance to offer him my shoulder to cry on if he so chooses.

Toeing a big, heavy rock closer to the house so I can test the last latch, I try my best to get it to move, curling my fingers under the short ledge. Right when I think it might give, dead leaves crunch behind me. My heart beats up my throat, and I pull my hands away from the house to reach for the Mace that I stupidly left in the car.

A deep voice skips up my back and fills my ears. "What the hell are you doing?"

I end up putting too much weight on one side of my body when I turn to look over my shoulder and find Colson. My ankle rolls over the side of the rock, and I fall. Right into a flowerbed of dirt and stone. My elbow smacks into something hard, another rock perhaps, and pain blossoms around my ankle.

"Goddamnit, Violet," Colson growls, as if it's my fault he snuck up on me.

I'm a bucket of emotions that spills the second I tip over. I groan and try to right myself, but it almost feels like my arm is stuck under the weight of my body, and while I'm concerned about my throbbing ankle, I'm more focused on Colson crouching next to me, his frustration with me evident.

My eyes fill with big sloppy tears. I can't get the words out that I'm okay. That my emotions have nothing to do with my fall and everything to do with seeing him. I try to mumble out a pathetic apology. Over what? Me trying to break into his mom's house? The fact that he caught me?

He tucks his hands under my armpits and hoists me to my feet. "I can't believe you. You're lucky I saw you before I went inside. Can you stand?"

I apply pressure on the ankle that rolled. It responds with an inflamed sensation that circles my joint. I hobble my weight over to my uninjured foot. "It hurts a bit."

"Fuck." He blows out a breath then says, "Okay, just lean on me. We'll go slow and in through the back."

I find a comfortable way to hold my foot up and do as he says. He turns into a human crutch as I limp beside him.

"Why are you here, anyway? I thought I made myself clear when I didn't respond to your calls."

Screw making things clear.

It was unfair for him to walk out on me with little explanation. To strip away my own voice when it came to us.

I wince when I shift my foot higher so it doesn't snag on the concrete at the back patio. "I wanted to see you."

What he doesn't know is that I *needed* to.

"I haven't answered your calls for a reason, Violet." His voice is cold and lacking all the affection I'm used to. I decide I'll do whatever I can to hear it again.

"If you would have answered your phone, I wouldn't have felt the need to—"

"Felt the need to what? Break into my house? You're lucky the people in this neighborhood don't give a shit about breaking and entering."

He pulls keys out of his pocket and unlocks the back door. "Put your weight on the doorknob if you need to, then use the counter. I'll pull a chair over for you to sit on long enough to check out your foot."

The house is as dark as it seems from the outside until Colson flicks on the kitchen light and closes the door behind him. It's a lot cleaner than last time, the countertops cleared off. There aren't loads of dishes in the sink, either. I sit down when he drags a chair over and motions for me to sit.

"You gave me no other choice," I tell him, swallowing my nerves. "You just…left."

He yanks open the freezer door, shuffles a few things around, then pulls out a bag of mixed vegetables that are old enough for the label to be worn off. He kneels down in front of me and gently lifts my leg. I grimace when he twists my shoe off. His strong fingers curl around my foot, elation zooming through me at the contact. It's barely anything, and his least favorite body part, but it doesn't slow the butterflies that sweep low in my belly or take away from me wishing it were more.

He gently rotates my foot without looking up at me, checking the damage. "It's not bruised, but a little swollen. Should be fine. Take the vegetables. You can ice it in your car."

Is he serious?

I'm so taken aback, my scoff gets stuck somewhere in my body. "Ice it in my car?"

He stands tall and swipes his thumb over his nose. "That's what I said."

Tears threaten all over again. My words come out in a pitiful whisper. "Why are you being like this?"

"You know why."

"Because your mom is gone? Because you don't know how to deal with it? Let me be here for you, Colson. That's all I'm asking."

He scrubs his hands over his face, twists so his back is facing me, then spins around so fast that I don't see it coming. His abrasiveness. "I don't *want* your help, Violet. I don't want Sebastian's. Get it through your thick heads. I want to be left alone!"

I press the cold bag to my ankle. Every word he says cuts into me like a razorblade, and I just know they'll scar long after this conversation is over.

Because I'm so damn exhausted from the last few days of worrying about him while multitasking with studying for finals, I finally snap. It doesn't matter how nice I am, how kind my words are or how compassionate my actions, he isn't hearing what I'm saying. And I'm done—*done*—with him treating me like what we have is nothing.

Like I'm easily disposable.

He's kidding himself. Delusional if he thinks I'm going to give up on him as easily as he's giving up on me.

I clutch the chilled bag of food, caring less about the mild twinge in my ankle, and throw it at his stupid chest. It thuds against him then smacks to the floor. I can tell he's close to the end of his rope. That if I act out more, it might have him tossing me over his shoulder so he can haul me out to my car himself. Well, I'm at the end of my rope, too, utterly fed up with him and the days he let go by without responding to me.

His gaze drops to the makeshift ice pack on the floor. He picks the bag up and tosses it on the counter. It skids to a stop against the wall. "You don't want to ice your ankle, suit yourself."

"You're a coward," I insult, hating the way it sounds on my lips and makes my stomach curl in on itself.

His brows push down, and without warning, he steps closer. I'm still sitting in the chair he brought over, but I don't care how tall he is or how close he stands. He's not the man I thought he was if he can't even *try* to fight.

I lift my chin against his intimidation. His jaw clenches. "You want everyone to think you're so strong." A choked laugh leaves me. "You stood in the alley at Lucy's and told Sylvia you'd *beg* someone to end you if you ever did something as low as Nelson."

"Don't fucking compare me to that guy. He was a piece of shit covered in sprinkles. I'm not forcing myself on you. The exact opposite, actually."

There's enough space for me to stand, and I do, wishing I was this close to him for a different reason. My chest presses to his. He doesn't back away. Neither of us stand down for the sake of the other. "Tell me how pushing me away and telling me to ice my ankle in my car makes you *any* better."

"I didn't put my hands on some woman when she didn't want it." The muscle in his jaw twitches. "I'd *never* do that, and you know it."

He's seething, fumes coming out of his ears at the

comparison. He's right, in a way. He's not on the same playing field as Nelson, and I do know he'd never force himself onto anyone who didn't want it, but I'm distraught over him not giving me the time of day.

I hate myself for resorting to hurting him with my words, but what else am I supposed to do? Get down on my knees and beg for his love? For his attention? Attempt to break into his mother's house all over again?

"Maybe I do, but it doesn't change that you're still cowering. That you're being a pussy instead of being the man I know you a—"

He reaches for me so fast, one hand grasping the back of my head and the other grabbing my thigh on the side opposite of my hurt ankle. He wraps my leg around his waist and swings me around until I'm flat against the refrigerator door.

My heart jumps in excitement, and embarrassingly so, a rush of heat travels low in my stomach. I keep my arms by my sides, too scared to reach out because I don't want him pulling away, as he presses his forehead against mine.

I'm gifted with the clean spicy scent that always follows him. I breathe deeply. His touch, no matter what emotion it stems from, feels like home. Like the warm baths I've gotten so used to these last few months, it comforts me.

His tone trembles when he speaks. I imagine his chest tightening along with the way his voice breaks. "What do you want from me?"

I swallow at the lump in my throat, incapable of words.

"What? Don't have anything to say? You were fine running me down into the ground a second ago. Have you run out of insults, or are you just surprised that I'm finally giving you what you want? That I'm finally touching you?"

His face hovers so close to mine that all I can focus on is the weight of his body against mine. We're chest to chest, and with a little bit of effort, we could be lip-locked and drowning out all this hurt with something sweeter.

Just as I'm about to say something, he nudges his nose against mine, his warm exhale spreading over my skin in the best possible way.

"I'm sorry," is what leaves my mouth when I finally find the courage to talk.

He tilts his head to the side and drops his face to my shoulder. His nose climbs up my neck, running slowly across my skin until goosebumps pebble under my clothes.

"Don't ever apologize for how you feel," he whispers in his delicate voice I'm used to, pressing his beautiful lips to the spot below my earlobe. Tingles ignite under my flesh and move in every direction. His hand that hooks my leg to his side squeezes into my thigh.

This isn't exactly what I had in mind when I came over. My plan was to talk, not to seduce him, but I'll take anything he's giving. And maybe, just maybe, he'll be real with me when it's over.

Hell, maybe it's already over, and I just don't realize it yet.

I grip onto his hoodie, twisting the fabric in my palms as he continues to kiss my neck. Most are quick pecks. Others are more languid and end with his tongue sweeping over my sensitive skin.

"I don't want to hurt you," he hums, nipping at my earlobe.

"Then don't." It's difficult to focus on his honesty when all I want is to melt into him.

"I can't focus on not hurting you when there's so much other shit going on in my head." His hand, the one at the back of my head, slides down my neck and goes as far as tucking into the collar of my jacket. He tugs and the top button pops free.

"One minute I want to break things," he confesses. "The next, I want to cave to the pressure of it all, say fuck it, and down a bottle of booze so I can forget what it feels like."

I really shouldn't say it.

Shouldn't give in because when I look back on it, I'll realize how fucked up it is, but Colson and I have always had a certain way of doing things. We give ourselves up to the other when it's needed most. And I know, without a doubt, that Colson's favorite way to let go is when I give myself to him fully.

No different than the night we made out at Lucy's.

Or when it happened again in this very house.

I'm at his mercy.

I'll *always* be at his mercy.

"Forget all that," I whisper to him. "I'm right here. Use me. Drink *me* until you're too drunk to notice the difference."

NINE

COLSON

I WISH she wouldn't have offered herself up, but if there's one thing I know about Violet, it's that she cares tremendously, sometimes too much, when it comes to certain people. I just happen to be on that list. It'd be easier if I didn't know how the hell I ended up there, but I do.

For months, we've bonded, created this link between our hearts and souls that's almost unexplainable. She gets me. Understands what I need at every moment. Like now. If I caught anyone else trying to break in through one of the windows, they would have curled into themselves at my hard tone, but she didn't let it bother her. At least not enough to leave. She lashed out, got under my skin, and now look at us.

I want her so goddamn badly it physically hurts. Not just because I want to forget about what I'm feeling inside, but because it's always good with her. I'm well aware I'll never meet another girl like her. One who is so willing to give herself up for the sake of pulling me out of the shit-stinking mud I'm stuck in.

I'm a selfish bastard.

I don't tell her no when she tells me to use her as my drink of choice.

For the life of me, I can't force that one-syllable word out of my mouth, and if I'm being honest, I don't want to.

I left her.

Told her we were over.

But as she stands in front of me, spitting insults, I'm reminded of how much I fucking care for this girl. How much she makes me feel and how easy it is to forget the rest of the world when she's near. She's the greatest magician on the goddamn planet.

I slide my hand down the line of buttons on her jacket, each one of them popping one after another. I go slow to grant her the opportunity to pull away if she has a change of heart. Her arms go slack, and her coat drops to the floor instead. Her shirt comes off next, leaving her in nothing but her pants and the flimsy bralette she wears when she's kicking back at the apartment. This one is light pink but almost looks purple and does nothing to hide her nipples. They're right there and as my thumb draws closer to them, I wonder how I got so lucky.

How the *fuck* did I lock her down?

How the hell is it possible that *I'm* the one she's looking at with unapologetic desire pooling in her eyes?

I wish I could dive into them and sink into the pureness of her irises. As much as she calls me a coward, and as much as I allowed it to get under my skin, she doesn't mean it. Violet is too genuine to cut me with those razor-sharp words when she already knows I'm hurting from everything else.

She's doing it for a reaction.

Not to upset me.

But to draw me in.

My thumb slips under the loose band of fabric covering

her, and in a windshield-wiper motion, rolls over her. She presses her eyes closed, and I am intensely aware of the scent of her floral bubble bath soap, the kind that smells like a summer rain shower and a hint of jasmine.

I lower my face to hers. "You and that scent. It drives me crazy. Makes you smell so good."

"I needed to de-stress tonight."

I hate that she needed it because of me. That I've been a big enough asshole for her to need a bath at all.

My kiss starts slow but turns feral quickly. My teeth graze her sweet lips, and when my tongue begs to glide against hers, she opens for me. Over and over again, our tongues tangle, and each time they do, a needy throb pulses in my jeans. A line of fire trails down my spine, prompting the thought of sinking into her sweet, wet center.

She presses her palms to my chest, pushing me away and breaking our kiss. She averts her gaze, but I grip her chin and make her look at me. We've always had this uncanny ability to communicate through our stare, and I don't want it stopping now. She can be upset with me all she wants, but I want to feel the burn of those golden eyes against my own.

And that's exactly what I get when she peers up at me. She sucks her bottom lip into her mouth, and I wish it were mine doing the sucking instead. Her gaze, though heady, packs a punch behind it. She might be giving me this moment, but it's only a matter of time before she knocks me on my ass. I can feel it. Sense it. And yet, I continue on with my inconsiderate need to have her.

I don't get the chance to lift her bralette off because she pushes me backward. My ass drops down into the chair she sat in a moment ago as she hobbles on her feet in front of me. I know her ankle hurts. It had already started to swell by the time I got her inside, but she pushes through, stretching her hands over my thighs. My dick bristles in excitement, strangling itself against the elastic band of my boxers.

She sinks down onto her knees. I'd rather this be happening anywhere other than Mom's kitchen, but a tiny, hedonistic part of me loves knowing that I'll be adding a better, more magnificent memory of this house into the mix.

I tug my hoodie up a bit, remembering where I came from tonight. After sitting in this house for days, I needed to get up and get out. I landed at Gulliver's. Llewellyn let me work for a couple hours to get my mind off shit. Afterward, he suggested I take a few days for bereavement leave.

Violet peels my belt off, her fingers slipping it out of the loops. She finds the button on my jeans and rolls the zipper down with ease. I shimmy just enough to get my pants down my legs. My mouth waters in anticipation, my stomach clenching.

She eyes the hard ridge settled in my lap, finds the cut in the fabric of my boxers, and pulls me through it. I don't miss the way she licks her lips or how her hand lazily moves up and down me.

Fuck.

I bite down on my cheeks and rest my head back.

I don't know what the future holds, and because of it, I want to take in every second of this I can. I want to be fully overwhelmed by the woman in front of me.

"I need to hear you say what you want from me." She says it so softly, I have to put some of the words together on my own. She's being a little more shy than usual, but if guidance is what she wants, it's hers.

I look at her.

She's so fucking pretty on her knees for me.

"Grip me and lick your way up." She looks up at me like she's about to give me the best blow job of my life. I reach forward and run my thumb across her lower lip. "Get my cock nice and wet for that pretty mouth."

Her tongue flicks out at my thumb and then she moves her attention to the stiffness in her hand. She holds me with the perfect amount of pressure. Her tongue starts low, and it's so fucking hard to stop the groan that races up my throat.

Goddamn, she feels good.

She leaves a trail of wetness as she glides her way up, her tongue circling the head where she knows I like it most. She forms her lips into a kiss and moves to the sides of my shaft, slicking them up and down in a way that makes it feel like she's grinding her pussy lips against me.

I want to reach out, let my hand caress her face, but I don't allow myself that connection. I grip the sides of the chair in efforts to control myself. To keep from reaching out.

"Just like that. Now open wide and let me have you."

The groan in my throat breaks free the second she suctions her mouth on me. She's slow at first then picks up speed when I gently press my hips upward. I love every inch of this girl's body, but there's something about the way she sucks me off that lights a fire down my spine. It's embarrassing to admit how close I am after only a few minutes, and she can tell.

My cock springs out of her mouth in a tease, and she's at it again, licking me without abandon, all the way down to my balls where she softly sucks one into her mouth.

"Oh, fuck."

She carefully runs her tongue over them in a way that makes me want to finish down her throat. The thought of it paired with what she's doing only overwhelms me more.

"You take me so good," I praise, watching her as she lifts her gaze to mine. There's a dare in her eyes when she shifts my cock closer to my stomach. My balls quiver as her hot tongue sweeps over my skin, going low enough until she hits that strip of skin under them.

"Jesus Christ," I breathe out heavily.

I can't control myself. My head tilts back and rests on the chair. My eyes screw themselves shut, and I sink into the bliss of having her mouth on me, on what it feels like to not *feel* anything but her.

She's never touched me there before but this sensation that causes my skin to shudder and my balls to tighten is heavenly. So much that I wouldn't give a fuck if my time came the second I released, which grows closer the more she plays with me.

"Does that feel okay?" she asks between pleasuring my balls and the space below.

"Vi, baby, it feels so fucking good that it has me wanting to fuck your throat until I come." I shift my head and look at her. "Is that what you want? To taste me?"

Her cheeks match the same shade of pink from after we fucked that first time. The night I led her into her apartment, and we got lost in each other. I've craved her every day since, and now is no different. She's made me long for these moments only to hoard the memories in the deepest recesses of my mind. I never want to forget this—her—but I know when all is said and done, all I'll have left is the box in my head I've scribbled her name on.

"Mmm, maybe I would like that," she mewls. "Would you?"

"You know I would," I grind out roughly.

She laps at me until I can't take it and brings her mouth back up to my tip. I guide her back onto me, and she takes me whole.

A few times, she pushes me back so far that if I close my eyes, I swear it's her pussy I'm lost in. Her gags are the only reminder that it's not. I push deeper every chance I can, and when that familiar heat swishes down low, I let my orgasm rip through me like a hurricane in the night.

Ribbons of tension paint the back of her throat. It's so fucking hot that it spurs my release on longer than I expect, giving her a mouthful that she proudly takes.

TEN

COLSON

I ZIP MY PANTS, the sharp hissing of metallic causing tense sparks in the air. If this was a week ago, I would've clasped Violet's hands in mine and brought her up to her feet. I would've dragged her leggings down her long legs and placed my mouth over every inch of her skin, and after, I would have eaten her out until she trembled and stars scattered her vision.

Unfortunately, it's not a week ago, and as much as I'd love to let this continue, it needs to end. I hate how selfless she's being and how easy it is to take advantage of that. I don't want to be the guy who depletes her and makes her realize that she deserves so much more than she's getting. She's already had a similar experience with Webber, so how fair is it to turn around and do the same to her?

She drags the back of her hand across her mouth and clears her throat. She takes a step back, giving me the space I need to gather myself and stand, then moves for her belongings that lay in a heap of fabric by the fridge. I cringe over how dirty the floor is but revel in the notion that the kitchen light isn't all that bright. It doesn't illuminate the entire space. Only offers a soft yellow-orange glow over half the room.

I make a mental note to clean the entire house from top to bottom when I feel up to it. I used to keep up with the cleaning when I still lived here, so it wouldn't be anything new. It's just a matter of getting out of my head enough to make it happen.

I sniff, the sound of it cutting through the quiet. I don't know where we go from here, but I do know that what just happened a minute ago can't mean that we're back together again.

I meant it when I broke up with her. I should've put what was happening between us to a stop the night outside of her apartment after she got a glimpse of the dysfunction in my life. Instead of saying fuck it and putting my lips on hers, I should've retreated.

I should've let it be.

Because she deserves better than what I can offer.

Better than cold shoulders and ignored texts.

She deserves more than the lies I've kept to protect a person who's no longer here.

God, what the hell would she say if she knew that I spent weeks paying off my deceased mother's drug dealer? And in place of getting her help no less.

She pushes her arms through her jacket when I finally work up the nerve to approach her. Even in this disgusting house and in the glow of the tangerine light, she's beautiful. I wish things weren't so fucked up. That Mom was still alive. That I could smooth my hands into Violet's silky hair and kiss her with all the love in my body.

I reach for her wrist. She stiffens and double blinks. There's an obvious roll to her throat when she speaks. "It's okay," she murmurs, her voice so goddamn quiet. "We don't have to—"

"That was..." I move my hand up her arm and thumb her

chin. She looks up at me, and the misty look in her gaze nearly sends me over the edge. I'm torn between wanting to drag her out of this house and dropping to my knees with an endless string of apologies. She stares at me, and I can't help but praise her for a job well done, for the way she suctioned that mouth around me like we were the last two people standing and it was our last day on earth. "You were goddamn phenomenal."

Pinkness slants over her cheeks.

My eyes flick between hers. "You like hearing that, don't you? And knowing that you can distract me so fucking well."

She's been doing it since the beginning of our relationship, occupying my mind with other stuff when I've needed it the most.

I need to put an end to it.

She can't show up unannounced. Can't be breaking into windows on my behalf. Whatever line of connection is left has to be severed. Whatever tether exists needs to be macheted clean off.

Because I can't have Violet when my head is so fucked up. Every time I think of Mom, boulders of guilt crush me. I sit in this house, and I think about the what-ifs, about what I could've done differently, about her having more time. About me being parentless.

I hate that something so greedy took her, that her heart was too weak to carry on, to fight, to give me more time with her. I'm irrevocably helpless. And then there's the shit with Finn and the Lincolns.

Forcing rehab should've been my priority over paying them back. My entire existence went to that, and I know I promised I was going to get Mom help after, but then everything happened so fast.

Finn was right.

This place embeds itself into you, and it doesn't leave.

I'm not about to let that happen to Vi. I care about her too much, which is exactly why I'm putting an end to this tonight.

For good, this time.

"Thanks for helping me out. You know, when I fell out there." It's soft on her lips when it comes out, and she limps a step away. "I think I can make it out to my car without help. It's actually, uh, starting to feel better."

I glance down at her ankle. I might be seconds from breaking her heart all over again, but I won't let her go out in the dark alone and fend for herself. I'll at least make sure she gets to her car okay.

"I can help you outside."

Her eyes meet mine. "You can do something better for me."

"Hmm?"

"Answer your phone when I call."

I roll my lips into my mouth and three, two, one…

"That's not going to happen."

She covers the hurt on her face remarkably well, but she forgets that I can read her like the back of my hand.

"What do you mean?"

"I told you I don't want to be bothered. You can't come around and push your way into my life, Violet. You can't show up, suck my dick, and think everything is going to be back to normal."

"I didn't—" She rubs her hands over her face and pushes her fingers up into her hairline. "I didn't do *that* just to convince you to get back with me or convince myself that everything is okay. I know it's not."

Violet will keep trying to right a wrong that has nothing to do with her. She'll continue to try to be here for me because it's who she is, it's who *we* are together. Only we're not a we anymore, and if I have to be the biggest asshole on the planet for her to see that, then so be it.

"Are you sure about that?" I question.

She's offended by my audacity, rearing her head back. Fuck, I am, too. "You truly think that I risked breaking in and rolled my ankle just so I could get in your pants and convince myself that life is just fucking dandy, Colson?"

"What matters is that we're done."

I don't want anything to do with you, I tell her in my head, even though it makes my entire body revolt.

If we were still only friends, and some other guy was pulling this shit on her, I'd pound him into the ground. I'd take one look at him and know it would be easy making his life a living hell.

She brings her fingers to her lips and shakes her head. She's seconds from cracking, from being consumed by the heartbreak my words stir, and it's so goddamn painful to have a front row seat to it.

But I have to do it.

"It doesn't have to be like this."

"Get it through your head, Violet." I tap my knuckle against my temple. "I don't fucking want to be with you anymore."

"What is so wrong about me being here for you? Even as your friend?"

Everything.

Nothing about that set up would work.

She takes a step forward, that jasmine scent invading my senses all over again. I twist around because I can't handle that right now and move over to the other side of the kitchen. She watches me despite my words manhandling her.

"You *don't* want to be here for me."

"Yes, I do!"

"No," I yell back, stomping over to her. It's the first time I've raised my voice at her like this, and I feel like the shittiest guy on this side of the Sycamore Memorial. "You fucking don't. You don't want to see me like this. You don't want to know what it feels like *here*." I punch my chest. "And you don't want to be on the receiving end of it."

"I'm not afraid of you...or your pain," she mutters softly.

"You should be."

"You're not the kind of man you say you are. *Think* you are." Her hands come up to my chest, playing with the strings from my hoodie while she tries to catch my gaze.

I pluck her hands off me. "Don't touch me."

"You didn't seem to mind a minute ago."

I turn to grip the countertop, my back to her. Again. "That was different."

She huffs, and I wish I wasn't this fucking stupid. "Of course it was. It's always different when you have your dick shoved down the back of someone's throat, isn't it?"

My teeth nip at my cheek and my jaw clenches. Her sucking me off *wasn't* nothing. I felt every ounce of her in the way she pleasured me, but I'm not about to tell her that. I'll never admit to wanting more of her in these moments where I'm so goddamn broken I can't tell left from right.

"Oh, nothing to say to that?" she goads. "Go figure."

"Please just go. For the love of fucking God, get me out of your head. What we had never existed." It's amazing how good I've gotten at spouting off bullshit since I found her on that rock.

She winds up her bow and that mouth of hers sends her insult flying. It lands in the center of my back, a stab above my kidneys. "Screw you, Colson. How dare you try to take that away from me, away from *us*."

We were always meant to go up in flames. I think I understand that more than ever. It was easy to think otherwise when I was so focused on Finn, thinking about getting Mom help, and working out my next step in life.

She sniffles and then yelps. I twist around to find her holding her ankle. She must've tried to take a step, but it was too much. I immediately spring into action and move to her side.

"No," she screams, shoving me away. "Get away from me! You don't get to say those things and then help me."

"You can't fucking walk on your own, Violet."

I hoist her back to her feet, her tiny fists flying at my chest in frustration. She lacks all the power in the world behind each punch, but it hurts more than when Nic and I got into it in that alleyway. Each time her closed palm connects with my body, my heart threatens to beat out of turn. To halt completely.

"Stop."

"No!" She's crying now, big sloppy tears rolling down her cheeks, and all because of me. *I* did this. I told her that what we had was worthless. That we'll never be together again. I've shown her that her mouth is worth more than loyalty and love.

I really am a fucking coward.

I grab her shoulders and shake her. "You have to."

"Fuck you for telling me what I *have* to do," she wails, yanking herself away from me. She stumbles on her foot then turns for the back door, breathing through the pain each time she limps.

Wiping her tears, she flings the door open like she doesn't care if it slams against the wall. She moves as fast as she can with her bum ankle, but it feels like it's happening in slow motion. Her barreling out the door, wisps of her dark hair reaching for me. She's a blur as she moves farther and farther away.

Out of sight.

Out of reach.

It's like watching a piece of myself leave, and I spring into action, following her out the back door to the side of the house.

She hobbles with each step, her body shaking. I don't know if it's from the discomfort in her ankle or the agony in her heart. I don't understand why the universe had to bring her into my life just to make me watch her leave.

I amble up next to her. She ignores me, wrenching her arm away when I offer her weak side support.

Don't worry, I wouldn't want to be touched by me, either.

At the front corner of the house, she stops and gathers her breath. Her tears have slowed and what's left of them, she wipes away. I wonder if her ankle is throbbing as much as my chest.

I know a moment will come where I'll regret this, but I also know we'll both be better for it. I can't cater to Violet when I'm sifting through the sandy shores of grief and guilt.

"I can walk the rest by myself." The darkness of the night shrouds us. There's not a star in the sky tonight. No moon to give us that little bit of light to make out our faces. I can't make out the tiny beauty mark on her face or her permanent frown.

"I'll watch from here," I offer because I'm hearing exactly what she's *not* saying. She doesn't want my help.

"I don't want us to throw insults at each other," she says calmly. I don't know how, in the space of seconds, she mellowed out the anger and pain flowing through her. "I don't want to cause more hurt than what's already here. I'm sorry for not controlling my tongue back there and saying hurtful things. I didn't mean them."

I've already told her not to apologize over her feelings, but I keep my mouth shut. I'm in the same boat. I'm fucking exhausted after the days I've had. I don't want to fight. I just want to let her go.

Her face turns in my direction, I think, but it's hard to tell since it's night. "Are you talking out of grief and everything you're feeling with your mom, or are you being serious? Are we r—" Her voice cracks, and fuck, if it doesn't make this ten times harder. "Are we really done?"

I chew on her words, and for a split second, I think maybe we can work this out. We've done well together this entire time. Even though I had other shit going on, I never let it affect my relationship with her. I promised her I'd try and told myself I wouldn't roll over and die at the first signs of defeat, but...

Something deep inside of me says to release her. That I'll eventually screw her up, that even though I can try to convince myself I'm good for her, I'm really not.

She doesn't even know about my past with Finn or the secrets I've kept. Staying with her would only be delaying the inevitable. I'm speeding up the process by ripping the roots out before they grow too strong and can't be removed.

"It's the end, Vi."

I swear I see her nod. That, or my eyes are playing tricks on me. She doesn't say another word. Maybe she can't. It's difficult speaking when emotions clog your throat and you're trying to gargle your way past it.

She makes it to her car, and I watch her get in as the moon shuffles between the clouds, offering me a sliver of temporary light. She doesn't look back, doesn't send me one of her cheeky smiles over her shoulder that I love so much. She turns over her ignition and vanishes into the night.

I trudge my way back into the house, grab a glass from the cabinet and fill it with water. I drink it down in large gulps as I walk back to Mom's room. An overwhelming sensation fills me to the brim. It drowns out the tick of the oscillating fan I set up on the dresser next to the Jack Daniel's. It darkens the room despite the light being on, and because I have nowhere to put it, because I'm already feeling everything, I rip the seal off Jack and bring the rim to my lips without thinking twice.

ELEVEN

COLSON

Aunt Bess: Sebastian told me you're at your mom's.

Aunt Bess: We have stuff we need to discuss.

Aunt Bess: You're giving me no choice but to drive there.

MY HEAD POUNDS as if a sledgehammer has come down on it repeatedly, my face and neck pulsating. My arms are hundred-pound weights each, and when I reposition them to roll over to my back, a low groan tumbles out of me.

Fuck.

I don't know how much I drank last night. I stopped keeping track after that initial sip hit my tongue but judging by the way my body is one move away from combustion, I must've downed quite a bit.

I peel open my eyes, my gaze fuzzy around the edges.

Nausea immediately implants itself in my stomach, reminding me of the flu I had when I was eleven. My insides churn at the memory of being in bed for those two days and vomiting up everything I ate.

The steady thump of pain behind my eyes worsens when I turn my head and peer over at the nightstand. I grab my phone and brighten the screen. It's like someone is in my face with a flashlight. I squint through the newfound sensitivity behind my eyelids and note the time.

I slept through breakfast and nearly lunchtime.

Brown eyes invade my memory when I turn back over, their color matching the liquid of the Jack Daniel's.

I want to hate Violet for showing up last night, for pushing me, and finally making me snap. I was doing so good at keeping Jack at an arm's length. But then I had no choice but to crack her chest wide open. I saw the look on her face. She came to get me to see reason, to get me to open my ears and heart to the fact that I can trust and lean on her. I didn't listen. Instead, I took advantage of her. The thought of it triggers the gnawing pain in my gut to pinch sharper, causing my throat to spasm with the possibility of a heave.

What the hell is wrong with me?

Why did I let her give me a blow job?

Why didn't I tell her *no* and immediately walk her out to her car?

Mom is gone, and now Violet is, too.

All thanks to me.

This sense of anguish trickles through me, not near as potent as last night, but it's there nonetheless. I find the bottle of Jack on the floor at my feet when I sit up and make it to the edge of the bed. What's left of the golden liquid sloshes when I kick it out of my way.

I make it to the bathroom and splash cold water on my

face. It's the best thing I've felt since before Aunt Bess's fundraiser. Even though Mom was in lockup, life felt hopeful back then. I had the girl of my dreams. Finn was paid off. I was in the clear and finally ready to figure out my life.

I cup another handful and toss it at my face. It helps calm the nausea stirring in my gut, and when I look at myself in the mirror, I'm met with blue eyes I'd rather not see. Blue eyes that are submerged so deep in a murky marsh that they can't see clearly. Blue eyes that are desperate to get a handle on the grief stirring them into obsidian swirls.

A heaviness I don't see coming hits me square in the chest and pushes itself up behind my eyelids. The pressure comes next. Before I know what's happening, my chest cracks wide open, and I'm crying at the bathroom sink. I clutch the porcelain like there's something grabbing at my feet, trying to pull me away.

"Why?" I bellow out, pressing my fingers to my eyes to get rid of the sting. "Things were messed up, but why did you have to go and do this? You could've gotten better."

Just like all those other times.

The possibility was there. It existed.

Until she took those drugs and blew it all away.

The truth of never seeing Mom again knocks me off my feet. I slide down to the bathroom floor and knock my head against the sink as I try to catch my breath. The sobs worsen, the pain engulfing me like a goddamn wildfire, burrowing its way under my skin and into my bones.

My mind goes on a wild goose chase, searching and seeing all the different ways this could have played out. It won't make a difference, I know that, but it helps lessen the panic in my chest and brings me back to the awful reality that is my life.

If I were only a few years younger, I'd be orphaned by Mom's departure.

I'm thanking fuck that's not the case when I hear someone at the front door. I wipe my mini meltdown from my face and cup another handful of cold water to throw at it. Something tells me it's Sebastian. He's the only one who's shown up regularly, and it's always in the mornings.

The knocks sound again, so I head out and open the door to find Aunt Bess. I have to do a double take to make sure I'm looking at the right person, but she's standing right there. Four feet away from me in the flesh and blood with eyes that look like they've been through a waterfall of tears.

Relief settles on her face, and it's the exact thing I don't want to see. Sadness and sorrow. Sympathy and empathy. She wishes she could take away what I'm going through, but she can't because she's going through it herself.

I let the door hang open and walk into the house. She follows silently, shutting it as I make it to the futon and sit. I prop my elbow up and run my finger over my lip.

She blows out an unsteady breath. "I can't remember the last time I was in this house."

Neither can I.

Maybe when she brought Mom back from rehab and promised she'd be there for her every step of the way. Suddenly, I'm angry at her for not trying harder. For not being in her sister's life more. For not *helping* me.

I stare at the wall. "Does it even matter?"

"I guess in the grand scheme of things, it doesn't." She sits down next to me. "I wanted to check on you. How are you holding up?"

"I don't really want to talk about it," I tell her, trying to cover the bite in my tone and the sting in my eyes.

"I know this must be hard."

"Do you?" I snap, looking over. "Is it hard for you?"

Her brows pull together, an indent creasing between them. I've offended her. "How can you ask me that, Colson? Of course, it's hard for me. She's my sister."

"One you stopped coming around for," I mutter.

She shakes her head and clutches her bag on her lap like it's her lifeline. Like it'll help her find her way out of this house, out of this town. Like if she touches anything else she might succumb to the same fate as her sister. "There are reasons for what I've done, the decisions I've made. Janie was a flight risk. If I didn't walk away and take care of myself, she was going to take me down with her. She already was beginning to."

I don't remember Aunt Bess succumbing to the pressures of dealing with Mom. But maybe I was too young. Too in my own head to see how much it affected her. I don't care to pick apart the pieces of that puzzle right now.

"I wanted to wait for you, but you haven't been around. I had to make the executive decision on her burial." She rubs an open palm on her leg, and I realize this is more than uncomfortable for her, and it should be. We're talking about *her* dead sister. *My* dead mother.

I move my elbows to my knees and drop my head in my hands. Just thinking about her being six feet under makes me want to fucking puke.

"I wasn't sure what her wishes were or if she had any."

"What did you choose?"

"I wanted her close to her family," she says. "We picked a burial site for her at Willow Creek Cemetery near Chatham Hills. She'll be laid to rest tomorrow morning. It'll be private, just family, but we want you there, Colson. It'd be wrong to send her off without her son present."

My heart kicks at my ribs.

"And if I don't show?"

"Don't do that to yourself." I can feel Aunt Bess's eyes on me again, burning a judgmental hole in the side of my head. "Don't give yourself a lifetime of regret."

I thought dealing with Mom's erratic behavior was difficult. The mood swings. The cravings. The mornings she'd walk through the door like it was no big deal that she stayed out all night while she had a kid at home. The guys she'd bring back with her just to manipulate into giving her drugs or money. The money she stole from me—directly and through the money I gave Finn.

I'd deal with all that ten times over if it meant I didn't have to have this conversation.

A thought hits me, one I've had many times since Uncle Thad finished the words Aunt Bess couldn't say at the fundraiser. "I don't understand how she got the drugs in the first place."

"You know how it is. Even when everyone is supposed to be locked up and doing their time, things still sneak through the cracks."

My gut knows that's true, but I also get the feeling that it's not the entire story. I hate knowing that someone handed over the very thing that took her life without caring that they were taking away someone's mother and sister.

Aunt Bess gently rubs my back. "Your mom was a recovering addict who was in the thick of her addiction. Withdrawal can turn someone into a totally different person. Can desperately convince them that they need more of what they long for than they do. It was a tragic accident; one we should be grateful didn't happen sooner."

I rub my hands over my face to keep the emotions that want to wrack my chest all over again at bay. Perhaps she's right in saying it was just a freak accident. Maybe it all came down to Mom taking more than she could handle. She was always good at biting off a bigger piece than she could chew.

"There's something else we need to talk about," Aunt Bess announces. "As you know, your grandmother left me and Janie an inheritance. It's the same money that we used to set up the recurring payments on the mortgage and utilities here. My lawyer is drawing up the paperwork to have it transferred into your name as we speak."

I remember Sebastian saying something about money.

"I don't want it," is what comes out of my mouth instead of asking more questions. I don't want something that was hers. If I take it, it writes her death in stone. It makes it permanent.

"Yes, you most certainly do," Aunt Bess rebukes. "If you don't claim it as her next of kin, the bank will absorb it. Do you want to say no to almost a hundred and thirty thousand dollars, Colson?"

My ears perk at her words.

A hundred and thirty thousand dollars.

I've never known how much money existed in that bank account. I was too young to understand the details of my grandmother's death. The only thing that mattered was having a roof over our heads and knowing that Mom and I wouldn't end up on the streets or have the power shut off.

I look over at my aunt. She's wearing an expression like she knows I won't say no to it. How could I? That's a…literal shit ton of money. The kind that takes people *out* of this town.

So, as much as I want to, I can't pass it up.

I swallow at the bulge in my throat, ignoring the way my stomach wants to upchuck the alcohol I drank last night. The nausea just won't quit.

"What do you need from me to get it transferred?"

"We have an appointment with my lawyer after the burial

tomorrow. He'll go over all the details with you, and you'll sign the paperwork, but you'll need your social security card and birth certificate to prove your identity as Janie's son."

"I only have my social security card." I carry it around in my wallet even though it's heavily frowned upon. I didn't trust that I'd get it back if Mom held onto it. Or that I would remember where I put it if I hid it.

She takes in the house around us. The dingy carpet. The yellowed walls. "What's the likelihood that she has your birth certificate stowed away in this house somewhere?"

My teeth cut into my bottom lip. "Your guess is as good as mine, but I'll look around. If I can't find it?"

She pats my back. "We'll cross that bridge when we get to it. Pointless to worry about what hasn't happened yet." Her gentle hand hooks over my shoulder and rests there. "I won't bother you any longer. I'm sure you're enjoying your space, but if you need anything…"

…*you know I'm here,* I finish for her in my head.

I watch as she walks out the door and closes it behind her. I inhale a steadying breath, hoping to tamp down the urge to vomit. I find myself in the bathroom with my head in the toilet a minute later.

TWELVE

VIOLET

"I DON'T THINK this is a good idea."

Sebastian leans against the doorframe in his funeral attire, looking every bit of nonchalant while I freak out. He has a mini bag of M&M's in his hand—the kind little kids get at Halloween—and empties the rounded candies into his palm, dumping most of them into his mouth a second later.

It reminds me of the obsession Olive and I have with Sour Patch Kids, the memory highly welcome since it's been a few days since I've talked to her. I make a mental note to text her later when I'm not so distracted that it feels as if my head might burst if I add one more thought into the mix.

"Maybe. Maybe not. But what's he going to do when you show up? Kick you off cemetery grounds like he owns them?"

I tug my black pantyhose up my legs. Sebastian kindly puts a hand over his eyes when I have to shimmy them up under my dress. I should've put them on first, but again, I'm so overwhelmed that even executing getting dressed in the proper order proves difficult.

"Colson broke up with me. Made it very clear that he

doesn't want to see me. I shouldn't be showing up at his mother's funeral like we never parted, like I knew her, like..." I'm at a loss for words and so tangled in my emotions that I don't know what else to say to convince Sebastian that I should stay home.

He dusts his hands off before moving into my room. He showed up fifteen minutes ago, as he promised he would yesterday, and has been keeping me company while I finish getting ready. I thought I wouldn't mind him being here before heading out, but it's making this all seem a lot more intense.

Like I'm about to make a huge mistake.

I saw the way Colson looked at me the other night.

Understood it clearly when he told me we were done, and I hobbled to my car. If I have one thing going for me, it's that my ankle is feeling a lot better. But the rest of me?

He's going to freak if I trek up to his mom's burial ceremony after what happened the last time I saw him. My heart and ego still ache any time I muster up the courage to think about how he left me hanging that night. How he watched me make it to my car in a series of limps. How he stood there and watched me drive out of his life like it wasn't worth calling me back to stay.

Sebastian knows that I showed up at his house. What he doesn't know is how many times I've visualized his cousin running after my car, yelling for me to stop, just so he could tell me what a huge mistake he was making.

Sebastian presses his hand gently against my arm. I look up into his eyes, and I'm so glad to have a friend like him. Sylvia and Tristan are too busy with Fletcher and Nelson to care about anyone else. And there's no way I'm falling back on Webber to get me through. Space is the best thing for us. Which circles me back around to Everleigh, who's trying her best to offer support after going through her own break up, and Sebastian.

"He's going to flip shit when he sees me," I tell him, bringing my thoughts back to the present.

"No, he won't."

He sounds so sure of himself. As if he and Colson are the same person, and he can guarantee that he won't take one good look at me and tell me to leave.

"He'll be too distracted over what's going on. Sure, he might see you and wonder, but he's not going to kick you off of Willow Creek Cemetery property. He doesn't have the authority to do that."

I scoff. "We hope."

"I *know*."

Part of me hates that Sebastian is wasting his time with me when he could be living it up with his gaming buddies and hitting up parties with Tristan and Webber.

"He's already having a hard time. Add on that my mom has him going to see her lawyer afterwards to deal with legal shit, and it's going to have him wanting to shut down. He's going to need you there, both of us, to help him get through it," Sebastian explains.

"I'm not so sure about that." From what I saw the night I went to his mom's house, he seemingly had himself under control. Yeah, he didn't want to see me, and his tone was callous, his eyes jarring, but did he appear two seconds away from breaking into a tiny million pieces?

"Your lack of trust in me is insulting," Sebastian cracks, dousing out the tension with a teasing tone. My shoulders sag in relief that only one of us is freaking the hell out.

"I'm sorry." I bring my hands to my face, pressing my fingers into my cheeks, careful not to smudge the little bit of makeup I have on. "It's just that...I have a hard time believing that he's suddenly going to be okay with me around." My stomach swoops with the fright of a big, scary monster being under the bed. Standing this close to mine, it really does almost feel like one is about to reach out and take me. It certainly would save me from what I'm about to walk into. "Do I need to remind you of how he reacted?"

"Yeah, and if you ask me, he's a dumb shit for even thinking about pushing you away, but he's going through his worst days, Vi. Something bigger than either of us, and it's going to take him a minute to walk through it." Sebastian's voice is usually so upbeat that it nearly knocks me back a step when it trembles. "Don't give up just because the going is a little tough. Stick it out with him. *For him.* He's worth the fight."

The awful part is that I know that. I know Colson is worth it. I know that I care so deeply for him that I'd do anything to help him through what's been tossed in his lap. What's difficult is that I don't want to step on his toes. I don't want him to think of me as less than he already does. I don't want to risk pushing him so far away that when this is all said and done, when he's recovering from the impact, he's still too far away to grasp my hand for me to help him to his feet.

"You know how much I care about him, Sebastian."

"I know." He drops his hand and squeezes mine once before tucking his hands into his pockets. He grabs another small bag of chocolate candies out of his pocket and tears it open. This isn't the first time I've gotten hints of his obsession with the sweet treat, but it is the first time I'm noticing that he's falling back on it to help him get through his stress.

I watch as he dumps them out in his hand again and eats all of them at once.

My brow arches at him, and I let out a breath. "I'm sorry I'm making this all about me when you're going through it, too. Are *you* okay? It can't be easy seeing him hurting as deeply as he is. Or your mom."

He cracks an easy grin as he chews with a closed mouth, the corner of his lips tugging upward and shooing away the frown that was there a minute ago. "The great thing about things stinking like shit is that everything else smells a helluva lot better in comparison. Today will suck, but it'll be the beginning of their journey to healing."

I can't help it. I shove his shoulder softly.

"I can't believe I've known you for over two years and have never truly realized how much of a softie you are."

He rolls his eyes and crumbles his second empty M&M wrapper into his pocket. "It's not a big deal to care about people," he mumbles around a mouthful of candy.

He's right. It's not, which is why I brush my hair off my shoulder and tell him I'm ready to go.

SEBASTIAN PARKS his Aviator in the cemetery parking lot. As he shuts off his car, I notice the two other black SUVs that belong to his family. Tombstones of varying sizes and shapes outline the area, putting a nastier chill in my bones than the lower December temperatures. In the field up ahead, there are a few chairs next to a raised casket. Sebastian's parents and Colson are already seated and waiting.

I glance over at Sebastian. "Are we late?"

"Nah, they're early."

"Are your parents expecting me? Is Colson going to be the only one blindsided?"

"They know." He pulls the latch to open his door. "And

one day he'll be thankful as fuck that you blindsided him. Let's go."

I hop out of the car and smooth my dress down. My black peacoat keeps me warm as we cross the lot and descend onto the field. I'm careful where I walk, not wanting to disrespect graves. The closer I get to my ex, the harder my heart thrashes in my chest.

The way I see it, I'm walking into what could very well be a war zone.

Sebastian clears his throat to voice our arrival. His parents look up and notice him. His mom gets out of her chair and envelops him in a hug. I hear the quiet, "Hi, Mom," he gives her and shift my focus to the ground.

Colson is in my peripheral, sitting in that damn chair like a statue. His gaze is set forward. Most likely on the cherry-colored casket, and his body hitches forward at the waist, his elbows on his thighs. His chin rests on his hands, and all I imagine is walking over, squatting to my knees, and looking deep into his blue eyes. They'd tell me how he's really doing.

I rally some semblance of self-control as I watch Bess pull away from her son and come for me next. There's a sorrowful smile playing on her lips, making her look more put together than she did the night at the hospital. It must be eating her up that things are the way they are. She lost her little sister, and her nephew isn't doing so well.

Her worry and stress present themselves under her eyes, in the shadowing that sits below her lush lashes. She murmurs into my ear. "Violet. I'm so happy you could make it."

I move my hands to her back and squeeze gently. "I'm so sorry for your loss, Bess. There's nowhere else I'd rather be." And I mean that, despite my logic telling me to back away and leave.

"I'm so glad Colson has someone like you." She says it so quietly that I barely hear it. I'm not sure if it's done out of respect for where we are or so he doesn't hear. Does she know that he's broken it off with me?

She pulls away, and I look at her. "If there's anything you ever need, please let me know."

She clutches my hands. "You're the absolute sweetest. Come sit."

I find myself following Sebastian's mom to the only empty chair, which happens to be next to the one person I'm worried about seeing. I gulp down my nerves as I cross into his line of sight. He continues staring straight ahead. Pretends he doesn't notice me. I'm quiet as a mouse as I shuffle onto the seat and make myself comfortable. I get one semi-reassuring glance from Sebastian on Colson's other side, but it does nothing to calm the unsteadiness in my bones as I sit and do what everyone else does.

We stare at the closed casket before us. It's perched above the ground, and at some point, it'll be lowered into the hole beneath it. There's a picture of Colson's mother from when she was younger close to it. She was gorgeous, with long glossy hair and clear hazel eyes. It's easy to see her resemblance to Bess. Before her life choices impacted her appearance.

Time passes, but unlike a normal burial service, there isn't someone to say a prayer or offer a eulogy on behalf of the deceased.

I pick at my nails and glance at Colson's back. I wish I was brave enough to reach over, extend my condolences, and comfort him. I'm deathly—a real fitting word considering our surroundings—afraid of reaching out and ruining this for him. Frightened he'll snap like one too many rubber bands wrapped around each other.

A single rose sits atop his mom's casket, and I realize that if roles were reversed, I'd want his comfort. Even if it felt like I couldn't take one more breath and all I wanted was to be left alone with my thoughts, I'd want someone there for me.

I scrutinize my cuticles one last time and breathe in a steadying breath. *I can do this.* My hand is cold, chilled down to the bone from the winter air, but warms as soon as my palm glides over the scratchy sweater stretched over his back.

Turns out, I am brave enough. That, or I just really like to torture myself when it comes to Colson. I hold my breath, half expecting his muscles to jump, for him to jerk his shoulder in a way that says, *get the hell off me.* My eyes flutter shut when that doesn't happen.

My chest nearly caves in, and Lord knows I'm about ready to sob as if I personally knew Janie Moore. I've missed this man so much. I miss his stoic expressions, the goofy text messages he'd send throughout his workdays, how he'd come back to my apartment in the evenings and never once left me wondering if he missed me.

Someone sniffles. I'm pretty sure it's him, and my eyes snap over to his back where my hand gently moves up and down. Sebastian gives me a conspiratorial glance as if to say, *this is it. I hope you've been lifting weights because you're going to have to hold up your side of the crumbling man between us.*

I fold my lips into my mouth and endure the back and forth of wanting and not wanting to curl closer into his side. When his shoulders wobble with a weep, I can't hold back. The fight in my head vanishes, as does everything around me.

My hand moves from his back to the top of his leg where I can access it from the way he sits. His elbows are still perched on his thighs, but the second he feels me there, he drops one of his hands to mine. A jolt of comfort shoots through me, and I'm quick to entwine my fingers through his. He holds onto me like he slipped on a rock and tumbled over a cliff, and I'm the only one available to pull him back to solid ground. His other hand moves to his face, and he presses the heel of his palm to his eyes. It kills me every time his shoulders wrack the tiniest bit.

What was I thinking?

Not wanting to come today?

Sebastian was right.

He *needs* me.

Even if he might not see it.

Even if I'm scared.

Even if he broke up with me.

I scoot to the edge of my seat and run my free hand over his sweater-clad arm. The material is coarse, but I bet it's the last thing he's thinking about. No one cares about the little things when their heart is so tragically close to splintering.

"I'm here," I promise in a muffled tone. "I'm here, and I'm not going anywhere."

He doesn't respond, but I know he can't right now. He's lost at sea in the middle of a storm. Holding my hand doesn't immediately draw him out of it but guides him to shore. I'm his lighthouse, throwing out bright, luminous light every other second in hopes it'll bring him closer and closer to home.

Closer to me.

THIRTEEN

VIOLET

AFTER A WHILE, Bess and Thad quietly rise from their chairs and walk over to the casket. Bess places her palm on it and gazes at Janie's picture. I imagine she's saying goodbye and wishing she could have done more for her. I can't be certain, I'm not in her head, but I feel like it's something I'd say if I were in her shoes.

Bess offers a reminder to Colson before they retreat, saying that they'll have to head out soon. I assume for the appointment Sebastian told me about. Thad clamps his hand down on his shoulder with a reassuring squeeze. His way of telling him that he's not alone.

I like his uncle even more for the gesture; his one small action speaks the weight of a thousand words.

He and Colson have that in common.

They're gone a minute later, and it's just the three of us. Sebastian is so inaudible you wouldn't think he's there, but I can sense him wanting to provide help, if needed.

I wish I could take Colson's pain away every time his body shakes with emotion. He does a decent job keeping silent, but I know he's up to his chin in grief. That it's so goddamn hard for him to say goodbye to his mom that he's probably contemplating canceling his appointment with his aunt and spending the night in the cemetery.

I scoot another inch closer, my hand numb from the way he's holding it. It's unbearable but nothing compared to what he must be feeling so I take it and deal. I gently rest the hand that's been rubbing his back on his shoulder and lean close to him.

I can't find it in me to turn away. Despite how cold he's been, my heart still beats for him.

"Do you want to go up and say something?"

His fingers pulse between mine, and his hanging head barely lifts. He swipes the back of his other hand over his face and clears his throat. I wait for an answer.

It comes in the form of him tugging my hand even closer. It's so out of our *new* ordinary that my heart lurches for him in response. He pulls a second time. It's rough enough to pull my butt the rest of the way off my seat and get me to my feet.

"If you don't want to, that's okay, too," I tell him.

My goal is to assure him that whether he's ready to say farewell now or another time, she'll know and won't be upset by it. But maybe the reason he's pulling me out of my chair is because of what I feared before we arrived. That he doesn't want me here. That I've outstayed my welcome. Embarrassment grips me over inviting myself to an event as intimate as this. Sebastian and I should've reconsidered this before just assuming it'd be okay.

I try to pull my hand free and take a step back. "I'm sorry. I shouldn't have come. This is entirely about you, and I made it about me by showing my face when you've been clear on where you stand."

His hand is a vise around my fingers, which makes it that much more difficult to pry him off me, but I need to get out of here. To give him space. To let him bury his mother without his ex-girlfriend making a big deal out of it. And also before pieces of my broken heart fall into the grass, and they're impossible to pick up.

How could I have been so damn stupid?

Colson looks up, and his bloodshot eyes convey how broken he is. This isn't the Colson I ate burritos and did yoga with. This Colson is an empty shell.

He sweeps his hair back, and since it's longer than it was when we first met, it messily falls back over his head. Colson's stormy blues meet mine, and it's just like old times, him telling me exactly how he feels with one simple look.

You don't know what the hell I'm going through. How hard I'm trying to get through each and every fucking day. The emptiness that threatens me every waking moment.

And then it dawns on me.

He wasn't pulling me to my feet because he was telling me to leave. He was pulling me to my feet because he wants me close.

His grip on me tightens, as if that's possible, and he hauls me close enough that his knees bump my legs. He releases my hand to circle his arms around my waist.

My heart is like a fish out of water, flip-flopping inside my chest to get back to where it belongs. I grip Colson's shoulders and rest my hands on the back of his neck where I lightly run my nails over his skin.

I almost forget Sebastian is sitting next to him. When I glance up at him, he's already watching me, his eyebrow hitched up in a fashion that says, *what did I tell you?*

He retreats a moment later, getting smaller and smaller until he joins his parents at the edge of the cemetery underneath a big oak tree.

I don't dare speak, too afraid that what might come out

of my mouth isn't what Colson needs. He's so close, so vulnerable, that I don't want to ruin it. I know it won't take much.

He leans his forehead against my stomach. It almost feels like an eternity passes before he speaks. "This isn't how it was supposed to be."

I take in his rumpled head of hair.

"She was supposed to get help. *I* was going to help her get it, but then she fucked it up, got thrown in a jail cell. And who the hell knows what she was up to then." A saccharine laugh comes from him. It lacks all humor, putting more strain on my already aching heart. "Well, I guess that isn't entirely true. We know exactly what she was doing," he comments. "Getting high enough to die."

I run my fingers up the back of his head. His hair curls over my knuckles, but I don't stop rubbing circles over his scalp. "What happened is not your fault."

"Yeah, I keep trying to tell myself that, but deep down I should've gotten her help, Vi. She should've been in rehab months ago. Goddammnit, she would've never been in lockup. She wouldn't have been dealing the drugs that got her there—which is a whole other conversation—and that needle wouldn't have been in her vein. She wouldn't be in that casket. She'd still be *alive*."

"I wish you still had time with her," I murmur.

He pulls away, looking up at me with all the hurt in the world etched into his frowning features. "Why did you come? You didn't even know her."

I nibble on the corner of my lip, strongly disliking that he's making me say it. Isn't it obvious?

"I came because I want to support you."

His eyes harden. "Support sending my mom six feet under?"

"That's not how I meant it. I mean that I wanted to be here to offer anything you needed. Company. Comfort."

He lets me go and sits all the way back in his chair. His gaze flicks to what's behind me then moves back to my eyes. His nose is red from wiping and pinching it. The color under his eyes isn't much better. It's nowhere near the shade it should be.

"I hate myself for not being there for her in the way she needed most," he mutters.

"Colson—"

"No, let me finish."

"Okay."

He blinks. "I hate myself for what I'm putting you through. I don't deserve to have you here after what I did."

Yet here I still stand.

Because *I love you*.

"You do deserve it," I insist, holding back the urge to crawl onto his lap and give him all my strength and love.

He grimaces. "I fucked your mouth the last time I saw you, Violet. Mercilessly. Then kicked you out to the curb when your ankle was fucked. After I *broke up* with you. I don't deserve your kindness or generosity."

My shoulders sag, and I clasp my hands in front of me. It would've been nice if he had been a little less prickly that night, but I understand it more than he knows. Even if it did feel like a sucker punch to the face at the time. "You're having a hard time, Colson. We all go through stuff. What matters is that you don't stay where you are. You can believe what I'm saying or not, but it doesn't matter what life throws at you. You're not your circumstances. And you know I've never judged you, so why would I start now?"

"Maybe you should've done that from the start. Would've kept you the hell away from me."

"I didn't want to be away from you. I wanted to be *with* you." I still do.

"That's the thing, Violet. I don't want that for you anymore. I don't want you to want someone like me."

I huff out a breath, hating how he's resorted to putting himself down because of what happened. It's not his fault she was addicted to drugs, and it's not his fault that her last breath was taken while strung up on them.

"*Someone like me*? What's that even supposed to mean?"

"You know what it means."

"I don't." I refuse to let him tell me with his stare.

I want him to spell it out with words, so I can pick up the letters and mix them into something decipherable. I want to put them in order like I used to do with my SpaghettiOs as a kid.

He licks his lips, looks away, then back at me. His shoulders knot under the pressure of our conversation, and *good.* At least I'm not the only one who feels like a tea kettle on the brink of a whistle.

"There's shit you don't know about me, Vi."

"Maybe so, but I don't need to know everything to know that I care about you."

I've known from the start that there were things he's kept private. For instance, the night he showed up at my apartment looking less than stellar. Does he think I haven't wondered about that? *Obviously*, there's shit going on that I'm not privy to, but I trust him. I trust how safe I feel when I'm by his side. I trust that I can share pieces of myself with him without feeling criticized. I trust that his heart pumps as ferociously as mine does when we're together.

What's more important than that?

"If you knew what I've done, you wouldn't be saying that."

"So then tell me," I push. "Whatever you've done in the past, it's not your future."

He chuckles softly again, and it's wild to witness considering he was weeping for the woman who raised him a minute ago.

"Don't you see? Everything from my past has built me into the person I am today. All the bad shit I've done is embedded in my flesh and bones. I'm carefully crafted from all the situations I've willingly—and unwillingly—participated in. You think you're looking at a gold mine, Violet?" He scoffs. "More like a giant fucking black hole. You dive in and you'll be lost forever."

"Don't you think that warning is a little late?"

I've already jumped headfirst into what we have, and I'd do it all over again if I could. *I'm not afraid of the dark.*

"Yeah, well, I tried telling you back then, too, but you weren't having it. Then again, neither was I, huh?" He smacks the side of his head suddenly. I flinch. "You've invaded every goddamn part of me, and do you know how fucking tough it's been to get you out?"

"Stop."

"What?" When he leans forward, I know it's in challenge. He wants this. The fight. For me to put my fists up and battle him for the opportunity to stay in his life just to walk away at the end of it. He wants to feel something other than his mom being gone.

I remain close enough that he could wrap his arms around me again if he wanted to. "It doesn't have to be this hard."

"It was hard long before either one of us ever made it so."

"Okay," I relent, "It's fine if you don't want me to be in your life as anything intimate." I'm lying. It's not fine. I'll never be fine being less to him. Not when I've already experienced what it's like to have all of him. "We can do this as friends."

His expression turns rueful, telling me exactly what he's thinking. "How did that work out for us before?"

It didn't, but I'm grasping at straws, wanting to do anything to keep him in my life. Can't he see that?

"We did it before, we can do it again. Besides, what happened then doesn't matter now."

"Everything always matters," he murmurs in a broken voice, and then he lifts his hands to my hips so quickly I don't see it coming. In the matter of seconds, I'm uprooted and hauled onto his lap. My legs naturally spread for him and wind around his waist. I don't question it because I live to be pressed close to this man.

His fingers glide down and pinch into my thighs. I'm lost in the moment, aware of our surroundings but also not. My breath lodges in my throat. "What are you doing?"

"The very thing I shouldn't be."

I've always admired his ability to tell me how he's feeling at any given moment. The way he cracked his shell wide open for me and hasn't been able to fully close it ever since. As much as he says he doesn't want me, he wouldn't be doing this if it was true. Every interaction we've had since the fundraiser has been a push and pull of emotions. One minute we're arguing, and he's trying to convince me how he's done. In the next, he's pulling me close. I'm a frisbee, curled into his chest just to be thrown farther than the last time. What he doesn't know is that, for him, I'll always be a boomerang.

"Close your eyes," I tell him.

He narrows his gaze but listens nonetheless. He's curious and tired of putting up so much of a fight. I unbutton my peacoat and let it fan open. I don't know if I should be doing this in the middle of a cemetery, but I need him to feel my love for him.

I take his wrist and slip his hand under my dress. It's poofy and loose fitting enough that it falls back down over his forearm without showing much. My panty hose are dark enough to not give anything away. My peacoat acts as a shield, too.

We inhale a sharp breath the instant his fingertips brush against me. They climb my body until they're at my rib cage, and then I stop him. I press his palm flat against the spot just under my breast and let him feel the erratic beat of my heart.

I slither my other hand up under his sweater. I'm met with ridges of abs but have no problem finding his heart. It beats just as fiercely as mine.

When he opens his eyes a heartbeat later, I'm met with my favorite shade of blue. My heart knocks against my chest and reaches for him.

"I know you feel it, too," I murmur. His hand kneads into my thigh like he's not sure if he should let go or touch me more. Or maybe like he's holding on but also on the brink of losing his grip. "As much as you want to believe it doesn't exist because you're hurting, we're bound. So much that I can *feel* what you feel, Colson." He swallows and his gaze flits down to my lips once. "Your pain is my pain. My strength is your strength."

A mix between a warning and plea leaves his mouth. "Vi, baby. Please fucking kiss me."

"Is that what you really want?"

"I always want you. Fucking desperate for you, always."

"Then why do you keep pushing me away?"

"Because something as good as you shouldn't be in a life as fucked up as mine."

"That tactic will always feel more like punishment than protection to me," I tell him.

He inches forward. As much as I'd love to give him what he wants, I can't. I can't continue to play this game with him. It's not fair and every time it happens, I leave with my heart more bruised than it was the last time.

If I keep doing this…eventually, I won't have a heart left.

I remember the times I've told him to be selfish with me, each instance that I was willing and open to giving myself to him without a second thought, and while I'd never take them back or regret them, it can't be how we operate moving forward.

If we keep approaching our relationship this way, we'll never make it. We'll be shells of two people, an outline of a relationship that's bound to destroy us both.

I push him back and move my palm out from under his sweater. He must get the hint because his drops, too. He doesn't let go of my waist. He holds me to him like he's not ready for me to leave quite yet.

"I can't. I'm here as your friend," I reply in a whisper. "Everything else has to stop."

His chin dips. It's enough for me to know that he doesn't need more of an explanation.

We're better than throwing our bodies at one another, especially in a manner as indecent as this—in the presence of his mom's casket. If we're ever going to get through this, we need to be smart about it. We need to stop maiming one another and giving ourselves up just to walk away even more depleted.

We need to heal.

Colson needs to heal.

FOURTEEN

COLSON

JITTERY ISN'T the word to describe how I feel as Aunt Bess, Uncle Thad, and I walk into the law offices of Langlon, Tucker, and Rosenburg.

I didn't expect Violet to show up at the cemetery. Something tells me Sebastian had something to do with it. I don't know if I should be happy about him interfering or punch him in the throat for even considering it'd be a good idea.

He has to know that I've pushed her away along with everyone else, though I'd be downright lying if I said I didn't feel the smallest amount of relief when my girl quietly sat down in the seat next to me. Sure, my head was elsewhere, filing through the memories I've had with Mom throughout the years and the sad fucking truth that she was minutes away from being buried six feet under, but the bombardment of it felt a little bit lighter with her there.

I loathe knowing she has that kind of ability over me.

That it's so easy for her to sidetrack me and pull me from the shit that's going on in my head. When I pulled her hand in mine, I knew I wouldn't be able to let her walk away without talking to her. Without hearing her voice wrapping around me and scaring away the negative energy I always seem to find myself blanketed in.

I *physically* ache for her. Miss her so damn badly that I want to compare it to withdrawal—even if I don't know exactly what it's like. Was this how it was for Mom? Having one true love and always chasing it but never being good enough to catch it half the time?

Violet broke off a tiny piece of herself and let me have it. She was the corner piece of a chocolate bar, and I greedily ate it up, licking my fingers clean of the smudges that melted against my heated skin just to immediately want more.

But today, she rejected me.

I can't get it out of my head that she told me no. I'd never pull the same kind of shit Nelson did the night in Lucy's and take a woman's innocence and choice from her, so when she pulled away, I let her go.

I'd be lying if I said I was okay with her throwing my words back at me. Fucking friendship? That's what she's offering me after repeatedly hurting her?

I want *nothing* and *everything* to do with it.

I want my fingers flying over my phone's keyboard, texting her about the kind of day I've had. About the thoughts that constantly stream through my head on a never ending current. About how desperately I want to *hate* my mom for the years of neglect but also love her like hell all the same. How I still wish I could've gone back and helped her in ways that mattered. Ways that didn't involve paying off her drug debts.

I want Violet in my bed at night, her lithe waist pulled back and pressed into me. I want her mind and heart and *soul* shackled to me forever.

A pang of guilt pelts me like hail. I nearly keel over as we step into the elevator. I clear my throat, and Aunt Bess glances over. I don't make eye contact. I stay in my own lane, keeping my eyes forward until the doors spring back open and we exit.

Aunt Bess checks in with the receptionist before we're taken back to a private room. In the middle of it is a long conference table where I'm sure all kinds of meetings are held. How many times have people had to sit here and listen to every detail of a loved one's will? Just thinking about the amount makes my stomach twist with sickness.

"This should be quick," Aunt Bess states. She's holding a stained envelope in her hand. The one I gave her when I showed up at the cemetery this morning. Turns out it wasn't too hard to find my birth certificate. I just had to sort through half the shit in Mom's closet. I slipped my social security card in it for her, too.

I stand by the wall near the table. I sat long enough at Willow Creek Cemetery, and my legs are too restless to sit.

"We'll get this over with then be on our way," promises Aunt Bess.

I don't know why she chose to do this after burying Mom, but I guess time is of the essence. If we wait too long, thousands of dollars will be handed over to the bank. Once that happens, there's no way in hell they'll entertain the idea of giving it back.

Stingy motherfuckers.

Can't say I blame them, but this is the last thing I need this morning.

Mom was already too much. Add in Violet fucking with my head more than she already has, and I'm ready to say screw it all and buy another bottle of Jack to replace the last one.

I know it won't solve my problems. Despite the possibility of addiction running through my veins, I know I can't continue to turn to it when life feels like too much. I don't want to end up like Mom or even her dad, but I don't know how else to cope with all the loss.

Resting my back against the wall next to the door, I focus on the fancy fluorescent lighting. Chandeliers that cost more than an entire year's salary for most hang overhead, shiny metal leaves welded onto it and stretching out like they would on a branch.

Little time passes before the door opens and a man in one hell of an expensive looking suit strolls into the room. He's about my height but older. Way closer to Uncle Thad's age. He has a thick, dark beard with grays mixed in.

"Hello," he greets, addressing me the second he notices me near the door. "You must be Colson. Stewart Langlon," he introduces as he extends a hand and props a folder under his armpit. "Circumstances be damned, it's nice to meet you. I'm sorry to hear about your mother."

I swallow down my thanks and give his hand a firm shake before sinking mine back into the pocket it was in a second ago.

He undoes the button on his suit jacket before gesturing for me to take a seat. I'd rather walk out of this room than sit and listen to all the legal jargon that's about to be crammed down my throat, but I remind myself that this is what's left of Mom.

I owe it to her—and myself—to mind my manners and get this over with.

"Let's get right to it, Stewart," Uncle Thad encourages. He's barely said a word today, but that's how Uncle Thad is, light on his words. "It's been a long morning already."

Stewart smooths his palms down on the table before opening his folder where an abundance of paperwork lies. My attention skates over the pages covered in text. My head swishes with this funny feeling. I chalk it up to not eating since midday yesterday. Stomaching food isn't exactly easy after losing a parent and going through a breakup.

"Right," Stewart agrees. "I can imagine."

"Just a few signatures and we should be set?" Aunt Bess reaffirms with her question. She's looking a little worse for wear this morning, too. I couldn't see it earlier. My head was too far up my own ass to notice, but I see it now. It's there in the little lines creasing around her eyes when she gives Stewart a brief smile. The way her shoulders slump even though she's repeatedly tried squaring them and sitting straight.

"Well…" Stewart raises his bushy eyebrows. "There's actually something we need to discuss. Something my paralegal found last night that I didn't get a chance to call you about." Aunt Bess glances at Uncle Thad, and my stomach sinks to an impossible depth.

My aunt claimed this would be easy peasy, but Stewart is making it seem like there's a roadblock in our way.

"Why didn't you call?" she asks.

"It was late." He waves his hand in the air while rifling through a few pieces of paperwork until he plucks one out. "I didn't want to disturb you and figured we could discuss it this morning."

"What is it?" Aunt Bess questions, her tone lacking patience.

Stewart looks up, and I gotta say, my entire body twists into knots with the way his expression suddenly falls. He was doing a decent job at keeping his spirits up for the sake of us, but now that we're getting down to business, he wears his emotions on his sleeve. It's the exact opposite of reassuring. I file it away as one of his flaws.

"When I work with families who have lost someone, I typically have my paralegal dig a little deeper into family history. Distant relatives have the tendency of coming out of the woodwork like roaches. We've known each other for a long time, Bess, and you know I like to be prepared for everything. When wills land in my office and relatives insist that part of what's in it belongs to them...well, normally, it's pretty simple to handle. If your name isn't on the will, you get nothing.

"What's problematic is when a loved one passes and there's *no* will. No legal document that binds certain family members to what remains."

"Mom didn't have a will?" Then again why would she? Her attention was always elsewhere.

Aunt Bess clears her throat. "I tried getting her to sign off on one after your grandmother died, but she wouldn't do it." A grim line draws between Aunt Bess's brows. "What are you saying, Stewart?"

Yeah, Stewart, get to the fucking point.

Stewart slides the piece of paper in his hand over to my aunt and uncle while briefly giving me a look of...remorse?

I swallow my nerves and flick my eyes back over to my aunt, who suddenly has a look of horror on her face. That's the best way to describe it. Along with the fleeting gasp that rolls out of her mouth onto the table in front of us.

"The point is that we initially thought Colson was next of kin for your sister. As you can see on that paper there, he's not."

What the hell is he talking about?

Mom doesn't have anyone else.

I drop into the chair next to Aunt Bess and rip the paper out of her hand.

"This can't be right," says Aunt Bess. I don't know what

her face looks like, if it's still holding that expression from a second ago, because my eyes are planted elsewhere.

"I'm afraid it is," says Stewart.

"What does this mean moving f—"

The sheet of paper is so damn glossy, like that premium photo paper you buy at office supply stores. It's a copy of the original. *Marriage License* stares back at me in that fancy old-time government script and below it is Mom's name.

Janie Moore.

I drop the paper as if it burns me when I read the name next to hers. It sails, ever so slowly, to the conference table. My chair skids back from the strength of my legs against them, the ones that were restless a minute ago but have now solidified into rock.

My world collapses to pieces.

I'm in a brick building getting hit with a goddamn cannon. Broken shale sprinkles down over me. The shrill, overpowering boom of the heavy artillery coming in through the wall causes a ringing in my ears. I swear my vision blacks out.

I sweep my hand over my head and hate how itchy this stupid sweater is on me. Panic settles into my chest as I pace to the other side of the room, my head spinning out of fucking control.

Aunt Bess, Uncle Thad, and Stewart talk in the background, but I can't hear a goddamn sound. My brain focuses on one thing, and that's the person who my mom has secretly been married to all these years.

As if the universe is trying to tell me something, four very hulking words—*just like yer father*—pop into my head at the exact moment I overhear Aunt Bess say, "There has to be a paper trail leading back to a divorce."

What I think she means to say is, *This has to be total bullshit.*

I mean, props to Stewart for finding this but…

I walk back over to the table and grab the paper again, bringing it so close to my face that it practically bops my nose. I'm hoping I read it wrong the first time.

But nope…

This is definitely happening.

"She never said a word about this," my aunt says, and I believe her because this is the first I'm hearing about it. Janie always had a way of keeping shit to herself. "Why wouldn't she tell us that she was married. Much less to him? Everyone who's ever stepped foot in Harrison Heights knows he's bad news."

I toss the piece of paper back on the table a second time, glad to give my fingers a reprieve from its scalding heat.

I finally speak. "Would you want to go around telling your family that you married the best of the worst?"

"What was she thinking?" Aunt Bess murmurs rhetorically.

"We'll never know the answer to that," replies Stewart.

Mr. Captain Fucking Obvious.

"This changes how we move forward. Spouses are next in line to receive what's left behind, Bess. I'm sorry but intestacy laws state that the one hundred and thirty thousand dollars, along with the house, will be inherited by the surviving spouse, which in this case is Clyde Lincoln."

FIFTEEN

VIOLET

Sylvia: Who the hell took my bottle of red?

Everleigh: Not me.

Violet: Didn't touch it.

Sylvia: One of you bitches did, and now you're
going to lie about it?

Everleigh: Hate to break it to you, Syl, but I'm
pretty sure I saw you take it back to your
bedroom like a week ago.

I'M forty minutes into looking over my notes for my language
and literacy development class when the soft piano music on
my phone comes to a sudden stop. My ringtone blares in
place of it.

I texted Olive earlier to see what her plans were for the
holiday break, but she said she was in the studio this evening,
so I know it's definitely not her.

I pick up my phone. Sebastian's name fills the screen. When he drove me home from the cemetery earlier, I gave him a quick farewell, waved goodbye and flew up to my apartment with a heavy heart.

Watching Colson sink into himself, his eyes pleading for my help, for me to give myself over to him when he knew I couldn't, was too much. While this push and pull might've been cute at first, it's just hurting us now.

And I don't want that for either of us.

I'm quick to answer the call, averting my gaze from my notebook. "Hey. What's up?"

"Violet." My name comes out of him in a winded breath.

My stomach swoops low. I drop my pencil on the desk. I don't pay attention to it as it rolls off the edge and bounces to the floor. "Please just tell me he's okay."

"Physically, yes. For now, anyway. Emotionally…he's fucking wrecked."

I push out of my chair and slip on a pair of tennis shoes as I hold the phone to my ear with my shoulder. I don't care that I'm in sweats and an oversized sweatshirt or that my hair is up in one of the messiest buns imaginable.

My throat is lodged closed when I ask, "Where are you? Where is he?"

"His mom's place. I just stepped outside for a second because…" Noise filters in from the background, but I can't make out what it is.

"Sebastian?"

"Sorry, I, uh, can you just get here? He's losing his shit, and I've tried to calm him down, but he's drinking. My only other option was to call my mom, but I think that would've just made it worse. He needs someone to ground him. You're the only one who I thought might be able to do that."

"No, it's okay," I insist. "I'm leaving now."

"Be careful on the 401. He needs you in one piece, and Violet?"

I grab my bag and keys off the hook by the front door, my studies quickly forgotten and my body humming with alarm. I jab the elevator button repeatedly until the doors open. "Yeah?"

"I've never seen him like this. Just…prepare yourself."

I ride the elevator down. My call with Sebastian ends, and I shove my phone into my bag as I race out of the building to my car. I fumble with my keys as I start the ignition and barely brake at the stop sign leading out onto Main Street.

Traffic isn't as horrendous as I expect it to be, but dusk makes it difficult to see as the sun sets on the horizon. I take my time when it's an absolute must and cross the Sycamore Memorial Bridge, pedal to the metal. I tap my brakes when necessary, then floor it.

I find Colson's mom's house easier than last time. My car comes to a screeching halt at the curb behind Sebastian's Aviator, my body purring with nervous energy.

It's like déjà vu as I follow the sidewalk up to the house. Not so long ago, Colson warned me about what we'd find inside the walls of the home he grew up in.

I believed him then, and I believe Sebastian now.

My legs are weak, threatening to buckle, as I skip up the steps and land on the stoop. I'm not sure if I should knock or just walk in. It's hard to gauge which option is smartest but when I hear a crash and my stomach jumps up the back of my throat, I bolt inside.

The futon in the small living room is a crumbled mess in the middle of the floor. The coffee table is on its side against the wall. There's a new dent in the drywall where the corner of it is stuck.

Someone shouts. It takes me seconds to realize it's Colson.

It's the angriest I've ever heard him.

A chair flies across the back of the living room where the room opens up to the kitchen. It smashes against the wall, tearing the wallpaper before thudding to the floor in a broken mess.

"Dude! You need to calm down!"

It's slightly calming knowing Sebastian is here. That I'm not walking into this alone. I'm not scared Colson will hurt me. More so that he'll hurt himself—that he already has—and I won't know what to do to help him.

"Go the fuck home," Colson shouts in a slur at his cousin. "I don't want you here. Never fucking did."

I make it to the edge of the wall and peek around the corner where I hear the commotion coming from.

"You think I'm going to leave you like this? Spit all your insults at me, be the piece of shit you want to be," Sebastian barks back. "I'm not bailing on you!"

Colson's gaze turns to the ceiling for half a second before he brings it back down to Sebastian. But then his eyes flick in my direction, and my cover is blown.

Not that I was hiding exactly. More like finding the perfect moment to interrupt.

His blue gaze pierces into me like a thousand tacks breaking skin. It's the worst feeling in the world as I watch him bring his tongue over his top teeth in disgust. He stares at me, and his words cut into me deeper than ever. "Why the fuck did you invite her?"

"Because you won't listen to me." Sebastian tosses his hands up. "You keep throwing shit around! Breaking furniture. You're spiraling, man. You need someone to haul your ass back to the surface."

"You think she's gonna be the one to do that?"

I take careful steps toward the man my heart breaks for. I don't know what happened after I left the cemetery or what transpired from the meeting with his aunt, but...something led him to drink. *Something* has to be responsible for this.

"Yeah, actually, I do," Sebastian says, turning to look at me for the first time. His next words are directed toward me. "As you can see—"

"Don't fucking talk about me like I'm not in the room."

Sebastian's nostrils flair. Colson doesn't see it, but he does run his hands through his hair and grip the disheveled strands. He tugs at them like he's outraged. Like he can't breathe. As if he doesn't know how he's going to get through the next five minutes let alone the next day.

He twists on his heel and trudges down the hall.

"What happened?" I mouth quietly.

Sebastian shakes his head. "He found out his mom was married. Kept it a secret. There was a lump sum of money that was supposed to go to Colson. The house, too, but it turns out he doesn't have a right to any of it because it all belongs to Janie's husband now."

"Oh my God."

"Yep." He nods back in the direction Colson took off in. "They went to sign everything over and found out then. He's been like this ever since."

Talk about a hard pill to swallow.

"That's not the worst of it."

I wet my lips, listening intently for Colson, but he's gone silent. "There's more?"

"The guy she was married to is a big-time drug dealer in Harrison Heights, according to my parents."

"Wait, what?" I can barely wrap my mind around what he

says. Janie was married to a drug dealer? My mind goes back to Thanksgiving night. Was it *that* man? Was Colson's stepfather in the same house as him without him even knowing?

Fuck, this is bad.

Sebastian glances down the hall and nods. We follow in Colson's footsteps, on edge ourselves. We make it to the doorframe of his mom's bedroom. Colson picks up a bottle of amber liquid from the nightstand and guzzles it down like it's apple juice. I can't imagine the burn that settles into his throat as he swallows. Maybe he's had enough at this point that it doesn't feel all that bad.

Sebastian is brave enough to approach and hold out a hand. "Don't you think you've had enough?"

"After the day I've had? Hardly."

"Give it to me," Sebastian says. It's less of a demand, more of a plea.

Colson glowers back with an angry stare. He points at Sebastian with one finger while the rest curl around the bottle. "Do me a favor...get her ass the fuck out of here." He sways on his feet, and I hope to God it means he's done throwing and breaking things. That now that I'm here, he's ready to calm down. "Fuck, I don't even care if you use her to keep your virgin dick warm. Just as long as she goes."

Sharp, impaling arrows.

That's what his words are as they come out of him. They hit me one after the other, biting into my skin like pesky razors, seesawing back and forth.

How can he say that to Sebastian?

How can he even *think* I'd entertain being with his cousin when the only person I want is him?

"Don't talk about her like that, man. It's disrespectful."

"Oooh." Colson's icy glare turns into a mischievous

smirk, and I just know he's not done spilling blood. I may be bleeding out, but Sebastian isn't yet. "Always the good guy. Little do ya know, she sucks cock so fuckin' well, you'd never want another woman again."

"Just *stop*," I holler, my heartbeat pounding out of my chest like you see in the cartoons.

Colson's eyes meet mine in the doorway. As much as I know that he's trying to hurt me and that I should take everything he's saying with a grain of salt, it presses down on my love for him, cracking what's left of my heart.

Shame and embarrassment coat my cheeks. If there was ever a time I wanted to slink out of a room, now would be it. But I've already spoken. And I can't let myself leave Sebastian to deal with him alone.

"Oh, and she swallows," Colson adds, digging the knife deeper.

He's too damn drunk to understand what he's saying. Maybe he'll wake up tomorrow filled with guilt or maybe he won't remember at all. It doesn't change that it's not right. That he's hurting two people who care about him.

My stomach is a water balloon falling from the rooftop of a ten-story building. It drops until it smacks against the sidewalk. "Tell me that gets you as hard as it gets me. Then again, maybe not. When was the last time you were with a woman?"

Sebastian's fist swings straight into Colson's face, and it's so unlike him that I gasp and stare in shock. Colson reacts in a snap. He shoves his cousin out of his face with the bottle of liquor still in his hand. Alcohol sloshes up out of the rim. He grabs Sebastian by his shirt and puts all his weight into pushing him backward. Sebastian manages to get out of his hold and shoves him back. The bottle of liquor stays glued in Colson's palm. And then Colson gets the upper hand and twists Sebastian's shirt in his grip. They move toward me so quickly I barely have enough time to get out of the way.

A scream bursts out of my throat. Sebastian's back crumples against the wall next to me. Surprisingly, he doesn't push back against his cousin but stands there and stares into his eyes. Like he's not afraid of him one little bit. And maybe he isn't, but I'm terrified Colson might do something irreversible.

"Stop!" I try to pry Colson's arms off Sebastian. He's so much stronger, and the alcohol enhances his strength.

"You should be fucking happy I'm offering her to you." Colson spits it out as if I'm not standing right next to him. I tell myself he'd never say these things if he were in his right mind, but it doesn't fix how my entire body deflates with each word that comes out of his mouth.

I jostle his arm. "That's enough. Let him go!"

"That's what you want?" Sebastian growls back. "You want me to take the only girl you've ever had feelings for and fuck her so good she forgets about you? You want some other guy to fill the void for her because your dumb ass can't get his shit together?"

Oh...no.

Colson's blue gaze turns a smoldering red. Sebastian shoves at Colson's chest. It knocks him back half a step. Sebastian is stronger than he lets on. He may not constantly spar with a boxing bag nor is he under the influence, but he used to tackle men for the fun of it. He could easily take Colson down.

Their gazes catch. I don't know who's winning in the game of war they're playing. It's deathly quiet, and then, in a flash, Colson's hand expands over Sebastian's throat in quiet fury.

I clamp my hand on his arm urgently, doing everything I can to pull him off. "Colson, no. *Don't* do this! Let him *go!*"

He ignores me again. I smack a closed fist against his bicep as Sebastian's nostrils flare for oxygen. He lets out this stutter of a noise and stands there and just *takes* it. Like he's under Colson's heel. Like he doesn't care if Colson empties his lungs of air. But then I realize that he's not reacting on purpose. He's letting Colson burden him with his emotions if only to get them out.

My body fills with a mix of fear and dread.

Colson and Sebastian love each other. They'd never do this on an ordinary day. They'd never lay their hands on one another or throw low blows and cheap shots.

Colson holds Sebastian to the wall and brings the rim of the bottle to his lips. He gulps down three swigs while looking at the green eyes across from him.

And then, *wham*.

He bashes the bottle into the wall beside Sebastian's face. His cousin flinches. Shards of glass spray in all directions. A streak of blood appears at the corner of Sebastian's mouth from the bottle's flying shrapnel. The stench of whiskey overtakes the room. Whatever was left in the bottle drips down the wall, and without prompting, Colson releases him.

Just like that, he lets go.

Sebastian wheezes out a massive breath. Colson stomps out of the room. The bathroom door bangs so fiercely the walls shake. I immediately reach for Sebastian and cling to his side while glancing over my shoulder. He rubs his throat and looks past me in the direction Colson disappeared.

What the hell did I just witness?

That person...that is *not* Colson.

But then I remember how there's an array of stuff I don't know about him. How there are details of his life he's kept to himself, hidden away. I recall all the warnings he's given me, saying how rotten he is. How I don't deserve him.

And I recant on that initial thought.

This updated, grief-ridden, bitter version of Colson... maybe this is *exactly* who he is and the man I got to know and learned to love... is just a lie.

SIXTEEN

COLSON

I OPEN my eyes and squint against the bathroom lighting. It's way too fucking bright and makes my head throb unnecessarily. I resituate my body, straightening against the wall behind me. It protests with an ache setting deep in my bones. My arms and legs are as weak as they were when I was a prepubescent boy with no muscle. My stomach wavers with each movement. So much that I have to actively try to force away the nausea that settles into it.

"Fuuuuck," I groan out. It gives me a tiny bit of relief but not enough. It lasts all of five seconds before my gut is back where it started, which is wanting to upheave every ounce of stomach acid that rests in it.

And that's all there is.

Because I sure as shit know I didn't eat much yesterday.

Thinking about it makes the rest of the day come back in a rush.

The cemetery.

That casket.

The lawyer.

The marriage license.

Booking it out of there so fucking fast.

Sebastian showing up.

Violet showing up.

Me spitting venomous words.

The memory of four specific words—*just like yer father.*

I'm not the one who'll be getting Mom's money and house. Clyde Lincoln, the man who Mom secretly married without anyone knowing, will be.

I also have the gnawing suspicion he might also be my father because who else would it be?

I stormed out of Stewart's conference room before Aunt Bess or Uncle Thad could get two words out. I walked until my legs got tired, stopped at a liquor store where I grabbed another bottle of Jack, and drank way too much on my way back home in an Uber.

Everything hit me at once yesterday. Every facet was like another million-pound boulder on top of me until I couldn't handle it anymore. I snapped. Went right back to the angry teenager I was years ago, but that's not saying much considering I've been riding the line of that person since Mom died. Back then, I would let it get in my head that my mom was a raging addict and the one person who could've saved me from it—my father—didn't think I was worth sticking around for.

Trudging through yesterday was like being a quarterback on an empty field and continuously getting sacked by an invisible force. I tried to get back to my feet but inevitably ended up on bruised and battered knees.

Visions of my fingers wrapping around furniture and chucking it filter in. One time wasn't enough to control my temper, so I kept picking shit up. Kept throwing it. Tossing it into the walls without a care in the world. Without worrying about the mess I'd wake up to or the damage it caused.

It felt helpful in the moment, but now, as I sit here and dwell on it, I feel like a giant piece of horse shit.

I see Sebastian's face. How he tried to quell my outrage but wasn't successful. He stood in front of me, nearly got hit with a kitchen chair and still didn't leave.

Then, he had to go and invite her over. He had to show Violet just how fucked up I am. That I'm nowhere near the man she needs or deserves.

Everything happened so fast after that. Sebastian and Violet followed me to Mom's room where I left my trusty bottle of liquor. I drank down more, and when Sebastian tried to interfere, I told myself there was no way in hell he'd take that bottle out of my hands.

Not when I was desperate for every last drop. Anything to make me forget about all the shit conspiring against me and that would continue to unravel. Because if there was one thing I was certain about, it was that this revelation with Clyde wasn't going to be swept under the stain-infested rugs I grew up walking on.

Aunt Bess wouldn't let it. Once he found out that Janie was gone and he was next in line for over a hundred grand, he wouldn't let it, either.

Where did that leave me?

With my hand around my cousin's throat while the girl I loved watched me fall apart.

I stand in front of the bathroom sink, turn the water on and wash my hands. The cold water falling over my hands brings me back to life. Splashing it against my face feels even better, but when I look in the mirror the guilt and dread hits me all over again. Shame becomes a second skin as I think about the way I taunted Violet with cruel, vulgar words she didn't deserve.

I have no choice but to go out there and face my mistakes.

That is, if Violet and Sebastian are still around. Who the fuck knows if they are. If I were them, I would've left last night without a lick of guilt. I don't know why they continue showing up for me. All I've done is continuously treat them like they're worthless and put them through a hell neither of them earned.

After I shut off the water, I take a quick piss, then wash my hands again before I open the bathroom door and listen for my cousin and my girl. How fucked up is it that I still consider her mine? That I can't stand the image of her being with anyone else yet said what I did about her?

Sebastian's words hit me all over again.

You want me to take the only girl you've ever had feelings for and fuck her so good that she forgets about you? You want some other guy to fill the void for her because your dumb ass can't get his shit together?

I want none of that, which is precisely why I reacted the way I did. I'm ashamed that I've fallen so far off course. That I don't consider myself good enough for her or worthy of her helping me through this season of my life.

The hallway is quiet, so I trudge into the kitchen with light footsteps. It's empty, along with the living room, but fuck, the place is a mess. A different kind than Mom used to leave. Broken furniture is scattered throughout the space. Dents are formed into the drywall where there isn't wallpaper. There's broken glass in the sink. I faintly remember tossing a glass of water into it before I cracked the top off my whiskey.

I drink a fresh glass from the faucet and decide it's best to check the rest of the house before the sun rises any more than it already has. The sunshine is slowly starting to slant its way in through the windows, but it won't be long until the day is in procession, and it's Groundhog Day all over again.

My bedroom is the first place I check. I'm relieved to find it empty and untouched. Apparently, I gave my belongings a pass last night when I was pulling a Tasmanian Devil. Mom's room is next, and I'm hesitant to get to it. Mostly because it's where I've been spending most of my time.

Life was far from perfect with her, but when I sit and think hard enough, I find crumbs of memories I want to hold onto. Times she made me laugh or fleeting moments when it felt like, for a minute or two, we were normal. When her issues with dependence weren't cackling in our faces and our lifestyle wasn't miles away from the closest version of perfection.

I stop short when I walk through the threshold and see a brunette curled under Mom's comforter. Wearing sweatpants and an oversized sweatshirt, she looks entirely too comfortable. My heart seizes in my chest, and I'm not sure if it's because she's so beautiful or if it's because she's still in this house.

I've told her before that she doesn't belong here, and I still believe it, but she just looks so...peaceful. The glow of the sun coming in through the window hovers above her, creating a halo above her body. I want to hold on to her forever, but she's angelic in every way that I am not. I don't forget that as I quietly make it across the room and sit next to her.

Resting my hand on her arm, I squeeze it gently, hoping it'll be enough to stir her from her sleep. It is, and she rubs the sleep away from her eyes.

I said shit last night, and when I did, I didn't give her the time of day. I acted like she wasn't there. The foulest words blew past my lips, and now I have to sit here and tell her how much I didn't mean them while hoping and praying she grants me a level of forgiveness I can't justify.

I need her to know that the alcohol morphed my reality. It put a twisted spin on my thoughts and made everything seem uglier and harsher. It turned my heart black.

"Hey," I croak quietly. She pulls her arm closer to her body, effectively making my hand fall from it. She doesn't want to be touched by me? Cool. It's like the grenade I threw last night boomerangs back and explodes from within, my heart and blood coating the walls of the room with black sludge.

"Hi." She says it in a hushed tone. I get the biggest urge to wrap my arms around her and pull her to me. To rest my head on her shoulder and let it all out. To voice how close I am to losing myself altogether.

"You didn't leave," I murmur, my throat dry as hell.

She shakes her head and sits up. It only creates more space between us. I only have myself to blame for it. I'm the one who caused this. Who gave her the stick she's pressing into my chest in warning.

"Sebastian had to head back, but I didn't want to leave you on your own."

She looks at me with careful precision. Like she's trying to get in my head and figure me out. "Are you okay? I understand if you don't want to talk about it, but Sebastian told me…"

Told you what? I want to ask, but I already know.

I drop my chin and suck my cheeks into my mouth and try to think of what to say, but for once, I don't want to bullshit. I don't want to brush off the nagging sense of unease that I wake up with and go to bed with every night.

"I'm the farthest from okay I've ever been," I admit in a low voice.

Her lips morph into a frown. Her eyes do the same. It reminds me of that saying to smile with your eyes, only hers are downturned and lacking the brightness they held before Uncle Thad ruined it the night of the fundraiser.

"I can tell," she murmurs.

Every cell in my body begs her to touch me. To curl her fingers into my hand, to brush the back of my neck with her nails, to pull me in and never let me go.

"Last night was…" My words trail off as I try to find the word I want to use.

"A lot?"

"No."

"Oh."

"I don't have a word to describe it, but I remember saying and doing things that should've never happened. I don't know why I put my hands on Sebastian other than knowing I needed to feel something different than I was."

"Is your jaw okay?"

I nod, realizing that there's a stiffness to it as I talk. The image of Sebastian hitting me comes back in full force. "Nothing I can't handle."

"I feel like you've said that before."

"Because it's true."

"Is it?" she asks. "How can you say it's nothing you can't handle when you're destroying things, Colson?" Her voice turns pleading. "I thought you were going to choke him out. There was a second there when I was *afraid* for his well-being. And the things you said…"

"Were fucked up. I know."

Her features grow solemn, her frown growing more pronounced. The emotion in her eyes drowns out the golden hues. And her eyebrows cave to the weight, her forehead wrinkling in effort to hold them up.

I squeeze my eyes shut and run my hand through my hair. I'm still in the jeans I wore yesterday. My sweater got discarded when I returned home after the lawyer fiasco. The plain white T-shirt I wore underneath stretches over my back as I lean my elbows on my knees and hide my face in my hands.

A moment passes before I sit up and give it to her straight. "I shouldn't have said any of that stuff. I wasn't speaking from a place of honesty. I said it to hurt you." I swallow, hating how it feels to admit that. Honesty is a bitch. So is accountability. "I said it so you'd leave, because it pissed me off that Sebastian invited you over when, clearly, things were not great."

"I'm glad he did."

I scoff. "How can you say that? I don't understand why you continue to show up. I don't deserve it, Violet. Look at me. My life is one wrecking ball away from being reduced to rubble. You want to get buried beneath it all? Because I sure as hell don't want you to be."

"Maybe things would have ended a lot worse if I didn't come."

"They did end badly."

"And why wouldn't I be here for you?" she asks, steering backward in conversation. "Remember when I was having a hard time with my dad? You listened to me countless times, gave me advice, and got me out of my head when it mattered most. It's only fair that I offer the same back."

"So, you're not mad at me for telling Sebastian to fuck you? That you're damn good at sucking dick and that you swallow?" My voice hardens, and I arch a brow at her. I almost wish she'd stand up for herself. That she'd look me in the eye and tell me what a jerk I am. "Because if I were you, I'd sure as shit be pissed."

She pulls at the hem of her shirt. "It was hurtful," she says. "I won't lie and say it wasn't."

I wind my hand up underneath the comforter, find her foot, and grip it. It doesn't matter if I like feet or not. At this moment, I'd fucking lick them to make sure she knows how sorry I am for acting like the biggest asshole in America.

Her eyes lift to mine the same time I squeeze my hand around her arch. My apology pours out of every crevice in my body. "I'm so fucking sorry, Violet." It's like my heart is under an ice pick, and my stupid actions come along and chisel it clean open. "You never deserved that. You haven't deserved anything I've done lately."

"I feel like...I don't know what to say to you anymore," she voices shamefully.

That makes two of us, baby.

I've been on autopilot. The logical side of my brain has barely been powering through. Everything I'm doing, it's not because I'm talking myself into it. It's because I'm not talking to myself at all. The fucks I originally gave have vanished, and my emotions are running the show.

"We used to be able to come to each other for whatever. Or well, at least I did."

"What's that supposed to mean?" I question.

She purses her lips. I keep my hand on her foot because I need to feel connected to her in some capacity. Even if it's through the most disgusting body part ever created.

"I think you've been open with me when it comes to some things. More open than you are with other people but..." She pauses, and my heart sputters. "Then there's other stuff that I know you haven't been very transparent about. I keep telling myself that it's okay, but I don't think it is anymore. This is new for me, too. I've never had a boyfriend who has lost a parent, much less to addiction, and it's clear how that's affecting you. But communicating about it has suddenly been bumped higher on my list of importance. Outside of your emotional rollercoaster rampages, I feel...in the dark. And I don't know how to help you fully, even as a friend, when I'm so far out of the loop."

I don't know where this is coming from, but as much as I wish she were wrong, she's not. I have been reserved on certain topics, or rather, one in particular, and that's Finn.

"This isn't anything like I've ever experienced," she continues. "I know who you are to an extent, Colson. I've told you my deepest, darkest truths. I don't need to know every single detail of your past to see that you really are a decent guy. But what I saw last night...it's like you were a totally different person. The guy that saved me at Lucy's would've never said those things. I can't help but think there's more going on than meets the eye. I can't help but be jealous and hurt over Sebastian relaying information to me that—"

"That what?"

"That a boyfriend would typically tell his girlfriend." She holds a hand up. "And I know we're not together anymore, but we're *something*, and that has to count. It has to, Colson."

Her palm slides across my cheek and the warmth alone from it makes my lips part. I am *dying* to be close to every part of her, but see, I pushed a big, heavy boulder in front of me when I was strong, and now that I'm weak, it's too heavy to move aside.

"I don't want to fight with you. It's only going to hurt us more. The only one who thinks you're a piece of shit is you. You're going through stuff, but so am I." She shakes her head and sighs. "I don't know why I'm saying all this or if I'm even making sense. I guess I just wish we could talk to each other and take the burden off one another like we used to. That we could confide in each other fully."

She rubs her thumb over the tired skin under my eyes.

From all my lack of sleep, I don't look as well rested as I should. Her eyes trail over my face like she's ingraining it into her memory, and her face turns sheepish.

"Maybe this isn't the time to say it. Maybe I'll regret it the instant it comes out of my mouth, but if things keep up like this, I don't know if I'll ever have the opportunity to tell you again." Her eyes land on mine. It's blue against brown, but at this moment, we're this swirly color of azure and roasted pecans. I feel it and so does she. A short reprieve in an otherwise long-lasting battle.

"You are...unlike anyone I've ever known. We all have our flaws and situations in life that seem to tear us down, but you used to walk around as if they were no match for you. You were so light even when I could sense the heaviness trying to cloak itself over you. I loved that about you. That you could go with the flow of life and still be okay. But more than that, I love *you*. The good and the bad, Colson. And one day, you will make it out of this. You'll find that man again, the one who let the worst slide off his back, the one who is worth more than what he's currently putting himself through."

This is not where I was expecting this conversation to go.

Things truly are royally fucked if me running my mouth about her last night has turned into her confessing her love for me.

I shouldn't allow her confession to wiggle its way into my chest and spark new life in me, but I do. Her loving words are a shawl over my coldness. A blanket tossed over someone who has spent days on a snow-covered mountain covered in frostbite. I need the heat more than she knows. And she's so, so fucking warm.

"Don't feel like you have to say anything back. I know you're in a difficult place, and this isn't about me, but I want you to know that people care about you. That even in your darkest moments, when you don't love yourself, and especially when you have your walls up too high for anyone to see in, we're here for you."

My jaw clenches. My hand around her foot twitches. "I want to pull you into my lap right now," I confess. *Just for a minute*.

It's an invitation more than anything. She made it clear yesterday morning that we can only be friends if we're going to make it out of this unscathed. I don't doubt that she won't make it. It's me who I'm worried about. When I remove the shit-covered glasses, it's hard for me to see her standing there with me.

She's not always going to be this kind. Her experience with Webber has only strengthened her need to stay true to who she is, which is stellar for her. But that person isn't the same one who stays with me; the guy who continuously fucks up and drags her down. The guy who doesn't open up entirely. The guy who has secrets.

When I find my way across, she's going to be long gone. On the back of a white horse with her knight in shining armor. Which is why I'm living in the moment and being selfish enough to steal a tiny, little piece of her again.

She unfolds her legs and climbs the short distance over to me. We were practically knee to knee before, so it takes no time for her to plop down into my lap and wrap her arms around my neck.

My hands fall to the bottom of her shirt. I can't help it when they find their way beneath it. I need to feel her. I need my skin touching her skin. I need her warmth snuffing out my chill.

She murmurs against my neck, "You will get through

this." And when her lips briefly brush over my skin, I want to take way more than a hug from her.

I want her underneath me, so I can make love to her. So she can give me the strength to wade through this awful storm as I fill her and ask for love in return.

Tell her you love her back, my mind scolds. *Before she finds someone else.*

I don't want another dude making her forget about me. The thought of it alone sends me into a gut-wrenching spiral of madness.

I mean, look where my hand ended up last night.

Even if there is someone out there who's better for her, I don't want her with him. I want her with me so fucking bad, but I don't know how to make it work.

I don't know how to cater to her when I'm the broken mess I am. I don't know how to give her what she needs when I don't even know what *I* need.

My palms run over her smooth skin, and we sit there for a long while as I contemplate all the ways this chapter of my life can end. Not all of them include us walking toward a sunset together.

But if I ever want that possibility to exist, something has to change. The problem is, I have no fucking clue how to do it. And more than wanting to consider the future, I want to ignore and forget and pretend that the agonizing pain ripping through me like a storm in the night doesn't exist.

SEVENTEEN

VIOLET

IT'S BEEN days since I sat in Colson's lap, and we held each other. As much as I hate the distance and wouldn't have imagined saying this a week ago, I'm glad for it. I'm hoping that when the time comes that he needs someone, he remembers that I'm someone he can confide in.

Until then, my main goal is to distract myself. Finals are doing a decent job of reminding me where my attention needs to be. I'm wholly focused on my notes, running my finger over the text repeatedly and then scribbling the information I need to know on notecards so I can memorize the material I need for my upcoming exam.

Finals week starts tomorrow. Less than twenty-four hours until I find out if I've fucked myself on all the hard work and effort I've given this semester because I chose to get caught up with a guy.

Then I remind myself that I need to trust my abilities, that I've never screwed up too badly on exams before and that my love for Colson is bigger than any tests I've ever had and any I'll ever endure.

It's strange to think about how I so willingly gave up

trying with Webber but am acting like an entirely different person when it comes to Colson.

Because you actually love him.

"Focus," I tell myself, squeezing my eyes shut then opening them to look at my chicken scratch. I normally pride myself on how neat my notes are, but I don't have much in me to perfect them. I've lost the desire to keep everything neat and legible.

I try keeping my attention on studying, but when I eventually fail, I leave my desk for a glass of water. I lean against the kitchen counter and drink, filling it again and chugging a second once I finish.

I spent time in the apartment gym this morning. I let the yoga music take me away and only allowed myself to feel the sting of the stretches. Everything except for the strain on my heart faded. But my muscles are stiff and achy, and I know it's because I haven't hydrated myself well enough this week. I've lacked taking care of myself to be there for others, but if I don't get a handle on it soon, everything is going to feel about ten times more overwhelming.

I put my cup in the dishwasher then turn for the cabinets. I'm rummaging through them, searching for something to snack on when someone enters the room. I know it's not Everleigh because she's with her sister, which means it's Sylvia.

I twist around with a bag of tomato-basil crackers in hand and spot her at the other end of the kitchen, her blonde hair pulled back in a French braid. A hot pink skirt stretches over her thin waist and ends about five inches from her crotch. She paired a matching halter tank with it, and I'll be honest, it's a cute combo, but it's not something you wear out if you're just meeting up with friends in broad daylight.

"Hey," I greet with a careful smile because as much as I'd

like to bypass this awkwardness, that'd be rude. It'd be something she'd do, and it isn't right. Even after all the messed-up things she has said, I push down my feelings and play nice. "Going out?"

She wears her best poker face, and I can't tell if she's zeroing in on a fight or if she's going to let the tension float away. My hope is for the latter. The last thing I have the energy for is fighting with someone who sees nothing wrong with the way they act.

She makes her way to the alcohol cabinet in the corner and eyes the selection inside. "Meeting up with Fletch and the guys."

"Sounds fun."

Who am I kidding?

It sounds like the worst idea ever, but I've given up on trying to convince her otherwise. For some unknown reason, she's become friends with them and sees them daily. I don't know why, but I'm at the point where I understand it isn't my business. We've grown too far apart for me to insert myself in her life.

She grabs a clear bottle. I catch *vodka* printed across the label before she reaches for an empty stainless water cup in the next cabinet over. You'd never know what's inside of it unless you popped the lid and sniffed. She drains the vodka into the cup, then takes the little bit that's left like a shot. She licks every last drop off her lips then sucks the straw into her mouth and drinks it easily from her canister. Like it's water.

I ignore the urge to tell her what she's doing is not okay. She hasn't been her usual self since last year. It tears at my heart to see her so distant and turning to external vices that will only amplify her problems.

She turns to place the empty bottle into the trash bin and moves for the foyer. Before she gets very far, I step forward and pull at her wrist. She turns her gaze on me in slow motion. Her eyes flick down to my hand on her, but it's almost like she's in a daze and zoned out.

She's not the girl who laughed at the thought of Colson breaking up with me a week ago.

Sylvia has always been known to have strong opinions and not sugarcoat anything, but this is something else entirely. We may not be on the best terms, but her walking in, barely saying a word, and just leaving is so unlike her character that concern immediately washes over me.

"Sylvia, are you okay?"

Her brow lifts in challenge as my eyes bounce between hers. Her voice is flat and lacking life. "Why wouldn't I be?"

My attention moves down to the cup in her hand, and I choose to tread lightly. Maybe she has convinced herself she's good, but she most definitely is not. She's not around much, and when she is, she's cooped up in her room sleeping or getting snappy with me and Everleigh. I don't know if she's going to her classes like she should be or if she's planning to show up for her finals. Just because she was in the quad the other day doesn't mean she's actively participating in her studies.

I don't mention how we both know her cup is filled with eighty-proof liquor. I have no idea how she'd react, and I'm not certain I'd be able to handle one of her outbursts amped up on alcohol and whatever else seems to be in her system.

Not when I'm going through my own stuff.

Stuff she doesn't even know about because we've grown so far apart.

It hurts knowing how attached she, Everleigh, and I were freshman year, and now we can't even be bothered to keep each other up to date with what's going on in our lives.

So quickly, we've gone from friends to complete strangers.

"We just haven't really talked or hung out," I say, giving her space by dropping her wrist and taking a step back. "Just checking in."

"Do us both a favor, Violet, and don't."

My bottom lip curls into my mouth when she reminds me of the type of person she is, and I nod, leaving it at that. There's nothing I can say that'll end with us laughing it out or in each other's arms.

As soon as she walks out the door, I track down my phone and send a message to Everleigh, telling her about Sylvia. That it's only a matter of time before her behavior catches up to her and she makes a mess of her life, if she hasn't done so already.

I SET my pencil on the pull-out desk in front of me. The auditorium my professor teaches Language and Literacy in is a temporary placement until his classroom gets the fresh coat of paint the administrative department promised three weeks ago. Only, when they went in to start the project, there was a leak they had to deal with first.

It's pushed back completion, bottling us up in a different room. It's not all bad, but the desks are small, the area between each seat miniscule. I don't know how some of the guys are fitting into them, especially the jocks with their thick thighs and meaty torsos.

I send a quick glance around the room then start flipping through my exam. It's ten pages, front and back, with an essay section on the last page. My nerves are all over the place. I need to just push everything else out of my mind, but it's hard when I'd rather run in Colson's direction.

I want to see him.

Hug him.

Make unrealistic promises, like tell him everything will be okay.

He lives in all the nooks and crannies of my mind as I check boxes and try not to second guess myself. My eyelids are heavy, and my eyes have this overwhelming dryness to them that always seems to come every spring when pollen coats everything. Not to mention I've been up since five, because I couldn't fall back asleep.

When I think I've finally answered all the questions correctly, I collect my belongings and hoist my messenger bag over my shoulder. I'm at the end of the row, so thankfully, I don't have to shimmy and excuse my way past peoples' legs. I quietly set my packet down with the other few who are already done on the professor's desk and offer a smile. He gives me a subtle nod and turns back to his laptop.

I head in the direction of the closest coffee spot on campus. They're sprinkled all over the place, and usually have the same menu. I wait in line to fill up on caffeine since I plan on heading to the gym after. I have a short break in the day before having to show up to my Family Child Care class and finish that final.

One step closer to winter break.

I'm waiting to collect my order when strong arms envelop my shoulders. I see the hint of a green shirt and smile, knowing exactly who it is. Green is Sebastian's favorite color, and I'd be doing him an injustice by saying that it doesn't match up against his slightly darker skin tone damn near perfectly.

"You good to share what you ordered?" he asks with a cheeky smile.

"No way in hell."

"Aw, come on. I'm working hard over here, too, you know." He releases his hold on me, and I twist around to see his full frame. He doesn't look like he needs coffee, that's for sure. In fact, he looks like he woke up on the right side of the bed this morning. As if his cousin's life and sanity aren't up against the test of time. As if said cousin didn't have his hand around his neck a mere few days ago.

"Are you almost done?" I ask him, referring to his finals schedule.

"Two down this morning," he confirms, hands on the straps of his bookbag. "One more this afternoon and then I have two tomorrow, but one is more of a presentation than an actual exam." The lady at the coffee kiosk calls my name and hands over my coffee. I fall in step with Sebastian, heading in the direction of the campus gym. It's a trek, but it'll be worth it when some of this tension in my body melts away. "What about you?"

"Two today, two tomorrow." I blow through the small slit in my coffee cup, hoping it'll cool down its near-lava temperature.

"Think you did okay?"

"I mean, I think I definitely passed." I tilt my coffee just enough for it to scald my tastebuds. I wince and blow on it more. "But I don't think I'm going to get the straight A's I initially wanted."

He bumps his arm into mine. "I'm sorry all this shit is happening right now. It's the worst possible time for it, but we all appreciate you being there for him."

I mean, I wouldn't exactly say I've been there.

Every time I've tried, Colson has pushed me away, but I don't remind him of that.

"I just wish he'd realize that he's not alone. That there are people a call away who would drop everything for him." Sebastian frowns, and I think our minds both go to the same thing. "Has he talked more about what happened at the lawyer's office?"

"I haven't been around since..." *Since Colson had his hand wrapped around his throat.* "I needed a little bit of space to focus on my finals." He shakes his head in this solemn kind of way. Sebastian's naturally grinning expression fades and replacing it is a version of him I don't see often. I think he's genuinely worried about Colson. And maybe wonders if we'll be able to help him. I understand that. I've had moments where I think the same. Where I'm unsure if we're strong enough to hold Colson up while his legs aren't able to do it for him.

"What happened has been a lot. It's normal to need a break from it. To have your own space. I'm sorry he did that to you, Sebastian."

"It's not your thing to apologize for. Besides, I know that isn't him," he tells me as we follow the walking path. "He's never crossed those lines with me or with anyone I know. He's just trying to redirect his pain onto someone else. Easier to make it through the day that way."

"You don't deserve it."

The insanity of the swampy, crocodile-infested waters Colson can't seem to swim out of is not something any of us deserves, but I also know we'll all be there for him regardless of what any of us says. Because it's what you do when you care about someone.

"None of us do," he murmurs, his eyes slicing to me as if

we're talking about me now. "Are you going to see him any time soon?"

I shrug. "I need to finish these finals. Need to keep my head clear for them. I want to know what's going on with him," I admit, "But I also feel like space is good for us. All we do when we're together is argue."

Besides, he probably doesn't even want to see me.

He sighs, and I feel it in my bones, tracing its way from one to the next until my entire body seizes silently from the pressures of life.

"For the longest time, I thought you were the only one who could lift the blinders he had super glued over his eyes. I don't think that's true anymore," he concedes. "I don't think anyone has what he needs to see clearly. And I'm not saying that because I'm giving up on him, Vi. I think the only person who's capable of saving himself…is him."

MAINTAINING MY STANDING FORWARD BEND, I relax my body and let my head hang heavy. My ponytail swishes to the ground as my hamstrings pull tight. When the burn mimics a line of fire ants, I sink into the stretch deeper.

I push every thought out of my mind, focusing on the violin that accompanies the piano in my earbuds. It's melodic and curls around me in a way that almost feels like a hug. I breathe deeply and allow my lungs air for the first real time today. All morning, I made it through campus on half breaths. Enough to keep me going, but not sufficient to the point my body was getting what it needed.

A pressure I'm used to from doing lots of downward dogs fills my head. It's like hanging upside down but not as prominent. I relish in the fullness of it, trusting how it's regulating my nervous system and giving me the chance to come down from the stressful high I've been riding for days.

When my music cuts out and a new melody graces my ears, I stand tall, take one last belly-deep breath and release my stance. I roll up my yoga mat, pressing the Velcro together so I can loop the strap over my shoulder. My messenger bag with my books and water bottle sits off to the side. I head over, grab it, and look across the gym through the windows in the yoga room. It's more muted in here than the rest of the gym, where boombox speakers pump uplifting workout music. College students are all around, and it's not a surprise since it's cold outside.

Pushing out the door and into the open space with weightlifting equipment and ellipticals, I hoist my messenger bag over my head. Somehow, it gets tangled in my ponytail. The smart thing to do would be to stop, set my water bottle down, and fix it.

But I'm not on my A game.

I keep walking, struggling to separate my hair from the metal buckle of my strap. Rounding the corner for the main entrance, I free the strands with a relieved breath.

The strap comes down to rest on my opposite shoulder at the same time I bump into someone. I stumble on my feet, the grip on my water bottle loosening. It crashes to the floor, the spout opening and water gushing out. One of my earbuds falls victim to the jostling as well, slipping out of my ear and skidding across the floor. I lose sight of it and reach for the water bottle to save it from creating a tiny flood where someone could slip.

"Shit, I'm sorry," a guy says as his hand clasps around my purple stainless steel cup.

Surprise skitters up my spine. *I know that voice.* I spent

two years of my life looking forward to hearing it after a long day and enjoying the way it murmured sweet words into my ear after nightfall. But I also remember how it cracked in brittle sadness when I broke up with its owner.

I glance up to find the same light green eyes that used to shine in the morning light that drenched my dorm room. "Webber," I breathe out.

"Violet?" His gaze trails over my body, taking in my workout gear and disheveled look. He snaps the lid shut on the water bottle and holds it out. "You okay? I didn't see you coming around the corner. You barreled right into me."

I shake my head and drop my chin as I take the cup from him. There's a hairline crack in the plastic lid. I run my finger over it as I mutter out, "Yeah, I…" I grab the strap of my bag, "I was having a bit of a malfunction with this. Got caught in my hair, and I was trying to walk and fix it at the same time."

He steps forward, letting someone move around him while telling them to keep an eye out for the spilled water on the ground. I follow his lead when his hand comes up to my elbow to guide me out of the way. "How have you been? I haven't seen you around."

When I ended our relationship, Webber promised to give me the space I needed. Looking at him now, I notice the lightness in his features. The way his pretty eyes glow. The way he looks well rested and refreshed. Nothing like the last encounter we had.

"I'm…" I start, wanting to lie and tell him life is great. The reality is…life is a complete horror, and yoga is barely keeping me sane. "Hanging in there."

His brows draw in, his gaze more observant than before. Concern flashes across his features, and when my eyes fall to the ground again, he reaches out and softly touches my upper arm. "Vi, what's going on? I know things ended with us, but you can still talk to me."

He says that, but see, I know otherwise. I *can't* lean on Webber when it comes to me and Colson. Whether or not he would understand isn't the issue. It's that...I don't want him thinking it's an open invitation to rekindle what we had. The flame we shared was blown out, and there's no match in the world that could relight it.

I'm quiet for too long. His gaze bounces between mine as I think of a response.

His tongue darts out of his mouth and smooths over his bottom lip. And that brow of his, it arches in question, joining his words for one hell of a ride when he quietly asks, "Is it Sebastian's cousin? Did he hurt you?"

I glance away because *yes, he did hurt me,* and I want to shout that from the tallest building in Chatham Hills. However, the only person I really want to hear it is Colson. Not my ex who stands in front of me with assessing eyes and judgmental words.

"I know that look, Violet. You look fucking wrecked. I know you two have been seeing each other, and I'm good with that. Just want to make sure you're good, too. If something happened..."

I conjure as much strength as I can muster and raise my head. My spine straightens along with it. "I'm okay," I answer, looking Webber in the eyes. "He didn't do anything. Finals are just dragging me down." *It's on me for falling for someone who's tragically damaged yet beautifully made.*

"You say that, but I'm having a real hard time believing it." He rubs his lips together. "If you don't want to tell me, fine, but at least talk to Sebastian. He'll help you through whatever you're going through, and he won't be afraid to call his own flesh and blood out on his bullshit."

Webber's name comes from behind me, someone shouting it over the clunking of a nearby weight machine. He lifts his gaze over my shoulder before I have the chance to thank him for being decent. With everything we've been through, it's nice to know that he's not holding grudges.

"That's a buddy of mine I've been training with," he explains, tossing a thumb over his shoulder. "I gotta go."

"Yeah, sure. Go ahead."

He looks at me for one long stretch. Almost like he doesn't want to go to his friend at all. But we both know he can't stay rooted in front of me. We're living two different lives now, and his is calling him back into its orbit.

"Keep your head up, Vi. And never fucking forget that you deserve the world. You know you do. Don't settle for whatever shit you're going through. Go after what makes you happy."

I nod with a tiny smile, holding my water bottle to my chest despite my ribcage trying to reflect the crack in my cup. Webber steps around me, getting lost in the mix of chaos happening in the gym. I don't turn around to see where he goes or if he turns and steals one last glance of me. It's not until I'm halfway home that I notice I never picked up my earbud from the gym floor.

EIGHTEEN

COLSON

THE THWACKING of fists against leather helps me zone out until I put in my headphones and hit play on my usual playlist. My gloves are next. I tug them tight over my knuckles as I prepare to let all my fury out on the bag in front of me.

After the ordeal with Sebastian, and Violet inevitably settling on calling me her *friend*, I need to get my frustrations out. I have no right to be upset about the lines she's drawn after I tried forging my own—and said the things I have—but I fucking detest them.

It's so much different being the one who's lacking control. I have no say in the thick rope she's laid between us. No jurisdiction over it vanishing or thickening. Over if it moves or stays there forever.

I don't want it to be there that long.

It's hard as hell getting her pretty smile out of my head. Harder forgetting what she tastes like when I fall into bed at night. She's the only one out there for me, but it has to be this way.

I drive my fist into the boxing bag.

I've never despised my life more than I do now. How I didn't have a mother to teach me how to work through my emotions. How I don't have a father who I can trust and turn to for girl advice when I've fucked up. Being branded the name "prick" wouldn't do me justice. Bastard is more like it. Not just because I've acted like an idiot but because it's a fact. I *am* one.

That's the other reason I'm at Gulliver's. I'm still trying to wrap my mind around Mom being married to Clyde. I've been trying to look back at my life, the timeline of my childhood, but none of it makes sense, and I only get so far before my memory cuts off. I don't recall if he was around when I was young. Did he show up at the house when I was a toddler? Did he sneak around with Mom, coming in through the back door past my bedtime?

I have no answers, and it only tests my patience and the theories I've been fed, making that pit deep in my stomach that thinks Clyde could be my father even more assuming.

I used to wonder how Mom got caught up with the Lincolns so easily. It makes sense now. She was doing business with them because she knew Clyde. Their relationship gave her a shoe in the door despite them not playing house. It was easier for her to seek him out versus finding someone else on the streets. And she was so caught up that she never once questioned his motives or why he continued to keep their marriage going while he was off living with Finn's mother.

If they didn't want to be together and no one knew about it, then why didn't they get a divorce? Clyde went on to have a son with another woman. I don't know what Finn's mom's name is, but I recall seeing her a time or two when we were still young enough for parents to show their faces at school.

My fist hits the leather again before I lay down a killer of a combo.

Clyde had, single-handedly, poured fuel on Mom's fire by giving her drugs to sell then forced me to helicopter in the gallons of water, chiseling away at my exterior bit by bit until my entire focus was on paying her debts and not on what truly mattered; her addiction and need for help.

How could he do that?

I shouldn't be surprised, but I can't help but to be. Not when he's Clyde and the Lincolns have the reputation they do.

My gloved fist drives into the leather harder. I go with a simple jabbing pattern and welcome the way it pulls at my muscles. It's been a minute since I've gotten to beat the shit out of something. It doesn't help that I've been drinking and haven't been sleeping well. It takes me a little longer than normal to warm up, but once I do I put my entire focus on my movements.

My mind, however, doesn't get the hint that it's break time. It goes right back to considering everything that's been going on and settles on Clyde again. Could he really be my father?

It doesn't fucking matter.

Music thumps in my ears, and my heartbeat plays along to the drums. Thump, thump, thumping in a way that brings me back to life. I haven't felt like this since before the fundraiser, when I spent most of my days outside of work with Violet.

A reprieve curls up over my shoulders and trickles down my arms and into my hands. A sizzling current makes way, and by the time I'm done with my set, sweat drips off my forehead and temples. I'm a disgusting mess, so much that I have to pull my clinging shirt away from my sticky skin. I peel my gloves off and sit on the bench near my bag and electrolyte drink.

I should've gotten out of the house sooner.

A hand clamps over my shoulder, and I look up to see Llewellyn. He's wearing a gym polo and is clean-shaven, which is nothing new. I've never seen the man with facial hair. What gets me most are his watchful eyes and the questions conveyed in them.

He gave me time off from working, and here I am, in his gym, anyway.

I tug my earbuds out and pocket them. "Hey."

"How you doing, kid?"

"Alright." I motion to the gym. "This helps."

"I sure as hell hope so." He sits next to me and crosses his arms over his chest, legs spread out and heels propped on the cement below him. We look out at the expanse of the gym. There's a new girl working the front counter. A redhead who offers timid smiles to everyone that comes and goes. I overheard a dude in the locker room say her name is Kelsie and how she's Llewellyn's niece from an estranged sister he doesn't ever talk about.

Old me would have greeted her properly when I arrived earlier instead of ignoring her, but no one needs me as a friend right now, so I ducked my head and ignored her altogether.

The last time I let a girl in she got in my head and heart, and I haven't been able to get her out ever since. And now everything with her is one giant fucked up mess.

Llewellyn takes my silence as something being wrong.

"Can't help you if you don't tell me what you need."

I glance over, momentarily stunned by what he says but then also not. Ever since I've known the guy, he's gone above and beyond to help those around him. It's his purpose in life.

The thing that gets him out of bed to open the doors to this place every morning. It's wild how he can take one look at a person and know how much they're suffering.

I'm not there yet.

I'm not ready to talk about it in depth.

To get down to the nitty gritty of how goddamn broken I am. For a multitude of reasons.

I shake my head and look down at my feet. "I don't know, Llewellyn."

He purses his lips, but it turns up looking more like a frown than anything else. "When Gulliver died, it was like he stole my heart from my chest and took it with him. Sure, my body was still here, but the rest of me?" He wags a hand in the air. "I was gone. Didn't give a single shit about anyone or anything. For a long time, I was fine living in the outrage that consumed me from it. Used to ask myself, *how?* How could it be that we both went over there, and I came back but he didn't? Didn't seem right. Still doesn't some days."

Jesus.

I can't imagine what it was like for him and his brother all those years ago. From the way I've always heard it from Llewellyn, they were thick as thieves. Did everything together, including signing up to fight for their country. One came back and the other did, too, but in a flag-draped casket.

"Gulliver was older than me by two years. Had more knowledge and life behind him, but it didn't matter. He was still taken in combat, and for a long time I goddamn hated him for it. Myself, too. Years went by before I could look my ugly mug in the mirror. All I saw was him. In every little thing."

I'm not sure what to say so I settle on, "Wish I could've gotten to meet him."

"So do I, kid. But that doesn't change what you're facing.

I know the struggle when I see the struggle because I've been through the struggle. Ya get me?"

"I get you."

"Good, so tell me, you at rock bottom yet?"

I swallow at the tarantula-sized lump in my throat.

Rock bottom.

I guess that depends on who you ask and how they define it. Then again, when I look back on time since Mom passed, all I see is me losing it on the people closest to me. Going from having some semblance of love around me to none at all. Maybe I have hit the rubble of bedrock and stone beneath the surface of the earth.

"I stared at a bottle of Jack Daniel's for days," I utter, knowing he won't judge me for it. Llewellyn has been through too much to cast a single stone. "Trying to decide if I wanted to run from my problems and risk the same kind of life she had or deal with my cards head-on."

"Yeah? Which way did the ball roll?"

Addiction is no joke in the Moore family. My body's tolerance is higher because of it. The absolute last thing I want is to end up like Mom or her dad. I don't want to have to answer to something that's embedded in my flesh and blood and lose out on the richness of life.

The richness of Violet.

In the end, I wasn't strong enough.

I sniff, pushing away the shame that tries to replace the sweat all over my body. "I drank the Jack."

"For what it's worth," he nudges me with an elbow, "I drank the Jack, too."

I glance around, noting the people filling the gym and getting their workouts in while chatting with one another. Eli is over by the ring with the same dude that's always training him. I linger on the last conversation I had with him, wondering for the first time what it would be like to take him up on his offer to get in the ring with him. How would it feel to push my pain onto someone else? Would it help me forget? Would it make this all a little more bearable?

I shift back to Llewellyn. It's like we're in a bubble, watching and observing what's around without anyone having the opportunity to do the same back.

"Grief is one of those things that appears out of the blue. It doesn't give you a heads up. It's like that genie in a bottle, except for granting one wish, it sets out to drag you down any way it can. All because of the love you have for the person who's no longer here."

"I don't know what to do," I admit, but my thoughts stretch to Eli again, and I don't know what to make of it. I was so quick to turn him down before but now...

"Most people don't."

"One second, I'm sad as hell and wish I could have more time with her despite everything she put me through. In the next minute, I'm angry. So fucking angry that I want to put my fist through something." I sigh and let out a staggering breath. That shame from a minute ago grasps me, and I can't believe what I admit next. "I almost strangled my cousin."

Llewellyn clicks his tongue and slants his head, giving it a shake. "And now you're here. Sounds like rock bottom after all."

I scrub my hands over my face, pushing what's left of my sweat back into my hairline. "I've fucked everything up, and I don't know how to fix it. Not when it feels like it just keeps getting worse."

I don't mention Clyde's name like I want to.

For some reason, I want to keep that information private. At least a little longer until I figure out what the hell to do about it, though I'm not sure there is anything I can do. How am I supposed to handle it? Walk up to the guy and demand that he should've never married my mom? That he should've kept his dick in his pants? That he's not taking her house from me or the money?

Everything is irrevocably screwed.

"I broke up with my girlfriend," I admit next.

"That pretty little brunette you showed me a picture of?"

I nod, guilt wracking my chest for the thousandth time. Back when things were good with Vi, I came in one night, high off my ass from her stunning smile and playful text messages. Llewellyn saw me grinning up a storm and asked what had me in such a good mood. I didn't tell him but showed him a picture of Violet instead.

"How'd you manage that?"

"The night Mom overdosed, I was out of my mind with emotions, and thought it'd be better if she were nowhere near me while I figured out how to navigate it all. And shit has happened since then. She keeps showing up for me, and like the asshole I am, I make it worse every time I'm around her."

"That's how you know she's a keeper, kid. Some of these women," he blows out a breath. "They're wavin' goodbye at the first sign of hardship."

"She wants *every* part of it. But I can't...I can't bring her into this shitshow. She's already seen me at my worst. She was there when that happened with my cousin. I don't want to drag her knee-deep into the quicksand." I wouldn't be able to save her when she needed it. Not when I'm stuck too. If I can't protect myself against my inner demons, how the hell can I ever protect her?

"Sounds to me like she's already in it."

I consider that.

Fuck.

Maybe we've already passed the point of no return.

"Listen, Colson, I get all you must be feeling. Your mama didn't make her life easy. Didn't make it that way for you either, and now she's gone. You can choose to handle this the way she would or in your own way, but if you want to stop hurting the people you care about, then you're gonna have to work on yourself." He thumps one fist over his heart and uses his other finger to tap his head. "You're going to have to get in here and up top if you want to make it."

I hear him loud and clear, I really do, but...

"What if I'm not ready for that? What if I have no clue what my first step is?"

What if I'm scared shitless over losing someone else, except this time there's so much more love involved? What if I can't be the man I need to be? What if being stuck like this is my fate?

"You'll know when you're ready. It'll click and you'll just start moving in that direction because nothin' else makes sense. And after that, you know your steps by trusting yourself. The process. Everything beyond what you already know."

He makes it sound like it can be easy.

I know from experience that it never is.

My eyes slice back over to Eli, watching him as he sidesteps and ducks when his trainer throws a fake swing at him. I hear his voice like he's standing in front of me again with the promise of having a remedy that works like no other.

It isn't Jack or drugs but starts and ends with my fists.

For the first time ever, I wonder if he might know what he's talking about.

NINETEEN

COLSON

Old text messages...

Colson: I took Sebastian's bag of M&M's. Let's bet on how long it takes him to realize they're missing.

Violet: Oooh. What does the winner get?

Colson: One hell of a kiss.

Violet: Just a kiss? This seems like a trick. I think he'll figure it out today.

Colson: I'm saying a month.

Violet: No way. Purposely trying to lose now?

Colson: Absolutely.

Colson: I never said where the kiss would be. Though I have a pretty good idea on where it should be.

Violet: I always knew you were a tricky trickster.

I SHIFT my car in park and look up at Stewart's fancy law building. The last time I was here, it changed my life. I can hardly wait to see what's in store this afternoon.

When Aunt Bess called after leaving Gulliver's and asked if I'd meet her, I was reluctant. I haven't spoken to her since the last time we sat down with her lawyer. I don't really want to now but would rather get it over with and not have to leave the house once I go home.

I'm hanging onto the small chance that Stewart found a way around the marriage license ordeal. Maybe it was a scam all along. A copy of a fake, and Mom wasn't truly married to Clyde Lincoln after all.

I don't let myself think about that possibility for too long as I ride the elevator up and approach the same receptionist Aunt Bess spoke to last time. She guides me back to Stewart's conference room, Aunt Bess and Uncle Thad already present when I walk through the door.

"Colson." Aunt Bess gets up from her chair and walks over to me. There's worry in the depths of her eyes. She wants to know if I'm okay but is afraid to ask. It's probably best that she doesn't. For a split second, I wonder if Sebastian told her what happened, but then she wraps me in one of her hugs, and I know he didn't.

He's still loyal to me, even after I screwed up.

Warmth encases me, and it's hard to let go of it when I've been shivering in subarctic temperatures for so long. I've purposely forced myself outside in blustering temperatures so I'd go numb, but Aunt Bess has always been a fireplace.

"I wish you wouldn't pull away," she says softly, pulling back and looking me over for harm. "Things didn't go so great last time we were here, I know that. I'm hoping Stewart has better news for us today. He's the one who called the meeting. He's trying to find a way around our current predicament."

"You had no idea that she was with him?" I ask her for the first time.

"When we were teenagers, her and Clyde would spend time together," she discloses. "I had no clue it had gotten serious enough for them to get *married* behind everyone's backs."

"They hung out?" She's never mentioned this before. "So, Mom and Clyde were friends?" If that's the case, then at what point did it go south, and where does Clyde's lifestyle fit into all of this?

"Yes, they were friends at one point, I think, when we were in high school. Long before he got deeper into his illegal activities."

I give her a hard look, unsure of how to feel about this. "Why didn't you ever mention it?"

"Why would I? It was a long time ago, and I was under the impression that they stopped speaking. Not long after they graduated, Clyde got strung up in a bad situation. Ended up having to do a couple months in jail. I was under the assumption that they stopped talking when he was sent away. I had no idea they resumed their connection when he was released. By then, my relationship with Janie was already starting to take a turn, rebelling in ways that didn't have to do with drugs yet. She didn't see eye to eye with me when I tried to help her. I met your Uncle Thad shortly after that."

I run a hand over my mouth. I guess she has a point. It really was a long time ago. But even if it was, somewhere along the way, my mom and Clyde reunited. Enough for them to get fucking hitched. "When would they have gotten married, though? That friendship they had must've been serious enough for them to show up at the courthouse and sign some papers."

Aunt Bess shrugs and rubs her palms together. She's normally so put together, so in control of what's going on around her that I barely ever see this side of her. The side that lacks answers and is uncertain. "I don't know, Colson. I mean, yes, at some point that clearly happened. But your mom would participate in activities back then that I wasn't aware of. She would go to parties and drink. She would hang out with groups of people I wasn't involved with. I wasn't her keeper, and it was hard to nail down any real answers with her when I did have questions."

I nod, accepting her answer and trailing around to the other side of the room to claim a chair. "Why would someone get married, just to *not* be with that person?" I've been thinking about it a lot. It doesn't make sense, and as much as I trust Aunt Bess, instinct tells me she's holding back. It's not just this that has me thinking about it, though. It's also that conversation I had with her when she was waiting for me in my apartment to tell me about Mom getting arrested. When I asked her about my father.

I stretch my legs out underneath the table and watch as she paces. Uncle Thad nods his hello from across the table. "I see the way you're looking at your aunt. Her loyalty isn't something you should be questioning, Colson. We've only ever wanted the best for you."

My gaze lingers on his, and bravo to him for reading me so easily. I'd give him a round of applause if I had the goddamn energy.

"There's a lot going on," Uncle Thad continues, "but if anyone is on your side, it's her."

Just like that, I feel like an asshole for wondering if there's something she's not telling me. I chalk it up to my own paranoia and all the shit that's been going on, the lack of sleep catching up with me.

Stewart walks in a moment later, but he's not alone.

The tall man behind him dwarfs his height and steals all the attention in the room. Dark blue engaging eyes. Scruff on his face. Entire body clad in midnight black. Just like his son, who stands behind him.

My body goes rigid at the sight of Clyde and Finn. My mouth clamps shut, and my muscles work overtime, clenching under the guise of this being the most fucked up family reunion ever.

Across the room from me is my stepfather—Mom's *husband*—and Harrison Height's most known drug dealer.

TWENTY

COLSON

THE THREE FILE into the room, the air uncomfortably tense. Stewart offers his best manners and gestures for them to find a seat. They round the table. A whole fucking lot of chairs in here, and they choose to sit next to me. I'm at the end, Finn is in the middle, and Clyde is on the other side of him. I stare straight ahead as the chair legs screech with the same protests I'm having in my head.

"Stewart." My aunt awkwardly shifts in her seat. Uncle Thad's hand moves to cover one of hers on the table. An act of comfort. My eyes track the movement of his thumb brushing the back of her hand as my aunt adds, "What's this about?"

Stewart sits tall. I'm sure this isn't the first time he's been in a situation as fucked as this. In fact, he looks as laid-back as the two sitting next to me. Like their stomachs aren't filled with wasps buzzing to protect their queen. Like it's no big deal when it's the biggest goddamn deal of the century.

I get why Clyde is here, but why the hell is Finn? Where does he fit into all of this?

Stewart tents his hands on the table. "I thought it'd be

best for all of us to sit down. I'll act as a mediator in order to make sure everyone walks away happy."

Aunt Bess purses her lips then acts as if it's just her and Stewart in the room. "We both know where that money belongs."

"That might be so, but there are legal documents that say otherwise. I wouldn't be doing my job unless we dealt with that appropriately. Mediation is the next step to take before dealing with the expenses of going to court."

"We could've done this privately," she gripes.

Stewart nods in understanding, but I'm not sure he realizes just how much of an overreach this is by not consulting with his client before dropping a bomb such as the Lincolns in person.

Clyde interjects, his voice deep and unapologetic. "Let's not pretend like we don't already know each other, Bess."

I keep my focus ahead of me, even though I want to look over at the men next to me. They know me, and I know them. But Aunt Bess and Uncle Thad don't know that. They *can't* know that. I lied to Aunt Bess's face about Mom's well-being in their own kitchen. She can't know about my involvement with them or why it exists.

I suck my cheek into my mouth and use it as a means to cope. My molars edge into the sensitive flesh and do little to calm the monster traipsing in my gut.

Aunt Bess glowers at Clyde, her eyes flaring with fire. It's so much worse than when Sebastian and I got up to no good as kids. "How dare you intrude, thinking you can say whatever you please."

"I belong here," he states simply. Like he's not crashing a party he was never invited to. "Just like any of you. It's no secret that Janie and I were married."

"See, that's where you're wrong," Bess plainly asserts. "It *was* a secret. Why couldn't you leave her the hell alone?"

Clyde shrugs. Finn lazily rests his elbow on the arm of his chair, ignoring me like I'm ignoring him. In this room, we're strangers. On the streets of Harrison Heights, we know each other quite well. I think of everything he's done to me. A lit cigarette to my neck. Having his muscle beat me down in that alleyway. Breaking my finger at his father's instruction.

"Your sister did her own thing. We've always known that. It just so happens that we made a couple of stupid mistakes when we were young one night."

"What was the point of it?" Aunt Bess questions. "Why marry her if you planned from the start to never be with her? To never *support* her?"

"Oh, I've supported Janie." His smirk is slimy. Like a snake that slithers out of water on a hunt. "Just not in the conventional sense."

I stomp down the accusations threatening to come out of me. The only way he supported her was by feeding her the drugs she was desperate to have. By getting her involved in a deal that I had to make better. He's only ever been selfish with her and has done nothing to help the woman he was legally bound to.

"Listen," he starts. "If I'm being completely honest, I forgot all about the marriage license."

Yeah, that's a crock of shit.

"I don't believe you," Aunt Bess accuses. "You chained her down with that all these years without anyone else knowing. I want to know why."

Stewart sits back without saying a word, steepling his hands at his chin like he's proud of himself. I don't like him. Not that I did before, but I really don't care for the guy now that he's pitting Aunt Bess and Clyde against one another and calling it mediation.

"Janie didn't seem to mind. Never brought me divorce papers, so I'd say she was happy with the turnout."

"You know why she never did."

She was always too worried about coping with her addiction. Feeding it. Figuring out how to give it what it needed to thrive. A divorce was probably the last thing on her mind.

"Janie's addiction had nothing to do with me."

What a fucking liar.

I grit my teeth, my jaw clenching, and sit straighter. Finn knocks his foot against mine. It's the first time he's made himself known aside from showing up with his dad, but where does he get off?

"You took advantage of it. Why? You had a son with another woman and have been with her all these years. You'd think you'd eventually want to marry *her,*" she says, referring to Finn's mom, and how the hell does she know this much?

I can see how she might know a little bit about him from my mom hanging around him when they were in high school and shortly after she graduated, but that was decades ago. How would Aunt Bess know anything about Clyde's current situation, about Finn, about Finn's mother?

"I think this is getting out of hand," Uncle Thad throws in. Stewart hangs on to every word like the rest of us. This conference room is the stage and we're just the pathetic chumps being featured in today's episode of Jerry Springer.

"This is normal for situations like this," Stewart's stupid ass says. "Let's allow them to share the floor."

Clyde meets Aunt Bess head-on. "If you want to throw all my business out there for everyone to hear, then it's only right to make it fair, don't you think?"

"Don't you dare." Her warning piques my interest,

blowing my assumptions out of the water. She knows something I don't. Something she hasn't told me. Something she's *kept* from me.

I'm like a little kid, watching a dodgeball soar from one team to another. Eventually, someone is going to catch the throw or get pegged in the face. I have the nagging suspicion I'm that someone.

"Afraid your husband and nephew will see that you're not the perfect person you claim to be?" Clyde taunts.

Uncle Thad clears his throat, his voice taking on an authoritative tone. "That's enough."

Clyde's voice turns threatening, reminding me of the way he spoke to me before Finn broke my finger in that car. "Don't fucking interrupt me. I came, wanting to be decent, but seeing as how it's not being offered in return, my patience is done. You want the goddamn truth? Yeah, Janie and I got married. So fucking what? It's none of your goddamn business how or why or when it happened."

"It's *all* my business. She was my sister," Aunt Bess argues.

"My involvement with her has nothing to do with you so butt the fuck out of it. Unless of course you want to hear about all the places I've fucked her. Might've been hooked on whatever she could get her hands on, but she never protested a good lay."

Aunt Bess rears back. "You're a pig."

"The money she left behind is mine. It always fucking was, whether you like it or not. I'll be the one leaving with it. Her failure to tell you the shit she was doing isn't my goddamn problem."

"*Please.* Don't sit there and act like you're better than you are."

I glance over at Clyde, my stomach in my throat. This is

so fucking bizarre that I barely hear it when he says, "If there's anyone at this table who has pretended that, it's you. Tell me, have you ever told the kid who he belongs to? That you've spent the last two decades paying me off to stay the hell away from him? Was your cuckold husband over there in on it, too, or was this all your doing, Almighty Bess?"

My heartbeat stutters in my chest.

What did he just say?

Aunt Bess's face falls. Once ready to go up against the storm of Clyde Lincoln, she recoils, a tiny gasp leaving her mouth as her hand comes up to cover it.

Gravel fills my throat. I've had the sneaking suspicion, but wondering about it is much different than finding out it's the truth. "What is he talking about?"

"Yeah, I'm with him," Finn speaks. I wish he didn't open his mouth at all. "What the fuck is she talking about?"

Uncle Thad rubs at his temples. I stare blankly at my aunt. The woman who sat across from me and lied about it when I asked her what Mom was talking about that night. "Is what he's saying true? Have you known all this time that he's my...my father?"

"Colson, it's not that simple," she says.

"You've always had a way of making situations sound a whole lot less than they are," Clyde comments with a smirk painting his lips before muttering, "Piece of fucking work."

"Not that simple?" I'm reeling, losing grip on my emotions like a fishing line being yanked out farther and farther because a fish is hooked and taking it with them. "I asked you if you knew anything about my biological father. You looked me in my eye and lied after keeping it hidden for *years*?"

"For your own good," Aunt Bess responds, face stricken from Clyde airing out her dirty laundry.

I narrow my eyes on her. "Who are you to tell me what's good for me?"

"You know the reputation the Lincoln name has across Harrison Heights. Did you want that imprinted on you?"

A laugh tumbles out of me. "Mom tainted my name the second she gave birth to me."

"Your mother was a *good* person who got herself swept up in something that ruined her. He…" She points at Clyde, who's sitting back with his arms crossed, a pleased expression on his aged face. "He's rotten. He impregnated your mother and then *left* her. He had no intention of being there for you or raising you. Not like he did with that one."

I ignore her comment about Finn. "Then why pay him off if he was never going to be around? Why stand there," I point over to the door where we stood when I arrived, "and lie to me about not knowing about them being married."

She shakes her head. Maybe it made more sense to her all those years ago. "I *didn't* know they were married. That was as shocking to me as it was for you. I wanted to ensure he kept his distance." Her eyes dart to Finn. "I didn't want you to become some protégé to him. I didn't want him to influence you into his way of life."

Oh my God.

This is fucking rich.

She wanted to protect me from them, but Mom forced me into their lives, anyway.

When Clyde chuckles, I want to laugh right along with him until he stops and adds fuel to the fire. "Now might be a good time to mention that none of us here are really strangers. You might've paid me off to stay away from him, but your sister dragged him into this life right under your nose."

"What are you talking about?" asks Uncle Thad. His stare

is hard, a divot forming between his brows as his attention bounces between the man across from him and me.

I inwardly cringe. I was a fool to think that I'd be able to keep my involvement with the Lincolns hidden. That my family would never find out about me lying to them. Everything always comes back around and catches up with you.

It's comical, knowing that we've *all* been hiding our truths and burying them beneath the surface of day-to-day life. Death has forced our hands, our honesty. Now, we have no choice but to claw our way out of the dirt and rise above the truths.

Finn brings his hand up and runs it through his dark hair. He's dressed in the same black attire as his replica next to him, but for the first time ever, I think he does it out of nervousness. His sleeve of tattoos slips out from the wrist of his long-sleeved shirt, and he shifts in his chair uncomfortably.

Aunt Bess's gaze lands on me. It reminds me of times when Sebastian and I got into trouble as kids. When she'd try to get the truth out of us but we'd both just stand there, unwilling to rat the other out. She always found a way, though. Always figured out how to get into one of our heads to give the tiniest of details for her to put it together.

Now is no different, but rather than hiding behind my cousin, I have to step forward and take responsibility. Something I should've done a lot sooner.

"Colson? What is he referring to?" my uncle asks again.

I run the tip of my tongue over the inside of my bottom lip, hating the storm that beckons over us, threatening to destroy the little good that remains. Storm clouds so fucking dark they make day feel like night.

Weeks ago, we were as close to one big happy family as we could get. Now look at us.

As I meet Aunt Bess's eyes across from me, I realize that we're not very different from one another. She thought she was protecting me by paying Clyde to stay away. I thought I was helping Mom by paying off her debts. Neither did a goddamn thing to protect the woman who's now gone.

I inhale a deep breath even though the air that's circling us is thick and strained. It pushes into my lungs and does nothing to scatter my nerves. My foot bounces underneath the table, my knee brushing the bottom of it with each lift and fall.

I glance over at Stewart. I'm not about to incriminate myself in front of him. Nor will I risk him eavesdropping and running with the information since he clearly can't be trusted. "Mind bailing for a few minutes?"

He lifts his palms to me and glances around at everyone. "As long as everyone promises to keep their hands to themselves." He rises from his seat when he seems confident that no blood will be spilled then slips out of the room.

"Mom was buying drugs from the Lincolns," I concede, feeling as if there's this negative energy hovering over my shoulder from my dumb ass choice to help her in all the wrong ways. "I don't know the details behind the transactions, but she ended up not following through and owing them a bunch of money."

Aunt Bess's eyes cut to Finn and Clyde before sliding back to me. "You were paying for your mom's drugs?" She balks at the idea. Like she has a hard time believing it's true.

I scratch the back of my neck. "I mean, she already had them because of some deal she made with them, but then she did who the hell knows what with them. I guess in so many words, yeah, you could say that, depending on how you look at it."

She blinks in quick succession, as if she's having a hard time understanding what's happening.

Join the club.

"When she didn't have the money or she'd go back on her promises to them, they'd come knocking for what she didn't have. What was I supposed to do? Let her fend for herself?" I ignore the fact the Lincolns are next to me. "They would've held true to their threats. I didn't want that to happen."

"How much money have you given them?" Aunt Bess asks as if the devil isn't sitting at the table with us.

Clyde chuckles, and I only now realize how much of a good mood he's in. All the times I've seen him with Finn, he was the complete opposite.

Sinister.

Mean.

Out for blood.

His cruel laugh slices through me.

"How much, Colson?" Aunt Bess prods.

"It was...it was a lot. At least ten grand." I don't tell her that amount only includes this last time.

"Why didn't you come to me?"

I give her a look. Like, *really?*

There was no way I wanted deeper ties to the Lincolns. Or to get more people involved.

"It was easier to deal with it on my own than pull anyone else into her mess."

Her gaze drops. Confusion coats her feminine features and then a wave of guilt hits me so hard, I would be down on my knees if I weren't already sitting.

This could have been avoided. Mom's dealings with the Lincolns. The fact that I'm Clyde's son—Jesus, I still can't believe it. And one he never wanted at that. For years, I wondered what it'd be like to have a dad. Hell, I even went as far as thinking that he could've been better than Mom. That a childhood with him wouldn't have been as fucked up as life with her.

How wrong I was.

There's no way in hell Finn had it better than me.

Sure, Clyde isn't an addict, but he's bad in every other possible way.

My chest seizes from the very real fact that my father—a deadbeat—is two seats away. After all this time, I finally know who he is. He's no longer a figment of my imagination, but a living, breathing human. And not at all the person I expected him to be.

Clyde *fucking* Lincoln.

A man I despise.

One of two men I'll never give the benefit of the doubt.

Not finding out would've been better than this.

Aunt Bess doesn't bother turning her attention to me. It's not me who's her enemy, after all, but the man with the buzz cut and dark, assessing eyes across from her. "You sold drugs to Janie? You two were married. All this time, you've handed over the thing that killed her?" She chokes on a tearless sob and rubs her palm over her clavicle. "I can't believe this."

Uncle Thad rests a hand on her back. "Deep breaths, Bess."

"He…" She swallows around the difficulty of talking. It reminds me of when her and Uncle Thad approached the fundraiser table. She tried getting the words out, but ultimately, it was him who had to finish for her. She doesn't give her power over to him this time. She pushes through, and all the while, her eyes blaze with a heat so hot that it sears just to be in the same room as her.

Clyde teases, "Cat got your tongue, Bess?"

"You planned this," she snarls accusingly.

"You're going to have to be more specific than that."

"You didn't forget that you were married to Janie. You didn't care that Janie never tried to divorce you because you...you *wanted* that paper legally binding you to her all this time."

Why would he—

"You knew that there would be money if she died, and you kept flushing her system with the one thing everyone knew was going to be her demise. Were you the one that got it into Harrison County Jail, too?"

"Gotta say," Clyde taps his knuckle on the table. "I thought it'd take you a lot longer to put all the pieces together. Shame you don't have any substantiating proof that I have contacts everywhere, isn't it?"

"You knew you'd be next in line for that money if something happened to her."

"Not necessarily," he blinks.

"Don't sit there and lie to us now."

"Okay, fine." His lips turn up like the Cheshire cat's. "Janie might've gotten loose lips one night and said there would be money if her parents ever kicked the can. Never said how much. It could've been five dollars for all I fucking knew." He shrugs. So nonchalant. "Figured it'd be worth it to stick out and never push for a divorce she didn't give a flying fuck about to see, and boy, am I glad I did. Over a hundred grand?" He whistles his surprise. "Well worth the wait."

Finn kicks back and pushes up out of his chair. His hand swoops through his messy hair again and then he moves for the door, his boots trudging with each step. He walks out without saying a word, and I have to say, I'm about ready to follow in his footsteps.

My knee bobs faster under the table. My heart moves along to the same rhythm. All the while, my stomach is in my throat. I'm on the brink of flipping this table in disgust. A numbness courses through me as I'm stunned into silence.

I always knew the Lincolns were bad. Rumors of them doing whatever they could for the things they wanted floated around Harrison Heights when I was a kid. I ignored them as much as I could. When I was young, it didn't matter as much because I wasn't in their crosshairs. But then I had no choice but to step in and help Mom.

It never made sense why they wanted her dealing for them. That they'd hand over copious amounts of product to a drug addict who couldn't be trusted.

Fuck, I never even trusted her with crackers and peanut butter. Yet they gave her so much more. *How stupid of them*, I used to think. *They're not the criminal masterminds they think they are.*

They appeared so goddamn dumb.

But they weren't, were they?

This was a transaction to him just like any other. A means to an end. It only backs up what everyone knows of the Lincolns; that they'll do anything for money.

Even enable a drug addict until her body turns cold so they can inherit the life insurance money her parents left her.

TWENTY-ONE

COLSON

Aunt Bess: Just checking in.
Aunt Bess: I know you're mad at me.
Aunt Bess: I never wanted you to find out like this.

I PUSH through Gulliver's entrance and catch Kelsie's greeting out of the corner of my eye. I don't let myself feel bad for being a prick and ignoring her. I'm not here to play nice with Llewellyn's new employee. I'm here for Eli.

His words from weeks ago popped up in my head—yet again—after confirming my thoughts on Clyde as my biological father and Finn as my half brother. Both drove the last nail in the coffin.

I have to do something besides drink it away. I don't want to carry on the Moore addiction lineage, but I also can't sit still and just work my shifts at Gulliver's.

The gym is bustling. A couple of guys and a few women are on the ellipticals. Two people are in the ring and a few dudes are around it, training with different boxing equipment. I make my way around, adrenaline pumping through me as if I'm about to jump out of an airplane. And hell, maybe I am, in a figurative sense.

Life certainly has felt that way lately, but I'm almost certain that what I'm about to do is going to help with that. It'll calm the commotion in my head, giving me the intermittent reprieves I'm so desperate for.

I find Eli in the back corner with his trainer. He's focused on the bag in front of him, his gloved hands protecting his face. His stance is stellar, and his gaze holds enough weight to set the leather on fire. I get close and nod a chin at him. He lowers his hand and tells his trainer he's taking five minutes.

"This is a new development," he comments, tugging his gloves off his meaty hands. Christ, the dude is all muscle. I remember back to what it was like watching him on Gauntlet Sundays. I haven't been back to one since I paid off Finn. I never planned on needing cash that badly again. Now, it's not about money but something much harder to attain. *Peace.*

"I want to take you up on your offer," I tell him, ignoring the nerves gnawing at me. "I want in the ring."

He glances over his shoulder at the one in the center of Gulliver's where the sound of one of the guys taking the other down on his back ricochets through the gym. Eli tucks his gloves under his armpit and crosses his arms. "You want in the ring?"

"Don't think I stuttered."

He cracks a grin and levels with me. "You sure about this?"

"Would I be here if I wasn't?"

"You want in *that* ring?" he questions, gesturing back at it. "Or *any* ring?"

"Don't care where the ring is as long as I can get inside of it and get my hands dirty."

"I train here," he tells me as if I don't already know that. "I get my hands dirty somewhere else."

"Okay, care to share?" I rest my hands on my hips. So much adrenaline is coursing through my legs it's like I'm going through a bout of restless leg syndrome as I stand in front of him.

He openly sizes me up, eyes scanning me head to toe. "Not sure if I should."

"Why?"

"Still trying to get a read on if you can be trusted."

You know what? I don't need this shit. Why the hell walk up to me and offer just to let me down by expressing his lack of trust in me when I'm finally ready?

"Forget it." I twist on my heel, ready to weave my way back outside and leave. I'll figure something else out. I'll show for my shifts and stay after to work out every goddamn day if it's what helps.

"Wait up," Eli calls out when I make it two boxing bags down. He stares me down as he catches up to me. "All I'm saying is I don't know you that well."

"We went to school together," I remind him, calling him on his bullshit.

"That don't mean shit."

"Cool," I twist on my heel again. If he can't give me what I want, there's no point in sticking around. "See you around."

"Jesus fuck, would you just wait?" He huffs out an annoyed breath. Welcome to the fucking club. I'm annoyed, too. "I got something I think you might be interested in, but it's exclusive. Can't go telling your girlfriend what you're doing."

That's easy. "I don't have a girlfriend."

"You got your phone on you?"

I pull it out of my pocket to show him.

"Add my number." He reads off his digits. "I'm almost done. Wait for me out in the parking lot, and I'll tell you more about it."

I make sure to save his contact and double check that it's there. Whatever I'm about to get into can't be any worse than what I'm currently enduring.

I DON'T KNOW what I was expecting when Eli dropped me the location ping to meet him where we are now. It's like Gauntlet Sundays but more stripped. Like street fighting but also not. He refers to it as The Battleground where dudes go up against each other and the crowds bet on them.

I watch two men fight until their faces turn bloody, and the crowd cheers, albeit some of them boo. The losers, I assume. Three more matches occur, the last one being Eli, who goes up against a guy who never had a fucking chance.

Eli is a force to be reckoned with far behind what he showcased during Gauntlet Sundays. He's meaner, strikes harder, and draws blood every instance he can. He's a madman, light on his feet but heavy with his fists. His opponent wails until he's a writhing mess on the ground.

We're in a shut-down gym, mirrors lining the walls. Only there isn't a ring here like there is at Gulliver's. It's just a solid slab of concrete. I catch all the drippings of blood on it as Eli stalks off, taking his place next to a group of guys who look like they're banded together.

After the crowd winds down, Eli finds me. I follow him as winnings are doled out. All I'm interested in is figuring out how I can find my place in a fight. Even if it's just one, it'll help a hell of a lot more than anything else.

I need to get rid of this clawing sensation in my gut and the way it hangs around like a kid brother. The heat of alcohol didn't drown it out as much as I wanted and left me feeling like literal crap the next day.

This has to be the next best form of physical pain.

It's easy to see that most of the guys Eli stands near are stoked. They get cash slapped into their hands and their eyes go heart-shaped. Like they're at the end of the rainbow and just got a brick of gold placed in their palm.

"Give me a sec," Eli mouths to me when he makes eye contact and holds up a finger. I wait on the sidelines, taking it all in. After long, he comes over and motions us toward the back of the gym. It's dark, illuminated with just enough light to see the fights. The front windows are barricaded with over-sized curtains but it's night, so even if the sun was out, it'd have no way to stream in.

We find a separate room that looks like it was used for extra stock. It houses a washer and dryer along with empty shelves.

"Tommy is going to meet us here in a minute. It's not exactly a professional setting, but this is how it goes. Locations are only used for so long. Either until a better one is found or someone snitches."

I nod. "Who's Tommy?" I cross my arms and lean against the washing machine, my eyes facing the door, because I'm not about to turn my back on a situation I'm not one hundred percent comfortable with.

"He's our boss. He brings guys in and sets up fights with the other leaders in The Battleground."

I quirk a brow. "So, he's your pimp?"

Eli chuckles like he didn't just get done beating the shit out of someone. My gaze drops to his knuckles. They're split to shit with blood smeared down over his fingers. Fuck, he really has made fighting his entire life. It reminds me of how much I've been fighting, though most of my battles haven't required my fists.

"That's one way to put it, but don't let him hear you say that."

A moment later, the door creaks and in walks Tommy. He's older than Eli and me with a dimpled chin and short black hair. His brows are permanently set in a scowl, the wrinkles there giving away his overall attitude. His nose comes down to a point, but the bone is slightly misshapen as if it's been broken.

"Eli." He says it like he's giving Eli permission to speak. I ignore the red flag it raises.

"This is the good friend I was telling you about."

Tommy sizes me up, sinking his hands into his coat pockets. "A good friend," he murmurs, mostly to himself.

"A *trustworthy* friend," Eli counters.

That seems to get Tommy's attention more. He nods at me. "What do you want with The Battleground?"

I glance over at Eli then back. "I want to fight."

"To fight," he enunciates the words, ending with a harsh 't' sound. "Not everyone has what it takes. Why should I take a chance on you? I don't trust just anyone to mosey in and fight under my name."

"You probably shouldn't," I answer honestly. I haven't been myself and so perhaps it'd be a bad business move for Tommy to bring me in but... "If you don't take the chance, I'll make sure someone else does."

I don't know what I'm saying or even who that someone else would be. I don't have connections in this scene, but it doesn't matter because it sparks a glimmer in Tommy's eyes.

"I run a tight ship, which means you always show up for your scheduled fights. Your job is to provide entertainment for the crowd and make me money. You decide to go against me any step of the way, and you'll wish you never stepped foot into The Battleground."

I ignore the fact he says *me* and not *us*.

"If business suddenly starts to go south, I'm going to link it all back to you, pretty boy," Tommy continues. "You'll be the one who pays hell for it, and if it just so happens that it turns out that it isn't you." He shrugs. "I'll still enjoy breaking the legs off you and the other guy."

"Nothing is going to go south," I assure. Why the fuck would I rat him out when I'm desperate to find myself in a similar position as Eli was only a bit ago?

He bypasses my promise. "I care about two things. Money and loyalty. You fuck me out of either of those..."

And I'll suffer the consequences.

Yeah, I get it. Loud and fucking clear.

"I can fight, and my loyalty is unmatched." I mean, look at Mom. Despite her betraying me, I still showed up and paid her debts like a fool.

Tommy keeps his hands in his pockets and continues to stare at me. I feel the weight of his eyes but like hell if he thinks it's going to break me. Besides, that'd almost be impossible since I'm already in pieces to begin with.

"Eli, what do you think?" Tommy inquires. "Should I give him an opportunity to prove himself? Should I let The Battleground swallow him up?"

Eli just smirks, crossing his arms over his chest. The hardness that took over in the ring melts off him. "I think Pretty Boy deserves a chance. I've seen him with a boxing bag, and it's not a pretty sight."

"You enter the mouth of the beast," Tommy says to me. "He won't spit you out, and if you're one of the lucky few he doesn't want, it still won't matter. You won't be whole by the end of it."

An out isn't something that's on my mind. But even if it was, being mangled beyond anything I ever knew wouldn't be new or scary for me. It'd just be another day in the long tumultuous life of Colson Moore.

TWENTY-TWO

VIOLET

Violet: When are you heading home?
Olive: Wrapping up what I need to then getting the hell out of here! Hallelujah.
Violet: You'll miss it.
Olive: Will I?
Violet: Of course. Need I remind you how much you dreamed of attending school there?

"AND THAT IS A FUCKING WRAP," Ev beams, walking into the living room with two wine glasses cinched in her hand. She lifts a bottle of sauvignon blanc above her shoulder and drops onto the couch next to me, the cushions sighing as she comes down on them. I take the glasses long enough for her to pop one of the two hundred dollar bottles of spirits Sylvia told us to go to town on from the kitchen cabinet. She was supposed to celebrate with us as per tradition, but she messaged Everleigh an hour ago explaining she wasn't going to make it.

I changed out of my stuffy day wear when I walked in through the door an hour ago. Ev was already out of her finely pressed skirt and blouse, and together we decided it was time to celebrate.

"No more finals. We are *finished*. No studying, no thinking about class for the next few weeks." She bypasses the appropriate amount of wine and fills our glasses to the tippy top.

"You love your classes." I push my toes into her leg, teasing her. There have been times she gushes over her creative writing instructors and the assignments they give. "You sure you're not mad over not having anything to keep you busy?"

She makes a pfft sound that rolls off her tongue. "While you're right, and I do usually love my classes, I'm ready to say goodbye to this semester. I'm excited about the TA gig I have starting when we come back, but I really need this break, so I'm stuffing it down until we're back." Her eyes drop to the drink in her hand, and I can't help but wonder if Tristan is still on her mind, if their breakup has affected her more than she shows.

I nibble the corner of my mouth, take a sip of my wine, then murmur, "I've been so swept up in my own life that I haven't asked how you're doing with the Tristan situation. I know you loved him, Ev, but if he can't see past the glitz and glam…"

She smiles sadly, lifting her glass to clink into mine. "Then he doesn't deserve me."

"Exactly."

"It's been hard seeing him around, but...I have an entire backlist of an author I've been wanting to catch up on. So, there won't be a minute I won't have something to distract my mind. Plus, a friend from class gave me a manuscript she's been working on. I told her I'd look it over and have it back to her by the end of break. It's the same one you caught me with the night you went to see Colson."

She's always had a love for romance books. And honestly, I find it kind of endearing that she lets go of her stresses and winds down with characters who spend more time holding each other at arm's length until they realize they love each other than choosing to do anything else. "As long as you're happy."

"Lord knows that the books I read have *way* better sex in them. Bet I can learn a thing or two by the time I find interest in men again."

I cackle. "Everleigh!"

She shrugs. "Can't blame a girl for having a strong sexual appetite."

I smirk. "Tristan couldn't keep up?"

"Oh, he could. He had all those muscles and what not, but it's more than that for me." She sips her drink. "I need to have that emotional, mental connection, too. Sometimes it felt like that was lacking with him, especially toward the end. Sometimes it felt forced, like he wasn't really in the present moment."

"What a mood killer. I'm sorry."

She waves my apology off. "It was, but thankfully, it's not something I have to worry about anymore. I am free at last and plan to be for the foreseeable future. I want someone who wants me. Who uses me as their main distraction. Who would move mountains to get me in their arms, Vi."

"Ever the romantic," I crack with a grin. "You'll find him. There's a guy out there just like that with your name on him. It just might take weeding through some tall grass to get to him."

"No kidding." She gulps down more sauvignon blanc. I do the same. "But let's not worry about me right now. I bet we can find a movie to watch while we devour this fine bottle of *vino*." She says the last word with an Italian accent. I can't help but smile. It's the first time I've been able to relax in a while.

I plan to use the next few weeks to recharge and prepare for next semester. While also trying to heal from the broken heart that nips my chest every time I so much as breathe.

I have no idea how I'm going to do it. I am inexplicably in love with Colson, and being away from him only makes my heart scream that much louder. The wine helps mute it out, though.

We spend the next forty-five minutes commentating on an old Amanda Bynes movie, *She's the Man*, where she dresses up as her brother to prove girls can play soccer, too, but also has the biggest crush on her roommate, who just so happens to be played by Channing Tatum.

Everleigh falls back against the cushions and visibly swoons. The flick is cheesy as hell, but hilarious in its own way. She wants them to get together so badly but secretly loves that Amanda has been covering for her brother this entire time. For a little while, everything else gets pushed to the back of my mind and it's just me, Everleigh, and Amanda with sideburns.

That is, until we're interrupted by a knock at the door.

Everleigh is so into the movie that I offer to get up and check it. We don't normally get many visitors, but I have a steady stream of wine coursing through my veins to care too much about who might be on the other side of it.

I don't check the peephole. Just twist the knob and pull it open. I lean my shoulder into the door but then nearly choke on my spit.

Olive has one hand on her suitcase, the other clutching her phone, and her lips split into a bright, blinding smile. "You said you weren't going to stay at Mom and Dad's for the holiday. Did you really think I was going to let you spend your break alone?"

"You're kidding me."

"Does it look like I'm kidding?" She pushes me out of the way and rolls her suitcase inside the apartment. "I thought it'd be good if we had some good ole sister bonding time since we never got it over Thanksgiving break." The door clicks shut behind us, and she whirls on me. "What do you think?"

"I think I'm shocked as hell that you're actually on my doorstep." I have to blink two times to make sure it's not the wine. "Are classes over for you?"

"Last one was yesterday. I booked it out of there so fast they definitely ate my dust."

I laugh and finally pull her into a hug. "I'm so glad you're here."

"We're about to have so much fun."

I sigh in her hold, realizing how much I needed this—a loving, soul crushing hug. "I'm ready to have all the fun with you," I murmur, sadness clutching me in response to her presence. I've missed her so damn much. She's exactly who else I need in my corner right now.

"Violet?" Everleigh calls from the living room. "Who is it?"

I pull away from my sister. Olive sing-songs from the entryway, "Only the best sister in the whole wide world!"

And then I'm left following her into the living room, watching as she takes my seat on the couch and comments on how stupid it is of Amanda to dress up like a boy rather than bone the hotness that is Channing Tatum.

TWENTY-THREE

VIOLET

IT'S the night before Everleigh leaves to head home for winter break. Her parents are a couple hours away, and it'll be a drive for her, but she's looking forward to getting away and putting more distance between her and Tristan. Unfortunately, he's one-sixth of our friend group, which means there are times we're all together. Like tonight.

All of us, minus Sylvia, are at Lucy's. Olive is here, too. It's our end-of-the-semester celebration as a group before we go our different ways for a few weeks.

"I'm going to miss you so much," I admit to Everleigh over drinks at the bar. It's less congested than normal since a lot of students wasted no time leaving campus.

Everleigh pulls me into a side hug and squeezes me. "I'm so glad we've had the chance to bond these last few weeks. It's made things easier." She means her break up with Tristan. As much as she likes to play it off that she's not bothered by it anymore, I know she is. She's longed for a meaningful relationship ever since I've known her, and she put so much time and effort into the one she had with Tristan just for him to push her to the side.

Now isn't much better, not when we can see him on the dance floor, flirting and groping a leggy blonde in a halter top two sizes too small.

"I seriously don't know what I'm going to do without you." That's not a lie. "This stuff with Colson would have been grueling without you around."

Olive, who's on the other side of me, butts into the conversation. I don't mind. I like having her around. It's making the fact that Everleigh is leaving easier. "When was the last time you talked to him?" my sister asks, her gaze swinging from the dance floor to our drinks on the bar top. She hasn't had any alcohol tonight, and I plan to keep it that way since, last time I checked, she was taking antidepressants.

I've kept her in the loop where Colson is concerned, texting her with the latest updates. I've leaned on Sebastian and Everleigh, too, and it's been one of the smartest things I could've done, especially after the situation with my dad.

It's so much harder keeping things to yourself when you don't need to. I learned that lesson the hard way. In such a short amount of time, I've done a complete one-eighty in how I operate. All because of Colson but also because *this* feels better than what I put myself through for months keeping Dad's infidelity a secret.

"Not since the night his mom was laid to rest."

Olive blows her fringed brown bangs out of her face. She has her hair pulled back, but they're too short to fit into the ponytail or stay tucked behind her ears. They give off these Zooey Deschanel vibes, and I'm here for it. "I don't get why he's being so difficult about it. If he likes you, why not lean on you for support?"

"Some people have a hard time doing that," I tell her,

giving her a glance that hopefully reminds her that I was no different just a few weeks ago.

"Yeah, well, I guess you two are a match made in Heaven then."

"We're not together anymore," I remind her, pretending like it isn't a shock to my system every time I think or speak about it.

Everleigh frowns and sips on her straw. "I hate that it has to be this way for you guys. You two were so good together. I mean, I wasn't even with you half the time, but I could definitely feel it whenever he spent the night and would hang around even if it was primarily in your bedroom."

I felt it, too. How right we were for each other. *But then it all went up in flames.* I'm learning that death makes a person reevaluate everything in life. It causes wedges. Massive craters the size of the Grand Canyon.

"Sorry," Everleigh apologizes with a sad tone when I don't reply. "I didn't mean to upset you. I should keep my trap shut."

"Believe me." I huff out somewhat of a laugh. "Nothing you say is going to make me feel any worse than I already do."

"Which is why we need to party it up," Olive declares, lifting her arms and shaking her shoulders. "Do you know how hot we are? There has to be a couple of guys who want to show us a good time. Maybe buy ya girl an alcoholic *bev-er-age*."

I give her a look. "I said you could come with us if you didn't nag about booze."

We both know I would've let her come regardless.

She waves her hand in my face. "Fine, fine." She looks over at Everleigh. "She's killing my vibe. We need to loosen her up. Shimmy those titties and get that bartender over here so this one can knock back a shot or ten."

My friend cackles as if I'm not sitting next to her. "I think I'm in love with your sister."

"While I think you're absolutely gorgeous," Olive compliments, "I'm definitely in it for the dick."

"Olive!" I shriek.

"What?" She smirks. "I'm just saying. I'm flattered but also no thank you."

"Please ignore her," I say to my friend as I feel someone come up behind me.

Sebastian's voice falls over my shoulder. He reaches forward, grabs one of the waters on the bar top, and chugs it. "Who are we ignoring?"

"Apparently me," coos Olive, visibly gawking at Sebastian like it's no issue at all that she's checking him out. I've never seen her flirt as hard as I have tonight. It's actually kind of entertaining. That, and I know Sebastian isn't about to cross that line. "Want to take me out there and show me how to get jiggy, Sebby?"

Everleigh catches my eye, a smirk testing the corner of her lips as she mouths, "*Sebby*?"

"Ah sorry, Olive. I'm all danced out. I was just coming over for a bit of a break. Pretty sure Webber wouldn't mind if you interrupted him, though," he taunts back in jest.

She nearly gags. "Ew." Then she realizes Sebastian is just trying to rile her. "That was wrong on so many levels."

He cracks a cheeky grin. "Sorry. Had to after you pulled the 'Sebby' bit." He shudders. "Never say that out loud again." His hand settles on my shoulder, and he squeezes. Ever since things have gone awry with Colson, he's gone the extra mile in checking in with me when he's around. "You good, Vi?"

"I'd be better if this one didn't always have something outlandish coming out of her mouth." It's true. My sister has been on another level since she arrived. I'm not sure if I should be happy about it or concerned. Instead of worrying, I've opted for going with the flow and not putting too much thought into it. I trust that if something was up with her, she'd tell me.

"Afraid I can't help you with that."

I softly press my elbow into his ribs. "Shame," I joke lightly.

"Man, you don't want to know how handsy some of those girls are getting. The second you step away, they pull you back in for more. One even pulled the invisible rope move out of her back pocket."

Everleigh lifts her brow at him. "I hardly think that's a problem for you guys."

"It's a problem when I need to get the fuck away because my throat feels like an overcooked piece of chicken."

She looks out into the club's dance floor, ignoring Sebastian's odd analogy. "Tristan and Webber don't seem to be having an issue with it. You being a softie tonight, Seb?"

He gives that lazy grin of his. The one that has my sister looking at him like he's a delicious red apple. Too bad he's dangling from the Tree of Knowledge and is off limits. "If you want to talk dirty, Ev, just give me the heads up, and I'll pluck *softie* right out of that vocabulary of yours. Show you exactly what it means to be hard."

She smacks him in the chest with a flush on her cheeks.

All of us laugh.

The three of us girls head out to the dance floor and move with the music after that. We dance to songs like Usher's "DJ Got Us Fallin'" *in Love* and Beyonce's "Naughty Girl". The air is extra warm even with the overhead fans misting us with water. Sweat coats my skin under the knotted crop top I'm wearing. My free-falling hair swishes over my shoulders. And my body feels more and more weightless with each song change.

I grind back into Everleigh, ignoring the few guys who linger close behind. Olive eventually grips one by the collar and drags him over to dance with us. He's respectful with his hand placement. I'm enjoying how carefree it feels to wiggle my hips and let my hair fall back.

We spend what feels like forever like that. Just letting loose and having a blast until we're like Sebastian and need to break away from the crowd to replenish our energy. I switch to water after downing a shot with Everleigh, and we spend more time out on the floor. The guys do their own thing, too.

We allow for distance between us, and I think it's important we do it. It's been an eventful semester. Two breakups in our group. Another friend who has distanced herself so much that I'm not sure how to help her. It's clear, more than ever, that we need this night. To unwind and be free.

Our time at Lucy's ends not much later. The DJ calls out the last set list. We decide to wind down and head out before it's closing time, and it's a pain in the ass to get out the door. We head out as a group, Everleigh on one side, Tristan on the other. Sebastian's arm is slung over Olive's shoulder, and she laughs at something he says. Somewhere through the night, her eyes switched from lovey-dovey to something calmer with him. Like friendship. And I can understand why. Sebastian is an easy person to connect with. It's so uncomplicated falling in sync with him. To talk to him and feel like you're being heard. He has this natural ability to make everyone around him feel important.

We form a circle out on the sidewalk to figure out our

plans. Webber looks down at his watch, and I already know he's not ready to call it a night. "I know a dude from my Econ class that's having a rager tonight. Anyone down?"

Tristan's finger immediately shoots up. "You know I'm always in."

I feel the invisible dig in his words as it rides the breeze like a wave and crashes into Everleigh. Always being out and not prioritizing his relationship with her is part of the reason she ended it with him.

Webber's eyes turn to Sebastian in question. "What about you?"

Sebastian checks his phone and sucks air through his teeth. "It's still early. Fuck. Okay, fine."

It's nearly midnight, but the guys always have an easier time pushing the limits than us girls.

Olive nudges my arm. "Are we going?"

"Not tonight, sis."

For a second I think she's going to complain, but then she nods. "I'm kind of tired, anyway."

"Same," says Ev. "You guys have fun."

The guys hail down a cab for us, and we squeeze into the back seat. We ride the short distance to Spring Meadows. Everleigh slips the driver some cash, and we file out of the back. We're relatively quiet as we head for the main entrance, Everleigh already prepared to swipe her keycard. She mistakenly drops it on the ground, and when she bends to retrieve it, I spot movement out of the corner of my eye.

It immediately puts me on edge.

Spring Meadows is only a couple blocks from campus, and security around Chatham Hills is always top notch.

Cigarette smoke wafts over to us, and for some reason, my brain links it to the guy with tattoos up down his arms and dark hair that approached Colson.

A bad feeling swoops low in my stomach. The door beeps, letting me know that Everleigh finally scans her card for access. The shape I thought I saw out of the corner of my eye walks out of the shadows, a tiny orange glow at the brightest point of it.

And I just know it's him.

I can't explain how I know, but it winds through my body and settles low in my gut. It amps up my heart rate and causes the slick of sweat that appeared on my back at the club to return.

I look over my shoulder to see Everleigh and Olive holding the door open for me, not at all concerned about the strange guy coming out of the shadows so late at night. But maybe that's because they haven't seen him yet.

"Vi? You coming?" Olive asks over her shoulder.

I don't know what to tell her, but suddenly it's as if I'm being tugged in two directions. Maybe neither of them mean for it to happen that way, but it's like I'm divided, in a bind over staying with Stranger Guy or following my sister and friend up to our safe apartment.

"Violet?" My sister's voice rings in my ears, and I decide on telling them that I'll be a minute since I have a visitor.

"It's late. And dark," she points out.

"I know, but it's safe. I promise."

"It really is," Everleigh adds, backing me up. "Campus security is always circling the first couple surrounding blocks."

"I don't know." Olive's gaze cuts to the side, finally catching sight of the guy who makes himself more known by taking a couple steps closer. He clears his throat, and in a low voice, she says, "I don't like this, Vi. It's giving me bad vibes."

"It's fine."

Her tone remains low, like she doesn't want Stranger Guy hearing her. "Do you even know him?"

"Yes, he's, uh, Colson's friend," I reassure her even though I'm lying through my teeth. I don't know Stranger Guy at all, but what I do know is that he's connected to Colson, and it's been far too long since I've heard from him. "You want to stay with me?"

She said she was tired at Lucy's not even twenty minutes ago, so taking a walk with me after midnight isn't at all what she's interested in. I know her answer as soon as she looks past my head and takes in the dark sky.

"You better not be lying to me. How long are you going to be? I'll wait up."

"I don't know, but I'll be up soon."

She sighs. "I swear to God, you better come up. If you disappear, I will beat you into a grave when the search team finds you."

I give her a soft smile. "I love you. Be up soon."

They give me one last glance before the door clicks shut, and I watch them disappear into the apartment building's foyer. When they wrap around the bend in the hall where the elevators are located, I turn back to the man in the shadows illuminated by the soft glow of a cigarette.

TWENTY-FOUR

VIOLET

STRANGER GUY REPLIES by turning on his foot and leading me to the side of the apartment complex where there are benches periodically spaced along the sidewalk.

"If you're looking for him," I say to his back, taking in his mysterious appearance—the dark clothing, his equally dark hair, and the abundance of black ink on the skin I can see—while also tamping down my nerves. "You won't find him here."

He motions to the first bench we come across. I have no plan on putting myself in a vulnerable position so I ignore the way his hand sweeps toward it and stand far enough away that I can make a quick run for it if needed. I cross my arms over my torso, too.

It's difficult making out his features and what kind of mood he's in when it's so late, but there's enough lighting around the building and parking lot to see his eyes and the shimmer of what looks like a lip ring. The long sleeve thermal he wears fits his upper body like a glove. The chilliness in the air falls away, and my body heats. Not because I find him overwhelmingly attractive but because, deep down, I get the inkling that I'm making a mistake.

If Colson felt the need to protect me from him before, I probably shouldn't be standing outside with him alone. But I can't walk away knowing he might have information regarding Colson.

"I didn't come looking for him," he says simply. "I came for you."

Surely, he must have it wrong.

I glance toward the entrance of Spring Meadows before turning my focus back on him. "For me? What did you do? Camp outside my apartment building all night until you saw me?"

He pinches the cigarette out of his mouth and blows the smoke away from me. "I saw you leave earlier. Knew you'd come back eventually, so I waited it out."

I curl my lips into my mouth, bothered over him openly admitting that he's been following me. But at least he's being honest. "Why? I don't even know who you are."

"It doesn't really matter who I am—"

"It most definitely does. You think I don't remember you from that day?" I ask him.

"That day is the least of our concerns."

"*Our* concerns?"

He shuffles on his feet and flicks the butt of his smoke on the ground before snubbing it out with the toe of his boot. "Your boy is getting himself into some serious shit."

My stomach takes off like a bird in flight. "What are you talking about? Wait." I squeeze my eyes shut and tighten my arms around myself. "You can at least tell me what your name is before you say more."

"Finn."

"Okay, Finn. Well, I'm—"

"Violet, yeah, I know. Can we cut past the pleasantries? You need to talk some sense into your boyfriend before he fucks up his life worse than it already is."

I rub my lips together and inhale a deep breath, wanting to reach out to Colson but also knowing it's not my place to do so. He took that away from me, from him. "Colson and I aren't together anymore. What he does isn't my business."

"Fuck that."

"Excuse me?"

His voice turns harsher. "I said, *fuck that.* Whether he wants help or not, he needs it, and it can't be from me. So it's either you or his rich, money-whipped cousin. Pussy always wins, which is why I came to you first."

"You don't need to be rude." I balk but then curiosity gets the best of me. "What's he doing that's so bad?"

Last I knew, Colson was holing himself up in his house and drinking straight from the bottle. What could he possibly be doing that could fuck up his life more? Part of me wants to walk away and not give Finn the time of day, but then I think about the what-ifs.

What if Colson really is in trouble?

What if he needs someone?

What if he needs *me?*

What if he needs me and I...I ignore that?

"Talking is pointless. It'd be better to show you."

"You think I trust you enough to get in a car with you?" To this day, instinct tells me that he's the reason behind Colson showing up at my door with a bloody lip and bruised torso. Nothing good can possibly come from following his lead. What if he's just saying this to get me alone and then, I don't know, something bad happens?

I don't know the full story because Colson never shared it

with me, but there's something there. I can feel it in the way my stomach squeezes.

"You don't need to trust me. You need to ask yourself how much you care about him."

I swallow and croak out, "I care about him more than you'll ever know."

"So then let me show you." He starts walking and leads the way as if it's just that simple. That easy to follow him into the unknown.

"Wait," I call out, watching his retreating form. He's a silhouette in the night. A dim and mystifying outline of a man who can't be much older than Colson. "I'm not...I don't think this is a good idea. I need more from you."

He takes three large strides back until he's a headspace away. "Listen, Violet, I don't really feel like standing here and shooting the shit with you. Facts are, Colson is losing his fucking head after finding out that *his* father is *my* dad. And maybe that doesn't mean shit to you. Maybe it means a whole fucking slew of things. Either way, he's making decisions based on emotion instead of logic, and it's going to get him killed just like it did his mom. Is that what you want? You want to see him go out even faster than she did? Because the people he's associating with will put a bullet in his goddamn head and put him six feet under if he so much as thinks about double crossing them."

My head spins.

His father is my dad.

Bullet in his goddamn head.

Six feet under.

My arms fall to my sides, my knees threatening to buckle and crash to the pavement.

Finn is his half brother?

He never mentioned that before. Before, when Finn

showed up, Colson acted…strange. Like it wasn't safe for me to be around him. Colson couldn't have known this then. It makes me wonder if Finn knew. Or maybe I have it all wrong. Maybe he did know and that's why he didn't want me around him.

Confusion swirls in my head, and I don't know how to get a grip on it.

"Did you know this when you were here that day? About being brothers?" I decide to ask, putting a stop to my whirling thoughts so I don't have to overthink it.

His response is a one-worded, "No."

"So then why wouldn't he want your help? If both of you were in the dark about it…"

He rubs his hands over his face as if his patience is dwindling that it's taking so much for me to agree to go with him. But I need proof. I need *something* that tells me I'll be okay. That he'll lead me to Colson, and I won't end up disappearing after I just promised Olive I'd be okay.

"Because a lot of fucked up shit has gone down. Shit you don't need to know." He digs his wallet out of his back pocket and flips it open. He fishes out his license. "Take a picture and send it to your friends. They'll know exactly who to come after if you don't come home."

Because I don't know what the hell is going on, I do just that. I slip my phone from my small clutch and snap the picture. I decide not to send it to Olive and make her worry unnecessarily but send it to Everleigh and ask her to cover for me. She sends me a thumbs up, and then I find myself following Finn to his car.

The interior matches him perfectly, everything set in shades of grays and blacks, and as I slip into the passenger's seat, I can't help but think how stupid I am for getting into a car with a stranger. Until I remind myself that this is for Colson.

And for Colson, I'd be a lot more reckless.

Finn straps his belt over his chest and reverses out of the space before heading toward Main Street. The tension in the car is constricting, squeezing me as if it has nothing else better to do. It's hard to ignore, even when he turns the knob on the stereo system and soft rock streams out through the speakers.

"So," I start, glancing out my side of the car, as I watch the streetlights pass us by. "Where are we going?"

He doesn't bother looking my way, but I feel his gaze all the same. He has that presence about him. Dark and alluring. Mysterious and moody. Could also be that I'm hyper aware of my surroundings. I have no clue if he's going to reach under his seat and whip out a pistol or grab the closest thing that can be used as a gag and yank the car to the side of the road to tie my hands behind my back. The thought sends my nerves into overdrive, tiny little goosebumps dotting my skin.

"Harrison Heights."

It doesn't take long for us to reach the mouth of the Sycamore Memorial Bridge. "I don't understand why you can't tell me what's going on. It'd be nice to know what I'm walking into. The mess you *say* Colson is in."

From the glow of the dash lights, I catch the tensing of his jaw. It took courage for him to show up at my place, to wait for me, and get me into his car. Perhaps he isn't coated in that hard gobstopper layer after all.

He repositions his hand on the wheel as we make it to the bridge's peak before bringing both up to grip it. There aren't a lot of cars out at this time of night, which means it doesn't take as long to cross the Sycamore River. I notice the way his hands relax, and he goes back to his one-handed grip on the steering wheel once we hit solid ground.

"He found his way into The Battleground."

He says it like it's a place. "The Battleground?"

"Underground fighting essentially. No one knows about it unless you're in it."

My stomach coils the way it always does when it comes to fighting. I've never understood why grown men fight or how it's even considered a sport. I can't fathom the idea of wanting to bloody an opponent. To make them bleed and hurt for no other purpose than to call yourself a winner.

When Colson initially told me about his love for boxing, I was revolted by the idea of seeing him in a ring with another man. But as much as using fists to deal with life doesn't make sense to me, I've pushed my opinion down for Colson's sake. I know how boxing is an outlet for him to release whatever stress he may have. I just never thought he'd take it any farther than a boxing bag. I never thought he'd willingly *choose* to hurt people to make himself feel better.

Disappointment fills me. I try not to let it come through in my voice. "So he likes to box. I'm not sure what you want me to do about that."

"I'm not talking about just boxing. If he was just slipping on some gloves and pounding away at a bag, I wouldn't give a flying fuck, nor would I have you in my car. I said he's underground fighting. The opponents are a lot meaner than a leather boxing bag. And the guys that run it are fucking heartless."

I turn in my seat and look at him. "How would you know? How do you even know what he's doing? Are you following him around, too?" There are so many gaps in what's going on, and it all comes from the distance between Colson and me. However, if we *were* still close, and he didn't let his current circumstances get between us, I'm not entirely sure he'd come to me about this crazy want to slip into this underground scene, anyway.

There have always been things he's kept from me. Hell, one of them sits next to me. And while I was okay with that for a while because we both had our own stuff we were going through, I'm realizing how terribly wrong that is. How off is it that as close as we were he never told me about Finn? It makes me wonder what else he's hiding.

My curiosity about him pushes up through the dirt and reaches for the truth. "How did you and Colson know each other before? He didn't want me around you that day, so what was he doing with you if he didn't know then that you're his half brother?"

"Not my story to tell." His hand changes position on the steering wheel. "Listen, I'm just trying to fucking help." He says it in a way that tells me he doesn't do this often. They're the most uncomfortable words that fall from his lips. I remain quiet, stuck inside my head over not getting the answers I seek. Suddenly, I'm mad at myself for not pushing Colson harder on the matter when it happened.

"There's a lot of bad shit that's gone down between me and Colson. To him, I'm his enemy, and I deserve that title, but a few days ago, that all changed."

I swallow against the ball of tension nagging my throat. I can't believe Janie was married for years, and it never came out. I can't believe Colson's mother died and now he has a sibling. How does that even happen? Did she know all along that Finn and Colson shared the same father?

God.

I choose to skip ahead. "So, you followed him, but how do you know he's messing with the wrong people if you're not part of that world, too?"

"I saw him talking to a guy we used to go to school with that's real big in the fighting scene. He's been doing it under the radar for years."

I shake my head. "Maybe they were just talking because they're friends."

He glances over at the same time his hand slides down the steering wheel and pulls it into a turn. "I called a contact of mine who was able to get me in on one of the fights to verify it."

I glance over at him, my gut pointing a finger at me and saying, *I told you he's not the kind of guy you should've gotten into a car with,* because if he has a contact that got him into a fight that means he has to hang out with some pretty shady people.

"Did he see you there?" I ask.

"No. I know how to stay out of sight, but to be honest, he looked way too fucking in his head to notice any of the faces in the crowd. The Battleground is known to snatch people up and when that happens, they *don't* spit them back out. They'll keep Colson tight knit until he's physically unable to walk into the ring again. And if he tries to escape before then—"

"You make it sound like he joined a gang."

"Consider this the next worst thing."

"If Colson is set on fighting, me walking in there isn't going to suddenly make him come to his senses." If I've learned anything about him in the last few weeks, it's that he's irrevocably stubborn.

He sniffs and shifts in his seat. "You're right, but if he sees you with me, he's guaranteed to freak the fuck out and pull away."

I blink three times. "You plan on pitting me *against* him?" My tone is a shriek when the words come out. "No. *Hell* no.

He's going through enough. He doesn't need this on top of that. You are out of your mind."

He looks over at me as the car rolls to a stop at an intersection. "You said you cared about him."

"I do," I insist. "But that's pushing it too far. He's the most fragile I've ever seen him." I'm not sure if that's saying much since I've only known him for a few months. "Presenting him with another, I don't know, *shit sundae* isn't going to make it better."

"He's hopping fences, Violet. The only way to get him to see reason at this point is to do the goddamn same."

I hate how much sense that makes, but I don't know what Colson will do if he sees me with another man, much less with Finn after he admitted Colson considers him the enemy. This is going to end one of two ways. Him still moving forward with fighting or raising his fists to spar with Finn instead.

"This isn't going to end well," I warn, my nerves tying themselves in knots as we drive farther into Harrison Heights.

"Never does when your biggest opponent is yourself."

I'VE ONLY BEEN to two places in Harrison Heights. The gas station Colson took me to Thanksgiving night when I showed up at his apartment an absolute mess and his mom's house.

We slowly drive down side street after side street. We pass a block of businesses, all of them looking as if they've been out of business for the better part of the last ten years, their windows dusty and smogged over. It's clear an economic decline has the town in its grasp.

Streetlights illuminate the bare minimum, and I take note

of how most of the sidewalks need repaving. They're not the only thing that could use a fresh coat of love. Random bushes, though dormant, could use trimming. Shutters on homes could use replacing. Awnings over closed businesses could use patching.

It's devastating to see, knowing that on the other side of the Sycamore River, life is bustling, the economy thriving. To know that there's not much opportunity that exists in a place like Harrison Heights hits the deepest parts of me. That Colson grew up in such lackluster circumstances is annihilating. There aren't even any doctor's offices around. No window clings with *therapy* or *healthcare* promising to make you feel whole again.

The farther we get into town, the more desolate it becomes. Everything is bleak and unlively. When Finn rolls to a stop at a curb, I peer out the window into the night to spot a laundromat, the windows of it in need of a good washing.

"I'm parking here, but we'll have to walk another two blocks."

I nod, and the instant I open the door, a wall of cold hits me. I forget that I'm wearing a skimpy top with skin-tight leather skinny jeans that do nothing to protect me from the chill in the air. "Do you—"

Finn knows what I'm going to ask before I finish because he reaches around to the back seat and deposits a black zip up sweatshirt on my lap. "Make sure I get it back."

I mutter out a thanks—*sheesh*—and put it on. The sweatshirt hits me mid-thigh.

I get out of the car and shut the door. In a hurry to fall in line with Finn, I leave the sweatshirt unzipped. We walk in silence before we come across an old, abandoned candy warehouse. Cement chocolates are formed into the front of the building around the entrance and Coco's Chocolate Warehouse is imprinted on a sign above it. The building takes up the corner of the block. There are a few broken windows on the second floor, but the brick work is absolutely stunning and reminds me of the university buildings in Chatham Hills.

We round the corner of the building and end up in an alley. "What now?"

Finn points to a door twenty feet ahead. "I'm going to knock on that door. You're going to keep your mouth shut and pretend you're just another ditzy airhead until we get inside."

I stifle a response because is he always this rude?

All night, he's seemed to know more than me, so once again, I have no other choice but to trust that he has my best interests at heart. Colson's best interests.

We approach the door, and he glances over his shoulder. "Now would be a good time to tell me if you have a problem with blood."

"Huh?"

"Blood," he repeats, enunciating every letter in the word. "Do you get faint or queasy when you see it? You gonna go down like a sack of potatoes at the sight of it?"

The image of scarlet liquid enters my mind, and my attention flicks to the heavy metal door in front of us. This weird sensation takes over my stomach, a twisting and burning feeling that trapezes into my limbs.

What the hell am I doing?

Have I really lost all common sense? Is my love for Colson persuasive enough that it made me get into a car with a stranger in the near-middle of the night just because he *said* Colson is in trouble?

The heaviness in Finn's question loops in my mind even though it's probably not that big of a deal. Blood. We all have it. It's in us all and yet…I don't know if I'd faint at the sight of it. I didn't when I helped Colson all those weeks ago or all the times Olive and I scraped our skin open as kids.

But that was different. So mu—

"Get rid of that look on your face. You can't fucking bail when we're this close. We're one door away from you seeing exactly what I'm talking about. So, I'm going to ask one last time, Violet. Does blood make you want to throw the fuck up or can you handle seeing it gush from a dude's nose without getting real close and personal with the floor?"

I shake my head, finally catching up to the moment even though apprehension finagles its way into my bone marrow. The door is daunting, staring me down like a detective wanting answers.

I hate how I'm backstepping. That I'm wondering if I should even walk in there. Colson and I have drawn a clear line. He wants to deal with his life on his own terms, and I'm supposed to be giving him that.

Then I think about what Finn said. I consider that if it wasn't as bad as it was, he wouldn't be trying to help. And he definitely wouldn't have camped outside my apartment to wait for me.

I give him all I can muster, which is a nod.

"Stay close in there, and we'll be fine. As for Colson… don't be surprised if you don't recognize him."

That's what I'm most worried about. Then again, I haven't recognized him in weeks, so how bad can this be?

"Remember him the way he was and try to stay out of sight." Finn pauses for a beat then finishes with, "He can't see help coming. Otherwise, he'll just prepare an escape route." And then he pounds his fist on the door.

TWENTY-FIVE

COLSON

"LAST RESORT" by Papa Roach roars in my ears, and I look down at my bare hands. My knuckles are scraped open and barely scabbed over from my last fight, but I can't seem to find a single fuck to give. When I go out there, my scabs will tear off and my blood will mix with my opponent's. That should worry me, except it doesn't.

I've moved past caring about things out of my control. Things like death, Mom's secret marriage to Harrison Heights's biggest drug dealer, and the intrusive fact that I share his DNA. Oh, and that my half brother is a replica of him who put me through hell.

It doesn't get worse than that.

It can't.

Which is why I said, *fuck it all,* and sought Eli out the way I did.

I could bury myself in endless amounts of Jack Daniel's, or any other bottle of liquor for that matter, but this is the better of two options. Getting my hands dirty wins out over continuously twisting up my insides from the booze and risking an addiction of my own.

In a weird sense, I'm at least mindful of that.

Being in this old shut down candy warehouse on the outskirts of town makes me feel a little less overwhelmed and a little more clearheaded. It's in an area where a lot of businesses went under a decade ago. When unemployment rates rose so high people had a hard time keeping the money coming in.

The distinct smell of stale cocoa powder permeates the air. If that's even a thing. I'm not sure if powdery food substances can create their own odors, but there's definitely a strange smell floating around. It's as if the mustiness of the building intertwines with the sweetness of the bean. Add in a little bit of bad fermentation and it's exactly what the place stinks of. I imagine at one time, when the place was bursting with business, it was much more pleasant. Something sugary with floral hints here and there.

Not like it matters tonight.

Pretty soon, the metallic scent of blood and the tanginess of B.O. from too many bodies packed in one space will take over. Then no one will pay attention to the old equipment mixers and conveyor lines to the side. Nor will they care about the bags of sugar that have long since been eaten through by rodents.

If I sit and think about it long enough, disgust will swish through me, so I lightly jump up and down. I roll my shoulders. I crack my neck from side to side. Sweat drips from my forehead into my eyes even though it's mid-winter and it's been a long time since this building has had heat. I sprinted here from where I parked my car a quarter-mile away. Eli warned me about the ramifications of having it too close. *In case shit turns for the worse, it's easier to disappear if your vehicle isn't close enough to draw attention.*

Between that and my nerves, I'm heated and ready to

walk out there with my chest glistening. That's another thing Eli shared. The crowd loves it when they see blood, even more when it's dripping down your chest versus soaking cotton. If you ask me, it's kind of stupid, but I go with the flow, knowing that their cheers will be one of two things that put the power behind my fists and the endurance in my step.

I grab a towel out of my bag and wipe it over my face. A hand lands on my shoulder, and it causes me to swivel around and pull my earbud from my ear.

Elijah McPearson's bulky frame comes into view, and while it should make me relax to see it isn't someone else, it doesn't. He may have brought me into The Battleground, but I can't say that I exactly trust the guy. Even back when we were in high school, we weren't close enough to share secrets. We were acquaintances at best and laughed over the same dumb shit that happened during class. And now, we're both part of this forbidden, probably illegal, fight club.

Outside of that, I don't know much about him or why the hell he trains during the day to get into the National Fighting League yet spends his nights in the world of underground fighting.

Seeing each other come and go at Gulliver's isn't enough to suddenly hand over my deepest, darkest secrets. However, his offer from a while back was enough to break me—along with life circumstances—and allow myself to get swept up in the same shady shit as him.

Life has pressed its pointed stiletto in the center of both our chests. I have a feeling the impact of it will scar me just as I assume it has him.

He hands me a roll of athletic tape for my fingers and wrists. I accept it with a nod of thanks.

"Amped crowd tonight," he comments, moving to the radiator at the other side of the small office. I've gotten used to the space. It's where I prepare and collect myself before every match, and tonight will be my fourth.

Now that music isn't drowning out all noises, I hear the racket in the other room where the fights occur. There's hooting and hollering, and like every other night I've been here, I'm glad for the location. The area is so run-down that no one will drive by or walk around and notice the warehouse has been breached. Especially not this late.

"Yeah?"

"Oh yeah." Eli runs his hand through his hair. It's gotten longer since the day he approached me at Gulliver's. I remember it like it was yesterday, and yet here I am, doing the one thing I told him and Llewellyn I would never do.

Beating a person to hell was never part of the plan. I wasn't lying when I told them I got what I needed out of a dangly punching bag. Slamming my fists into one was enough to silence the thoughts and break through the stress that continuously gnawed at my back. But that was before.

Before Mom died.

Before I lost the only girl I've ever loved.

Before I learned Mom was married to my father my entire fucking life and chose to keep it a secret. Before I found out Aunt Bess *paid* to keep him away. Before I found out that I have a brother.

"You're up after me tonight," Eli tells me.

I rip a piece of tape off the roll and wind it around the worst of my knuckles. They're still healing from two fights ago, but because I haven't given myself much of a break, it's taking longer than normal. The night I busted them, they swelled something bad. When I uppercut my opponent, a scrawny kid who lasted all of two minutes, they didn't crack the way it did when Finn took that mallet to my hand, but it was nearly as painful.

"Think you're going to come out on top?" I ask, making small talk, which seems to be all Eli and I do. We talk about fighting and the matches and how to keep Tommy from raging over not making his money. In my short time fighting under him, I've learned he's as greedy as the Lincolns, a common personality trait of residents of Harrison Heights it seems.

He cracks a cocky grin. "You're really asking me that?"

"They seem eager for something promising tonight."

"They'll get what they came for. They always do, and with all the fresh blood, they won't be able to get e-fucking-nough."

Eli has told me that I'm not the only new guy representing Tommy's side in The Battleground, but I have yet to meet the others. They fight on the days I don't, so our schedules never quite line up. I'm not out here to make friends, so I don't pay much mind to socializing. I'm here for the fight, to silence my thoughts, and drown out the heartache by feeling something else entirely.

"Yeah, well, that's what it's all about, isn't it?"

He crosses his arms over his chest and gives me a look like he's trying to figure me out. When I walked up to him in Gulliver's two weeks ago and told him I was ready to get in the ring, he didn't ask me once what my deal was or why I changed my mind. He simply nodded and told me to wait ringside until he was done training. He gave me his cell number, and when we met outside, we chatted a bit about what he was getting me into.

It's been fight after fight ever since.

"How's your head? You ready for that winner's roll of cash?" he inquires.

These fights bring in more money than Gauntlet Sundays did except Tommy always gets a percentage of what we earn.

While the extra cash is helpful and would've been even better when I was scrambling to pay Finn back, it's not why I'm here.

"The money doesn't matter, but yeah, I'm focused."

"Well, it matters to Tommy."

"Your boss has nothing to worry about," I grunt. A week from now, I'll still show up for the fights, and he'll continue to earn what he does. I'm a decent fighter, and so far, I've gone up against opponents who match me well, a promise that Tommy made that first night I fought. My desire to run from my life is a lot fucking stronger than anyone else's, which is why I've pulled out the win every fight so far.

"You mean *our* boss?" Eli goads back.

I hum in response.

"You were dead set on not getting in the ring at one point. What changed?" he finally asks, pressing me for details he should've asked when I approached him at Gulliver's.

"Life."

"Vagueness never got a guy anywhere."

I finish wrapping my last finger. "Nothing you say is going to help the battle I'm facing. Being out there, though? Just what I need."

"Put a lid on boiling water, and eventually, it blows."

"Let me guess, you know from experience?"

He shifts on the radiator he leans against before straightening. "Protect your face, Pretty Boy. Wouldn't want you fucking it up."

I toss the tape to him. He catches it with ease. "I'll be sure to take a picture of it for you after I go out there and make Daddy proud."

He chuckles and winces at the same time. "Please never refer to him as Daddy again or my dick might shrivel up and fall the fuck off. Besides, I'm his best earning fighter." He gets up and heads for the door. "Nothing makes him prouder than when I pull out the W and make him a shit ton of money. He can't look at me *without* dollar signs in his eyes. You, on the other hand..." He sizes me up, and I can sense the insult brewing.

I flip him the middle finger. "Get the fuck out of here."

He smirks. "Sure thing, Fresh Blood." And then he's gone, the door closing behind him while I prepare to go out there and knock a guy's lights out.

TWENTY-SIX

COLSON

I SWING my arms back and forth and roll my shoulders a few more times. I'm off to the side of the area where the fights occur. There's a lot of fucking people in attendance tonight, but because I'll be in the ring in less than twenty minutes, I get a front row seat with Tommy and his other fighters. On the other side are our opponents and the guy that manages them. The guy glowers at us like he's the Grim Reaper and one glance will take us out.

"Eli is about to wreck that fucking guy," Remy, the guy next to me, says. He's the last fight of the night. I won't see it happen. After our rounds, we typically head somewhere in the back of the building or return to our area where we got ready. Turns out, grown men don't take to losing very well. We like to lick our wounds in peace without an unforgiving audience. Eli told me they had to enforce that rule when one fighter put another in a coma *after* the fight. The winner didn't see him coming, but the sore loser peeled his back off the ground and got a cheap shot in at the back of his head.

Fights were shut down for weeks until the dude came out

of his medically-induced coma. He walked away with brain damage, still can't talk or eat on his own to this day.

I try not to think about all the risks that come along with what I'm doing. I know why I'm here, but if I let my mind wander on all the horrible ways my fights can turn for the worse, I'll be back in Mom's room with a big ole bottle of amber.

And no one needs that.

"Look at the weight he has on him." Remy snickers, running a hand over his bald head. He's in his thirties and lives for this shit. Literally. He's known Tommy since getting locked up in juvie for fighting and pickpocketing his way through his teenage years. "How long you give him?"

"You don't think he'll make the full three minutes?" I question, knowing by now that it's best to just go along with Remy than ignore him altogether. The dude rarely shuts up.

"Fuck no. No way in hell he makes it to the third. When he goes down, he's going down like a fucking pebble." He chuckles at his joke, and I have to say, Remy isn't wrong. Eli's contender is tiny. His muscles aren't as corded or ripped as Eli's. Nor does he have height on his side. He's lean like a swimmer, not ripped like a weight lifter, which makes me wonder why he's not going up against someone who's more of an equal in terms of weight class.

"Have to watch out for the small ones," I chime. "They can be scrappy."

"I'm not getting those vibes." He slaps my shoulder with the back of his hand. "How about we have a little wager? I'll throw a couple hundred on it."

"Not tonight."

His lower lip pushes out when he blows out a breath. "'Fraid you might lose? We both know you've made a pretty penny since you started working with Tommy. You can afford it."

Maybe so, but… "I'm here to fight. That's it."

He rolls his eyes, mutters that I'm a fucking prude with my money, then walks off to the other guys in our group. Probably to ask them the same thing. The dude can never sit still, and if it wasn't already noticeable, has a problem with gambling.

Eli ends up winning, and just like Remy suspected, the guy goes down easy. When he's carted off to the side, I swear I catch a glimpse of familiar brown hair. The perfect shade that I know way too well, but when I glance back over, it's gone. That quickly, it gets lost in the crowd, and I wonder if my eyes are playing tricks on me.

There's no way in hell Violet would be here. She doesn't have a clue that I'm fighting. She'd flip if she found out I took pleasure in beating the shit out of other guys. I can still remember that look that overtook her face when I told her I was into boxing and offered to show her a few moves. It was around the same time she offered to teach me yoga, and I took her up on it.

But she drew the final line in the sand, and surprisingly, she's been respecting it. Whatever I see, must be some other chick with the same remarkably brown hair as my girl.

It only serves as a reminder of how much I miss her.

The beauty mark under her eye.

Her smile and the way it always softened when I walked into the room.

Her goddamn touch and how it always made me feel alive.

Even more than fighting has.

I guzzle a mouthful of water and listen to the roar of the crowd. I'm up and bring my thoughts of her into the ring with me, but I can't let her get in my head. She doesn't belong there. *Not anymore.* That flicker of hair I saw is just my ego trying to draw me back into more heartache.

I won't have it.

Not now.

I'm here to entertain. I promised that to Tommy and the crowd when I signed up for this shit, despite the fact that I'm mostly just fighting for myself. The only reason I risked joining Tommy's group of guys is because it's the only sure way I won't get charged with assault. I can't go out and pick fights for the hell of it. But out here, in the chaos of The Battleground, I can get away with everything but death.

Pushing Violet out of my mind, I settle my feet at my side of the ring. The crowd cheers. I hear my name from people's mouths. People I don't even fucking know. Their voices swirl around me. Get in my head. Pretty soon, they're my only focus. Them, and the mean mug across from me.

My opponent is well-proportioned. Except maybe for his legs. They seem to be a little longer than the rest of him, and albeit, me. Otherwise, he looks just as strong, just as hungry for this match as I am. I rest my hands on my hips. My lungs scream for oxygen. I swear, sometimes when I'm out here, it feels like I stop pulling in air altogether. Like I'm in this upside-down purgatory where I have to hold my breath to make it through.

Maybe it has to do with this anguish inside of me.

Maybe it has to do with maintaining control.

I walk in a circle and look over the guy's shoulder. Eli is there, standing behind Tommy and Remy. He gives me a nod of encouragement then disappears in the shadows of the crowd. He's off to sit with his win and absorb all the good things that will come from it.

Praise.

Cash.

Popularity.

A buzzer reaches my ears, indicating that we only have a minute until the match starts. It feels like it lasts three seconds. It doesn't matter. I'm ready to get this over with. Ready to impale my fists into this fuckboy and cover the hurt that blatantly shows its face every morning.

The fight signal comes next and before either one of us knows it, we're in the center of the makeshift ring, trying to eat up the inches between us until our fists fly.

I've always been adamant about keeping my face protected, and I don't stray from that now. My fists create the perfect shield to keep him from hitting me. He sends a jab my way, I block it by raising my arm. I swing for him, but he pushes his weight onto his back foot, and I miss.

We're dancing, and the crowd knows it. Booing comes from every corner. It creeps into my head and adds to my unworthiness. They don't think I'm good enough tonight. To them, I don't deserve to be where I am. *I'm* the chum.

I do what anyone else would in my position, I lunge forward and hit him with a combination that confuses him. My fists move quickly. One of them connects with his cheek. The crowd erupts with cheers, and I've done well, but it isn't enough. My stomach clenches with the need to do the same thing over again, so I tuck my elbows and rely on my balance as he shuffles around and tries to retaliate.

He swings.

I dip down, his fist haloing my head.

"That all you got, fuckboy?" I spit out at him.

Only we can hear it, and normally I don't give my opponent the time of day by conversing with them, but something is at my back, pestering and pushing me to be better than I ever have before.

He replies with an original, "Fuck you, scumbag."

My grin turns threatening. I imagine it looks as cocky as Eli's was not too long ago. "Think it's safe to say we're both scumbags, no?"

A grunt tumbles out of him, and he lunges for me, lowering to try and tackle me until my back hits the floor. It doesn't work to his advantage. I'm prepared for it and put all my power into my legs and arm as I squat lower and drive my fist into his stomach. He heaves out a gust of air. His bare knees fall to the concrete slab below us. The gym shorts he's wearing get caught on something on the ground and rip at the hem.

The flock of people around us erupts with elation. Beyond, fists pump the air. He gets a couple of cheap weak shots in at me and then the buzzer blares again. The first round is over. We have two more rounds to knock each other out before we're thrown into a tie-breaker fourth.

I don't want it to get that far.

Judging by the way he sneers at me while we get a ten-second break, he doesn't, either.

He mouths, "Coming for you," just as the bell rings and we begin our second round. Three minutes are on the clock. One hundred and eighty seconds until I'll look up and see the impatience on Tommy's face. He doesn't like it when we draw it out, when we give them more time to take the lead and claim power over us.

For the first minute, I settle with a cross-jab pattern that he gets the hang of quickly. A disconcerting smile spreads across his face. I see a glimpse of red shine over his teeth, an indication that one of my last punches busted his lip. Or maybe he bit his tongue or cheek. Either way, it motivates me to fall back a couple of steps. To circle him and figure out the best plan of attack.

After endless conversations with Eli and my own experience with boxing, I've learned that you can't always go into a fight with a plan. Each person has their own strengths and weaknesses, and you don't know how they'll play with yours until you're face to face.

So, I observe him. I ignore the crowd and watch as he advances but caters a little too much to his right leg. Just like that, I have his weakness nailed down. When he throws another punch, I dip my chin down and peek through my arms to see how his leg responds. He's quick to pull it back and switch out with his other foot.

I give him one of my weaker punches to open up a response. He does exactly what I expect, and when my opportunity is present, before he's able to switch his stance, I rear back, bring my leg up, and kick him where he's lacking.

A combination of a grunt and yell comes out of his mouth. His body careens below me and he falls. I rejoice in my hit, but surprise consumes me when he gets back to his feet just as fast. He has a weak area, but perhaps he's spent time strengthening it for reasons like this.

I roll my neck to the left as he gears up for more, because let's be honest, it's coming. He knows I targeted his leg for a reason. Just to feel complete, I stretch my head to the right as well, my peripheral catching the crowd bordering us, and that's when I see it again.

Beautiful chocolate-colored hair.

Golden brown eyes.

And the faint glimpse of the beauty mark I visualized earlier.

What the fuck?

I thought I was imagining Violet before, but perhaps I wasn't.

How the hell would she know to find me here?

I look over and see her, but just like how a hallucination poofs into thin air, she does, too. Dispersed into the musty air of this broken-down candy stockroom. My opponent's fists slams against my cheek like a hammer driving a nail into wood. *Shit, that hurt.* Stars invade the edges of my vision. Everyone is so *fucking* loud that I can't see straight. My head dizzies, forcing my stomach into a nauseous fit.

My eyes immediately start watering as pain fans out over my face. I don't realize my palms are splayed out over the cold floor until I'm kicked in the ribcage. *Goddamnit.* This guy proves he has no weak spots after all. Proves that *I'm* the one with enough vulnerability to bring this match to a close.

Agonizing pain disperses out over my torso, and I realize I have two choices. I can lay here like a ragdoll and let him have his way with me or I can get my ass up and do what I initially intended.

And then after, I'll search the crowd high and low until I find her.

Until I find *my* weak spot.

Adrenaline pumps through me at an alarming rate, but I'm not mad about it. It gives me the chance to get back to my feet and press up into my stance. I swallow the nagging pain in my head and blink away the stars. Something tickles my top lip. I lick at it. Liquid metal coats my tongue at the same time I'm met with a smirk.

He's happy with himself.

Proud over drawing blood.

If he were anyone else, maybe I'd give him a clap on the back but nah. Tonight, I'm out for the same kind of blood he is, and even if Violet is somewhere close by, I don't plan on letting him take my win. It'll be me who walks away with my chin held high while he mopes over his loss.

I screw my head on straight, force myself into a tunnel,

and make him my only priority. I envision my fist sailing through the air until it knocks every last thought out of his pea-sized brain. And then after that, I visualize his limp body spread out on the floor beneath me.

My attention turns to the crowd. So many faces stare back, cheek-splitting smiles on their faces as they whoop and holler. What I want to know is why Violet is one of them.

More importantly, I want to find her. I *need* to find her because no matter how permanent that line has become, she's mine to protect. Even if the person I'm protecting her from is me.

TWENTY-SEVEN

VIOLET

"YOU WERE SUPPOSED to stay out of sight," Finn seethes, his unforgiving gaze narrowing on me. "At least until after the fight."

I run my tongue over my teeth and pull his zip-up around me tighter. Even with all the body heat collecting inside, it's still cold. Georgia's December air has pushed its way underneath the doors and through the shattered windows on the floors above.

Finn runs a hand over his face, his features more disconcerting in the shadows. I learned when we were walking in that this is what merciless underground fighting looks like. Fighters and attendees meet at places like this, rundown and abandoned, so they can watch each other strip the life from one another. So they can see it leave the fighters' eyes when they've fallen.

I picture the image of Colson on his knees again, and my heart stumbles. His eyes landed on mine, and recognition like I've never seen washed over his beautiful crestfallen face. It was like time stood still for him but not his opponent, who took advantage of Colson's misstep. My body riots at the memory of the hit he took, guilt skirting through my veins like a go cart. All because of me.

Finn is lucky he was quick to yank me away by the wrist. I would have run to Colson. I would have wrapped my arms around him and held him up. I would have told him that he can come back from whatever this is. That there's still hope. That I don't care if he's doing something I hate.

"What did you expect was going to happen?" I huff, ripping my arm free from his grasp. "You brought me here."

"I know that, but we had a plan before we walked in," Finn reminds me, and yeah, maybe we did. We agreed that we'd watch the fights, then after Colson was finished, we'd track him back to his car. Finn didn't want to spook him by showing our faces too soon.

Little too late for that.

"You can't blame me for not knowing what I was walking into."

"I warned you, or did you forget about that?"

"You didn't exactly tell me how brutal it would be."

"You think that was tough?" Finn questions, irritation laced through every one of his words. "That was nothing compared to some of the fights I've seen."

I roll my eyes. "What are we supposed to do now that he saw me?"

Finn glances over his shoulder. We're backed in a corner but still in a throng of people who are ready for the next fight. It's hard to focus on them when all I can see is the blood dripping down Colson's face and the bruising that embellished the side of it in the snap of a finger.

God.

That must've hurt.

He must hurt.

In so many ways.

He's so deep in his pain, in his grief, that he can't see the light at the end of the tunnel. He can't see that he *can* come out of this, and he can't possibly know where to put those feelings, otherwise he wouldn't be here. In this frigid and dirty building, getting the literal shit kicked out of him.

Finn grabs my bicep. He's not exactly gentle but not rough, either. I follow behind as he pushes through people who move out of the way without a problem. They're apparently used to being strapped into a tight space with a million other people. A little shoving isn't new to them.

We stay close to the wall and when there's a bend in it, we follow that, too, my hand always close enough to skim the wall. Eventually, we find a set of double doors and push through them. The chaos behind us quiets some, but I can still hear the chants of the crowd.

Fuck him up!

Fuck him up!

Fuck him up!

It's disturbing how much they get off on seeing a grown man beg for mercy. My stomach churns, dropping like a flap-jack after being flipped. I swallow through the unease clawing at me as we walk.

"Where are we going?" I ask in a hushed voice, looking back from where we came.

"Just be quiet, can you do that much?"

I tug my arm out of his hold again. There's not a crowd of people to get lost in back here, but also, he could be less of a dick.

He stops but only briefly enough to explain, "The fighters usually have their own space away from the fights for them to get ready. We're trying to find Colson's."

The farther back we get, the more muted the roars become. Darker, too. I peek into one of the rooms we pass and find it lifeless. Papers scatter a table set in the middle of the room and filing cabinets line the wall adjacent to it. The only reason I can see at all is because moonlight shines in through the windows.

Finn opens a door, sending a creaky howl down the hallway. A colder chill blankets my shoulders, and I glance back for a second time. Nobody is there. Nobody seems to be back here at all. I doubt we'll find Colson.

I stay on Finn's heels, prepared to mention that, and to say that we're wasting our time. That if we want to find Colson, we're going to have to go where the noise is, but I never get the chance.

An arm curls around my waist and hoists me backward. My first instinct is to scream, but as soon as I try, a hand covers my mouth and my voice reduces to a muffled grunt. I kick my legs. Try and drive my elbow back into the hardness that now encases me.

I try to pay attention to what I see around me, but it's just a hallway. Dark, damp, and dangerous. It doesn't help that Finn disappeared down an adjacent hallway a second ago.

I focus on the sounds around me except there are none. I'm dragged into a room and then hear the door click shut. We're in one of the abandoned offices, I quickly put together. No sooner do I realize this, my body is spun and plopped on top of a hard surface. I try to scatter away from my assaulter, but it's hard when there's nowhere to go. My hand brushes against the hard, cool surface of...of a filing cabinet? The coolness of the metal eats away at my leather pants, but my body is suddenly very far from being cold.

I'm hot all over, instantly in sweat mode after being grabbed by an unknown person until I look up and see familiar blue eyes.

"What the hell are you doing here?"

I gulp down my fear when Colson flicks on a battery-operated lantern. His gaze is on me. It's nothing like I remember it. The man I knew weeks ago is gone and in his place is a different one entirely. All hard lines and clipped words. Markings of a self-inflicted war on his handsome face. His piercing blue eyes hold mine, and I wonder how long it'll take Finn to notice that I'm gone.

"I, uh…"

"Talk, Violet."

Now would be a good time to do that, but see, everything gets caught in my throat as I take him in. His skin is tinged red below his nose, as if he wiped at blood that was there with the sleeve of his shirt, but as my eyes flick down to spot the matching color on his clothes, nothing is there. Only the gray, soft fabric of a cotton shirt. I'm not sure how there isn't a drop of blood on it, but then I remember he was bare-chested during his fight.

At some point, he put on a shirt.

The side of his face is a watercolor sunset, pinks and blues and purples mixing together to create a smattering of a bruise on his skin. I glance down and take in his large body. Broad-ish shoulders that lead down to wet-dream forearms. He's never seemed bigger than this moment.

My eyes catch on his hands that can't seem to stay still. They comb through his hair, then they're at his side, then they're rubbing the ache out of each other. He's on edge. So totally out of his element while being *in* his element that it's startling.

I know exactly how he feels.

And those knuckles, marred and aggrieved from his bare-knuckled fight, catch the faintest of light dancing around the room.

"You have nothing to say? Well then let me say it for you, this is *not*—"

"A place I should be," I finish for him. "Yeah, you don't need to tell me what I already know, but I chose to be here and that's something you're going to have to accept one way or another."

Suddenly, I'm pissed. I'm tired of him telling me what's best for me. Tired of him thinking he can make decisions on my behalf. Tired of him thinking he can tell me where I can and can't be. How I can and can't feel about him.

"I don't need your damn attitude."

"Attitude? This is nothing, Colson." I huff out the start of a laugh. "You know, this doesn't seem like a place you should be, either." My voice cuts down to a whisper. "You're fighting now?"

He puts his hands on his hips after setting down the lamp. "I don't need your judgments."

"I'm not...I'm trying to understand."

I'm sickened over this whole thing. That I even have to be here. That we can't be back at the apartment cuddled under my bed sheets and lazily running our hands over one another like there's nothing else we love more in life than each other.

His jaw clenches and he looks away. "How did you get here? I'm taking you home."

"No, you're not."

"Yes, I am."

"Where do you get the right?" My heart stands at attention and salutes over the constant heartbreak where he's concerned. *I didn't deserve the shit Webber put me through, and now look at me*. Dealing with similar shit from a different guy. But not for long.

"Ever since your mom died you've been trying to make decisions for me, but I'm over it. Done with you thinking you have a say over whether I can be near you or not. If I want to be here, there's nothing you can do about it."

I hop off the filing cabinet, pushing out of his immediate space, feeling one hundred percent fed up. Finn was right. Colson does have himself tied up with the wrong people, but I'm done trying to cater to a difficult person. Done being pushed and pulled and ripped in every goddamn direction like what I feel and want doesn't matter.

It's never been more obvious that he doesn't want to fight for himself. He wants to fight for *them*. For people who don't give a damn. For people who would *clap* if they saw him sprawled out on the concrete, barely conscious.

It's a punch to every organ in my body because if that's what he cares about...then that means I'm not important enough for him to be better for. Sebastian isn't important enough. Nor his aunt and uncle. We're all *meaningless*. But it also means he finds himself so undeserving of the fight of life —the most important one there is. I don't know which breaks my heart the most.

He grabs my arm when I turn for the door. Finn's sweat-shirt slips off one of my shoulders. "You're not going out there alone."

I look back at him, tempted to get lost in his stormy eyes. "We're not together anymore. You can't tell me what to do."

And then he walks into my space, crowding me with that stupid masculine scent of his that makes me dizzy. "Well aware of that, but it's not me who's following you, now is it?"

"Someone once told me he was protecting me when, instead, it felt like he was punishing me. Consider this as me doing the same."

His hold loosens and his eyes drop to the exposed skin on my shoulder before settling on the thick fabric covering me. "Whose sweatshirt is this?"

I switch to a more appropriate question. "What are you doing fighting at a place like this with people who don't give a damn about you?"

"Don't change the subject." His eyes flare but not with the good kind of heat. He grips the sleeve of the zip-up. "Who the hell does this belong to, and why are you wearing it?"

"It doesn't matter."

He grinds his teeth and fists the black fabric tighter. It only ends up pulling us closer together. "Whose, Violet?"

"I don't owe you an answer."

"That's where you're wrong."

"How do you figure that?" My breath wanes with us so close, our mouths growing nearer to each other. If this was the past, he'd tug me close and slide his lips over mine. I would grant him access, and then he'd pour himself into me while also taking every last bit of me. He'd give me that throaty, masculine groan I got so used to hearing when he'd kiss me, and that'd be the end of it. We'd end up in each other's arms with sweat-slicked skin.

"You're the one who put a stop to us," he murmurs in a weak tone.

I scoff. "No. You did that. *You* broke up with *me*."

"Yeah, but you..." He bites down on his lower lip. As if he's in pain. As if he doesn't want to speak it into existence.

"Don't flip this." I push my palms against his chest. I'm not trying to shove him, but even if I were, he'd go nowhere. I just want more space between us. He's too solid, and I'm too soft. We're a mixture of hard muscles, intriguing eyes, and thumping pulses. I know my resolve won't last forever. Not where he's concerned.

"If you wanted me," I swallow down a breath, "you

could've had me. I would've given you all of me just like I was doing."

I would have been there for you.

His bloody fingers come in between us as he unzips the sweatshirt. Then he brushes a knuckle down the center of my very-exposing top. "Even this?"

My tummy whooshes. The waves in his eyes crash into me without abandon. "Especially that," I whisper.

The air shifts. The anger-filled tension turns physical and causes a line of fire where the pad of his finger trails. It hooks on the material of my top. A couple of inches lower, and he'd drag his rough finger directly over my nipple. My back arches of its own volition.

His blue, blustery eyes meet mine, and I see the question in them. But I also see the walls he has built. Allowing him a piece of me will do nothing to tear them down. Unless I find a way to pick away at the mortar, I can't give myself up like this.

I promised myself I wouldn't.

I can't be for him what I was for Webber.

I can't constantly give and expect different results if all I'm going to get is pain and suffering at the end of it. He has to be willing to meet me halfway.

But he's not even on the same road as me.

I'm gentle as I wrap my hand around his and unhook his finger. His expression doesn't change. It's as stoic as it was when he dragged me into this room, but he understands. The line is still there, and there's no erasing it. It's written in permanent ink and the only way around it will be to forge a new one in a different color.

But those thoughts fly out the window when Finn makes his entrance, pushing into the room with watchful, assessing eyes. Like he's on the lookout for me. I know then that he couldn't have picked a worse moment to show his face.

TWENTY-EIGHT

COLSON

I THOUGHT tonight couldn't get any worse, but then Finn walks into the room and knocks me into the past. Back to thoughts of my life revolving around Murphy's Law, and the whole idea if something can go wrong, it will.

I want the comfort of being close to Violet and the peace she brings me, but my body betrays that, and it's because of him. My hands fist at my sides, and I take one more glance at the oversized sweatshirt draped over her lithe body and know it belongs to him.

To Finn.

To my goddamn half brother.

Disgust coils in my stomach, putting a mean spin on a ride of teacups I rode once when Sebastian and I were kids and Aunt Bess took us to an amusement park an hour away. My head rages with the onset of a headache from my match. I want nothing more than to drag Finn out into the center of that room and not let up until he's the one on the floor with his tongue lolled out the side of his mouth. Give him a little bit of what he gave me all those weeks ago.

I'm not the same person I was when Finn and Clyde had

me by the balls and held Mom's debt over my head. I owe them nothing, which is the reason I lunge forward and give Finn no time to react. I crush him against the wall faster than it takes him to blink, my forearm pressed against his tattooed throat.

Long gone are the days where I fall in line to his every word. I'm not his puppet anymore, and if I knew I could get away with it, I'd press just a little harder and watch the familiar war that raged in my eyes not long ago spark to life in his.

He wheezes, his lips quirking into a smirk despite me constricting his airway, "Good to see you too, Brother."

Brother.

The urge to cut his tongue out and douse it in kerosene hits strong. It's so much darker than the thoughts I'm used to thinking. I tack it to the wall of my mind as a red flag but pay it no mind as I sneer, "Don't call me that."

"It's what we are, isn't it?"

I don't let up on my grip but bear down on his throat more.

Violet shouts out in an uncompromising tone I've only ever heard when I had Sebastian in a similar position. "Let him go, Colson."

Finn holds a hand up to Violet at her demand. She quiets, and I wonder, what the fuck has been going on behind my back for him to have that kind of control over her when, a minute ago, she put up a fight with me.

She wouldn't let me get an inch with her—granted, I didn't deserve it—but now she's letting him call the fucking shots? What makes him any more deserving than me?

"You and I are nothing to each other," I grit out, my voice harsh and unrelenting.

He squints one of his eyes in thought as a garbled noise

leaves his throat, and all I see are all the moments he tore me down. Him forcing me to pay Mom's debt because she was too weak to do it herself. Ambushing me in that alleyway and standing there while Nic gave me a bloody lip and bruised my ribs. My broken finger. The threats, mental abuse, and emotional stress.

And that's not even getting into his dad being the biggest piece of shit in the world. The person who fed my mom's addiction and waited for her to go just one step too far so he could claim everything she left behind. He stood there beside him every step of the way. Never once challenging how goddamn wrong it was.

I remove my forearm from his throat and grip his shirt. I shake him until his back thuds off the wall. He lets me. Allows me to turn him into a ragdoll. Outside of me head-butting him the night near the battery plant in Harrison Heights, this is the only other time I've put my hands on him. To be honest, it's marvelous. "Why did you bring her here?"

"Why did I..." He chuckles, low and deep and then suddenly stops. A line forms between his brows. He shoves me so hard that I fall back a step, then smooths a hand down his shirt, fixing the wrinkles. He clears his throat, freeing it from the strain I put on it a second ago. "Because you're out of your fucking mind. You pulled Janie out of her shitty deal-ings, and for what, if you're going to end up doing the same stupid shit?"

Violet pipes up, "It doesn't have to be this way." I don't need to glance over to know her eyes are burning holes into me.

"Fuck you and your brotherly act," I spit at Finn. "You didn't care about me then and you don't now. You enjoyed making me bleed—in more ways than one—and knocking me down every chance you could. And now you're using her to get to me?"

Finn's face falls, but he picks it up almost immediately. "Everyone fucks up, Moore."

"No. Some people fuck up. Others choose to be fuck-ups. Pretty sure that's the category you fit in, Finn."

"You don't know a goddamn thing about the way I grew up, about the choices I had and still have to make. About the things I choose and don't choose, or the categories I belong in."

"If there's one thing I know, it's that you're no different than the tree you fell from. I told you when I paid Mom's debt off that I was done with you, and I meant it. Finding out we share DNA doesn't change that for me."

Finn rolls his cavernous eyes. Almost like he's bored with me. "Very metaphoric of you."

I give him my middle finger, because as far as I'm concerned, he can fuck right off. Also, it's better than punching him in the throat, and my urge to do just that is growing by the second.

Violet completely strips the thought from my mind when she speaks up behind me. "Wait. What debt?"

My ears buzz with static noise. For a split second, I want to run from the truth of my connection with Finn, but I've kept it hidden long enough. Violet needs to know who I really am. That I'm not all the good she thinks she sees when she looks at me. That my upbringing and Harrison Heights are sewn into me with no plans of ever leaving.

I used to think I was better than Finn, but now...it's never been clearer how similar we are in that sense that this town is a part of who we are. It shouldn't, but it defines us.

If she wants to be involved in the drama...well, *consider*

yourself involved, beautiful. Because I don't have it in me to keep it a secret anymore.

"Yeah, Finn," I jut out my bottom lip and sweep my hand in her direction, "you want to clue Violet in on how we knew each other before the brother thing came out or should I?"

Violet's attention ricochets between the two of us. "What are you talking about?" I don't know who the question is meant for. I've spent months keeping my business with Finn under wraps, but they got exploited in that stupid fucking conference room with Stewart. The same is happening now. The only one who gets the protection of lying about it at this point are the Lincolns, and I've about had it with them thinking they can do whatever they please.

No more lying.

No more secrets.

Only truths.

She needs to know that the person who brought her here tonight isn't who he's trying to portray himself as—a brotherly hero who supposedly cares.

And it wouldn't hurt for her to know that the guy she's spent the last few months falling for isn't as honest as he's made himself out to be. We all have secrets and lies that we hold close, and she's about to find out both of ours.

Finn's tongue sweeps across his bottom lip. Violet steps closer. My heart races like it's in a marathon and breaks are off limits. She glances at Finn, but it's me her eyes ultimately end up on. The truth hits harder with me. I see it in her eyes.

"Colson, what debt?" she pleads, voice strong, but I sense the waver in her words. She used to tell me that it didn't bother her when I didn't give every single detail on a matter, but those things mostly revolved around my connection with the guy who waited for me outside of Spring Meadows and the reason behind my bloody lip and bruised ribs.

Now, she's tired of my shit and wants answers.

She's fed up with the go around, and I can't say I blame her.

If we were any other people in this world, she would've known by now.

A staggering breath rolls out of me, and I clamp my hands on my hips. I decide it's better to just come out and say it because what good is delaying the inevitable? My heart is already broken, seeing hers shatter in front of me won't hurt that much more, right?

"Finn and his dad sold drugs to my mom." My eyes remain on him. He stares back at me, no emotion on his face. "A few times, I had to pay off money that she owed them, but a few months ago, she ended up cutting a deal bigger than all the others. They gave her product to move, but she fucked around with it instead. Their dumb asses trusted an addict with ten thousand dollars worth of supply—which we now know is because his dad wanted her dead so he could claim the inheritance she left behind when she finally kicked the bucket—and guess who had to pay it back?"

Her eyes scan my face. They drop down to my feet, then blink back up to my mouth while she points at Finn. "You paid him *ten thousand dollars* because your mom took drugs from them?" Her face pales. *I'm sick over it, too.* Fucking wrecked.

She puts it together so fast. "That's why he was at the apartment that day, isn't it?" she questions. "He's the one that beat you up. That hurt you and had you bruised and bleeding a-and…"

She rubs her hands over her face and cinches Finn's sweatshirt tighter around her body. She turns to him. "And then you…you gave Janie drugs when you knew she was deep in her addiction?"

Finn meets her head on, and why wouldn't he? He's not ashamed of the things he's done, of the deals he's orchestrated alongside his father. Of the people he's harmed in the process. "It's not like that. It's just business."

"Business?" she scoffs, disgust sliding underneath each syllable.

"It wasn't personal, at least not for me. If it weren't Janie, it would have been someone else."

They fed her addiction. Put it right in her hands when she was weak and needed help. They took advantage of her, and all it gave her was a one-way ticket to the afterlife. "And that's not even the best part," I add on. "His dad got drugs into Harrison County Jail through some contact he knew when she was an inmate. Kept her addiction going behind bars. He's the one who killed her."

Violet takes a step back.

Finally, she realizes that she's in a room with two people she doesn't know, and her lips part to say something. But nothing comes out. She's speechless, and if I know my girl at all, she's questioning why the hell she came with Finn in the first place. Why she's fighting for a man she's not sure she knows. We're all a little too fucked up to be fixed.

The angel on my shoulder wants me to reach out and curl my hand into hers and convince her that I'm not the person she's making me out to be in her head. That despite saving my mom and working with Finn to get her out of the hole she ended up in, I'm a good person.

"Those things happened, but it's not everything we are," Finn claims. He doesn't stop trying to convince us that it isn't as bad as it sounds. He can eat dog shit. "Our dirty laundry is in the past."

"What?" I ask. "Don't like the smell of yours? Can't bear to talk about it?"

His gaze narrows on me. "I don't give a shit what you say about me or who you say it to. I won't apologize for the shit I've done, for the deals, for the way I make my ends meet. We both know you didn't tell her because you didn't want her seeing you in a different light. She's not here because she trusts me. She came for *you*, but you want her to believe you don't deserve each other. For fucking what? Who the fuck cares about what happened in the past?"

"If it doesn't matter then why the hell are you here?" I challenge.

I'd ask how he gained access to the warehouse. How he even knew I was fighting and where to find me, but we all know Finn. He either tailed me or knows someone who knows someone.

His jaw clenches. "To save my idiot brother."

It's almost laughable. Really. He came to save me. Now that's something.

"Where was the hero act when you pressed that cigarette into my neck or when you broke my finger?"

"Oh, my God," Violet murmurs. "You told me the bandage on your neck was from cardboard and…and your finger was because you didn't use your gloves."

It turns my stomach knowing it's all hitting her at once when I had the advantage of dealing with it as it came.

"I don't want your goddamn help, nor do I need it," I tell Finn. "In fact, I want nothing to do with you. How many times must I say it?"

"I was there, too," he says as Violet turns on her heel and runs her hands over her face again. She's gone mostly quiet since we dropped our truths, distancing herself, and I know why. She's having a hard time wrapping her mind around the lies and secrets and omissions. I get it because I've been there. I *am* there.

Finn continues to yammer on. I look at him, but my focus is leaned more toward the girl on the other side of the room.

Fuck, does she even know how beautiful she is?

Even now, like this, I want to run my hands through her hair and bruise her lips with mine.

"I had no fucking clue that he was hiding his marriage to your mom or that we're brothers. The asshole never said a goddamn word." He grimaces like he's working through his own internal conflict. "I wouldn't have—"

"Save it," I quip.

"Don't punish me for his fuck-ups."

A dry laugh comes from me. "Oh, believe me. I'm not. I'm punishing you for *your* fuck-ups. The ones you apparently want to forget exist. Didn't take you for the kind of person who doesn't want to take accountability for his actions, then again, you are a piece of shit, so I'm not surprised."

His jaw tenses. "You know what, fine. You want nothing to do with me..." He raises his hands in surrender but then they come down hard at his sides. "Heard you loud and fucking clear, but just so you're aware, your boss out there?"

I cross my arms. "Tommy?"

"Yeah, you think paying us back was bad? He's going to get you for a lot more. You think you're going to be able to show up for a few fights and then," he brushes his palms together as if he's wiping crumbs off them, "that's it? When you want out, he's not going to let you leave unless you give him what he wants. He'll cinch that rope around your neck and hang you for every cent you have. And if you don't have the money, he's not the kind of guy who's opposed to taking something a whole lot more precious."

Violet whips around at the sound of that. "Please tell me you're just joking and saying that to get under his skin."

He levels her with a look, his eyes narrowing and his lips pursing. "Why do you think I brought you here? For shits and giggles? I told you he was getting himself into some serious shit."

"You don't know what you're talking about," I tell him. Tommy may be a particular kind of guy, but I doubt he'd string me up like a piñata if things went sideways. Not so long as he got his money.

"You sure about that, Moore? Last time I checked, I was the alleged criminal, and you were the goody two-shoes trying to fight for his druggie mom."

My hands curl into fists. It's hard to tell if he's just being himself or if the dig is intentional. I decide to let it go for the time being because what he says about Tommy picks at my brain in a weird way that I don't have an answer to.

If the day comes when I'm done, all Tommy will care about is the fact that I made him a shitload of cash. He'll let me walk.

You enter the mouth of the beast, he won't spit you out, and if you're one of the lucky few he doesn't want, it still won't matter. You won't be whole by the end of it.

Finn watches me with rapt attention. It's like he's inside my head and can hear my thoughts. He clicks his tongue and shakes his head. "See things how you want, but remember which one of us is meeting up in a dingy, broke-down-as-fuck warehouse on the outskirts of Harrison Heights nightly. You're not much better than me now, are you, Colson?"

"Fuck you."

"Right back atcha. Violet, you want a ride home, then let's go."

She nibbles her lower lip. I'd give anything to make it my teeth there. To be the one biting down on that pink, pillowy lip and sucking it into my mouth. "I'll be right behind you."

"You got three minutes, then I'm gone."

She nods, and he walks out into the shadowed hallway.

"I know you two don't see eye to eye," she starts. "And a lot of messed up things have happ—"

"Why the hell would you let him take you anywhere?"

She rears back, offended, then makes a dig at me. "You could've easily made sure this never happened if you would have told me the truth from the start, but you chose to keep it hidden and lie." Hurt laces her words. "You could have trusted me," she adds, her voice dropping. "Like I trusted you with what I was going through but I guess...well, it's clear you didn't."

Doesn't she get it? "I couldn't tell you at the time. I needed you to just trust me." My adrenaline is beginning to wear, and my damn knuckles hurt. I want to get out of here, back to my car, and go home.

"And I did." She takes a step closer, but I can tell with how her shoulders are set back that there's no way I can touch her right now. "But how would you feel if you found out that I was slinging large amounts of money at drug dealers and... and fighting a bunch of dudes in this underground world of aggression and stupidity? I'm so fucking confused and hurt because I thought I knew you, and now..."

My heart blazes with pain as if it's been twisted between two hands. My throat rolls, wanting the anecdote to make it go away but there isn't one. There's nothing that would make Violet's disappointment in me hurt less. "You do know me."

She shakes her head, flicking my promise away like a pesky gnat. "I came with Finn willingly because he said you needed help. I just didn't..."

I clear my throat, forcing it to work despite my entire body flaming with the need to close this distance and get down on my knees in front of her. She's looking at me like

I'm a stranger. Like we haven't spent time twining our hearts together over the challenges we faced. "You shouldn't trust him," is what I choose to say instead.

"To be honest, I'm kind of having a hard time trusting you after what I heard. I asked you about him and your injuries, and I understand why you wanted to keep it to yourself, it's…a lot. But I thought we were closer than that, Colson. I thought we could trust each other with anything. I told you what happened with my dad. I confided in you, and you just…I don't even know."

I hate that she's right.

I should've told her.

Not for help, but because she *is* someone I can trust. Her being here is proof of that. "I didn't ask you to divulge that information to me."

"No, but I did because I felt…" She trails off again, and it's like it's all she can seem to do. Like her thoughts are taking time to catch up to what's going on. Like she has the beginning of them but not the end.

I take a meager step closer, breaching her bubble. I could really use her warmth right now. Or that jasmine-like scent that clings to her flawless skin. "I know what you felt," I murmur, my earlier irritation over seeing Finn fading quickly. Nothing else matters when I'm alone with her. I wish I could pick up her heart and piece it back together. "I felt it, too."

"No…" She points at me, and I don't dare take another step toward her. "You don't get to do that. You don't get to make your voice all soft and push into my space and touch me and try to make this seem better than it is. You lied to me for months. There were so many opportunities to come clean, to confide in me."

My emotion bubbles, because fuck, I hate this.

She shakes her head. "You lied out of omission. That

might not be the same in your book, but it is in mine, Colson. I spent months lying for my own father and you made a fool of me by letting me lean on you when you were doing the same in return."

I turn on my heel and bring my fist down on the desk. A few old, dusty papers float to the floor. "Do you think I don't know that?" I'm not looking at Violet to see if she flinches. "I do trust you, but it was too much. A separate part of my life than where you took up shop. I wasn't going to bring you into it and taint what we had. You were already going through the shit with your family. It would've been messed up to pile it on you."

Something crunches. It's not until I feel a hand on my side, right along my rib cage, that I realize it's Violet's shoes making the noise. Her voice is like the gentle stroke of finger-tips running over my bare skin. "It sucks knowing that I came to you with my deepest secret, and you kept all of yours to yourself. I wish you didn't have to go through any of this, but I've been here. There were so many times you could've turned to me, but I'm beginning to realize that I wasn't enough for the simple decency of honesty."

Fuck.

She was never not enough.

Always *more* than.

I squeeze my eyes shut and try to force down the emotions.

I lost Mom, and even though it felt like I lost Violet before, this feels even more permanent. Before, she may have been gone, but a part of me still felt like I had her. But now…it's like trying to catch steam or smoke in your palm. It just scurries around your fingers, impossible to catch. She's fading before me, turning into a pigment of my imag-ination where I'll only have the memory of her all because

I shoved down my truths and buried myself beneath the lies.

My heart, having had enough with the twisting and burning, splits in half. It's a chunk of wood and Violet's words are the ax that bears down on them.

A pressure forms at my back. I quickly realize it's Violet resting her head there. I focus on the fact that she's touching me and how it'll probably be the last time. I know that if I turned around and tilted her chin up, her eyes would glisten in the glow of the lantern. "She wouldn't want you doing this. No parent wants to see their child this low. The truest version of herself wouldn't want to see her son in this much agony."

It's incredible seeing how wrecked Violet is over what's gone down, and yet she still finds kind, uplifting words to give me. I don't know how she does it.

"Yeah, well, I don't know the first thing to do to get rid of it," I admit in defeat.

"The first thing to do is to *feel* it, Colson. You'll never make it to your destination if you keep taking detours. You *always* have to go through. Out of everyone, you should know that the most."

I miss her touch when she lifts her forehead off me. I hear the click and creak of a departure I'm not ready for. I despise how she's leaving with Finn, but it's so hard to speak up. To say...

Come back to me, Violet.

I'm so fucking sorry for everything.

I'm ready to rise above it all.

To get the help I know I need.

But more than all that I want to tell her something even heavier. That I love her. And I don't think that love will ever run out.

TWENTY-NINE

VIOLET

Everleigh: Merry Christmas! Love you both!
Violet: Happy Holidays!
Violet: Olive says the same!
Sylvia left the chat.

CHRISTMAS MORNING CREEPS UP like a fox in the night. I'm so distracted by life that I don't realize it until Olive busts through my door and jumps on my bed like she used to do when we were little. The mattress springs up and down, and she tugs the blankets off me.

I yank them back over my shoulders and nuzzle in. I didn't sleep well last night. In fact, I spent a lot of time staring at the ceiling thinking about Colson and Finn.

Even though I never got on Colson's case about being more open with me before, it hurts that he kept something so big from me. Part of me wonders if it'd be best that I close that door and never see him again. It's why I tossed and turned a lot last night. I was too engrossed in a real-life nightmare by imagining a world where he doesn't exist.

Even now, my stomach rampages at the thought of it.

"Oh, come oooon," she croons, pressing her mouth to my ear. "It's time to get up. We made a deal."

I groan, "Can I take it back?"

"No. No take backsies." She pulls my hair lightly, but it's enough to get me to swat her away. "I said I'd stop nagging to go to a strip club if you promised we'd go to Mom and Dad's for Christmas."

I roll over to my back. "I still don't understand why you want to go to a strip club."

She sits on the edge of the bed and shrugs. "For the experience."

That worry that's always present for her pushes to the front of my mind. My sister has always been the more neurotic one out of the two of us, but it isn't lost on me how she randomly showed up on my doorstep without mentioning it. I want to ask if something is going on, but I also don't want to ruin the holiday by being overbearing. I was so worried Dad's infidelity would destroy her in the same way that stupid boy did when she was in high school, but she stayed upright. She proved there are things she can handle. That she's not the same broken girl she was back then. So, maybe, it's better I let her feel like the woman she's growing into, instead of the little sister I'll always view her as.

Pushing my concern aside, I look at her, and ask, "You're dressed already?"

"I've been up since six," she admits.

"What time is it now?"

"The clock on the stove said seven-thirty before I came back."

"No," I whine and close my eyes again. "It's too early. And I'm too damn tired."

"Too bad. Besides, everyone loves waking up early on Christmas."

"That's where you're wrong. Parents despise it."

She picks up a spare pillow and whacks me in the head before bouncing off the bed. "Get up, or I'll force you to tell me where you really went the other night. Yeah, that's right. Everleigh might have covered for you, but I'm not stupid, Sister. You claimed to take a walk outside. I know that doesn't equate to being gone for hours." She claps her hands. "Chop, chop." And then she's out of my room, and I'm left staring up at my ceiling. Again.

I didn't realize I was gone for hours until I undressed and climbed into bed that night. Roadwork on the 401 interfered with us getting back across the river after we left Harrison Heights, but that's not the only thing that made time drag. Being at that warehouse did. Standing there and watching two guys go through the motions before Colson claimed their spot ate up precious minutes that I didn't have an excuse for.

Too in the midst of questioning what Colson and I had, and the truths he kept from me, I linger in bed. I think of Finn and their dad. He admitted to Colson's accusations, and I know I shouldn't ignore that. The way they took advantage of Janie's addiction just so they could win a game no one else was playing. He didn't apologize—at least not from what I remember—and I guess I can see why. He's not ashamed of the money he's made or following the only way of life he's ever known. But I think he *is* ashamed over how he's treated his brother. I like to think that this is his way of making up for it. Had he known Colson was his family all this time, maybe he would've done better.

I don't know him well, but it's clear he extended an olive

branch that night when he warned Colson about his boss, Tommy. He doesn't want to see him caught up, and I can appreciate that because I don't want to see it, either.

Once I'm near ready to walk out the door, I grab my phone off my nightstand and check for messages. There are none. I'm not sure what I expect. A message from Colson? *Do I even want that?*

I glance at the date on the phone, December 25th staring back at me. Holiday cheer is nowhere in sight this year. I'm not excited to exchange presents or spend time with my loved ones. Well, aside from Olive. I'm still not sure what I'm going to say when I show up to my parents'. I haven't talked to them since Thanksgiving. There's a lot that hasn't been said. A lot of words hovering in the air.

I push that to the back of my mind, though, figuring I'll deal with it when I get there. I pull up my text thread with Colson. Skimming back to a few of our last conversations when things were good between us. When life wasn't dragging him under water every chance it got. There was so much love in those exchanges.

It's absolutely mind-blowing how much I care for him. How quickly I'm tossing the idea of never talking to him again out the window. The truth is, my love for Colson expands to distances I never knew existed. It's almost toxic how I'd do anything, even get in a car with a complete stranger, to get to him.

I send him a simple *Merry Christmas* text. I can't imagine him being alone today. Not when he should be surrounded by at least one person who loves him.

I WALK into the foyer of the home where I grew up. Mom decorated it beautifully. As she always does for the holidays. Outside, icicle lights hang from the eaves and wreaths fill every window. It smells like cinnamon and pine trees inside. Just like it used to when we were kids and would race down the stairs to see if Santa left presents for us.

Spoiler, he always did.

Mom and Dad don't greet us as we close the door behind us and toe our shoes off. It almost sounds like no one is home. Our purses get propped on the hook near the door, along with our coats, and we find the living room. A fake Christmas tree reaches for the ceiling, the star on top only inches from touching it. Lights wind around it and ornaments hang from nearly every branch. It's full and beautiful and brimming with gift boxes underneath with carefully crafted wrapping paper. It should spark the holiday spirit for me but doesn't. I'm still thinking about that text and how I haven't received one back.

"Mom! Dad! We're here!" Olive makes a beeline for the kitchen, and I follow close behind. It's there we find Mom behind the stove, working to whip up our Christmas dinner. It reminds me too much of Thanksgiving. The way she prepared that entire meal for it to fall flat.

"Girls!" Mom's voice is light and airy and full of happiness. The opposite of how she sounded during our last conversation. She brushes a strand of hair out of her face and sets down the oven mitts that are in her hands. She rushes toward the both of us. "I am so glad to see you two." Both of her arms grab hold of us, and we get crushed to her chest, giggles coming out of Olive and me.

It's almost like we're little girls again, and I sigh into her neck. She smells like home. Like summer afternoons with homemade lemonade. Like brownie batter on winter days when we'd bake over playing outside in the cold. More than either of those two, she's pure comfort and tenderness. Like her hug is powerful enough and so full of love that it might weld the broken pieces of my heart back together. Even the pieces she and Dad broke last month.

As soon as the hug ends, guilt rips at me. Guilt over not staying on Thanksgiving. Over not listening. Over being too caught up in my own selfish emotions to hear where she was truly coming from when it came to Dad. Over not talking to her or Dad since.

What kind of daughter am I?

She looks at us when she pulls away, no signs of disappointment present like I worried about on the drive over. "You two are so beautiful it makes my eyes hurt." She doesn't look at me any differently after I walked out on her Thanksgiving night. She acts as if there's not a rift between us, and while that might normally bother me, I'm beyond grateful for it today.

"Mom," Olive whines, but she's smiling.

"What? It's true. Go look in the mirror; your eyes might hurt, too!" We chuckle at her ridiculousness before she motions us toward the island. "I was just about to take my cookie dough out of the freezer. How about you two roll it out for me? Just like old times."

We spend the next two hours making cookies.

Olive and I sit side by side. Mom puts on a holiday playlist, and we sing along while rolling chocolate chip cookie dough into small balls. We line three baking sheets with them, and eventually Dad walks in. His gruff voice is laden with sleep. Mom lifts her head in greeting and gives him the brightest smile I've seen in a long time. Or maybe she's always looked at him like this, and I was too caught up in his recent affair for months to see it.

I don't know how I feel about it anymore. All I know is I'm happy I'm not hanging onto the secret of it. That it isn't weighing me down. Still, it feels slightly uncomfortable to be in the same space as him, which only makes me think back on the conversation I had with Mom.

How she kept saying that love is endless. That it didn't seem to bother her about what he did if it was her and his kids he was coming home to. I realize just how open of a mind and heart she must have had all these years to be okay with that instead of seeing her as the doormat I thought of her as. To still be with him through those transgressions rather than run.

For a second, I consider she might not be weak at all. That she really is the strong woman who raised me, who I still look up to, who might know what she's talking about.

And maybe, just maybe, I'm more like her than I thought. Because if I had my way, I'd be with Colson right now even if I am mad at him. Wherever he is, I'd be by his side, helping him slay his demons instead of standing by.

Just like she's done with Dad.

I don't know what to make of that.

Dad rounds the counter, kisses her cheek with his hand resting on her hip then grants us one of his easy smiles. Somehow, he looks different than he did a month ago.

He flattens his hands on the granite countertops and leans in, sweeping his finger into the bowl of cookie dough while Mom slides the trays into the oven.

Olive leans over and does the same when he offers us the bowl. "Nothing like cookie dough on Christmas morning."

Mom swats both of them with a hand towel and laughs. "Get out of here. You're both old enough to know that you shouldn't be eating raw cookie dough."

"But it's cookie dough," they both argue cheekily.

Mom's brows raise, and I can't help but chuckle. "With raw eggs." Then she turns on Dad. "You. It's your fault, teaching her that raw cookie dough is okay."

He backs away from the counter, hands raised in surrender but grinning all the same. "I don't know what you're talking about."

Mom smiles just as hard in return. "Mmhmm. Sure."

He heads for the living room. "Who's ready to open presents?"

Olive hops off her stool and runs after him, both hands raised in the air. "Oh! Me! Me, me, me!"

It's crazy how much I've missed my family when just a few months ago I didn't want to be around.

I follow after them, curling up on the sofa with my feet under me as Dad hands each of us gifts and tells us to have at it. Just like he did when we were kids. We'd rip through the wrapping paper as fast as our little hands could, and then we'd lift our presents in the air with brilliant smiles while Mom snapped photos of us.

Olive and I carry our gift boxes in from where we set them by the door, most of which I ordered online and had shipped to the apartment. We spend the morning exchanging presents and eating the chocolate chip cookies while they're still warm.

I GAZE OUT into the backyard where Olive and I have spent hundreds of afternoons. The trees around the property line are more grown in, and the rose bushes lining the back fence are bigger and more beautiful than ever. They're currently dormant, but it doesn't take away from the expansive area or all the memories that were created back here.

I bring my hot cocoa up to my lips, basking in the warmth that rises from it while blowing on it for a minute before the chocolatey goodness smooths over my tongue. I sigh into the richness of the flavor at the same time the sliding door opens and closes.

"Little cold to be sitting out here, don't you think?" Dad slowly approaches the swing. It's big enough for four and was a custom piece he had built almost ten years ago. Before last summer, you could see the worn spots in the splintering wood. That was until Mom put a fresh coat of paint on it, and now, in a way, it almost feels brand new again.

I wrap the thick cozy blanket around me that I stole from the basket in the corner of the living room. It's been doing wonders keeping me warm along with my hot chocolate. "I don't mind."

He points at the spot next to me. We exchanged pleasant words during our gift exchange and a hug afterward, but I can see he's hesitating. He's still in his Christmas get-up. A matching set of thermals that have little Christmas trees printed all over them. He started wearing them for Olive and me when we were younger to make the holidays more exciting. I guess old habits die hard. I find myself missing the connection we had before everything turned to shit this past summer.

"Mind if I sit?"

"No. Go ahead."

The hanging seat sways back when he plops his weight down. Like me, he casts his attention over the backyard. "Lots of great memories out here."

"I was just thinking about that."

He sighs, and I know he wants to say something. We

haven't spoken since everything went up in flames a month ago. I've ignored texts. Forwarded calls to voicemail. I wasn't ready to discuss the elephant in the room, but if I've learned anything these past few weeks it's that things aren't always as they seem, and truths shouldn't be held for the sake of someone else.

"I know we haven't discussed things, and our relationship has been pulled taut."

I snicker. "That's one way of putting it."

"I don't want the strain, Violet. I love you and your sister. Your mom, too. Despite what you may think. What happened...well, it never should have. I feel terrible for doing that to you. It was your birthday, and I don't want to get into all the specifics, but I've known for a long time that I'm a borderline addict when it comes to..." He lets that last word hang in the air. I'm glad for it because *ew.* "I know that's uncomfortable to hear, so I'll leave it at that, but everyone has struggles they face. Including me and your mom. What makes our relationship strong is knowing that we don't have to face them alone."

"It's none of my business." I'm not sure how much more I can listen to without throwing up. I'm ready to move on. "You were right to tell me to stay out of it. Whatever challenges you face are for you and her to get through."

I take a deep breath, and for the first time in months, it feels like it finally reaches the deepest part of my lungs. To move on from his infidelity and openly talk about it without tension coiling in my body. It's progress I'm proud of.

"Thank you for saying that. Your mom and I haven't had a perfect marriage, but we love the hell out of each other. She has accepted who I am in all areas of my life, and I've done the same for her. Anyone else would have bailed. Not her.

Her love has gotten us over mountains and rescued us out of valleys. You remind me of her in that way."

"What do you mean?"

"Well," he clears his throat, "I just mean that your love is worth its weight in gold. Anyone would be lucky to have that from you. I know that's why you felt so horrible over that day and why you didn't want to talk to me for the longest time." He sighs deeply. "It doesn't take me being a rocket scientist to know I broke my little girl's heart."

"You did," I tell him, my voice quiet as I take another sip of my warm drink. My heart tugs a little in my chest, wanting a big hug in return for all the heartache. "I do love you so much, which is exactly why I took it so hard."

He nods. "I'm so sorry I took advantage of that. I'm sorry that it happened on your birthday, and I promise it'll never happen again. I fired Nina, and I'm…getting help. At the end of the day, you three are what's most important to me. It has always been that way."

I nibble on my lip and say three words I couldn't say months ago. "I forgive you."

He looks over at me, his hair swept back in a mess and a faint stubble growing over his cheeks that he'll wake up and shave tomorrow. "Yeah?"

"You're you. Can't be mad at you forever."

He huffs out a tiny chuckle. "Honestly, I thought you were going to be."

"Yeah, I was a bit bratty there for a minute."

"No, not bratty. You were hurt. And it was justified." He lifts his palm between us. "New slate, sweetheart?"

I smile and place my hand in his, glad to finally have a resting place for what happened. "New slate, old man."

We shake on it, and I scoot closer to him, offering him

half of my blanket. He situates it over his lap. I rest my head on his shoulder.

"I'm not that old," he balks.

"Eh, you're more gray now than anything." He sweeps his hand through his hair and kicks off the porch for us to swing back. "Just wait until Olive starts getting on your case about going bald."

"She better not," he says around a chuckle.

"Oh, she's going to. The second she notices your hair is receding," I click my tongue. "Done for."

He pats my leg and doesn't bother getting on my case about joking with him. That's the best thing about dads. You can beat up on them all day every day. Physically, emotionally, mentally. And they just continue to take it as if there's a shield covering their body and the teasing pings right off them.

When I glance up, he has a relieved expression on his face. So unlike how it was the last time we were out here. "You have no idea how happy this makes me. Us being okay again."

"I wasn't sure we'd get here, but I met someone, and his experiences have helped me learn that maybe I've been a little unfair."

"Met someone, huh?"

"It's complicated."

He pats my leg again. "All the best loves are."

THIRTY

COLSON

Old text messages...
Violet: Out of my mind missing you today.
Colson: If anyone is out of their mind, it's me.
Colson: Completely fucking crazy about you.
Violet: You like me that much, huh?
Colson: You don't even know.

MY CELL LIGHTS up my face, making the ache in my forehead worsen. Last night's fight was my first loss. I made the wrong move, didn't watch my balance as well as I should have, and lowered my fists at the perfect time for my opponent to knock the wind out of me. He also got me in the side of my head.

For a split second during the fight, I wondered if I'd see brown eyes when I looked up. A tiny part of me hoped I would.

It was enough for the dude to gain leverage. I've had a persistent pain in my head ever since. I've also had this nagging voice telling me to reach out to my girl. To respond to the text she sent me this morning, but I haven't pulled the trigger on it. I don't know if I should.

Actually, no, I do know.

I shouldn't.

I lied to her for the duration of our relationship. I'm in no better headspace than I was the day Mom died. I've collected all my mental shit in a black garbage bag and shoved it into a hole under the floorboards where I can't see or deal with it.

I want to lick my wounds in peace, without the sight of Violet's disappointment looking back at me. Though, that proves difficult because I see it every time I close my eyes.

I hate how much my need to see her has grown since the candy warehouse incident. Since she showed up to my fight and was kept warm by Finn's stupid fucking sweatshirt. I should've ripped it off her and tugged mine over her head instead. I should've pulled my head out of my ass and begged her for more than what she gave me. I should've gotten down on my hands and knees and requested forgiveness.

My stomach clenches, but I don't pay it much mind. I've gotten used to ignoring the underlying effects of my emotions. The physical symptoms that push in when I don't deal with what's going on inside.

Most importantly, I can't let her distract me. My focus needs to be elsewhere, like my fight tonight.

Tommy put me on the schedule despite the hits I took last night. Said it was my punishment, that the only way to learn the lesson of winning and earning him his money was to get back out there. When one of the guys spoke up about a possible head injury, he brushed it off. Said if I didn't want to worry about head injuries, that I should've never let my guard down to begin with.

I'm slowly learning that he might be a little fucked up. But it's also something to admire. Having that kind of conviction and tenacity with his fighters is exactly what makes them the best. What makes *me* the best. So, I shrugged it off and agreed to show up.

It's not like I have anything better to do.

Though, tonight, we're not convening at the candy warehouse. Someone ran their mouth and blew our cover. Tonight's location is being kept secret until an hour before the fights. Once the text comes through, I'll grab my shit and head out.

Until then, past me criticizes present me to make an appearance at my aunt and uncle's. I read over Violet's text one last time, pretend I answer, then shove my phone deep into my pocket. I head to the kitchen, grab a banana and protein bar, and leave through the front, driving in the direction of Chatham Hills.

I PULL into the long driveway outside of the Rodriguez household. Their brick house sits back on an acre and a half of land. The Christmas tree shines through the big bay windows in the front, and when I get out and walk across the front pathway to the door, I swear the smell of big happy smiles and warm delicious pie swirls in the air.

I walk through the front door without so much as a knock, like I've always done, and find Sebastian and his parents in the great room with *A Christmas Story* on the big screen. My cousin gives me a glance and, I'll be damned, even nods his chin in greeting. We haven't seen each other since the hand-around-the-neck incident, but it nearly turns me into a puddle because what kind of asshole would do such a thing?

My aunt and uncle would be horrified if they knew what happened that day.

Uncle Thad notices me next and motions for me to find a seat on the oversized sectional. I'm hesitant at first because I'm still pissed over what transpired at their lawyer's office. I'm beyond hurt that my own aunt kept my father from me. That all these years, I could've avoided a lot of wondering had she stayed out of it or, at the very least, told me.

The next hour passes with me watching the movie with them. We don't chat. Don't interrupt what the actors say or do.

As much as I want to feel out of place, I don't. This house has always felt like home. It's always been a safe haven from the chaos in and around my life. Even with everything going on, it's easy to melt into the couch and pretend like life is fine and dandy. I know I'll have to tear myself away at the end of the night. Right back into the shitstorm. To Mom being gone. To The Battleground. To ruining my relationships with the people I love.

When the credits start rolling, Aunt Bess is the first to make a move. She walks over to the tree, snatches a gift under it, and places it in my lap on her way back over to Uncle Thad. "We didn't know what to do for you this year. I think all of us have been a little scrambled, but it's something."

"You didn't have to do this." My eyes catch on the envelope taped to the small rectangular box. I don't want to know what's inside.

"We wanted to, Colson," she says. "Open it. Please."

All eyes are on me as I push my finger under one of the corners of the paper and tear it. My hands go clammy when I flip the gift over, yank off the rest of the paper and see Mom.

It's only a picture, but fuck. She looks so young in it. Her smile is stretched wide, and her palm is splayed out on her round belly. There are crinkles next to her eyes from elation. Most of all, she looks healthy.

My eyes sting with sadness, with happiness, with every fucking emotion under the sun. I miss her, and no one knows how badly I wish I could've gotten this version of her. The *clean* version. The version that was free-spirited and carefree, yes, but also loved and cared for those around her.

For *me*.

"Janie always did what she wanted, even back then, but she was close to her true self there. It's the oldest photo I have of her looking that way." Aunt Bess explains. "I wish we all would've gotten more of that."

I trace my thumb over her face.

"I think that's how we should remember her. How she looks in that picture. So happy and excited for the future. She was seven months pregnant with you, and…" She clears her throat, and I know seeing her is getting to her. "And she was just so excited to meet you."

I'd do anything to make this picture reality. To transform her from paper to person. It's a stab to the chest knowing I can't. Knowing that I miss her so goddamn much but can't do a thing about it.

Her reliance on her addiction was always the most important thing in the room. All the times she shoved me to the side, didn't fill the house with groceries, or made me feel a certain way. Now that she's gone, none of that seems to matter as much.

In a sad, fucked up way, I sort of wish I was still dealing with all of it. Because if I were, it would mean I'd still have her.

Now I'm alone in the trenches.

"Thank you," I mutter, pressing a knuckle to my eyelid and swiping the wetness away. I don't look my aunt or uncle in the eye as I ball up the wrapping paper and set it to the side.

"There's more," Uncle Thad announces. "In the envelope."

I dip my chin and open that, too. It's your standard holiday card. I flip it open, bypass the cheesy heartfelt poem and see a check.

Each line has Uncle Thad's scripted handwriting, and in the little rectangular box on the right is a one with four zeros behind it.

I look up at them—*What the fuck?*—then back down to the check. "What's this?"

Aunt Bess sighs. "It's what you used to pay off your mother's debt with Clyde. You shouldn't have had to deal with that on your own. I wish you wouldn't have been so scared to come to us. And since you won't be receiving her inheritance, we thought it'd be nice for you to have it back."

I snap the card closed and just like that her words stir a tsunami inside me. Water pelts my skin. Anxiety builds in my chest. "I don't want this."

Aunt Bess looks taken aback. Uncle Thad sits forward on the edge of the couch, elbows resting on his knees. Sebastian is so damn quiet I forget he's in the room with us.

"What do you mean?" asks my aunt, taking offense.

"I mean exactly what I just said...I don't want it." My jaw clenches. I'm pissed all over again at her for keeping shit from me. But how upset am I allowed to be? We both kept stuff from each other. That doesn't keep me from saying, "You can't buy my forgiveness. You can't give me a check for ten grand after the news drops that you paid Clyde to stay away from me all these years." My voice cracks, but fuck it. "I could've had a father figure in my life, but you kept that from me."

"She did it to keep you safe," my uncle says in that deep yet reserved voice of his.

"No she didn't. She did it for herself."

"Had I not done it, he would've eventually swooped in and convinced you to get into that lifestyle of his," she explains despite the hurt written in her eyes.

"How do you figure?" My brows pull tight. "He wanted nothing to do with me, anyway. Hell, maybe he would've stayed away entirely on his own."

She shakes her head as if she doesn't believe that to be true. "Maybe when you were smaller, but then he would've pounced on you. He would've dug his claws in and hooked you."

I look at her. "I don't understand how you're so sure knowing what he would've done."

"I know because it's what happened with your mom. With Finn as well."

I blink. "What are you talking about?"

Ever since I can remember, Finn always leaned into his upbringing. He was calloused long before we ever hit adulthood. Clyde's lifestyle was imprinted on him the second he was born. So what the fuck is Aunt Bess going on about? Why is she talking about them like she's been in their lives all these years?

Like she knows them.

What else is she keeping from me?

"Finn's mom fell pregnant with him months before your mom found out she was having you. He had a reputation for cheating when we were in high school and ran around on Janie, which is why I never cared for him much. I bumped into Finn's mom once years later in Harrison Heights. At the grocery store on the corner near your mom's."

I huff out an exasperated breath. "Wow, every time I see you, I learn something new."

"It was one of the times your mom just got out of rehab. I brought her home and stopped there before getting on the 401 to come home. You and Finn were young, but she warned me that while Clyde might not have wanted you then, that he had plans to recruit you for his drug running once you were old enough to take care of yourself. She told me that he'd sweep in, put on his charm long enough to convince you, and that'd be that. She was sick over him already having an influence on Finn at the time." My aunt purses her lips. "I wasn't going to risk the same thing happening to you. I wasn't going to risk *losing* you, Colson."

"So that was that? You just believed every word she was saying to be true?"

"You might not understand it, but she was coming to me as a mother, as a nurturer. I could tell she had already lost her baby boy to Clyde's money-hungry greed and illegal activities. The look on her face when she spoke to me...she was grieving the loss of a son she never truly had but had to raise each and every day, anyway."

"That doesn't make what you did okay."

"I didn't say that it did, but I wanted the best for you, so I did what I thought was right at the time. I did what I thought would keep you safe because your mom was already long gone by then. She didn't care enough to keep you out of trouble, so I did it for her. It's what family does."

I don't know what to trust.

What to believe.

I look down at the check again. I think about the money she must've handed over to Clyde to keep him at bay. I think about all the missed opportunities. Of what it would have been like to have a dad to turn to growing up. All the things I should have had but never got.

I reconsider the few interactions I've had with Clyde. I imagine the hardness in his stare when Finn nearly drove me off the road near the battery plant. I hear his cold voice in the back of the car before Finn broke my finger. And I hear his condescending tone in Stewart's office. The way he was so sure of himself. The fact that he didn't give a damn that he was taking something that wasn't his. That he did it in a way that proved his lack of conscience.

I think about his love for money and how Aunt Bess might be right. It'll always overshadow his care for me. Beyond that, part of me wants to forgive her for doing what she did. But then the other part is still so damn pissed over her ripping that choice out of my hands when I was so little. For never giving me the chance to make my own decision on the matter.

"It wasn't right," is what I murmur next. "None of that should've happened."

She scoots to the edge of her seat. "It shouldn't have, but it did. I understand that it might take time for you to forgive me. It's difficult to process, but always know that I did it for your own well-being. I did it because I love you. And yes, I also did it selfishly because I wanted you in *our* lives. I didn't want to risk that being taken from you or us."

She stands then, walks over to me, and leans down to

wrap her arms around my shoulders. Like the asshole I've been lately, I don't hug her back, but that doesn't stop her from whispering, "Merry Christmas," into my ear. Then she rounds the sectional and disappears up the staircase.

Uncle Thad follows her a moment later, but not before giving me a comforting shoulder squeeze to scare away all the doubt I'm treading.

The water is so close to my mouth, I can sense the sharp twinges of pain that'll come when it enters my lungs. I never expected so much turmoil out of Mom's death, but it literally ripped the rug out from under us. I think we've all felt like our feet have been in the air ever since.

Is it always going to be like this?

Am I always going to feel so out of control, so empty, so *alone*? Or will a time come when the tides turn and the water spits me out?

Sebastian moves to a sitting position once his dad leaves the room. "Surprised you even decided to show."

"You're not the only one."

There were a handful of moments I wondered if showing my face was worth it.

"How've you been?" he asks.

This awkward tension zips through the room. It's sporadic and doesn't flow in a straight line. I know I need to address that night, to apologize for the shitty way I handled myself.

I turn my face in his direction but don't look him in the eye. "I shouldn't have put my hands on you."

"But you did."

"Yeah, I did," I admit.

"Do you feel like shit about it?"

"More than you know."

He slaps his hands against his thighs and stands. "I guess we have nothing to worry about then."

I glance up. "Seriously? You're letting it go that easily?"

He shrugs. "If you're apologizing, it means you regret it ever happening. Besides, I fucked up, too. I shouldn't have egged you on like I did. I should've kept Violet's name out of my mouth even though you were insistent on pushing her away."

I *was* insistent on pushing her away.

I still am.

Even though she's taken away my ability to keep her close.

Sebastian's taunting from back then bothers me all the same. His words curl around me but instead of making me angry, they just make me feel pathetic. So damn pathetic that I have to rub my palm against my chest to shoo away the ache.

"You fix things with her yet?" Sebastian prods, pulling me from his taunting jabs that night.

"No."

"You should if you know what's good for you."

I shake my head. "She knows everything that went down. The shit with Finn and Mom's dealings with him and Clyde. I kept it from her, and she's pissed over it."

"She cares about you too much to allow herself to stay pissed at you for long."

Thoughts of Violet push into my head. All the time I've spent with her. Getting to wake up with her each morning with my arm around her waist. Feeling her silky skin against mine. Tasting her. Comforting her. Consuming her.

Loving her.

How she gave me it all straight back. How she always knew when to say things and when to offer me silence. How she'd trail her fingertip up my stomach and over my shoulders when we'd lay our sweaty bodies back on her sheets after taking everything we could from one another.

She's only ever been my truest and safest space, and my heart knows that as it twinges with sharp steadfast palpitations. And then it falls to the pit in my stomach because I know—*it* knows—that Sebastian is wrong.

I've already lost her.

THIRTY-ONE

COLSON

IF IT WEREN'T for the kid on the treadmill across the way and Llewellyn's niece Kelsie at the front counter, I'd have Gulliver's to myself. The entire floor and the silence that comes with it. I'm kind of wishing it were the case because my headphones are dead, and Treadmill Kid has been playing some weird angsty boxing playlist from his phone. I think he thinks it isn't that loud, but the volume is high enough that it's getting under my skin.

I need fucking silence.

To go at the bag without worrying about it punching back. That, and it's been a week since Tommy has had a fight for me. Tomorrow is New Year's Eve, and I need something to hang onto other than my own reality and the fact that I'll be entering an entirely new year without Mom alive.

Not to mention, Finn keeps showing his face at the house.

Three nights ago, he was waiting on the porch when I came home. I ignored him. Pretended he was nothing more than a giant piece of garbage wasting space before unlocking the door and slamming it behind me.

Two nights ago, he was there again. With a cigarette

pinched between his lips, he leaned against the dirty siding and nodded at me when I climbed the front steps. I stopped for half a second, watched him blow smoke from his mouth and did a repeat of the night before.

Ignore.

Unlock door.

Slam door.

Go about my business.

Easy peasy, right?

Yeah, not so much. Even though I had nothing to say to him, he has managed to get in my head. I've lost sleep over him trying to push himself into my life. I don't know why he's trying.

I lay in bed at night thinking what life would have been like if I had a brother. I guess in a sense I did. I had Sebastian, but it's different. Sebastian's upbringing was so distinctly opposite from mine that it would have been nice to have someone to understand what I was going through. Who could relate to having a fucked-up family life with a parent who only cared about themselves.

Then I recall the last few months. The way Finn treated me. The way he abused my love for Mom and threatened us if we didn't pay back her debt.

I don't trust him.

I *can't* trust him.

Which only makes it worse that he's brought Violet into this shit. Bringing her into Coco's Chocolates was a mistake, and I'm just waiting for it to catch up to us.

Treadmill Kid's music changes. It's some angsty teenage bullshit song. I pound my fists into my bag harder, ignoring the sweat that drips down the side of my face. My arms ache in protest with each hit, my muscles sore from the continuous strain I've put on them with little upkeep on my part. My sleep has been crap. My nutrition, too. I'm not taking care of myself, but at least my head isn't hurting anymore.

A crumb of a blessing in a dumpster of baked goods.

I finish my combo and drop to the bench near the bags. The front door chimes, but I don't pay much attention to it. People come and go all the time. A blur of black enters the corner of my sight and sits next to me.

"Think they'll mind if I get in a few jabs?" Treadmill Kid's music fades out, my half brother's voice turning into the only sound I hear.

"Leave," I snap.

"Well, that's rude."

"I don't give a fuck. You're not welcome here."

"Says who?" Finn looks around. "You?"

"Obviously."

He smirks and pushes his hair back. My eyes drop to the fresh ink on the side of his neck. Shame the needle didn't go just a *little* deeper. "How the hell is this place still running when there's only two of you in here?"

"There's three of us." It's pointless to mention, but for some reason I don't want to exclude Kelsie. Maybe the sympathetic part of me feels bad for ignoring her most of the time. I glance in her direction. She has her hair in an updo and is rocking a Gulliver's Gym & Ring polo, except hers is a different shade of gray than mine.

"Ah, yeah." Finn's gaze follows mine, and it doesn't take a genius to see the way he checks her out. I suddenly wish she wasn't there at all. Her copper red hair only makes it worse. I'd be lying if I said she wasn't pretty. She has a softness to her, similar to Violet, that I can't help but notice. She's shy, usually quiet aside from greeting whoever comes and goes. And she has this blinding smile with perfect straight teeth that tattle on her for having braces growing up.

"Pretty little redhead, isn't she?" Finn observes.

I don't answer him.

"I had a major thing for redheads when I was a teenager." I don't know why he's telling me this. I grab the bottle of water from my bag and start chugging. "Jessica Chastain. Emma Stone." He nods at her then glances over. "You get in that yet?"

I give him a hard-pressed, "No."

Why the hell would he ask me that when he knows I was with Violet?

"Why the fuck not? Ah." He grins. "Holding out for Violet again, aren't you? Hoping she'll eventually see past this toddler tantrum you're having and take you back?"

"Fuck off, Finn."

"Now we both know you don't want that."

I cap my water bottle. "It's exactly what I want."

"You mean to tell me that you haven't liked seeing my handsome mug at your house at all hours of the night?"

Sinking my bottle in the side pocket of my bag, I grab my gloves and shove them in the open pocket. I zip it up then toss the strap over my shoulder. No point in hanging around when one of my biggest stressors is three feet away from me.

He follows, and my irritation over him being near escalates like that carnival game where you whack the hammer against the big red button and the little thingy flies skyward. Kelsie gives us a timid wave and soft smile as we push through the doors and make it outside.

I don't bother waving back.

"Come on," he draws out. "Forgetting we're brothers?"

"No," I say to him. "We're not."

"Pretty sure we are, so you're gonna have to get used to it, Moore."

I twist on my heel, damn near ready to shove him up

against the old siding of the building. The only reason I don't is because I respect Llewellyn too much to cause a scene in front of his establishment. Hell, if he knew Finn was poking his snout around, he'd have a fit about that alone.

My blood morphs into smoldering hot lava as I stand in front of him and growl out, "I don't have to get used to shit. You need to stay away from me. We're nothing alike and whatever game you're playing at, I'm not interested."

I take a step closer. He holds his ground because he's Finn. I'm not stupid enough to think that he'd cower to me. The smirk playing on his face does drop, though. I consider it a bigger win than making his knees buckle.

"Remember when I told you I was done with you in the back of your car on the strip? I wasn't fucking around, and I'm not now, either. We're *not* brothers. We weren't three months ago. We're not now. We never will be."

"You keep forgetting that it was kept from me, too. I'm not saying we have to be best friends. Fuck, I don't entirely know what the hell I'm doing but…"

I don't know why I do it, but I ask. "But what?"

He grits his teeth. "He always preaches that blood is permanent and how it's the one thing you never cross. You fuck with family, and you pay the consequences."

I stare at him for a long second and then the sound barrels up my chest and pours out of my mouth. I wouldn't stop it even if I wanted to. I laugh. It's sudden and deep and hearty. He stares at me, but I can't help it. He actually thinks he can take back everything he did?

I don't fucking think so.

His audacity is truly admirable.

"I don't know what's so goddamn funny," he mutters.

"You," I tell him. "You are. You think you can come around, share some bullshit sob story about how you were raised by the same man who bailed on me and enabled my mom's drug habit and think that," I snap my finger, "it's enough to wipe the slate clean? That it's enough to erase the fuckery you've caused and kickstart some kind of brotherly bond you're suddenly searching for?" I pause for effect. "Well, I hate to break it to you, *Brother*, but you're shit out of luck on this one. Your guilty conscience is on you this time, not me."

THIRTY-TWO

COLSON

"TOMMY WAS OFF HIS ROCKER TONIGHT," Eli says as he comes up behind me and pulls a shirt over his head. He sent me a text, inviting me over to his place for a beer when I got back from Gulliver's. And because of Finn irritating the hell out of me, I said what the hell, why not?

Except Eli forgets to mention that he rents a room in a crowded house. Claims there's no point in renting one on his own when he spends most of his time training at the gym or out.

And I get that but these people he lives with? They weren't considerate when I arrived. No one greeted me, which honestly, I'm fine with. But the two people making out on the couch could have at least put clothes on. Or maybe even just left the common area.

It reminds me an awful lot like a halfway home, especially when some dude walks out from the back hallway and starts yelling at the couple on the couch and bitches at a guy in the kitchen scrambling eggs.

That's about when Eli brought me back to his room. It's a decent size and smells a lot better than it did out there.

There's a bed on one side of the room, a couch on the other. A flat screen is mounted on the wall above his dresser, and there's a few odds and ends floating around.

"Oh yeah?"

Eli went out earlier for a fight. I didn't show up to watch.

"Fucking out of his mind." He grabs a can of beer from his mini fridge, pops it, and hands it over. I shrug off the thought that comes when I take a sip. The one that says this isn't me. I don't go out at all hours of the night. I don't make drinking a regular habit. I don't kick back with guys who are one bad decision away from ending up in a hospital room or jail cell. And Eli? He's hugging both lines.

"Why? What'd he do?" I ask.

"Nearly had it out with Remy because he lost. The dumbass rolled his ankle two hours before he had to go out to fight. Didn't tell Tommy."

"Was it bad enough to sit out?"

Eli grabs a can for himself. His eyes fall shut when he plops down on the couch next to me and guzzles some. "Could barely walk."

I wince.

"It gets worse," Eli says.

"He decided to fight and lose?"

"He couldn't shuffle. Couldn't balance out his weight properly. Only made it to the beginning of the second round before his ankle gave out and his opponent took him out."

"Glad I wasn't there if shit hit the fan."

He hangs his arm over the side of the couch. "Tommy turns into another fucking person when he doesn't get what he wants. Even worse when people keep shit from him."

"Starting to see that."

Which only makes Finn come to mind again. With Violet in the same room as me, he warned me about Tommy. Told me that he wouldn't just let me go when I wanted out of The Battleground. I'm not looking for an out currently, but what if a day comes when I change my mind? What if I get my head out of my ass and go back to wanting to make something of myself? What then? Is Tommy going to shackle me down and force me to do what he wants? Is he going to take me out if I go against him?

Eli glances over. "You still knocking your socks off with it?"

I gulp down another mouthful of beer. It tastes like cold piss. "It's working for me right now." Finn's voice grows louder in my ears, and I find myself questioning Eli. "What about you? See yourself doing these fights forever?"

It comes out all calm and nonchalant, but inside my body is buzzing. I don't want him giving me an answer that validates what Finn told me. Because if he does, that means there's substance behind what Finn's claiming.

I don't want a reason to trust him.

Don't want to believe that he is looking out for me.

"I'm a fighter for life," he says. There's noise outside of the room. Someone shouting. I glance over at the door when Eli continues. "Knew that when I was still in high school. Why do you think I came in with a busted face half the time?"

"Were you fighting for Tommy back then?"

"I knew a kid who knew a kid and got introduced. A lot of shit went on back then and while I love getting in an actual ring, the elusiveness of his fights always made me light up." He shrugs and lifts his beer can to his lips. "Money's not bad, either."

I'm suddenly spinning down a spiral staircase of memories.

Mom's debt to the Lincoln's.

Ten grand in their greedy palms.

Over a hundred thousand dollars that was meant to be mine in the hands of a deadbeat father who never wanted me. Who has treated me like the shit stains lining the insides of a toilet bowl.

My chest grows tight, and just like that, I'm up out of my seat. I can't sit here anymore. I hand my beer to a very confused looking Eli. He takes it, but his brows pinch together. "What's going on, man?"

"Forgot I have a place I need to be."

Only there is no place.

I just need to get the hell out of here. I need to get out of this weird ass house and fall into bed where it feels safe. I need to get Finn's voice out of my head because I can't stand that he's trying to be there after everything he did. I need to get Clyde's dark eyes out of my thoughts before I go ballistic because the facts are simple: he took Mom's inheritance from my grandmother's death, and he's going to take the house, too. It's only a matter of time before the timer runs out, and I have nowhere else to go.

Eli glances at the watch on his wrist. It's shiny and new, a piece he treated himself with last week when he hit a new personal record. I don't ask him what the deal is with it. Everything else about him is used and worn. "You sure? Kinda late to have anywhere to be."

No, I'm not fucking sure, but I throw up a peace sign in response and walk out of his bedroom. The old dude from earlier is pounding on someone else's bedroom door as I make it down the hallway. He doesn't spare me a glance. My guess is this happens often. New faces coming and going, and there he is, trying to get a handle on whatever the fuck.

I push outside and jog my way to my car at the curb. My chest grows increasingly heavy with each breath. My hands tremble as I get inside, my heart racing like a stallion in an open field. I blink past the blurring in my vision and start my decrepit Ford. It purrs to life, and amazingly, I return back to the house without sideswiping the cars parked on the street.

My body feels like it's been thrown around and bounced off brick walls for the last fifteen minutes. My breaths are shallow, and I do my best to deepen them. It's difficult, though, because when I glance up and look out the window of my car, Finn is on the porch.

Again.

For the third night in a row.

After I told him hours ago at Gulliver's that he's nothing to me.

What the fuck is his problem?

It only strengthens these newfound sensations moving through me. My arms tense down to my wrists. My stomach suddenly turns like it wants to hurl up the few sips of beer I drank at Eli's.

I press my thumbs into my eyes and try not to think about the dull ache that's moving into my cranial cavity. I get out of the car and make it up the porch steps. My goal is simple: get past Finn as quickly as possible. *Get inside and remember how to breathe.*

"You look like shit," says Finn as I amble up the steps and unlock the front door. "I'll be here if you need a little brotherly love," is all I hear as I slam the door in his stupid face and trudge my way across the living room.

I stop in the kitchen for a quick drink, the old cookie jar I'm using to store my fighting money mocking me. I found it in the back of Mom's closet when I was looking for my birth certificate. The mouse on the front reminds me of afternoons I spent watching *Tom and Jerry* as a kid.

I nearly choke on my water from trying to breathe

through the onslaught of whatever this is and turn my back on the piece of ceramic.

Finn's words pirouette in my head.

I'll be here if you need a little brotherly love.

I'll be here if you need a little brotherly love.

I'll be here if you need a little brotherly love.

There is one person I need, but it's not Finn.

THIRTY-THREE

COLSON

SOMEWHERE IN MY haze of setting down my glass and moving to Mom's room, I end up with my phone in hand, the lock screen long gone as my fingers move over its brightness. I click open my messaging app and look at the last message she sent.

Merry Christmas.

Nothing has come through since. I never did reply to it, so she most likely got the message loud and clear that I have nothing to say. I wrestle with wanting to tap out a few quick words but find my thumb hovering over the tiny phone icon at the top of the thread and do the exact opposite of what I've been preaching.

I call her.

I fucking *call* Violet.

It's late and the room is dark, but I sit back on the bed as my phone rings. I don't turn on the lamp, too afraid that if I illuminate the space, I'll back out and hang up before I hear her voice. And I *need* to hear it. I need it to invade my head. I need it to soothe away the tightness in my chest and the crisp, sharp pains moving up the hollow of my neck.

Just when I think it's going to go to voicemail, I hear a hushed, "Hello?"

My eyes fall shut and a sense of relief washes over me. It's easy to pretend she's here with me when the room is so dark. I rest my head back on the wall and imagine her next to me. Her leg tossed over mine as she presses her cheek to my chest. The way she melts into me when I wrap her in my arms. The warmth that encases me when her subtle, flowery scent wafts over me and invades my senses.

I realize I haven't said a word when she lets out a worried, "Colson?"

"Yeah, hey, sorry." It all comes out in one hoarse breath, my heart beating wildly against my ribcage.

"You sound weird. Are you okay?"

"Been better," I admit, pulling in a deep breath.

"Seems to be life lately."

"Yeah."

The line goes silent. I appreciate it when she doesn't badger me over calling. She's being way more patient than I'd be, especially this grief-ridden, heartbroken version of me. "Sorry, I just…I needed to hear your voice."

"It's fine," she declares, even though it's not. None of this is fine. Treating her like shit isn't fine. Lying to her wasn't fine, either. "This is what friends do for each other."

I wince at that statement.

The *f* word.

The one I don't want to hear.

I bypass it and ask, "Tell me about your day?"

"Sure," she says easily, as if she didn't admit to not knowing who I am the last time we were together. "Olive is here so we've be—"

"Your sister is in Georgia?"

"She is." I can hear the smile in her voice. "I chose not to spend my entire break back at my parents, so she decided to stay with me so I didn't spend the break totally alone. It was sweet of her, really. I'm happy I get to see her."

"I'm sensing a but coming," I mutter, trying to get in deep breaths.

"She's just...hang on a second." There's ruffling on the other line, and I hear what I'd guess to be a door clicking shut. And then another one. "Sorry. We were hanging out earlier and she fell asleep in my room. I didn't want to wake her. Anyway...she kind of showed up out of nowhere. Didn't tell me or my parents that she was planning to stay with me. I'm trying not to be the overbearing big sister, but I'd be lying if I said I haven't thought about something being up with her."

"She loves you," I remind her. "I'm sure if anything was going on, you'd be the first person she'd come to."

"Yeah," she breathes out. "Maybe. The guys are having this get together tomorrow for New Year's Eve. She's adamant that we go."

My shoulders relax and the intensity in my tightening muscles waver, too. Hearing her talk about her sister and whatever else is exactly what I need. The perfect distraction. *As always.*

"You don't want to go?" I ask her.

"Um, no, not really."

"Why not?"

"Things have been kind of too much lately. I'd rather just be alone." A tiny twinge of discomfort hits me in the center of my chest. Her heartbreak ricochets through the phone, and suddenly I'm feeling it, too. The hairline fractures settling into my bones are nothing if not agonizing. "How have you been? Still fighting?"

Yes, I'm still fighting...

Against my grief.

Against knowing who my father is.

But also with my fists with no plans of stopping.

"Yeah," I choke out.

"Why?" she quickly asks. "Why are you doing this to yourself, Colson?"

I run my hand over my forehead and into my hair. The darkness of the room encases me in a cocoon. It makes me feel like I don't have to watch what I say. Like I'm free and it's okay, if only for these short moments.

"It numbs me," I tell her, figuring honesty is key at this point. I kept too much from her before and don't see the point in doing it any longer. I breathe through another ragged breath. "It just...I don't feel anything when I'm doing it." It's the best thing I've been able to give myself since Mom died. The truest and most honest form of reprieve.

After her, of course.

"You don't have to cover up how you feel when it's completely normal."

Normal or not... "I didn't ask to experience this, Vi, and it's crippling. I've pushed myself to do a lot of things in my life. Hell, I scrounged up ten grand to keep her safe, but I can't do this. I can't wake up each morning with this insurmountable misery knocking the breath out of me each step."

"You *can*. And you don't have to do it alone."

"I'm a nuclear bomb, Violet. Anything I do or say, there's a ten-mile radius under the fallout. You saw it for yourself the last time you were with me."

"It's not too late to make better choices for yourself. You taught me that, remember?"

I do.

When she wasn't sure what to do about her dad's cheating, I told her that it wouldn't help matters if she continued to drag it out. That, at any given moment, she could make a choice to relieve herself of the discomfort it caused. And she did. She told her family after months of living in fear.

"Your shit wasn't as fucked up as mine."

"I didn't know we were comparing." There's an edge of hurt in her words, and for a moment, I think she's going to hang up.

"We're not, it's just...*fuck.*"

"You can hang up, Colson. Really, it's okay. You don't have to apologize, because I know you're going through something and the reason you're saying these things is due to the film it's casting on you. That's not to say it doesn't hurt. Just that I understand."

A beat passes. "I don't want to hang up. I also don't understand how you're being so decent to me after finding out everything I kept from you. I'm doing shit I would have never done before..." Before Mom died. "But...I don't know. I was with a friend tonight. We were hanging out and then all of a sudden, I couldn't fucking breathe."

"You couldn't breathe?" There's alarm in her voice.

"I'm better now." I really am. Her voice has done the trick like I knew it would. It's taken over my senses and calmed me. I mostly just feel exhausted now with the remnants of an upset stomach. "But it took calling you to get me there. I miss my mom, and it's all so fucked up because I shouldn't. All the shit she did... Sometimes I wonder if I shouldn't miss her at all, but then this love for her pours through me and..."

"And what?"

"I'm left realizing I'd go through it all over again. I'd go through all the bullshit again if it meant that she could come back."

She sighs, but she's not upset with me. She's listening, letting me lean on her in a way she's asked for since my mom died. I don't know why I choose tonight to let her in when I've pushed her away every other time she's tried being there for me. Maybe it's because I want her to know that I *am* the man she got to know. That just because I lied to her doesn't mean I'm a different person entirely.

I'm still me.

"Then there's you, and if there's anyone I miss just as much as her, it's you. I miss you so fucking much, Vi. I *hate* seeing you because it makes me feel shit I don't want to give attention to. The other night when you showed up with Finn, it wrecked me. Seeing you in his sweatshirt? You know how badly I wanted to rip it off you and cover you with mine? How hard it was to hold myself back from touching you after I shattered you to fucking pieces?"

"Colson—"

"No, I know. I did this. I lied to you. I pushed you away. I told you I wanted nothing to do with you, but I don't know how to be with you right now. I can't taint the way you shine. My darkness will devour your light, right now, Violet. It will, and I can't do that. I *can't*. I can't be the one who diminishes how goddamn gorgeous and amazing and *perfect* you are."

But I also need you.

I need you so fucking badly.

I let out a shaky breath. My plan wasn't to drop all this on her. I just wanted to hear her voice. Pretend for a moment that I was the old me and she was still mine.

"Colson, I can't…"

I can't do this with you anymore.

A long moment passes before I reply. "I know, Vi."

Then I murmur a goodbye and end the call.

THIRTY-FOUR

COLSON

A FIST COMES at my face, and it's quick as a motherfucker. I don't see it coming, but that might be because it's my first fight in about a week. I'm starting to wonder if Tommy has something against me. I've never gone with so much time in between since I started, and he's been giving me looks that aren't exactly friendly.

I don't know what I did to him, but he's acting like I took a giant dump in his Cheerios.

He always works with the other ringleaders for equal pair ups. But tonight? Non-fucking-existent. I'm pissed because he could've at least given me a heads up. He could've pulled me to the side and told me to watch my back, to cinch my elbows in tighter, and lean into my weight for more powerful hits, especially since if I lose, he doesn't get paid, which then becomes *my* problem.

A grunt leaves me when I strike my opponent back. I'm big in stature at over six foot, but I swear this guy has a solid foot on me, which only means he has that much more muscle. I look like a hobbit compared to Bigfoot. My lack of control has my anxiety at an all-time high. I've made sacrifices to be here, to do this, and this is how Tommy does me?

It's fucked up, even if it is my choice to continue.

I make sure my fists are quick, my feet quicker. It gets me so far, but the dude is too big for me to gain a real advantage. Two steps, and he has me along the edges of tonight's ring.

Since the candy warehouse was ruined for us, we're underground in an old car park located near the 401 that's been out of service for ages. I don't think it's structurally sound enough for us to be down here, but then again, none of us care if the concrete decides to crumble around us.

I bob and weave until he hits me with a corkscrew across my jaw. It knocks me back. I thankfully catch myself, but I don't miss the sting that spreads over my face. He grins at me, the sadistic fuck, and when he pulls his hands back up to protect his face, I find blood on his knuckles. *My* blood.

It lights a fire under me, and I go at him hard, psyching him out so I can hit him with a cross, but if I'm being honest, my head is spinning. A dizziness takes over, and it's all I can do to stay on my feet until he ends the fight with a haymaker. It's a wild one, but I see it coming. I don't react fast enough.

I fall flat on my back, the cold, wet concrete soaking my clothes from the last rain we had. Even with coverage, it still managed to get inside the parking garage. I thought it'd be smart to dress in moveable sweats and a basic tee, but I regret it the more the fabric absorbs the water and soaks my skin. I'm overheating so I might not care a ton now, but when I come down from the adrenaline, it's going to suck.

The crowd circling us screams, yelling like a bunch of banshees. It never gets old, hearing the chants and clapping. It's not right. Fucked up beyond a reasonable doubt, but I can't say I don't use it to motivate me.

My contender raises a fist and spits. It lands on the

ground next to me. My jaw clenches. I'm not about to get up, break The Battleground rules, and challenge him, so I act like it didn't happen.

My body thrums from the ass beating he doled out, but I take my loss for what it is. I don't cower but push up on my hands and knees and get to my feet. I push through a section of the crowd when they part and make it over to the side where Tommy and his other fighters stand. There aren't separate rooms to hide away in out here.

"Couldn't take him?" Remy chuckles and shakes his head at me. "Maybe next time, Pretty Boy." When he tries to ruffle my hair, I shove his hand away and seek out my bag. I crouch to the ground and pull out the small medic container I keep there for situations like this. I pour alcohol on a clean towelette and smooth it against the cut at the corner of my mouth until I can clean it better when I get home.

The rubbing alcohol only enhances the sting. I grit my teeth against it until it fades away then toss it back into my bag and pull my hoodie over my damp shirt.

A closed fist comes into vision, and when I look up, I see Eli. I knock my knuckles against his. "That looked tough."

The same irritation I felt during the fight comes over me. "It was bullshit. That guy was twice my size."

"I wouldn't say he was that big, but definitely out of your weight class."

My eyes move to my boss about forty feet away. His attention is focused on the next fight about to start. We've been moving through the rounds quickly. Probably because we're not in closed quarters. Best thing to do is get through our matches before anyone gets wind that we're down here.

Eli catches my line of sight. "I'd be careful if I were you."

I narrow my eyes on him. "Why? He could've given me a heads up."

"Yeah, but that's not the kind of dude he is. Is what it is, bro." He clasps his hand on my shoulder. "You alright, though?"

I'm suddenly aggravated over the fact that he doesn't seem to care. In a way, Tommy did me dirty. If he makes a promise, he should learn to keep it. The way none of the other guys seem to care or notice? It's uncanny and makes me think of Finn yet again.

"I'm good."

"You ran out on me fast last night."

"What the hell do you care?" I grind out, not liking the way he switches the topic.

He raises his palms in surrender. "Just sharing an observation."

I clear my throat, guilt and irritation swirling inside me. "I told you I had somewhere to be."

"Yeah, okay. No problem, man. Just checking in with you."

"I don't need a check-in," I spit at him. "I'm fine."

He nods and eyes me warily, as if he doesn't believe me. I don't give a shit if he does. Not when I'm reeling over this fight and how it felt an awful lot like I was blindsided. My eyes cut to Tommy once more. As much as I try to block out the volume of the people around, my body vibrates with their chants and chatter.

The end of the night comes quickly. In an hour the ball is going to drop, and I'll be rolling into the new year with the shit of the last few months trailing behind me like a caboose. And yet all I care about is the moment everyone breaks apart and the crowd starts following the road back above ground. I've been waiting for this moment all night. For the chance to figure out what the hell tonight's fight was about.

When we're called over to collect our winnings, I know

I'm walking away empty-handed. I lost fair and square. I may be salty over Bigfoot, but that's what happens when you have the advantage, and he had it on me. He had the size, the strength, and me being off guard.

So, for that, cool.

For Tommy pulling a fast one on me, not cool.

I'm mixed in with a group of guys. Remy is to my left, running his mouth like always. He was one of the first fights of the night and pulled off his win before the third round started. Tommy calls his name and Remy's smile is the size of a canoe. Cold hard cash is slapped in his hand. "Thank you very much," sings Remy as he strides away, a pep in his step even though we all know he's going to blow it at the closest casino he can find.

"Keep fighting like you are." Tommy's eyes scan to the crowd. "All of you keep fighting and winning, and you'll always find yourself walking away with this sweetness." He raises a bundle of dollar bills and smacks them in his palm.

I'm the only one tonight *not* getting paid. And I mean, it may not be about the money for me, but it still sucks. I watch everyone take their winnings. Remy flaunts his, bragging to no end how good he is. Eli takes his quietly. He doesn't have much to say outside of getting on my case.

When everyone has collected their winnings, they disperse into the night. They trail up the road leading above ground, but I hang back. Tommy and the dude who trails him like a shadow—it reminds me a lot like Finn and his goons— hover by their car, an old school Cadillac with shiny, expensive rims that could use a paint job. It probably wasn't smart for them to drive it down here. I'm sure Tommy insisted. It offers him protection, a quick getaway, if need be, though I'm not sure how far he'd get.

I approach him, my hands deep in the pockets of my

bottoms. The sides of them are still damp, my skin most likely pruned underneath it. The cool almost January air slithers up my legs. I bring my shoulders to my ears and nod at the man in charge. "Tommy? You good to have a quick word?"

His blue eyes plunge into me like an icicle falling from a roof. He's not happy. Probably doesn't think my last few fights are the kind of quality he wants, but has he forgotten about all the others before? I have a damn good winning streak. Better than what the guys we go up against can say.

"Colson," he says in greeting, but I hear the sharpness in it. I also sense the impatience. As I'm gearing up to talk, he walks the short distance to the back of his car and says, "Not your best night."

"That's actually what I want to talk about. I thought our pair-ups were supposed to be equally matched." I must sound like a little bitch, complaining over this trivial shit. "That guy was pushing close to two-fifty."

"He's who we had for you tonight."

I scoff. "I find that sort of hard to believe."

"I never said this wouldn't happen, Colson. I like to match fighters up with their class, yes. Guess it's the wrestler in me from all those years ago being on the mat. But it's not written in stone and sometimes the payout is bigger when there's a bigger guy in the mix."

"I don't see you pairing the other guys with bulkier dudes."

Switching Remy's opponent with mine would've been a better match for the both of us.

His eyes narrow on me, and he takes a step closer. "Consider it a test, a means to see if you have what it takes and how you handle your business."

He has got to be fucking kidding me.

"I've won every match minus two. You put me in the ring after I got blasted in the side of my head, and I still fought *and* won. If that doesn't show you my commitment or how I handle myself then what exactly am I supposed to do?"

He shrugs. "That's for you to figure out, but the first step in proving you know how to fight is by bringing in cash and knocking your opponents out."

I blink and look off to the side. I don't understand how I'm putting forth all the action, showing up, fighting, and winning nine times out of ten, and it gives off the impression that I'm not serious.

"What's this really about, because I feel like you're giving me the jerk around."

Tommy smiles, but it doesn't reach his eyes. "I test my guys' limits. I want to see how bad they want it. The lengths they're willing to travel shows me how committed they are to the cause."

"There was no cause discussed when Eli introduced us."

I don't like this sneaky shit he's pulling. How he's going back on his word and throwing in other stuff that we never discussed.

"Well," he says, "Consider myself the cause. Either you go through the hoops like everyone has—"

"You've done this with the others then?"

He's being polite when he says, "Don't question how I manage my fighters," but I can see his eyes and they're anything but. "If you don't like how I run things, you're free to go. Just remember what we talked about."

"Remember what exactly?" When Eli introduced me to Tommy, my only priority was getting out of my head. I recall most of what was said, but now I'm wondering if I missed something.

"The buyout."

"What?"

"If you want out," Tommy says slowly. "You'll pay your way out, Colson."

Yeah, no. I would have definitely remembered that. "You never mentioned a buyout."

"Consider this an amendment to our prior discussion."

I blink at him.

"I only work with men who take this seriously. Men who want to be in the circle, fighting for their right at a prize at the end of the night. Doesn't matter what their reason is for showing up. If you can't find it in yourself to man up and take a fucking beating when it's to the benefit of me, well then, you can buy yourself out of the predicament you're in. Call it insurance, if you will. A guarantee that if you do walk, you won't talk, and I won't, either. Ten grand ensures I won't have to track you down to make sure you don't spill the beans on my profits. Or my fighters."

I get the sudden urge to ask if he's ever been the one fighting or if he's always pitted guys against each other to be ripped down and beaten. But what does it matter? I made my bed, and now I have to lie in it. I'll gladly come back and keep fighting if it means it'll put him in his place. If it'll have him eating all these words and admitting his wrongs.

"I'm not going anywhere."

I'll just remember that I can't trust him and bring my A-game every damn night. That way, if he puts me up against someone in a higher weight class again, he'll be the one who's surprised.

"Then I guess that settles this."

I dip my chin down, and he twists on his heel. He climbs into the back of his Cadillac. It purrs to life, then speeds out of the parking garage. I glance around and note I'm the last one left. A discomfort rushes down my spine. I want Tommy to regret what he said tonight, and I know the only way I can do that is prove myself more than I already have, but it doesn't stop me from thinking about him trying to pull a fast one on me.

I've worked with Finn in the past. I know what it looks like when someone is greedy for money and power. I also know what it looks like when someone will manipulate a person to get whatever it is they want. If and when the day comes when I do want an out, I'm not paying him shit. He can consider my wins as payment enough.

I shoulder my bag after his taillights fade into the night and begin my trek toward my car. It's a two-block walk, and when I get there, my phone buzzes in my hand. It's a repeat text from Sebastian. He invited me to some New Year's Eve party they're having at the apartment. I initially told him I wasn't going to make it, but as I stare down at the picture he sent of him, Tristan, and Webber, I can't help but wonder if she's there.

I also can't help but be annoyed at this game we're playing. I know it's mostly on me. I'm the one that called her last night. I'm also the one who hung up on her. It was uncalled for, a total dick move.

But I reached the threshold. The spot in our conversation where I needed to put distance there. As time goes on, I miss her more and more. And the more I miss her, the more I want her. And the more I want her, the more I wonder if I should be out fighting for Tommy and ignoring my problems at all.

Because if I have Violet, I'll have to face everything.

And I'm not sure I'm ready for that.

THIRTY-FIVE

COLSON

I DON'T MAKE it in time for the ball to drop. It's ten minutes after midnight. I wanted to stop at the house and get a fresh change of clothes. I also grabbed a quick shower. As I enter the apartment main entrance, it's quiet. I ride the elevator up to Sebastian's floor. It's weird to think that I spent months living in this building. In a way, I guess I still kind of do. I never moved my stuff out after Mom passed, and this is the first time I've been back since.

I make it to the apartment door and use my key to unlock it. Surprisingly, there's no music playing. I expected to walk into a full-on rager with red Solo cups littering the floor, liquor bottles spaced out over the countertops.

It's dark, too. Most of the lights are off, so I use my phone to light the foyer. I check the kitchen first and note about ten pizza boxes. I brush it off and head to the living room. Giggling sounds from somewhere, but I can't make out where.

Someone grabs my shoulders from behind and spins around me. I'm ready to let out a, *"What the fuck?"* but then my cousin starts whispering, "You made it, but you're late."

My face twists in annoyance. "Why are you whispering?"

"We're playing hook and seek. I'm it and don't want people to know I'm close to blowing their cover," he explains. It makes no fucking sense to me.

I feel my eyebrows wrinkle in question. "What the hell is hook and seek?"

"A tradition." I hear the grin in his voice.

"You gonna explain?"

"Okay, so. It's sort of like hide and seek. Everyone hides and then the seeker obviously has to find them, but the first person who gets found has to make out with the seeker for thirty seconds. But," he holds up a finger I can barely see and pushes the button on the side of my phone. It goes dark. "It has to be pitch black. You're not supposed to know who it is you're kissing. You can't talk, either."

I scratch the side of my head. "You realize how juvenile that sounds, right?"

"Yeah, it is, but it's a thing around Chatham U. Starts freshman year if you're lucky enough to get an invite to one, and if you are, you're supposed to continue it until you graduate."

"How much have you had to drink?"

"Barely anything. That's one of the rules of the games. You can't be wasted, but we all agreed to consent at the start of the game. It's a requirement, or you sit out." He slaps the back of his hand against my chest. "You in?"

"I don't know. I didn't expect to walk into this."

"Maybe I should've warned you," he confesses. "But you haven't been around. Thought it'd be good for you to get out and be back around your people."

I bite my tongue. Tristan and Webber aren't my people. Neither are Sylvia and Everleigh, though Ev and I have had a few random conversations because of all the time I spent with Violet at their apartment.

Giggling ensues again. I look over my shoulder, but it's too dark to really make anything out. Sebastian has to get back to seeking, but I have to know. "Is she here?"

"What do you think?"

"I don't know. That's why I'm asking, Sebastian." I forgot how annoying he can be sometimes. Or maybe I'm just keyed up and still tense from Tommy. From being back in this apartment. From wondering how close *my* person is.

"Seek and find out," is all he says in this mystifying voice before he walks away. It irritates me even more when two people shove past me, one of them driving a shoulder into my arm. I'm not surprised to catch a glimpse of Webber and Tristan speed walking their way into the kitchen when I glance over my shoulder.

I'm tempted to reach out and drag Webber—I know it was him trying to piss on my territory—back by the collar to get an answer as to what his problem is, but I'm a thousand percent positive it has to do with Violet. I'm not surprised he doesn't give me a chance to react. Ever since I've known him, Webber has been selfish in all the ways that count. Hell, Tristan, too. Now is no different, though I don't think either has the right to judge me for how I've acted when both of them lost their girls not that long ago.

My cousin's words ring in my head.

Seek and find out.

If Violet were in this apartment hiding, where would she be? I pocket my phone and roll my bottom lip into my mouth. *Where would Violet hide?* It'd be somewhere clever, I know that much. She's not a hide behind the shower curtain kind of girl. She'd put thought in it. She'd consider the places other people would go and then she'd make her decision.

Making my way back to the kitchen, I give it as much of a glance as I can, finding that Webber and Tristan aren't there after all. I don't know where they zoomed off to, but it's hard making anything out, so I mentally run through the layout of the apartment. Unless Violet turned herself into a human pretzel to fit into one of the cabinets, she's not in here.

She wouldn't do that, even if she is flexible enough.

I walk down the hallway, figuring Sebastian has the living area covered. If he happens to find her first, I'm shit out of luck. I like to think he'd realize it's her and wouldn't put his lips on her mouth, but I can't be certain. Everything is so different, so fucked-up.

I need to get the images of my cousin being lip-locked with the girl of my dreams out of my head before the drywall around me crumbles from sheer mind force.

I bypass the other rooms until I'm at mine. Deep down, I don't think she'd hide anywhere but in my space. Maybe it's self-centered to think, but it's where I would go if I were her. If my heart was broken over being told to fuck off multiple times by the only person I wanted, I'd find their space and wrap myself inside of it.

The issue, though, is there aren't many hiding spots in my room. It's bare beyond the few pieces of furniture. It's quiet as I make my way in. I try my best to make sure I'm light on my feet. My shoes don't even squeak. If she is in here, I don't want her to hear me coming. I want to catch her off guard. I want her heart hammering over me like mine is right now. Thump, thump, thumping in a way that shows our love for each other is explosive and endless and *electric*.

I run my hand over the bedspread. It seems flat, not like someone could be hiding underneath it. I feel around next to the dresser and leave checking under the bed as my last resort.

Making it into the bathroom, I investigate the usual places. Behind the shower curtain. Underneath the sink, but it's as tight of a space as the kitchen cabinets would be. I feel around the built-in closet where towels and wash rags go.

Nothing.

I can't believe I'm doing this.

Searching through the apartment like a goddamn teenager on New Year's Eve. Maybe I should've stayed home. Maybe she's not even here. What kind of fool would I look like if I came across another girl and had to kiss her?

Yeah, it wouldn't happen.

I'm certain I know Violet well enough to notice her breath and the feel of her skin. A single finger running down her arm, and I'd know it's her.

Hope blossoms in me like it did when I set forth down the hallway. I slowly walk back into the room. There's only one last place to check. The walk-in closet. Aside from trash bags filled with my belongings, I never put anything else in there.

I decide it'll be quick and easy to check before heading back out to find Sebastian and tell him how dumb this is. Shouldn't he be in front of the TV playing his video games? Or, hell, maybe this is a real-life simulation of one and he gets off on it. Fuck if I know.

The closet door gives off a soft creak. My feet are feathers as I amble my way in. My foot hits one of my trash bags, and that's when I hear it. An intake of breath. A faint nervous gasp. It ignites a flurry of nerves inside of me.

It can't be, can it?

I'm hoping, praying, *begging* it's Violet. I'm not close enough yet to make out if it is her, but fuck, it better be. After all, she's the reason I ultimately decided to come tonight. She's the person I want to see most. The one I've been missing in a way I can't effectively describe. The one I need to grovel my apologies to.

I reach down at the bag closest to me and feel around it. It's even darker in the closet than it is in the rest of the apartment thanks to the lack of windows.

My hand glides along the cool material of the plastic bag. That's it. No human flesh. No skin. No warmth. I walk further into the space, knowing there's a laundry basket somewhere with another bag. My knee bumps into the bag first. I do the same as I did before, feel around for her.

Where are you?

I huff out a breath, one that's a little too loud. I'm getting antsy. I want to find her. *Need* to but doubt trickles in. Maybe the person I heard is another girl. Or worse, a guy. I grimace at the thought but push myself to find the basket. If I don't come across anyone after that, I'll leave.

I'll take my loss just like I did earlier and walk out of the apartment.

My foot bumps into the basket a second later, but the strange thing about it? It almost seems like it slides off something. I take half a step further. My heart skips when my foot hits something hard but human-like.

Jackpot.

I crouch. No other gasps come from the person's mouth. No signs that they're scared their hiding place has been found, but that doesn't deter me. I reach out, and eventually, my palm catches skin.

I feel what I think is the edge of a knee. I trace my fingers over the boney body part until it fills my palm. I squeeze my eyes shut even if I can't see and slide my hand toward the person's foot. I'm getting a feel, figuring out if I can place the person's leg.

I get to their ankle, feel a dainty bracelet I've had the pleasure of running my fingertips over in the past, and all the air whooshes out of my lungs.

Violet, baby.

I found you.

THIRTY-SIX

VIOLET

Everleigh: How are fictional men so much better than the real life kind?

Violet: Because they're written by women?

Violet: Also, where is this coming from?

Everleigh: Tristan drunk-texted me. Sent me a picture, too.

Everleigh: Sylvia and Fletcher are in the background of it.

Violet: Soooo what exactly does this sexy book boyfriend of yours look like?

Everleigh: I always knew you were a keeper.

I'M NOT TYPICALLY SCARED of the dark. Next year I'll be a twenty-two-year-old college graduate, for crying out loud, but it's almost eerie how the guys' apartment goes from lit up to stark black.

Chatham U's tradition of hook and seek wasn't what I was planning on getting into tonight, but Olive wanted to celebrate and go into the New Year with a big bang. I couldn't bring myself to say no to her. Not when winter break will fly by, and she'll be back in Florida before either of us knows it.

However, the idea of another guy's hands on me...no, thank you.

Colson's are the only ones I want sliding up and down my body. His soft, feathery lips are the only ones I seem to think about every time the game resets, and we enter another round. I always seem to find the same hiding spot—this one in the closet—and so far, no one has found me.

Sebastian told everyone Colson's room was off limits. He had this serious look on his face when he said it. No one challenged him, too excited to get the game started to care about one room. I'm the only one who has dared to creep into his space and shut the door behind me like I'm not betraying Sebastian's trust.

For an unexplainable reason, I put an empty laundry basket on my lap, thinking it'll keep someone from finding me but what does it matter? No one has come in here so far, and I think it'll stay that way. I rest my head against the wall and wait for the commotion that comes at the end of each round when the seeker finds someone and gets in their make-out sesh.

The quiet and darkness envelops me the longer I sit. I wonder where Olive hides. Last round, she ended up in Webber's bed unknowingly. Her eyes went wide, and she gagged when I told her whose room she exited. There was nothing I could do but stand there and laugh while everyone rallied to hear the seeker of the next round. At the start, we agreed that tonight's seekers would only be guys.

Mostly, I'm glad Olive is enjoying herself and has found friends in mine. Even Everleigh came back for two days to hang out with us and bring in the new year. I just can't help but feel disappointed that I'm not spending a minute of it with Colson.

I'm still trying to work through the betrayal over him keeping everything from me. But waiting for things to change is pointless.

I think back to last night's phone call. It didn't take long for me to realize something was wrong. That he was calling because he needed me. I wish I could've physically been there. We may have this line drawn between us. We may say we're just friends, but I think we're both fully aware that we'll never be able to be only that. That six-letter word feels too wrong on our lips when we say it.

A sound sparks from the bedroom, a trace of two objects flicking together.

My breaths grow quieter.

What was that?

I listen intently for more details. Sebastian wouldn't come in here. Why would he if he told everyone to stay out? That wouldn't make sense.

Unless someone else is using Colson's room as refuge.

My stomach swoops thinking about a stranger being in Colson's space. I have this sudden urge to kick them out. To protect his vulnerability just like I wish I could protect his heart. I don't because the sound passes by the closet door.

A moment passes.

Then another.

I think I'm in the clear but then the worst thing imaginable happens. The person walks into the closet, an almost inaudible sigh leaving them. The energy shifts, curling around me like a cloak. I can't tell if it's good or bad. But I do know that it's uncomfortable in its own way. But also, maybe it's not uncomfortable at all just...different?

The person bumps into one of the large trash bags. Then something knocks into the basket on my lap, and it shifts off me, one end of it sliding to the floor. I don't reach out to catch it, thinking it'll blow my cover, but my breathing is now erratic as the person invades my space.

And then I feel it.

A hand colliding with my knee.

A palm spreading over the bone.

My heart, the traitor it is, drums inside of my chest. My stomach hops into the same boat, going crazy like a fish out of water. I'd berate myself over having a reaction as strong as this with someone other than the person I truly want, but I can't move. I don't *want* to move. I don't want to be found. I'm a whole hunk of stone. Even my mind freezes. The warm palm slowly coasts down my leg in the most delicious, drive-your-stomach-insane kind of way.

And.

I.

Am.

Not.

Okay.

A finger traces the bracelet clasped around my ankle. A dainty piece of jewelry I ordered from one of my favorite online boutiques. I can almost remember it like it was yesterday. Me on the edge of my bed, Colson watching from the other side of the room, his hair a wet mess after getting out of the shower. His towel so, so low that it made my belly burst with that same kind of need I'd always get when I saw a little too much of him. More so when he walked over and crawled his way up my body on the bed before he grabbed my ankles, yanked me down, and made himself at home between my thighs.

I didn't get to submit my order until the following morning.

The person unclasps the anklet, and I'm so close to berating them for it. There's no way I can give it up so easily with the memories it holds. But my words are stuck in my stomach, burning away from the flame that ignites when fingers circle my ankle and squeeze in a way that is all too familiar.

My stomach and heart switch places. *It can't be.*

I look up as if light suddenly streams into the closet, giving the person away. He *hung up* on me last night, and we're fooling ourselves if we think we're okay, so why would he be here now?

He wouldn't.

Not unless Sebastian invited him.

Wait…did he?

I reach a shaky hand up in hopes of finding a face. I end up touching a shirt instead. I breathe out a nervous but hopeful breath and whisper, "Is it really you?"

"Yeah, baby, it's me."

Relief moves through me at an unnerving speed when the voice sounds a lot like the man I got to know. I scoot over when he pats my leg in a way that asks me to make room for him. His warmth fills the space next to me, his arm brushing against mine. Seconds pass before his hand moves to my knee again, and it stays there, his thumb brushing back and forth tenderly.

It reminds me of the Colson I was lucky enough to get before his mom overdosed. I'd be lying if I said I didn't crave more of it. If I said I'd be okay with never seeing that side of him again. Because truthfully, I'm dying for it.

My voice is so low I worry he won't be able to hear me. "Why are you here?"

"Sebastian."

So, I was right. He did invite him.

"You missed the ball dropping," is what I choose to say instead of everything else I could pick from.

"Got held up."

I try to imagine what that means. I consider the very real possibility of him being with another female, but that can't be. He doesn't even want me around, so how could he possibly want someone else?

I push it away.

"Why were you hiding in here?" he asks.

"Would you have preferred I hide somewhere Sebastian or anyone else could have found me?"

"No. Have you been in here the whole time?"

Call me a love-crazed girl, but I secretly love that he asks if my lips have touched anyone else's. It shows he still cares. My heart runs with that knowledge, despite my memories reminding me of the secrets he kept from me.

I nod even though he can't see, then give him the honest truth. "I've hid in this closet every round. Pathetic, right?"

"Not quite the word I would use to describe you."

My admission is a featherlight breeze across my lips. "I miss you."

He squeezes my thigh just above my knee. My heart mimics it, clenching painfully. I can't tell if it's in reassurance or because he's hurting, too. All of this is asinine. That we've repeatedly pushed each other away. That we can't step out of our own way to be happy.

Desperation clings to me. All at once, I'm needy to keep him close. To keep him here with me. I'm not sure if it's smart to do what I do next—actually, that's a lie. It's dumb, but I'm tired of tiptoeing around him, worried each move I make will send him farther away.

I carefully push his hand off me, feel for his shoulder, then swing my leg over his lap until I'm straddling him. My skirt pushes up my legs from the motion. His hands find me effortlessly, magnetizing to my hips. He tugs me closer. I can't help but notice the electricity zipping through my body at our connection, at the friction of us touching.

"I'm still me, Violet," he murmurs, digging his fingertips into me and pulling me away from my admission. "I fucked up, and I'm doing shit that you hate. I don't blame you for being pissed at me. And you sure as shit shouldn't be crawling into my lap, but I promise that underneath it all I'm still the same person you got to know."

The darkness requires us to forgo our sense of sight, which only enhances our touch. It's all I can focus on as his fingers pinch into my waist. It's encouraging, *way* too encouraging, and has me wanting to grind against him with a simple arch of my back as I ignore his reminders. I don't but just thinking about it fills my stomach with undeniable arousal.

My hands skim up his shirt until they reach his neckline, the skin there so soft and smooth. My thumb traces up the center of his throat, curving over his Adam's apple until I feel the scratchiness of his stubble. I go up, up, up until my fingers curve around his chin. Another centimeter or so and it'll be his delicious lips against my fingertips. And *God*, I want to feel them. Not just on the pad of my fingers but everywhere.

My thumb moves until it stops over what feels like a cut. My brows push down in confusion and concern. *The Battleground.* I gently run along the rough skin and when he winces, I pull away.

"I'm sorry. I didn't mean to hurt you."

His hand finds my wrist so easily it's like he has night vision. He presses my hand back to his neck. He wants this as much as me, and I could fucking cry, because this is so much better than him breaking up with me and constantly pushing me away. "You're more than fine, Vi."

"What happened?"

"Nothing," is what he replies, but it's a lie. When he showed up at my apartment busted up, he was so nonchalant over not being able to tell me. Like what happened was nothing, but if that were the case, he wouldn't have been injured at all.

I don't want to go through that same thing again.

"It's not nothing. You're hurt."

His hand falls back to my waist. I love the weight of it there. "It's expected when you get into fights with guys bigger than you."

I try to say something, but nothing comes out. I hate the way my stomach sinks into a blackhole, wiping away the butterflies that were there a minute ago. "Why are you torturing yourself?"

"I told you...it's helping me deal. My life is a clusterfuck. Mom dying. Finding out she was married to my dad all these years and never told me. On top of that, Aunt Bess knew and paid him off to stay away. And then there's the fact that I have a half brother all these years. A brother, Violet. I had family out there and didn't even know it. Tell me how I'm supposed to react to all that without losing it."

My palm runs down the side of his neck. My thumb brushes higher until it smooths against his earlobe. I go as far as tracing his entire ear. "I hate all of that happened to you. I wish I could turn back time for you. Make it better."

His hands drop to my thighs.

"What's done is done."

"You get to choose how you react to it. You don't have to be so angry, Colson. No one is forcing anything on you. Not in a way where you have to push us away. We just want to be there for you when you need us. You matter."

His hands brush higher until they're under my shirt and on skin. "You say that, but you don't deserve this bullshit. No one does. I don't know how to rewrite reality. To turn it into a story where it's good enough for you, Violet, or anyone else."

"You spent years taking care of your mom, and I understand why, but don't you think it's time to take care of yourself? Isn't that why you pushed me into my apartment that night and had sex with me? Because you were tired of giving up what you want for the sake of others? She's gone but..." I'm nervous to say the rest, unsure of how he'll react, but I need to get it out. "She's still taking your autonomy from you. She's stealing your choices, your love, and your ability to receive it all back. You're letting all these circumstances victimize you."

"I hate it when you make so much fucking sense." His hands move up and down my sides, his thumbs rolling over my ribs before dipping back down and starting again.

"Stop fighting," I blurt out, holding his face in my hands and bending forward until I can place a gentle kiss wherever my lips land. This entire time I've been trying not to think if there are more marks on his beautiful face. It's hard for me to rationalize why it's so easy for him to endure so much physical pain but impossible to face his emotions. I'm at the point where I'm not opposed to begging. I can't stand the thought of him back in that candy warehouse or on the streets in the middle of the night, taking a beating that he never deserved in the first place.

"Don't leave. Come back to my apartment with me and stay. We'll work through what's happened and figure everything out as it comes up. It can be that easy if you let it be. I'm so angry at you for not telling me what was going on, but that doesn't mean I don't want this, that I don't want *you*."

I pepper kisses over his cheek, my lips brushing against parts of him I'll never stop loving. Maybe I shouldn't still feel this way. He took advantage of how easily I let things slide. He didn't confide in me to the same extent I did him, but we have always been there for each other. What we had wasn't fake. And I do believe that he's the man I got to know. Underneath all the hurt and pain, he's that person. He has to be.

He tips his head against me. I rock my forehead against his, our noses nudging one another.

I sigh. "Doesn't this feel good to you?"

His hands slide back down to my hips, and like before, he tugs me as close to him as I can get. My knees bump into the wall behind him, but my pelvis molds against him perfectly, grazing a very hard something.

He rolls me into him, causing my heat to drag over him. The butterflies in my stomach revive, flapping up out of the darkness. "You always feel good to me, Violet. That's the problem."

"I don't see how that's an issue," I murmur.

"Because you're this beautiful fucking gem. Polished and sparkly, and I'm the tainted jeweler who will cut you in half and mold you into something else just because I can."

"We're all a little fucked up. Just not in the same ways."

"I don't want you fucked up at all," he whispers, bumping his nose against mine again. God, how much would it take to seal my mouth over his?

My hands rest against his upper chest. He keeps my hips planted over his hard length. It'd take nothing to drag my panties to the side and revert back to who we used to be. "Colson."

"Vi."

"Ever think of yourself as the gem? But also the jeweler? You're polished and sparkly in your own ways, but you won't let yourself shine because you're constantly dirtying your hands before handling yourself."

"Mmm, maybe."

I blow out a breath, my sigh rolling out of me like tumbleweed. I don't know how else to make it clear that I want him no matter where he's at mentally and emotionally. No matter what's happened in the past, I want to forge a new and better future together. Why doesn't he want the same?

It reminds me an awful lot of my mom and how she stuck by Dad, despite his issues. My words are a mumble out of my mouth. "Are you going to stop?" I almost don't even want to hear the answer.

"This?" He grinds me against him again. My stomach coils tighter. I'd love nothing more than to keep going. To do things to each other in this dark closet, but...

"No. The fighting."

"Maybe I can be convinced," he teases, giving me a bigger glimpse of himself. This is who he is. Why can't he see that? Why can't he see that he can choose this for himself? That we can be us again?

"Liar."

"Now you're learning."

I nibble on my lip, unsure of what to do next, but then Finn pops up in my head. "What happens when Finn turns out to be right?"

"Finn is a piece of shit who will say and do anything for his own benefit. Don't believe a word that comes out of his mouth." His tone is unrelenting, that prior flirtatious charm gone. "And don't go anywhere with him again."

"He told me you were in trouble, Colson, and when I followed him, you were in an abandoned warehouse with a mob of people chanting for you to beat the hell out of another guy. I get you have history with him, but how is that for his own benefit? Sounds to me like he's trying to be there for you, and you won't let him. You're pushing him away just like you're doing to the rest of us."

"I told you the kind of stuff he did to me."

"I know," I sigh. "But don't you think that people can change?"

Colson's shoulders stiffen. I rest my hands on them regardless. I assume it's from my prodding, from discussing topics that make him feel ashamed and uncomfortable. "Jesus fucking Christ, why are you pushing me when it comes to him?"

Annoyance builds in me. "Because there are people that care about you, and you're too stupid to see it."

"You never used to be this brash with me," he comments.

"Yeah, well, you're kind of not giving me a choice now."

"I'm not forcing you to do shit," he challenges back.

"Fine, Colson. You win. You fucking win. Waste your life away because you don't want to take a single step forward. Leap backwards. Go fight. Do what those guys are doing and get stuck in the pattern of going out every night to kick people's asses. Live a life where you wake up with *nothing* to look forward to and no one to turn to."

I move to get off of him. I'm so done all of a sudden that I can't be around him. The closet is too dark. Too stuffy. Too freaking small. I need out. To go back to my apartment and put this night behind me like I have all the others.

He doesn't let me get up, though. His hands grip me

tighter than they have in weeks, and when I push on his shoulders to stand, he keeps me glued to him.

"Don't go," he pleads.

I ignore it. "Let me up."

He repeats himself. "Don't, Violet."

"I don't want to do this with you anymore. Like, I'm done with the back and forth," I choke out, sadness clogging my throat. I need to get away from him so I can let the tears fall. So I can let go of trying to be so goddamn strong for him. "So, please, I'm begging you. Let me go."

He bends forward, pressing his forehead to my chest. I don't give in to the need to run my fingers through his hair. I'm so exhausted with him settling on being so angry instead of working through his issues. With him being okay with me one second just to fight me the next. I'm not his human fucking punching bag.

"I'm sorry," he breathes out in a rush. "I'm fucking sorry. Okay?"

My heart crumbles at his apology, at the conviction in his tone and how sad he sounds. "I can't keep doing this," I tell him. "I'm trying so damn hard, Colson. You push me away, and I still want to be there for you. I find out you've kept your deepest secrets from me, and I still miss you. I want to *be* with you. Do you know how heartbreaking it is knowing that it isn't reciprocated? I don't know why I constantly fall for guys who don't want the same things as me. Who don't mirror back what I feel for them."

"That's not true," he's quick to say. "I do feel the same about you."

"No, you don't." My heart is so heavy, the agony of this moment searing into me like a branding tool. "If you don't want this anymore then you have to let me go. For good. You can't saunter back into my life when it's good for you. You can't call me in the middle of the night. You can't show up and act like this. And I can't do that to you. I can't suddenly pop up in your affairs. If Finn shows back up, I'll mind my own business." I sniffle past the pressure of wanting to cry. "Good luck with everything, Colson."

I didn't think I could feel any worse than I have, but this is a knife to the chest. It's soul-shattering and heart-wrenching as I sit and wait for a reply I know he isn't going to give me.

Instead, he releases me, and I don't stop walking until I make it back to my apartment and fall onto my bed in one big crying heap.

THIRTY-SEVEN

VIOLET

Old text messages...
Colson: I see you.
Violet: Of course you do, I'm right next to you.
Colson: How about I tell Sebastian you have a
   headache, and we can go back to your
   place?
Violet: You're funny, but I'm not doing that. He
   invited us out for dinner, and right now you're
   ignoring what he's saying to text me.
Colson: He'd understand.
Violet: Go away.
Colson: Never.

WITH MY CHEEK pressed into the pillow, it's like someone is stepping on my back, holding me down. I have this feeling, this uncertainty, this *knowing* that I'm in the eye of the storm.

It follows me through breakfast, lunch, and dinner. It climbs in bed with me at night, squeezing between Olive and me.

I grab my phone off the nightstand and check the time. It's a little after eight but not obnoxiously early for me. Olive snores from her side of my bed. Even though I've told her she can take the couch, she has claimed my room as her spot more often than not.

We were up past midnight watching movies and eating trash food. Sylvia walked in while we were in the middle of *How to Lose a Guy in 10 Days* to a coffee table of junk food wrappers and crumbs. She scoffed at us before moving to the privacy of her bedroom. Ever since she walked out of the apartment with that cup of vodka, it's like walking on eggshells when she's around. Not to mention how there was another letter from Ireland waiting for her the other day on the kitchen counter where we keep our mail.

My belly gurgles for breakfast, but I push it away and unlock my phone, swiping until I find my message thread with Colson. The last message I sent was on Christmas. I swipe my thumb over the screen until I'm on a thread from a few days after we returned to our normal schedules after Thanksgiving break.

> **Colson:** Llewellyn has me on laundry duty, and fuck, it's horrible. These dudes smell like ass.
> **Colson:** I have this weird theory that if I close my eyes when I toss it into the washer, it won't stink as much, but nope, it only magnifies the odor.
> **Violet:** Funny how we do those things thinking it'll make it better.
> **Colson:** It is. Not funny how horrid it is, but yeah.
> **Violet:** I bet.

Colson: Okay.

Colson: I'm getting the sense that something is up.

Violet: Thought all your senses were tied up with smelly towels?

Colson: Touché, but my Violet senses are always up and running.

Violet: Oh yeah?

Colson: Definitely. So, what's up?

Violet: Why would anything be up?

Colson: Where are you?

Violet: Campus gym, but why does that matter?

Colson: Because it tells me everything I need to know. What has crawled into that beautiful mind and is bothering you?

Violet: The fact that my ass isn't round enough.

Colson: Yeah, we both know that's bullshit. Your ass is marvelous. Top notch in all the best ways. So give it to me straight, before I have to leave work and spank that ass for not telling me what's really going on.

Violet: You'd do that? For me?

Colson: Baby, it'd be more for me than anyone. Just thinking about it...

Violet: Interesting.

Colson: Don't make me ask again.

Violet: Nothing, really. I'm fine. Just an off day.

Colson: I don't believe you.

Violet: I guess it's because I had a dream about my dad. It sucks because I never asked for things to end up this way. They just did but now it has me missing him and my parents in general. Then I bumped into Sylvia on my

> way to classes this morning, and she acted
> like she didn't even know me. We made eye
> contact and then she just walked away in a
> huff without saying hi. So, like I said, just an
> off day.
>
> **Colson:** The hardest part with your family is
> over.
>
> **Violet:** I know, and I'm happy about that.
>
> **Colson:** The rest will get better in time. Not really
> sure what to say about Sylvia because
> there's no covering up how I feel about her.
>
> **Violet:** Me and Everleigh think something is
> going on with her, but we don't know what.
>
> **Colson:** Everyone has their secrets, baby. Just
> do me a favor?
>
> **Violet:** Hmm?
>
> **Colson:** Keep that pretty chin of yours up
> for me?
>
> **Violet:** Only because you called me pretty.
>
> **Colson:** I'll remind you every damn day if makes
> it easier.

My belly somersaults the same way it did the day he sent me those messages. I scroll until I find more.

> **Violet:** What else are you bringing to the table?
>
> **Colson:** There something specific you want, Vi?
> Gotta ask, if so.
>
> **Violet:** You.
>
> **Colson:** That can be arranged. Anything else?
>
> **Violet:** I don't know.
>
> **Colson:** Try again.
>
> **Violet:** Maybe your mouth pressed against me.

Violet: *sends picture*

Colson: What have I told you about sending me photos while I'm at work?

Violet: It's nothing bad.

Colson: You saying that doesn't stop my mind from going places.

Colson: Fuck, here goes nothing. It better not be your feet again…

Colson: *opens multimedia message*

Violet: See, I told you, nothing bad. Just showing you the general vicinity of where I'd like your mouth on me.

Colson: You know it doesn't take much to get me between those magnificent thighs of yours. I'll never get over how fucking delicious you taste, how hard you make me, or how goddamn tight you are when I slide inside of you. It's like you were made for me, baby.

Violet: Okay. Now you're getting ME horny.

Colson: Face the facts. You already were.

The minute he found me in my bedroom that evening, he closed the door and flipped the lock. He tugged his shirt off and tossed it into my laundry basket. His jeans folded down his legs next, and it was no secret that he was ready for me. My belly dove low at the sight. Even more so when he told me to strip out of my own clothes and start touching myself so he could watch.

I followed his request until I was on the brink of an orgasm, and he took over, slanting his tongue over me in the best of ways.

My heart beats in quick succession as the memory fades,

and it takes all that I have to let go of my phone and set it back on the nightstand. I've been finding myself looking back at our messages a lot lately. It makes me feel close to him, but at this point, it's just self-inflicted torture more than anything.

I can't take it anymore and get out of bed. I pad my way out of the room and into the bathroom across the hall. I twist the water on, watching as it sloshes over the bottom of the tub and starts collecting, but then images of my accidental meet-cute with Colson rush into my mind, and I turn the water off.

I comb my fingers through my hair and decide brushing my teeth is a better bet. I quickly get myself together then decide if I'm ever going to get him out of my head, I need to do something different. Something he hasn't embedded himself into.

I grab a pair of leggings and a loose top from my clean clothes in the dryer. It's easy to slip into them along with my sneakers, and then I'm out the door and down the elevator.

The second my soles hit the pavement, I start running.

Away from my thoughts.

The love in my heart.

I run so far away from it all that my lungs are nearly ready to explode by the time I loop back around and walk into Spring Meadows's lobby. I even have a not so wonderful case of boob sweat happening. I ignore both for a cup of water once upstairs and almost jump out of my skin when Olive waltzes in with a bagel in hand.

She takes a bite and props her hip against the counter, her stare unwavering. The kind that I know holds questions and won't rest until she gets answers. "What's going on with you?"

I wipe my forehead with the back of my hand. "What do you mean?"

She chews and doesn't care that her words are muffled when she says, "Don't play that game with me."

"I'm fine."

"You're not, and even if you keep telling yourself that, I don't think you'll believe it. What happened the other night? No one could find you and then we were all in the living room when Colson walked down the hallway and left. Side note, really great job picking him because he is *hawt*."

I give her a look. "The hot comment is not helping."

"No?"

"No."

"Well then, clue me in. Give me all the dirty deets. Something happened between you two, what was it?"

I wish I had dirty details to give her, but I simply don't. Colson and I refrained from anything physical.

"There aren't any," I tell her.

Her brows wrinkle. "How?"

"We didn't do anything."

"That wasn't the walk of shame?"

"Not even close."

She looks perturbed more than anything until a thought hits her. "Oh, fuck." Her bagel gets forgotten when she sets it down on the counter and comes over with open arms. "You broke up already, but that night was like the nail in the coffin, wasn't it?"

I nod, my bottom lip trembling because I can't hold it in anymore. I've been keeping strong this entire time. It was hard for me in the beginning, too, but I was sure he'd eventually change his mind. I've always maintained that kind of hope.

Turns out I was just naïve.

I'm a used-up sponge, hanging on until the absolute end of my life expectancy but also knowing that I reached it about two weeks ago. I've been submerged, squashed, and strung out to dry just to have the process repeated.

The adrenaline from my run comes to a standstill. My feet slip farther and farther away and my knees give out, my hands splaying to the ground in my mind.

Olive's arms encase me like twine around a bundle of flowers, unforgiving and tight, holding me together. I lay my head on her shoulder and let it all out.

I've wanted to scream, sob, and stomp my way out of the despair, but this is it. It's staring me in the face, and as much as I want to keep running from it, I can't.

The corners of my eyes burn and pinch in the same way my heart does. Tears roll down my cheeks, staining Olive's sleepshirt, and for the life of me, I can't get the wrenching heartbreak to stop pouring out of my eyes or my lungs.

"Shhh," Olive coos. "It's going to be okay. I'll catch all the tears you wanna give me."

Her undying love only makes me cry harder. I don't know when I wrap my arms around her, but they cinch at her waist, one hand limply holding my opposite wrist so I can hang onto her. I'm afraid that if I let go, I'll drift away. That the current will pull me down like a riptide and no one will be able to save me.

Not her.

Not Sebastian or Finn.

Not my parents.

Especially not Colson.

I'm a measly piece of seaweed at the hands of the tide.

Olive's hand gently rubs my back. "It sucks, I know."

I know she knows. Not too long ago, she endured the horrors of something similar. Of something that sent her spiraling and forgetting who she was until she found herself again. If there's anyone who understands and can get me through, it's her.

Not for the first time, I'm happy she's here.

"It just..." My voice is a shredded mess and cracks with every word. "Really fucking sucks."

"He's an asshole if he can't see what he's throwing away."

Yes, but also no.

Colson is so far away from the asshole spectrum it isn't even funny. The only reason we're in this predicament is because he cares too much. His grief for his mother is a sure sign of that. Him not wanting me in his life because he's trying to protect me is another.

"I just don't understand," is what I mumble out in reply.

I don't get how things have flipped so far upside down that no one can seem to get back on their feet.

"He was supposed to be the good one," Olive says. "He wasn't supposed to be the one who broke your heart."

"I know."

"You didn't even cry this much over Webber, and you were with him for a lot longer."

"I know," I say again.

"You're going to get through this," she promises. "Even if I have to leave school and sleep on your floor."

"Real funny, but you're not going to do that," I hiccup, squeezing her tighter. "This has been building for weeks, and now I'm just done. Like, I can't get my bearings. Can hardly hold myself up."

"We'll get you crutches and an oxygen tank."

I can't help but laugh through my tears at Olive's off the wall response. It's so unexpected and comforting at the same time that I let out a guffaw of tear-streaked giggle-sobs until I'm pulling away and need to wipe my face.

Her face is crestfallen when I look at her.

"I'm willing to bet you disappearing that night we were all at Lucy's has everything to do with Colson, too. Am I right?"

I nod. "His half brother came to tell me he got into this underground world of fighting. He has no plans of stopping. Says it's helping him deal and is insistent on not letting anyone else in, but then when we see each other it's like there's this invisible force that wrenches us together."

"Holy fuck."

"Last night was the first time I asked him to stop for me. Long story short, he's not going to."

"I'm so sorry, Vi. I've caught you quite a few times just randomly staring at your phone. Even saw you in a text thread one time if I'm not mistaken. I know you miss him, but if he's adamant on pushing you away then maybe it's time to cut your losses." She looks at me with pity, but it doesn't bother me because in the next second there's so much love in her eyes. "I think I know what you need."

"What's that?"

"A distraction."

Distraction.

I almost hate that word. Colson and I have always been that to each other. I hate to think about someone else taking that job or claiming my position, but maybe Olive is right. Maybe it's time to get the hell away.

I let out a pathetic laugh. "I don't think I can handle any of your crazy ideas right now, Olive Garden."

She points a finger at me. "Just for that, you have no choice."

THIRTY-EIGHT

COLSON

Finn: Just going to keep ignoring my texts?

Finn: I can see that you're reading them, you know.

Finn: Whatever. Ignore me all you want.

Finn: Doesn't change the fact that we're brothers.

Colson: We're not anything. Lose my number.

Finn: Ah, he speaks. The blessing of the century.

Colson: The blessing of the century will be when you get it through your thick head that I want nothing to do with you.

GRABBING my polo and a pair of jeans out of the janky washing machine, I prop the gray shirt on top of it and yank the denim up my legs. I have a shift at Gulliver's, and while I'm not exactly looking forward to it, I have to go. I don't have it in me to let Llewellyn down despite doing it with everyone else in my life. Besides, he gave me enough time off as it is, and I like being at the gym. The atmosphere creates this resemblance of peace I haven't had in way too long, and it's probably a good idea that I get back to my daily routine—or as close to the one I had before Mom died.

I finish dressing then make my way back to Mom's room. It's become my own sanctuary, the one across the hall long forgotten. I haven't slept in it a day since being back. Being in it only reminds me of Thanksgiving night, and I can't go there.

Violet already pops up in my head at the most inconvenient times. Never mind the fact that it's been more prominent since New Year's when she got off my lap and walked away from me. I hate that she asked me to stop fighting. I hate even more that I couldn't tell her I'd stop for her.

I've done a decent job at making Mom's space my own and glance at a few of my belongings throughout the room. I grab my phone from the nightstand and light up the screen. There are unread messages. I get them every day, but I've gotten really good at ignoring them, at pretending they don't exist and there aren't people out there looking out for me. Their concern is relentless, and while I appreciated it back when Sebastian came through and let me move into his apartment with him, I just want to be left alone now.

Solitary is all my heart reaches for as I ignore everyone's texts, including Finn's. The loneliness that digs into me isn't uncomfortable but warranted. I deserve to stew in the ramifications of not helping Mom sooner, and instead, giving the Lincolns more of my attention.

I should have helped her, goddamnit.

Gotten her back into rehab and *then* paid them back.

But I didn't do it that way and now she's dead.

Fucking gone.

This pressure weighs down on my chest as I tuck my phone into my pocket and grab my keys. I don't bother giving the rest of the house attention as I leave through the front door. I jiggle the doorknob just to make sure it's locked and jog down the steps toward my car.

But then my feet come to a screeching halt halfway down the walkway. The car parked in front of mine doesn't belong there. It sticks out like a sore thumb but only because I've never seen that make and model on this street before.

The brazen man leaning against the passenger door is new, too. He's an older version of Finn and me. I send him a heated glare that's almost natural at this point. Clyde Lincoln doesn't look at me with fatherly love in his eyes or with that forgiving look parents often give their children no matter their attitude. He regards me as if everything about me and our connection is conditional.

Like I'm a business deal he has yet to wrap up.

It only confirms the kind of person he is, one I want nowhere near me or this house.

His conniving, sinister voice slithers its way over to me. "Could be happier to see me."

I stand there and stare at the man, a person I know I'll never be happy to see. He's taken too much from me. My money, my mother, and now everything she left behind, which has to be the reason he's here at all. I knew he'd eventually crawl his way out of the woodwork. I'm surprised it took this long.

The house behind me is the perfect backdrop for whatever he has to say. A reminder that the home I've lived in my entire life and have come back to now that Mom is gone will be ripped away from me just as quickly.

"Don't fucking act like I didn't speak to you." His tone is

sharper now, like he has every right to correct my behavior. News-fucking-flash, he doesn't.

My molars grind down, my jaw damn near breaking from the pressure. My chest aches in the same way it did when we were in Stewart's office. When I learned that the man across from me is my biological father. "What the hell do you want?"

His eyes flick to the house behind me, and he holds up a piece of paper. "Finally came to collect what belongs to me. Took a bit of time but the bank finally fucking pulled through with the paperwork."

"This house isn't yours."

"Not what your lawyer said, boy." He cants his head to the side. "He really did screw you right up the shitter, didn't he? Bet it was nice thinking about what you'd do with all the money your dopehead mother left behind." He lets out a contented sigh that annoys me. "Doesn't matter because this," he indicates to the paper in his hand again, "gives me the right to throw your ass to the curb. House is in my name now."

I wish my glare was strong enough to bring him to his knees. That it could act as pliers and torturously yank each of his teeth from his head one by one.

I get hung up on the way he disrespects Mom, ignoring that stupid piece of paper in his hand that I could easily take a lighter to and burn. "Don't talk about her like that," I counter with a venom in my voice that I've gotten quite used to the last month.

"Aw," he coos. "How fucking adorable. Even now you want to come to her defense. If mommy dearest were still alive, you think she'd give a shit about you standing up for her?" He takes a small baggie out of his pocket and wiggles it. "This is what she'd care about. Same thing she wanted when she was behind bars."

My brows push together, moving from what looks like a powdery substance in his hand back up to his face. How would he have known what she wanted then?

He smirks like he's proud of me for coming up with the answer to the rhetorical math problem he laid out for me. It dawns on me a minute before he brags, "That's right. Your druggie mom used her one call on me when those pigs locked her up, and guess what she asked for, Colson? No, wrong word. Begged is more fitting."

Fucking drugs.

I thought about this, wondering how it was possible for her to get her hands on illegal substances while she was property of the state.

I stay quiet, because I'm not sure what I could possibly say to this man to make him realize how fucked up he is. Sneaking drugs into a jail for an addict through some secret contact is on another level of messed up.

All the muscles in my body seize with irritation, anger, and sadness. I don't fucking know. Maybe all three wrapped into one. Either way, there's a conglomeration of emotions as my stomach fills with disgust. This is why I turned to fighting, because I can't deal with this, with *him*. With everything.

There's nothing I'd rather do than cross the sidewalk and turn him into one of the guys I go up against. They're all villains to me, this guy the biggest one. It'd be easy taking him down with how much rage boils my blood.

"What was I supposed to do?" he asks. "Deny her request?"

"You're a piece of shit," I spit.

"I was only giving her what she wanted," he rationalizes.

My body moves on its own, eating up the grass as I cut

across the patch of it in front of the house. "You're going to wish—"

"Watch your goddamn mouth," he snarls, lifting his hand to signal what I find is one of his guys across the street. A car door opens, and it's like all the times Finn ambushed me. A beefy dude stands there, face muscles pulled taut like they've never been given a day of relaxation. He's wearing a red windbreaker, and with the flick of a hand, pushes it to the side and rests his hands on his hips. A gun glints in the daylight, the back end of a blued barrel merging into a handgrip resting on a belt buckle.

"Put the tough guy act away. You're nothing to be scared of, but if you try and pull a fast one, Francis won't have a problem speeding up your chances of seeing Janie again. He'll make it quite the reunion."

I fist my hands at my sides and manage to get out, "What do you want?"

"What's mine. It's time to pack your shit and find a bridge to live under."

"Fuck you." I'm not the guy who fell into the trap of him using Mom as leverage. I have nothing left to fight for, so at this point, I'm done holding back with him. He can reap what he sows.

"I was going to give you a month to make it happen, out of the kindness of my heart. But now?" He turns for the street, making it around the car and pulling the driver's door open. "You got a week."

"You think I'm just going to fall in line?"

He arches an eyebrow. I hate how his eyes have a similar shape and color as mine. How our appearances are uncanny, and I never picked up on it before. "If I'm not mistaken, you always did before. Be a good boy and keep it up," he condescends with a smirk. He looks back at Francis. "He can help with that and will if you're not out by this time next week. You don't like that? Take it up with someone who gives a flying fuck. This house and the money are mine. Sooner you realize that, the better it'll be for you."

"I don't owe you anything."

Not anymore.

"Just the house," he smirks. "But you're right. If Janie did one thing right, it was teaching you the importance of following through on a deal."

"That isn't what this is," I grit out.

This is him doing what the Lincolns do, which is taking what isn't theirs.

"That's where you're wrong. Janie made this deal long before that last one you paid off. The night we took our hands in marriage, she put this into motion and just like you've always done, you're going to bring it the fuck home for her." His eyes drop to my feet then settle back on my face. "It's the only thing you're good for, but I guess that's what happens when you're a bastard child to a narcissistic junkie."

My bite holds the weight of a Malinois attacking an intruder. I want to walk right up to him and take everything he ever took from me and more. I want to see him wither under a force that's bigger than the both of us.

But I'm deathly still, my feet glued to the pavement below me. My body shuts down as it watches him retreat back into his car. He starts the engine and smoke billows out from the exhaust pipe, leaving my car and me in the dust.

THIRTY-NINE

VIOLET

I LOOK up at the blinking pink sign that reads, *WHERE DREAMS COME TRUE*. Below it is a flier for Amateur Night at The Landing Strip, and unfortunately for me, the date on it just so happens to be today. I rub my arm uncomfortably, my body raging with a plethora of nerves as the piece of paper stares back at me.

The strip club we're at is on a side of Harrison Heights I've never been to, but it seems to be one of the few places where business isn't lackluster, the parking lot filled to the brim with who I assume are regulars.

"I told you I wasn't up for one of your eccentric ideas," I tell my sister. I can't believe she did this—dragged me to the other side of the Sycamore River in order to fulfill one of her crazy bucket list items. This is *not* what I need. I don't need to be in the same stomping grounds as Colson.

Olive clicks her tongue and looks up at the paper. It's taped to a blacked-out window next to the entrance. "Don't be a prude. It'll be fun and definitely get your mind off things. Besides, this was the closest strip club I could find.

All the bars in Chatham Hills were too uptight for what you need."

I look over my shoulder, nightfall draping over us as we stand outside. If it weren't for me pumping the brakes on my sister's weird ideas, we would be in there already. Gooseflesh breaks out over my arms. Partly because I left my jacket in the car, but also because I'm nervous to go inside.

This isn't our town. Not that it belongs to anyone in particular, but it's not our scene. I don't know what the likelihood is that I'll walk inside and find Colson, but the thought sends my thoughts spiraling. I don't want to see him right now.

I also don't know how shifty the guys inside might be. We're two young, pretty girls. The last thing I need are guys barking up our trees because there are a bunch of gorgeous half-naked women grinding on poles in front of them.

"Where did you find this place, anyway?" I'm curious to know if she planned this—getting us to the other side of the river—or if it was an honest mistake.

"I Googled strip clubs in the area."

"The…" I glance up at the bright yet incognito sign at the top of the establishment. "*Landing Strip* is nowhere near *in the area* of Spring Meadows," I muse, dropping my gaze and mulling over the big block letters on the glossy paper again. "I think we should go to Lucy's. We can drink without worrying about being so far from the apartment."

"Why would we do that when we're already here?" She loops her arm through mine. "I've never been this far north. You know Mom and Dad basically banned us from ever crossing the Sycamore Memorial Bridge. I want to see what all the hype is about. Why you fell for a dimwit from around here and if it's worth giving him a second chance or writing him off for good."

My face scrunches. "How is hitting up a strip club on Amateur Night going to tell you that?"

She shrugs. "I don't know, but I have a good feeling about it."

I press the back of my hand to her forehead. "Are you feeling ill? Because nothing good is going to come from this."

She swats my hand away. "I'm fine, thank you very fucking much. I'd be better if you dug your heels out of the pavement and followed me inside."

"Olive." It comes out as an annoying whine.

"No. We're getting you out of your head. You promised you'd trust me."

"That was before you had me driving down the 401 in the exact direction I didn't want to go."

The door to The Landing Strip flies open, a drunk couple hanging onto each other as they stumble their way out. They're all giggles and heart eyes as the guy whoops and lifts his hand into the air for some unknown reason. They only get to the first car in the parking lot before she shoves him against it and pulls something out of her pocket that's hidden by her body.

Olive gives me a look and lowers her voice. "See. They're having the time of their lives. Ready or not, here we come."

Fuck, fuck, fuck.

"Okay, fine. But if this goes sideways…"

"Nothing is going sideways. Not unless some guy has one of us pressed against the wall with a pervy grin on his face and his dick in his hand."

Olive grabs the door handle and looks at me over her shoulder. When did my little sister get so damn confident?

"Maybe try to breathe a little bit so you don't look so uptight when we walk in."

I mumble out, "Rude," as we embark on an adventure I want no part of. It's darker than I expect it to be when we walk inside and nothing at all like Lucy's. Along the sides of the open space are booths and tables, in the center is one large rectangular runway with various poles spaced around it, and a bar at the far end. A pretty popular one by the looks of it. There are just as many younger people as older, and the farther inside we get, the more the song pumping through the speaker hits me. I've never heard it before, but it's seductive in that way that entices the dancers to sway their hips, keeping all eyes on them.

We find our way to the bar, my heart in my stomach. Nearly every stool is taken, but Olive squeezes close to the corner and looks down the bar top for a bartender. I'm pleasantly surprised how comfortable she seems since I'm still mildly freaking out. How is it that my baby sister seems older than me? How is she not freaking out right now?

I take in the establishment as she works her magic. The place is packed but not so much that you can't squeeze behind chairs or make your way to the back of the building where the bathroom sign hovers above two doors next to a staircase that twists and follows the wall.

My eyes flick to the dark ceiling but instead of worrying too much about what could be happening upstairs, I take in the walls. There's not a decoration in sight. No paintings or pictures of sexy women. It only amplifies the fact that we're in a strip club.

Not far ahead, there are women sliding their bodies down poles in skimpy—but honestly sexy as hell—thongs. Two of the four girls aren't wearing tops, their chests round and perky above thin waists and supple backsides.

Shelves of liquor line the walls behind the bar, and the two women bartenders work seamlessly, zipping from one customer to another in shirts that barely cover their boobs. I turn around at the same time one walks up to help Olive, her grin wide and charming as she wipes her hands on a towel before tossing it over her shoulder.

My sister leans in, says something I can't make out then holds up two fingers.

The pretty bartender winks at her. I have no doubt Olive sizes her up—because hello, she's gorgeous and who wouldn't?—but before she walks off, Olive slips a card out of her clutch and that's when it finally clicks. She's giving her a fake ID, and I can't believe I'm only realizing it now. How we shouldn't even be here because she's not old enough to legally drink. There's also the fact that she's on medication that shouldn't be mixed with alcohol.

She twists around and hands me one of the shots the pretty bartender slides across the bar top. She clinks it against mine. "We're going to pretend that for just one night I can have this," she says.

"Olive," I warn, glancing around before saying in a low voice, "You're not supposed to be drinking at all. Not with the antidepressants you're taking."

Her gaze darts off to the side, and she does this thing where her chin dips for half a second before she raises it and looks at me head on. "Actually...I stopped taking them."

Wait...she *stopped*? A million questions buzz around me. My parents took Olive to the doctor after a boy convinced her she was something special just to turn around and make a laughingstock of her. She needed the meds to help her see the glass half full again when all she wanted to do was cry. I had no idea she was considering stopping or that she even had.

"Olive, you can't just *stop* taking medication like that. You have to wean yourself and then—"

"Violet, relax," she interrupts. "Everything is fine. *I'm* fine. I did what the doctor told me to do when I was ready to stop them."

"But why didn't you tell me? Do Mom and Dad know?"

She glances down at our shot glasses. "No, and I don't want you telling them, either. I don't want them to worry about me when I'm better, Violet." She gives me a look that tells me I better not tattle. "I mean it."

"Why?"

"Why what?"

"Why did you stop?" I ask.

"Because I feel better. The doctor told me that only I would know when I was ready. That no one else could decide it for me. It's why I haven't told anyone. I was weak for a short period of time, and I needed them, but I don't anymore. I'm strong, and honestly, I just want to enjoy the night with my sister instead of talking about something that should stay in the past."

"And then tomorrow you're going to cut your fake ID in half?" I press my lips to my shot glass and down the liquid in a rush, breathing through the trail of fire it leaves in its path. Chills spread out over my arms, and I wince. "Oh my God, that's awful."

"Really? It's my favorite."

Olive guzzles it like a pro, and just like that we're no longer focusing on how she made a huge decision, one that closes a door to her past and opens another to her future. One with more happiness and love and spirit. I look at her, taking in the way her bangs fall over her forehead and the blush on her cheeks that enhances her beauty. She's right. We both deserve, for one night, to live in the moment and not let our pasts define us.

I glance back at the bartender who hovers at this side of the bar and lock every little emotion I've felt in the last few weeks behind a trapdoor. The liquor doesn't taste that great, but just for a little while, we'll stay. And then, we'll leave.

"YOU'RE SERIOUS?" I shout as loud as I can.

Twenty minutes after we got here, a few people at the bar vacated their stools and we stole them. There are guys on either side of us that we've been talking to. They're not quite our age, the man to my right has a dusting of gray hairs in his beard and fine wrinkles that sit next to his gorgeous green eyes, but they've been decent so far and haven't tried touching us inappropriately.

I told myself not to think about Colson and just have fun. To go wherever the night takes me, and if that's this man next to me, then what's wrong with that? It's time I live for myself. To let loose and say *fuck you* to anything that makes me feel like shit.

It doesn't hurt that Olive keeps shoving drinks in my direction. I happily accept them all because I'm a changed person. I don't run for the hills when Bret, the guy who's sitting next to me, leans close and tells me how beautiful I am. Nor do I ignore the way his eyes glisten with a suggestiveness that tells me he's looking for a one-night stand. Not that I'm about to follow him out of The Landing Strip or sneak back into one of the private rooms. I take it more as a compliment than anything.

He's cute in his own way with the stature of a man who

works with his hands for a living. Sexy as hell forearms with the perfect amount of muscle that reminds me of my ex. Biceps that could haul me out of this chair just as easily as he could strip me of my tight-fitting clothes. Shoulders that are stalky and wide. A thick neck with stubble that waterfalls over a very pronounced Adam's apple.

But right now, it's not him who I'm focused on. It's my sister, the one who just told me that she signed me up for Amateur Night.

"Stop fucking with me." My words come out in a slow slur, but I enjoy the way the curse comes out so effortlessly.

Her smile is full of trouble. "I'm not. At all."

"I'm not getting up there." I blink, still feeling the bite of the alcohol at the back of my throat from my last shot.

"You definitely are."

"When did you have time to sign me up, anyway?"

We haven't left each other's sides except for...

"When I went to the bathroom," she confirms.

She raced across the club before she peed her pants while I giggled until my cheeks hurt. Bret stole my attention after that, so I didn't see when she came out of the bathroom. When she dropped back in the seat next to me a few minutes later, I didn't think much of it because, honestly, this place isn't as bad as I thought it'd be.

She shoves another shot at me as the bartender slides two her way. The man next to her pushes the money over the bar top. I don't miss the mouthed *thank you* Olive gives him or the twinkle that sets into his eyes.

This shot goes down easier than the last two or three or four. My head is a little fuzzy at this point, my body a lot less tense. I flag the bartender back over. Because you know what?

Fuck it.

We're not at Lucy's where I attend college with a bunch of the patrons. We're not at home. I'm at The Landing Strip for a reason. For a little fun. For a night away from a hopeless reality.

If it weren't for Olive, I'd be in my bed, rereading text messages that no longer hold meaning while crying my eyes out over a guy who doesn't want me.

But the hand that gently rests on my lower back? The man it belongs to *does* want me, and hell, what would it matter if I climbed on the stage right now and gave everyone a little entertainment?

I've seen *Coyote Ugly*. I might not be able to hold a note to save my life, but I sure as hell can sway my hips. I can push my boobs together and be all seductive. I can laugh and smile and enjoy every minute of it.

I slap my hand down on the bar. "You know what, let's do it."

One of the bartenders cups her hands around her mouth and shouts that it's show time. The ladies currently working the stage slowly shift out of their very revealing positions and saunter off the stage, the man guarding the staircase off to the side assisting them down.

The music changes to something a little more upbeat and a few spotlights hovering above the stage change into a mix of light blue and purple while the booths and tables surrounding it remain shadowed. Then, the music cuts off altogether as a voice comes through the speakers to go over rules.

No touching or pulling girls off the stage.

Two participants on the stage at a time.

Girls must *remove their bras at some point during their dance.*

I clap like a madwoman, ready to take the stage and show

everyone what I'm made of. Showing off my boobs will be easy peasy. Like, who cares if these people see my puckered nipples? It's not like anyone else is looking at them. Well, maybe aside from Bret.

A hand presses to my back, and the warmth from whispered words steam against my ear. "You sure you want to do this, beautiful?"

I look into Bret's green eyes. "Of course."

They drop to my top, and he licks his lips. "I'll be here if you need anything."

I pat his beefy bicep and lean into his space as I scoot off my stool. I don't doubt that he'll be right where he is now since a bunch of stunning naked women will be front and center, tits out, nipples stretched against their bras until the fabric is pulled off them. *God, am I glad I wore a matching panty and bra set tonight.* "I'm sure you will be."

Olive comes to my side, looping her arm through mine like she did outside, only my stomach is a lot more wishy-washy than it was then. If I'm being honest, things are a tiny bit distorted. I haven't had this much alcohol since I would hit up parties with Everleigh and Sylvia our freshman year. I'm worried that between my last two shots, I've done myself in. More so when Olive's body moves in slow motion beside me. She drags me over to where a group of women line up. "Do you want me to do it with you?" she asks.

I shake my head a little too vigorously. "No. I'm going to get up there and jiggle my tits and take home the grand prize."

"I don't know if there is one."

I scoff, my head suddenly seeming ten pounds heavier. "There's always a prize."

"Maybe I missed it on the sign-up sheet?" We walk to the end of the bar near the bathrooms and staircase. I note the thin chain secured into two hooks before the first step. "Are you sure you don't want me to do it with you?"

"No way I'll win if I go up against you."

Olive laughs. "You've had one too many shots, but I kind of like this side of you."

"And you'll buy me another when I'm named reigning champ?" It comes out as a question, slurred beyond recognition. Olive's smile almost looks like it stretches off her face when I look at her, and then I frown.

"What's the matter?"

"You're so pretty. How am I not that pretty?" I sneer at her. "It's disgusting."

She holds me by my arms. "You *are* just as pretty as me. Maybe even more. All these guys are going to pop boners once they see your nips."

All these guys.

But none of them are the one I want.

God. I miss he-who-I'm-not-supposed-to-think-about. I wonder if it's even remotely possible that he could be in the crowd tonight. I bet he has better things to do. Like stay away from me for instance. Or go to that chocolate warehouse to fight.

My head snaps up, my eyes darting around the room. Moving so quickly only intensifies my dizziness, and I stumble back a step.

"Whoa there," says Olive, gripping my arms. "You sure you're good?"

My chest is awfully tight, my heart beating against it like it doesn't want to believe I'm doing this. Sadness overcomes me, and it's immense. Like trying to walk in three layers of clothing that are soaked and dripping wet.

Stupid, stupid clothes.

Stupid water.

Stupid Colson.

A rage rips through me in the next breath. I tear my arms out of my sister's grip. I turn on my heel, push through to get in line, and wait until someone guides us to a room in the back where we can keep most of our clothes while we're on stage.

Two girls go out through an entrance that's attached to the stage and the back end of the club. I wait my turn, standing next to a woman whose name is Yolga. In minutes, it'll be me and her on the stage. I barely need to look at her to see she's a lot prettier than me, her body tight and voluptuous in all the areas that count. For a second, I think about all the eyes that are about to be on us. But then it falls away, and my thoughts shift to

Me.

Colson.

Life.

I stagger on my feet and fix my hair, flipping it over my shoulder. A hiccup bubbles up my chest and "S&M" by Rihanna spits through the surround sound. The bartender announces it's time for the next rotation and introduces Yolga and me as we climb our way up the few stairs to the stage.

My six-inch high heels—a pair that belongs to one of the club's regulars—hits the surface, and a wave of heat rushes through my body. The weight of a thousand eyes are on me as I sashay my hips and stop at one of the poles. Yolga takes her spot at the one next to me, looking like she was born to be in front of an audience. It takes every bit of control to keep my ankles from rolling when I walk. Having the pole to lean on helps, but I've never twirled around one in my life. My body doesn't know how to blend in with it and use it as a prop.

From the corner of my eye, Yolga begins moving her body in ways I couldn't if I tried—even with my yoga background. She hooks her leg around the pole and slides into it. Then, she drops down to the stage and crawls her way to the edge. I don't realize I haven't done much of anything until a whistle pierces my ears and someone shouts, "Come on, honey, move a little for us!"

My entire body blushes, including the skin covered by my lavender lace bra and skimpy matching bottoms. The lights on me turn ten degrees warmer. Perspiration forms along the back of my neck when another deep voice bellows from the dark, "Unclasp that bra, sweetheart!"

I look at Yolga as I curl a hand around the pole, my head tilting in time with her body even though I'm barely moving. *Come on, Violet. You can do this.* It's up to me to put on show for the crowd. To give these men exactly what they want.

With Rihanna chanting how good it feels to be bad, I drop down into a squat. The pole slides against my butt crack as I descend. I press my chest out, keep one hand overhead gripping the pole, and lazily trail my index finger between my breasts to the waist of my panties.

Next to me, Yolga is already out of her top. Her nipples are the perfect shade of pink and pebbled into miniature saucers. She skims her palms down her sides and fake gasps, her mouth drawing into a circular shape before she brings her finger up and sucks it.

There's whistling. Cat-calling. The stage vibrates below me from people drumming their hands along the sides of it. For a second, I think Yolga really might be a pro with the way she twirls and displays her perfect round boobs to the crowd.

And then it's my turn to discard my top. My boobs are pretty nice, I must admit, but they're nowhere near Yolga nice. They're a decent handful, not the size of volleyballs. A queasiness sets in the longer I compare myself to the woman next to me. *She* is everything these men—and women—want.

And I am everything they don't want. It's very clear who's going to be the one walking off the stage with bragging rights.

The countless eyes on me are nothing against the fire burning below the surface. My body temperature skyrockets as Yolga walks across the stage to join me on my side. The alcohol, the rows of filled tables and booths, it's all too much. I'm a deer in headlights as my near-naked body sobers.

There's…so many people.

Too many people.

And I'm…standing on a fucking stage next to a stripper's pole with my body showing and Olive peering up at me with her eyes half shielded as she claps. Bret looks like he's going to devour me the second I hop down and *whywhywhy* does that make me want to throw up until daylight savings?

I need to get down.

I need to get out of here.

I need fresh air and familiarity.

I need so much that isn't easily accessible that I settle on twisting my body to the side so I can shield myself in a way that doesn't show just how much I'm freaking out.

Yolga is exuberant as hell next to me, her arms moving languidly in all different directions. At one point, I think she pushes her tits together and bends at her waist like she's waiting for some guy to paint them with something *very* specific. I catch an array of dollar bills on the stage that I must've missed while I was too in my head.

I grimace at the thought of them being tucked in the band of my panties and try to move away from Yolga because she's right next to me. And if eyes are on her, that means they're also on me. But then her elbow comes into my vision. It rears back so fast—but, like, also in slow motion—that there's no way for me to move in time with the alcohol in my system.

She drives it into the side of my head while her back is turned to me, completely oblivious to what's happening.

I wobble back a step—these heels were not made for me —and get the sense I'm falling back. I can't be sure. It's like my brain isn't moving with my body. It's some weird out-of-body experience that I have zero time to figure out because everything goes black.

FORTY

VIOLET

THE ROOM SPIRALS like a spinning bottle in a game of truth or dare. A gnawing ache cascades down into my temples, my cheeks almost feeling bruised. It doesn't help that my throat is dry as dust. That the thought of water causes my throat to spasm with the threat of a constricting heave.

I groan and roll over to my back, the bed creaking from the movement.

Wait a second...

The springs in my mattress are quiet as a mouse. They don't croak as if a frog lives in them. And now that I think about it, my mattress isn't as stabby as this one, either.

My eyes fly open, and I press my hands against the soft material around me just to be met with unfamiliarity. The walls are paneled and black, the ceiling that same color.

I take note of the window across from me, my stomach sinking because I've never seen it a day in my life. I squeeze my eyes shut and try to recall what happened last night. I remember the blinking sign outside of the strip club and the first shot Olive shoved in my dir—

Olive.

Oh, no.

If I'm in…here alone, then where the hell is my sister?

I must've blacked out.

I must've, *fuck*, I don't know.

My stomach drops about ten flights.

Where *am* I, and why was I so reckless?

Creaking sounds from outside the door, and I snap my head in its direction, frantically looking for a weapon to protect myself with, but there isn't much in this room. In place of a nightstand is a small stool, and oh look, my small clutch rests on it. I snatch it at the speed of light while also being really quiet. My phone clatters to my blanket-clad lap. I'm quick to check if there's battery left. Relief washes through me when the screen lights up and tells me the time. Just after five. I blink.

Five in the morning or five in the evening?

It's still dark outside thanks to the only window in the room. I have no bearings on if it's daytime or nighttime. Not only do I have no clue where I am, I also don't know how long I've been here. Or where my sister is. I scrub my hands through my hair and forget about the hangover pains.

What the hell did we get ourselves into last night?

I take a deep breath and push away the tears that creep into the corners of my eyes. I have to be strong. I have to figure out where I am and save the meltdown for later. I have to—

The noise out in the hallway sounds again. This time louder. Just like my heartbeat that thumps like a stampede of heavy-as-hell water buffalo in my chest. I grip my phone tighter. It's the only object I have readily available to protect myself.

If I have to, I'll peg it at the head of whoever enters.

I squeeze my eyes shut a couple of times and reopen

them, trying to adjust and gain focus. If I have to chuck my phone, then I need to make sure my aim is on point, and I'm actually going to hit my target.

The doorknob twists at a snail's pace. My eyes drop to it. I tighten my hold on my cell and rear my arm back. The hinges on the door groan in protest as the door pushes open. Just as I'm about to send my phone flying, a man in all black steps into the room.

The person closes the door, and I can't help but stare.

"Finn?" Relief like I've never felt rains down on me, all the tiny raindrops acting as pricks of tingles over my body. I don't understand. How is he here? And *where* even is here? I was at a strip club in Harrison Heights last night that Olive dragged me to.

My sister.

His dark eyes settle on the phone clutched in my hand. "You really think that'd protect you?"

I lower my arm. "I don't know where I am. I was—"

"You're safe," is what he says, and it does feel like I am, knowing that he's here. I don't think Finn would hurt me or let someone else do so. No matter his history with Colson. In fact, I think it's the very reason that he *wouldn't* do me harm.

"My sister. She was with me last night and now she's not."

He moves farther into the room and takes a seat in an old wooden chair that I didn't notice before. "She's fine."

"Where is she?"

He tilts his head toward the door. "Sleeping in the next room over."

My eyes slice to the opposite wall. She must've freaked out last night. She doesn't know Finn, and as I try to place the events of what happened to get me here, my mind draws a blacked-out blank. Still, my one and only concern is her.

"Are you sure she's okay? She doesn't know who you are."

"She's been passed out for the last two hours but if you want me to take you to see her, I can. Warning you, though, she was a bit...how do I put it?" He squints one of his eyes. "Untrusting and wild."

Oh my God.

I glare at him. "Did you hurt her?"

He glares back. "Fuck no. I explained who I was. You referred to me by name last night when I brought you up here, so I think that helped calm her down, but she was still pretty fucking accusatory. One of my guys is watching her room. Making sure no one goes in."

"So you're holding her hostage?"

"No." He gives me a look. "She can come out whenever she wants. She sat in here with you for a while until I convinced her she should sleep."

I glance around the room again, at the darkness outside the curtainless window. "Where are we?"

"Same place you were last night. The Landing Strip."

I scrunch my brows and look at him. He looks like he's still dressed from the day before or maybe from today? "Wait. The time...is it morning or night?"

"Morning." His lips raise in a lazy smirk. "You gave quite the entertainment a few hours ago. Based on how you're acting, I'm gonna go ahead and say you don't remember a blink of it."

No. I have no recollection of life before drinking my first few shots. I shake my head.

His eyes drop to my chest. Mine obviously do too and catch on my top. I collect the blanket over my legs and draw it up to cover myself.

And then it all comes back to me.

The Landing Strip.

Bret.

All the shots Olive fed me.

Being on the stage.

Yolga, her big boobs, and her elbow.

Embarrassment blossoms on my cheeks so extensively I feel them warm. "I don't understand." I shake my head. "How do you know?" Between the hangover and the confusion, my head hurts. I don't get why I'd get on top of the stage and start prancing around. How I'd ever be okay with stripping down to my undergarments for a crowd of people.

Those aren't the kind of things I do.

Sylvia, yes.

Me? No.

Finn rests back in the chair as if he can't be bothered, but I'll give him props for looking me in my eye the entire time. His legs stretch out, and he rests his hand lazily on his thigh. His tongue peeks out and wets his bottom lip. Almost as if he's thinking about what he should say. How *much* he should say.

"Finn?" I press.

"I sort of own this place."

"You own The Landing Strip?"

I mean, it is in Harrison Heights, but I've never looked at Finn and thought, *Oh, he looks like a businessman.* Because he doesn't. He's always dressed in dark clothes. Loads of tattoos cover his skin, swirling in this direction and that. He has a sharp tongue and an even darker persona.

His face pulls tight. "Doesn't matter but you should stay away from this place. Away from Harrison Heights. Keep yourself in lah-dee-da land on the other side of the river."

I shove my phone back into my little purse, realizing that Finn is absolutely correct. We never should've crossed the

Sycamore Memorial Bridge last night. Being here, with Finn, is just going to make me think about Colson, and I don't want that when I'm not even sure if Olive is okay.

"What the hell are you doing?" asks Finn as he watches me flip the covers off my body and stand.

"What do you think? I'm leaving. You just told me I shouldn't be here."

"Sit down."

"I'm going to go find Olive."

"Violet, sit your fucking ass down. You're already here. Have been all night. If something bad was going to happen to you or your sister, don't you think it would've happened by now?"

I pause and match his stare. "Honestly, how would I know? There seems to be a lot that I don't know floating around. Colson doesn't think I should trust you."

He grimaces, the muscles on the side of his face pulling tight, but recovers from it quickly. "I wouldn't let anything happen to you. I know how much you mean to him."

My heart seizes at the idea of outsiders seeing the love Colson and I share.

"You're lucky I was here last night. Otherwise, you probably would've been waking up in another room with some random guy hovering over you, asking for a lot more than I fucking am."

The thought makes bile rise up my throat.

"I still don't get it," I tell him. "I didn't see you last night."

"Was upstairs the entire time. We have cameras. Just so happened to be watching them when your smart ass decided to participate in our amateur event. Figured you would rather I save your ass than leave you to the wolves."

I narrow my eyes on him. "Something tells me you might be one of those wolves."

A mischievous grin coats his lips. "Some days. Other days, nowhere fucking near."

"Is that why you keep trying to push your way into Colson's life?"

His chin dips. "I didn't know he was my brother just like he didn't know I was his family."

I stare at him. "So that's it?"

I can tell he's reluctant to give me more. "I've spent my life being told emotions are a weakness. That they should be pushed down and forgotten about. That a real man does his business, earns a living, and provides for his family no matter the means. That family always comes first and outsiders last."

"What does that mean for Colson?"

He sits up and bends his waist forward to rest his elbows on his knees. "It's complicated. Long story short, he was the outsider for a long fucking time, but he's not that anymore. Not to me."

I look at him deeply for the first time since he forced himself into my life outside my apartment. He definitely has this appearance, one that looks like he has to keep up with. Skin covered in black ink. Long dark locks falling over his face. Clothes as dark as the night sky. Steel tipped work boots. He even sports a lip ring. He toys with it as he fumbles with his fingers.

It's hard to know what his true intentions are, and perhaps Colson has seen him in a different light, but he's only ever shown his heart around me. It's almost impossible to see the villain Colson paints him out to be when he looks like a guy who hasn't found his place and is just looking for love as he sits across from me.

"Have you seen him lately?" It's a whisper on my lips and

while going out with Olive was supposed to result in a fun-filled experience that made me forget about him, it didn't work. He's still there, tapping on the inside of my brain in the form of nagging thoughts.

Finn looks up at me and nods. "Yeah."

"And? Is he still fighting?"

"Far as I can tell."

I fiddle with a loose string on the bedsheet, forcing myself to wipe him out of my head. It's done between us, and I have to accept that. "Oh."

There's a pause before Finn replies. It speaks louder than his actual words. "He's a fucking idiot."

"Why do you say that?"

He shakes his head in annoyance. "Because it's the truth. I may be locked in a life in Harrison Heights with no chances of ever getting out. My goddamn blood bleeds with this place, but he's too dumb to realize that he has options. Yet he's allowing this fucking place's claws to dig into him and drag him under."

I swallow and glance down. "I don't know what to say, Finn."

He stands and shakes his head like it's an effective way to put a conversation to an end. "There's nothing left to say. Go wake your sister. I'll drive you home when you're ready."

Fifteen minutes later, Olive and I exit the room she was sleeping in. Her hand loops through my arm as we make it out into the hallway and hunt for Finn. The hallway, this narrow area with creaky floorboards, is empty, so we slowly trail toward the staircase.

"Okay, downstairs it isn't so bad, but up here?" Olive offers a slight pause for effect. "Creepy. I still can't believe you know the guy who owns this place. That he's Colson's brother. He was kinda cute until he opened his mouth and was rude as hell." She breathes out a sigh then asks, "Do you think they've killed people here?"

I look over at my sister and arch a brow. "Seriously?"

"Yes. This place has a weird vibe to it. And it took me forever to fall asleep because of it. Well, that, and I was convinced that this Finn guy was a lying sack of shit when he tried telling me that you knew him."

"Finn is...Finn."

"What are you doing even knowing a guy like him?" she whispers, her eyes slicing to the top step and down the stairs that curve near the bottom. "I mean, we come to a strip club and then you get elbowed in the face and pass out and some big ass bouncer looking dude barrels down the stairs and scoops you up like," she snaps her finger, "that. Anyone can look at Finn and see he's into some shit. My gut tells me he's bad news, Violet. Wait, holy shit, isn't he the guy who was waiting for you that night after Lucy's?"

"Maybe he's into some shady stuff," I admit. "But I don't think he's as bad as what he's made out to be. And yes, same person."

Olive blinks, and it's as if she's trying to connect the dots. "How do you think a guy like him owns a place like this? He's around your age, Violet. Unless his parents are loaded, which I doubt considering where we are, then he had to have done something illegal to get the money for this place."

I don't want to think about it. Finn is in the business of drugs. I know that much, but I don't want to consider the details or what he had to go through to become the owner of a place like The Landing Strip.

"You told me that it was just his mom, that Colson didn't have any other family."

"At the time, that was accurate," I tell her.

"So what changed?"

I make my voice as low as it'll go. "After his mom died, he found out that she was secretly married to some guy. Colson never knew this, but it was actually his dad, who ended up having a kid with another woman, too. Finn is that kid."

"She kept them from each other?"

"He was never in his life. They found out because Colson's mom had a lump sum of money that he was supposed to get." Her eyes go wide. "Except because she was married, it went to her husband."

"Holy fuck."

I nod. "Yep. So not only did Colson lose that, but he also found out about his father and Finn in the process of trying to gain access to those funds."

She looks down the steps again. "That's really messed up, Vi. No wonder he's fighting."

"So as shady as things seem around Finn, I trust him." Even if Colson warned me not to.

"Well, bonus that I don't have to worry about him digging a hole and dropping me into it, huh?"

"He wouldn't let anything happen to us." As odd as it is to say that, I know it's true. Finn cares about Colson more than he lets on. He wouldn't let anything happen to us because he doesn't want anything more happening to Colson.

Olive nods and blows out a breath, letting me know she's ready to descend the stairs. I know it's not easy for her, getting swooped up into all this drama. It wouldn't be easy for anyone.

Finn comes into view when we pass the bend in the staircase. He's leaning against the end of the bar, his elbow perched there as he loops his keys around his finger with one hand and types something on his phone with the other.

He doesn't look up. "Ready?"

"What about my car? It's sitting in the lot and will need to get back to Chatham Hills."

"One of my guys will follow us with it," he says, finally looking our way. His eyes cut across Olive for the briefest second then he asks for my keys. I slip them out of my clutch and drop them in his hand. "Let's go."

We follow him out of the building, which is a lot quieter than last night. There are no patrons sitting on stools. No bartenders catering to their drink orders. The chairs are propped up on tables and the booths are wiped clean. There's still the glow of the lights behind the bar that taunt me as we walk by, but I force myself to ignore the memories of being on stage.

My skin blooms with goosebumps and embarrassment at the memory of being in my lingerie in front of everyone. That, in turn, eventually led to my panic and walking a little too close to Yolga as her elbow connected with my head. There are fuzzy parts in between.

We follow Finn to a SUV at the back of the lot. He unlocks it with his key fob then, surprisingly, opens the back door for us. We clamber in, and I can't help but wonder how many times Colson has been in it. Has he ever smoothed his palm over the material stretched over the seats? Has he had the opportunity to breathe in the faint cigarette smell embedded into it?

Finn hops into the front and starts the car. The dash lights glow in the dark. Soon, the sun will rise over the horizon but before it does, I take full advantage of the night skies. Of how it casts a shadow over all areas of life, how it makes Colson seem so far away and that makes my heart scream out in protest.

Finn is quiet on our ride back to Chatham Hills. I turn to look out the back window to see if my car is following us.

Finn doesn't lie. Someone really is driving it back for me. I cast a long look out over the Sycamore Memorial Bridge as we cross, noting how the moon shines the last of its reflection atop the river. When we pass Chatham U and Finn pulls into Spring Meadows, I squeeze Olive's hand and promise that I'll be up in a few minutes.

"You promise you won't bail on me?"

"Yes. I just want to talk to Finn about something first."

"About what?" Olive prods.

"I'll tell you when I come up."

"You promise that, too? Because I'm tired of being out of the loop."

I grab her shoulders and pull her into a hug. "Thank you for trying to get my mind off of him last night. It didn't end how we wanted it to, but I'm still so glad to have you as my sister."

She squeezes me. "You're making it sound weird, but I'm going to let it go because I think you might still be a little drunk."

A laugh tumbles out of my mouth when I pull away and clutch my stomach. "You're probably right on that."

Her gaze cuts to Finn as he rounds the front of the car and sinks his hands into his hoodie pocket. "I don't care if you're Colson's brother," she snarls at him with narrowed eyes. "She better come up unscathed."

Finn only raises his eyebrows at her, and I can hardly imagine what he must be thinking. Olive is small, but she'd take down the Empire State Building to keep me safe.

"Have I done anything to harm either of you yet?" he questions, his features impassive as he regards my sister.

"There's always time to change that," replies Olive. I don't miss the snark in her voice or how she gives Finn attitude.

"I promise you," he says emotionlessly, reaching into his back pocket for his pack of smokes. "That won't be happening."

She regards his cigarette with disgust then looks back at me before we all head to the entrance. I swipe my card to let her in. Finn and I trail around to the benches.

I speak as the orange end of his ciggy glows. "I can't see him anymore, Finn."

He huffs out a cloud of smoke. "What are you talking about?"

"You know what I'm talking about. Colson and I are done for good. You can't bring me into his messes. I can't know. I don't *want* to know. I need space."

I know he cares about Colson and is trying to help him in his own ways, but gone are the days of me being strong for Colson. Sometimes, I consider how stupid I've been for hanging on to hope for so long, for continuing to show up for him when I need to show up for myself.

I need to be strong *for me.*

As much as I'd like to ask myself what's wrong with me, why I keep putting myself through his rejections, I know having a big heart isn't bad. And that's what this is. A curse and blessing rolled into one but never a flaw to be ashamed of.

That doesn't mean I need to keep putting myself last.

I've tried to be there for him. He doesn't want it. There's nothing else I can do but take care of myself now. Finn needs to know that even if he has only come to me once regarding his brother.

Finn looks off to the side and takes a hit off his smoke. "You sure about that?"

"I've never been more sure of anything in my life."

I say that, and yet, I don't believe myself one bit.

FORTY-ONE

COLSON

MY LEG BOUNCES A MILE A MINUTE, occasionally bumping into the steering wheel as I stare out the dash and take in my surroundings. *This* is where Finn grew up? Fuck. I always knew he had it bad, but this is worse than Mom's place. Metal and junk litters the yard around the small home. One of the shutters on the front window is missing, another window broken with cardboard covering half of it. There's a shed off to the side locked tight with not just one deadbolt but three. It doesn't make sense that they run drugs for money yet live in a place this run down.

The car in the driveway has seen better days, too. It's not the one Finn or Clyde drives around in. I wonder if maybe neither of them is here at all. The only reason I know this is where they live is from hearing about it back in middle school.

My thumb smooths over the worn leather of the steering wheel until it snags on a piece that I've spent the last few months picking at. My nail scratches into it and even though I don't want my car to look worse than it already does, I also need to keep my hands busy, so I rip it off.

When Clyde showed up outside of Mom's, demanding I leave the house, I skipped back in time. That familiar feeling of fighting that I haven't felt since before Mom died came over me, and I went into solution mode, trying to figure out what I could do to keep it.

It's not just that, though.

Mom's never coming back, and I guess my question is, what do I have to show for that? How am I going to carry her with me in this life? How am I going to build upon and correct the shit legacy she left behind?

I don't know what my future holds or where I'm going to be next week. I don't have a college degree to fall back on, and it's not like my job at Gulliver's grants me the opportunity of climbing up the metaphorical ladder. I hit the glass ceiling the second Llewellyn hired me.

I don't know if the house is the answer, but every time I think about handing it over to the Lincolns, my intuition sparks back to life, exiting hibernation.

He's already taken so much from us. I won't just hand over the house.

I can't.

I *have* to fight for it.

I just don't know what that looks like with a man who is greed-driven and doesn't give a single shit about anyone around him. I can't sit and think about what he'll do with the place I grew up in—the only place that holds memories of Mom, good and bad.

So, I have to fucking *think*. I have to figure it out.

I crack my window to let in the cold air. My heater doesn't work half bad and mingles with the coolness. Condensation builds on the glass, making it difficult to see across the street. I roll the window back up when the cold sinks under my jacket and threatens my skin.

My fingers waver on the door handle. I don't want to walk up that porch, but I also know I have to if I want any of this to go the way I'd like it to.

The roar of an engine catches my attention as I push my shoe against the door and prepare to push it open. Clyde's car comes into view, speeding down the quiet street and swerving toward the sidewalk to park. I watch as he steps out and slams the door shut. As he makes his way toward the front door, I look down the street, watching and waiting for his shadow—the guy with the red windbreaker—to follow. He never does. I take it as my sign to get this the hell over with.

I get out of my car and lock it before stuffing my hands in my pockets and damn near sprinting up to the door. I knock, pounding my fist against the splintering wood and wait. I suck in a lungful of air at the same time the door opens and a short, albeit attractive woman looks up at me. The shape of her face reminds me of Finn. He may look a lot like Clyde, but one look at this woman, and I know she's his mother.

Her gaze flits behind me before she turns and looks back in the house. Before I'm able to get a word out, she starts closing the door while muttering, "We're not interested."

My foot darts out before it latches shut. "I'm here for Clyde."

"I don't recognize you," is her reply. She has a voice that sounds as though it's naturally quiet. Or maybe like she's been told to shut up one too many times and now she's gotten used to maintaining a hush-hush demeanor that doesn't get any backlash.

"Who the fuck is at the door?" barks a loudmouth from inside. Concern flicks over her features, drawing her eyebrows close together. I catch the sight of a faint scar lining her jaw when she glances back into the home again. "Tell 'em we're not interested and shut the goddamn door. We're not heating the fucking outdoors."

She opens her mouth as if she's about to say something but doesn't know what. I wonder if Clyde has stripped her of who she is as a person simply because he likes having authority over people. Almost like their fear boosts his morale and increases his energy in some sick way.

My answer is directed at Clyde, but I keep my stare on her as I take a small step forward and shout into the house, "It's me."

A noise ricochets, sounding a lot like a refrigerator slamming shut. Footsteps thud through the house and then he's standing behind the woman before she slips back into the house without a word and disappears. "You got balls showing up like this. Let me guess. You're here to get down on your pansy ass hands and knees and beg like she did?"

THE ROOM IS SOMBER, the windows blocked off with dusty, sun-stained curtains that look like they've never been washed. The overhead light is on, but it barely does its job. Instead, it makes the area more daunting. I stand with my back facing the wall opposite the door.

I fucking hate this man.

I hate that conniving smirk quirking his lips to the water-stained ceiling, how he stands tall with confidence in a way that denotes this level of superiority he thinks he has—but unfortunately does possess—and I detest how easy it is for him to want to strip everything I've ever known away from me.

"I have no goddamn desire to entertain whatever you

came here for," he tells me, sinking down in the center of a sofa that has seen better days. He picks up a pack of smokes, plucks one out, and lights it. It reminds me so much of Finn it's almost scary.

My jaw clenches on its own volition as I watch him toss his cigarettes on the table in front of him. "I'm not giving it up."

"So you think."

I'd love nothing but to glance away. It'd be better than staring him head on. Every second I stand and look at him twists my insides more. Turns the simple knot that's there into an intricate constrictor's knot only a percentage of the population would be able to unwind. I meet his gaze and don't waver. I can't when I need him to know how serious I am.

I don't plan on giving up Mom's house without a fight.

"What do you want from me?" I inquire, knowing that I might not have a thing he wants. I'm willing to try, anyway.

His smirk pulls to one side of his face. He may not be the moody asshole that was yelling about who was at the door a few minutes ago, but in the snap of a finger it's almost like that has changed.

He flicks his ash off onto the floor, too bothered to lean forward and make it into the ashtray. "You got nothing I want, boy."

"I'm sure we can figure something out."

The cigarette glows orange when he props it between his lips and inhales. He pulls it away, eyeballing me from head to toe. "How do I know you won't try to fuck me over? Haul my ass right over the barrel top and pull my trousers down the second I agree?"

"Your DNA might be a part of me, but that's where our

similarities end. I'm not about purposely hurting people. All I want is the house."

He squints at me. "And you'll do anything to get it?"

"Just about."

"Hmm," he ponders, enjoying his smoke like we're not mid-conversation. His gaze strays off and then he says, "I know about Tommy Lescaro. About your little fights." My tongue finds my cheek. I don't know why I'm surprised by this, but it rubs me the wrong way. How he knows so much about me, yet I know jack shit about his affairs. "That motherfucker robbed me blind eight years ago. Couldn't do fuck all about it at the time because he was involved with too many people. Had fucking dreams about cutting his fingers off one by one and slicing his eyelids off with one of those miniature craft knives."

My lips form into a frown. Christ, cutting his eyelids off? What kind of sick bastard would do such a thing?

"What'd he do?" I dare ask.

"Stole money right out of my goddamn hands by poaching my best dealer. Lured him over to The Battleground by telling him he'd make double the amount of money fighting than he was making with me by pushing drugs."

I can see how that would be a betrayal for a man like Clyde.

"Killing him back then would've brought too much attention. Would've given me motive, so I hung back, always knowing the day would come that I'd get the chance to retaliate."

Acid rolls in my gut. "You want me to *kill* him?" Because that's where I draw the line. I'd do a lot to keep my childhood home, but murder is not on that list. I'm not risking the chance of going away for twenty plus for this man.

Clyde's dark eyes find mine. "That would be the best-case

scenario but no. You're going to do what he did to me. You're going to give him a taste of his own medicine and steal back from him what he took from me."

I cross my arms over my chest, unsure how I feel about this. When I drove over here, I knew I'd have to do some shady shit in order to get Clyde to agree to give me the house, but betraying Tommy isn't at all how I figured it'd happen. I thought, worst case, he'd have me do a drug run or collect money from some deadbeat who owes him some. Something similar to what I've always done for Mom, but this?

I think back to my first conversation with Tommy. How he harped on loyalty. How he has a hard-on for money just like the Lincolns do. How he warned me about the beast spitting me back out, but if it did, I wouldn't be the same as when I went in.

Doing this would mean war but not necessarily between Tommy and Clyde.

"If Tommy finds out that I stole from him…" He'll go ape shit. He'll have a fucking field day, and it'll be my head that's on the chopping block if he gets a whiff of it.

"You saying you don't have what it takes?" Clyde taunts. "No balls under that dick of yours?"

"I'm saying, is this the only way?"

"Once in a lifetime deal, boy. You want your dopehead mother's house, it's yours, but only after you replenish what Lescaro took from me." He wipes his hands off each other, then around his cigarette says, "Easy as pie."

"Not exactly. I have no fucking clue where Tommy lives. He's always got a dude with him that drives him around and his fighters are always circling him." I don't think the guy has a weak spot.

"That's the problem with idiots like you. Always think

you need a *weak* point to infiltrate when the best way is always right through the front door."

Did he not just hear me when I said I don't know where he lives? Mom's face materializes in my head, but when I reach for her memory, it falls away. Like sand through my fingers. Water through a colander.

Clyde didn't need to go in through the back with her. He manipulated Mom and took advantage of her from where he stood directly in front of her. He might've used her weakness as a way in, but it wasn't just that to her. It was her obsession.

And Tommy's passion is his fighters.

I look at him, and once again I catch on to what he isn't saying. "You want me to lose a fight."

"That'd be the easy way of getting the job done, but if you got something else planned, clue your old man in."

I grimace at his father-son innuendo, my expression morphing into disgust.

He snubs his cigarette out and comes to a stand. "It'll be real simple. I'll show up, place my bets. Everyone will think you'll win because you're one of Tommy's guys, right? That prick always had to be one of the top dogs. His minions were always his fucking rottweilers." He walks around the table and approaches me. "You're going to play a little game of possum, except you'll go one step further and take a dive."

"You want me to pretend to be knocked out," I conclude.

He tilts his head, so nonchalant. "I'll win my bet, get what I'm owed, and you'll live to see another day in that house. That's what you want, isn't it?"

Staying in Mom's house *is* what I want, but is this the way to go about making sure that happens? Calling Aunt Bess and having her go through Stewart to work out a deal is probably best, but I'm still pissed over what she did.

Besides, I always handled Mom's deals without issue—

most of the time. What's one more between me and the Lincolns if it means I'll get what I want and never have to deal with them again?

I extend my palm, waiting for him to shake on it. "I'll lose a fight so you earn big on the bets, but you're not going to let me stay in the house longer, you're going to sign it over to me."

His brow raises like he's impressed and clasps his hand in mine. His shake is firm and unyielding, on the brink of crushing my fingers if he squeezes any tighter. "You get me my money and the house is yours," he agrees on the spot.

This agreement is straightforward and simple. By the end of it, we'll both get what we want, except as I stand in front of the man that never wanted me and fed Mom's addiction under the radar but also directly *in* the radar, my stomach coils with distrust because...

I just made a deal with the person who killed my mom.

FORTY-TWO

COLSON

Old text messages...
Violet: You awake?
Colson: Am now. What's on your mind, baby?
Violet: Nothing and everything.
Colson: Which category am I in?
Violet: The everything one. Always.
Colson: Promise?
Violet: Pinky promise.

A BITTERSWEET STIRRING takes place in my body, swishing from side to side as I look out over the crowd. Tonight's matches are on a patch of land on the outskirts of Harrison Heights behind the old battery plant that was shut down years ago.

Finn and Clyde tried running me off this road not that long ago. That night, Finn pressed the head of a lit cigarette against my neck and melted my skin into a circular scar I still don.

My eyes keep skirting to Tommy from where I sit. I've decided to keep my distance until my fight is up, so I've gotten comfortable on the delivery landing dock. Behind me are huge garage doors with dents in them. Above those are windows busted from years of sitting and enduring ravenous weather. None of us should be here, the chemicals most likely still poignant in the soil. One touch and who the fuck knows what a person could contract.

But maybe it goes deeper than that. Maybe it took years of working under certain conditions for so many of the workers to end up sick. It reminds me a hell of a lot like the movie *Erin Brockovich,* a woman who was an environmental activist and built a case against an electric company that contaminated groundwater that eventually led to unexplained health issues amongst many in its town.

There was a solid two years when I was in middle school that Mom would fall asleep in the living room and that movie would play in the background. Sometimes, I'd sit with her while she slept and watch the whole thing through. Other times, I'd venture to my room because it was too hard to see her passed out when she was home.

I shake the memory out of my head.

Focus.

With the battery-operated lights someone hauled out here, I recognize the scars that litter my hands. The areas on my knuckles that have split repeatedly. The skin was supposed to grow back stronger, but I never gave it the chance to properly do so between fights. I run my thumb over one of the scars, and it immediately throws me back to the night I showed up at Violet's apartment after Finn got to me in that alley.

My lip was split, bloody and horrifying, but she swept me

under her arm, anyway. Didn't get on my shit. Made me feel important. I think that's when she really got in my head and heart. When everything around me started to blur just a little more each time I saw her.

The memory of her rolling my shirt up, her skin brushing against mine holds like the black of the night, finishing off the cracks in my heart where I've been worse for wear most of my life. I squeeze my eyes shut and drop my head, pretending like I'm in her room and her hands are featherlight against my damaged skin.

My entire body craves her presence, but then I open my eyes and remind myself how this—my current way of life—isn't her. Violet has always been a blinding contrast to what I am. Seeing random people shove each other and holler when Remy gets his win isn't something she approves of or needs to be around. She made that perfectly clear when she straddled my lap and begged me to stop.

It's something I dream about at night, how I refused to follow her guidance. The way her disappointment wove around me in a death grip. But in my sleep, she's not alone.

Clyde is also there, ripping Violet from my grasp, hauling her away, and forcing her to run drugs for him. When she returns from doing just that, he makes her test them, checking the potency by forcing them into her body and watching as she succumbs to the high. Her brown eyes drench me in sweetness and shame, and I'm fucking *immobile*. I try so damn hard to push to my feet to save her from his abuse, but I never can. All the while, scenes of Violet are projected across the wall of my mind. Her snorting a powdery substance. Her swallowing a pill. Her skin pricked and broke open with the fine tip of a needle.

Her body falls slack almost every time. She loses that brightness in her beautiful eyes. Her skin pales just like

Mom's. And then she's an outline of a shape. A human body that's alive but not living. An incredible, caring mind that isn't aware but still giving into the motions.

A cold sweat breaks out over my arms and back. The same kind that's always there when I wake up from the nightmare. Then someone clamps a hand over my shoulder and pulls me from the agony settling into my chest cavity.

I glance up to find Eli looking down at me, his face wearing the same distant expression as always when we're out at fights. It never fails to remind me how he morphs into an entirely different person on nights like these. He turns into a fucking killer in the ring. I haven't seen him lose one match since I've started, which reminds me that I need to lose mine tonight.

"I'm hearing the grass is slick as shit," he says. "Still wet from yesterday's rain."

Well, that sucks for most of the guys fighting tonight. I choose to see it as a small blessing in the deal I made with Clyde. It almost feels like the universe is on my side for once.

I'll take anything that'll work in my favor and make it seem less likely that I purposely screwed Tommy over. I don't include Eli in my plan. It wouldn't be wise to share it outside of the two people who need to know.

Besides, I have to do this. I can't let anyone talk me out of it.

Somewhere in the crowd is Clyde or his goons. They've already bet on me losing. If I switch up at the last minute, I'll lose Mom's house and have Clyde on my ass. The way it is now, I'll only have to deal with Tommy and that's if he finds out. This could all go down without him being none the wiser. That's what I'm betting on.

"You can try getting in my head, but it isn't going to

work," I tell him, playing it off like I'll still go out there and kick ass. On a normal night, I would.

Violet's face crystallizes in my head again. I blink, and she's gone.

Eli chuckles, giving me the more easygoing version of himself before he goes out there and brings his opponent seconds from passing out.

He smirks. "Ah, who said I was trying to rile you?"

I crack one right back. "Your name is Elijah fucking McPearson and you sat next to me in high school history. Pretty sure I've watched you get on the teacher's ass countless times in between your stints in the principal's office."

He sits next to me. "That was just fun and games."

"This isn't?"

"A more grown up version, sure." He knocks his shoe off mine. "You're shaping into a top fighter. You'll be fine out there, just watch your footing. Make sure you're solid before you swing and your balance is even."

"And now he's giving me advice," I quip.

"Must be something in the air. Tommy's even off. The dude is putting a percentage of his winnings back in the pot for the crowd tonight. Something to do with bulking up the crowd by the time the spring fights roll around."

A tornado of alarm swirls in my gut. If Tommy is putting in his own money, it makes my choice to throw my match a whole lot worse if he ever does find out. I say the only thing that comes to mind. "But he loves money."

"Which is why I don't fucking get why he's giving it up tonight. The nice weather is months off, and we've never had an issue with the crowd dying down before."

"Guess there's a first for everything?"

He shakes his head, watching the current fight from afar with me. "He's always been heavily invested in keeping the crown on his head. Being the top guy in The Battleground world. Making sure everyone looks to him instead of one of the other head honchos."

"Would one of them actually move in on him, try to take his place?"

I've never really put a lot of thought into the politics of The Battleground, but I guess in every structure where there's a top player, there's a chance for someone else to take him down.

Eli shrugs a shoulder. "They wouldn't survive it if they did, but that doesn't always scare people off."

"Hmm." Again, that pit in my stomach opens up like the size of the Red Sea. I ignore the nagging thought that what I'm going to do tonight is a bad idea, and instead focus on the guy next to me.

"So, go out there and kick some ass?" I reason.

He nods to the crowd. "Give 'em something to walk away with. They take something big home with them, they'll come back again and keep pouring their money in the pot, keep us fighting. And most importantly, keep Tommy happy."

ELI WASN'T KIDDING when he said the grass was the equivalent of a slip 'n slide. My feet glide every time I make a move. Every time I bob and weave, I worry about overextending my weight just to end up splayed out. My opponent, a guy around my age with a shaved head and scar tracing its way from his temple to mid-cheek, snarls at me. Literally. He's a jaguar in the rainforest, ready to annihilate and eat his prey, regardless if I'm his top choice. But, alas, I'm the sucker in front of him, and that's good enough to pull the deep growl from his throat and swing at me with powerful abandon.

I get him with a check hook, timing his movements out in my head during our second round. There's only one more after this, which means I need to figure out how I'm going to go out in a way that seems real. One wrong move, one discernable flick of my eyes in the wrong direction, and Tommy will recognize what I'm doing. I just fucking know it.

I have no doubt there haven't been guys like this before. Men who've tried to take advantage of the money that gets passed around. Guys who are okay risking their lives to put an extra thousand bucks in their pocket at the end of the night.

And then there's the fact that I questioned Tommy not long ago. If he had his fighters split up, I'd no doubt be on the shitlist. Even as I move back and forth with my fists protecting my face, I notice his steely gaze on my back, beckoning me to end this before I give this guy a bigger advantage.

The issue: I need to deliver an opening to him regardless.

The crowd wails around us, cheering and hollering. They don't care where we are. It doesn't matter if someone can hear them. They want blood, and they want their bet to be the winning one by the end of the night. I know a lot of them bet on me simply because I'm one of Tommy's guys. I've been around long enough to deduce that Tommy is nowhere near a bottom-feeder. Clyde further proved that when I saw him, and we concocted this stupid ass idea I'm about to follow through on.

My enemy swings at me. I duck down. It's the perfect storm of movement, granting me the opportunity to make it seem as though my foot flies out from underneath me, and my leg buckles from the movement. It twists back, and a grunt thunders from my mouth, though I doubt anyone hears it. It's too loud around us, but there are varying gasps that pull at my ears the second my back thuds against the muddy, wet ground.

My opponent beams at me with a nasty look in his eye, and then he's standing over me, his meaty legs caging me in. I wait a few seconds to act, pretending like it knocks the breath out of me when I go down. As he hovers above me, I use my right foot and push it against the ground. I slide upward to create distance, but he matches the movement and follows.

My stomach twists around itself. My neck and shoulders go rigid. This guy is about to knock me into a new goddamn dimension. I'm stuck, but it's a good shitty position to be in. One that will give me what I ultimately want.

I've already decided that I'll fix up Mom's house once it's mine. I'll work my ass off to pay the mortgage. I'll take care of it, make it into something she never had the chance to. Into something I deserved to have when I was a kid.

That's what I look forward to as my opponent's heavy fists come down. I block my face pretty well until he shifts and moves his focus to my ribcage. My torso absorbs blow after blow. His legs are so close to my body, it's impossible to roll to my side and protect myself. I'm wide open.

Agony twinges just beneath my skin. It's not long before it embeds itself into every part of me. When I have no choice but to lower my hands to protect my body, he uses it as an opening to my face. My head flies to the side, spit flying from my mouth when he strikes my opposite cheek. Stinging immediately takes root inside my mouth, and blood coats my tongue.

My body is an inanimate object as he beats me to oblivion. The only part of me that isn't hurting are my legs. My torso is on fire, and my face tails behind for second place. Wetness coats my forehead. I don't know if it's from the grass, the spit coming out of my opponent's mouth as he yells, or blood from a part of me that isn't my mouth. Perhaps a combination of all three?

Fuck. I don't know.

My head spins, and I have never felt like this before in my life. I get this false sense of motion. Like I'm running, but I know I'm not. I'm on the ground, my body flush with the crust of the earth.

My body becomes heavy. I try to keep my eyes open, but someone, or rather something, pulls down on my eyelids. My muscles shout to give up and give in. For seconds that feel like minutes, I fight it, but then my neck gives out, and my head lolls to the side.

Darkness consumes me a minute later.

FORTY-THREE

VIOLET

I STARE at the little red candy in my fingertips, sour white specks over the sweetness that lies underneath. I pop it into my mouth and ignore how the roof of my mouth is cut up from the bag of Sour Patch Kids Olive and I consumed yesterday.

I've always loved these candies. They take me back to being a kid. Back to when the only thing that mattered was what color we picked from the bag even if we did argue over which one was the best.

The hallway deposits Olive into my room as I rummage through the bag to find another red one, the redberry flavor my absolute favorite.

She balks. "You're eating SPK's right now and didn't even invite me?"

I take in her pajamas, a pair of flannels that cling to her skinny legs and an oversized sweater that drapes off her body. I don't understand how she can sleep in all of that. I'd overheat the second I got under the covers. I can't even wear socks to bed without feeling like I'm suffocating, but the craziest thing of all is that I don't need to wear one article of clothing to feel like I'm submerged in a pool of defeat.

"Sorry," I mutter, squishing the candy between my teeth. "Didn't know I was supposed to send out invites."

A sheepish expression comes over her face, the apples of her cheeks tingeing pink. She feels bad for me. Sad that I've kept to myself and my bedroom. It's the only place where I can let myself feel what I need to. After knowing how it felt to deal with Dad's infidelity, I don't want to hide from the emotions of Colson's and my breakup. As much as it hurts, I need to feel it all if I'm ever going to get to the other side of it.

"I hate seeing you like this," Olive tells me. She comes in to sit on the edge of my bed where there's an extra blanket she brought from Florida. She drops her chin but only for a second. "I know what you're going through. I mean...I may not have gone through a breakup, but I know how much it sucks to be where you're at. The heartbreak, the sadness, the feeling of not having anything to be hopeful for and everything being out of your control."

My brow wrinkles, and I instantly feel bad because this is a sensitive topic for her. We don't talk about what happened to her much but only because I never want to trigger her back into that time of her life. "Olive Garden," I murmur, patting the spot next to me where my Sour Patch Kids reside. I set them on my nightstand.

A sad smile quirks her lips and pretends like it has been there this entire time. She climbs up and flops down beside me, nuzzling her cheek into my arm. "It gets better," she vows. "Even if it seems like it won't. I promise it does."

"I know," I mumble. I watched her get through the hardest days of her life. And if she could do it, it's possible for me, too. I just don't know when that's going to happen.

When things will shift and this pressure on my chest will be more hope than dread.

The truth is, I'm spiraling after what happened on New Year's Eve and my choice to get up on that stripper stage. I know Olive meant well taking me out, but what happened at The Landing Strip fills me with a sense of shame and embarrassment. That feeling of waking up in an unfamiliar room has stayed with me the last three mornings also. And then there's the fact that I would've never been there if it weren't for Colson. If I wasn't broken over what transpired in that stupid walk-in closet.

"What's on your agenda for the day?" Olive asks after a few quiet moments. "Should we do something? We can walk around campus or go for a jog. Maybe go over to the strip and get lunch?"

"I was thinking about going out for a smoothie later." Then I plan to come right back here and laze the day away in my bed. Once classes start back up, the opportunity to take my time with my emotions will speed up, and moments like this will be almost impossible.

"Just a smoothie?" She lifts her head to look at me. "Nothing else? Have you eaten anything besides candy this morning?"

"I'm really not that hungry," I admit. My constant stream of thoughts has zapped my desire to eat anything with real substance. The only reason I want to get a smoothie is because I know it'll provide me with the energy I need without feeling like I'm really eating food.

She sighs and tugs me into a side hug. "I think now is a good time to admit that I'd love to kick Colson in the balls a whole lot harder than I wanted to inflict pain on Webber's."

I pick up the bag of Sour Patch Kids and offer her a handful. If there's anyone who knows exactly how she feels, it's me.

She stays with me until I'm ready to get up, get dressed, and head out. When we get back to the apartment after, I lock myself in the bathroom, fill up the tub and soak in the warm water. I don't bother wiping away my tears when they streak down to the corners of my mouth. I lie there as if letting them go will mend the cracks in my heart and glue them back together.

It doesn't.

"THIS IS the best mac and cheese I think I've ever eaten," Olive chirps from her place at the table. She stabs a piece of lobster meat and holds it up for Mom and me to see. "Look at this. Whoever thought of adding seafood to a delicacy such as this cheesy goodness is a freaking genius."

"I didn't know you ate lobster," Mom remarks across from me. Her hair is pulled back, and she dabs her napkin on her lips. She ordered a salad big enough to feed a family of four and is already done.

"I didn't until a friend had me try some when I moved to Florida. Been hooked ever since."

I roll my eyes at her even though there's a smile on my face. It was Olive's idea for us to get out and have lunch with Mom. She wanted the extra girl time before heading south after break, which is fast approaching.

The strip isn't overly packed since it's the middle of winter and most tourists book hotels in the warmer summer months. Before we sat down to eat at one of the more upscale restaurants along the mile-long shopping strip, we walked around for a bit, and it was nice, not bumping into elbows at every turn.

Mom reaches her hand across the table and clasps mine in hers. "Aren't you hungry, Violet?"

I glance down at my plate and the way my fork has gotten quite good at pushing my steak and vegetables in circles. I chewed through a few pieces, and while being out and about has helped my mood some, my stomach still boycotts the idea of wanting to process more than a handful of bites.

I sense Olive's stare from where she sits, hesitating on speaking for me.

A stinging sensation collects at the corner of my eyes. When I don't answer, Mom tries again. "Violet, honey, what's the matter?"

My heart, which was content a minute ago, speeds to a pace I can't calm on my own. For the longest time, I didn't understand where Mom came from when she preached about love being endless. I thought she was ridiculous, holding onto a silly little phrase that made her look like a doormat, but with her looking at me the way she is and with thoughts of Colson in my head, I wonder if maybe she wasn't that far off at all.

Maybe love *is* endless, knowing no bounds, considering the lengths I'd go for the man who has my heart, yet continues to push me away.

It's the way her eyes fill with concern on my behalf that makes the emotion bubble up the back of my throat. I try to clear it away and tell her nothing is wrong, but then I glance over at Olive. She mirrors Mom's expression, one filled with limitless love and care. And I know there's no way I'll be able to keep the hurt at bay.

"I—"

"Violet, it's okay, we're here for you," Olive reassures in a soft voice, forgetting about her lobster mac and cheese.

I lick my lips and squeeze my eyes shut. The smell of Olive's food sneaks into my nostrils, making my stomach even more unhappy than it already is.

Mom's gaze shifts to Olive, and I see the questions in her eyes. *What's going on with your sister?*

I bite the bullet, knowing it may just be inevitable to keep the tears away in this cute little restaurant running parallel to the Sycamore River. "I met someone, but it didn't work out. And I'm just…"

"Oh, honey," Mom croons sadly, squeezing my hand all over again.

Olive moves to sit in the chair next to me. She tosses her hand over my shoulder and pulls me into a side hug.

"Why didn't you mention it sooner?" Mom asks.

"Because…I haven't been the greatest daughter," I confess. *And I found it hard coming to you when I wasn't sure where we stood after Thanksgiving.*

"I hold no grudges over what happened during Thanksgiving break. I just want you to be okay. Dad said you two spoke about things during Christmas. I didn't bring it up, because I didn't want to resurrect something that was already laid to rest."

I nod, understanding where she's coming from. It's not like she was the one who had to apologize for her behavior. I was the one who turned into a brat and stormed out that evening.

I manage a thankful smile. If she weren't so forgiving, I don't know what I'd do. "Thanks, Mom."

"Always, sweetie. Now, what's going on with you and this boy you met?"

"It's complicated."

"Surely not too complicated to work it out?" Mom questions, and I love that she does. I love that instead of judging Colson without meeting him, she's giving him the benefit of the doubt and not assuming the absolute worst of him. She's giving him a chance beyond what his flaws may be.

"There's…" I take a minute to think about what I want to say. "He recently lost his mom, and it's been difficult for him," is what I decide to tell her, leaving out the bits that would probably make her head spin. It's not too much, but enough for her to know that things are rocky.

"Oh, no. How awful."

"Yeah, and so…it's been kinda hard to deal with. He wants to be left alone. We were solid, and so close." *The best of friends until it happened.* "And now it's like that never happened."

Her lips flatten into a thin line. "He'll come around, honey."

"And if he doesn't, I'll give him hell where it'll hurt the most," Olive promises, forever in my corner.

Mom gives her a look, and she seals her lips, fake throwing away the key.

"The best you can do is give him time and your patience," Mom suggests in that logical way of hers.

And I understand what she's saying but, "I guess I just don't know how to handle how it's all making me feel."

"You handle it day by day. When things were bad with your father," she starts, making me realize that, at some point, she must've told Olive about things. "I held onto the notion that even if I felt like total crap one day, the next could be so much better. I relied on the faith that all would work itself out. There were many uphill battles along the way, but your father and I found a place where we were able to put our feelings on the frontline and respect them, but it takes time. And you're so young, Violet. Sometimes it takes living through different experiences and gaining that wisdom to understand you don't like where you are and want to be somewhere better. And, sometimes, that somewhere better is exactly where you were to begin with."

I already know I don't like where I am. I hate how quickly the love Colson and I shared fizzled into nothing. I don't want this for either of us. I wish he could see that. That he deserves so much more than he's giving himself. And how I deserve that, too.

"But until then, you still have to take care of yourself, honey. That way you're strong enough when he comes back around and is ready to fix the turmoil the death of his mother caused."

Strong enough.

She says it as if strength is the easiest thing to obtain.

But it's not. Remaining strong when you're being cornered with insurmountable heartbreak is like climbing a dirt mountain while it's raining.

It's impossible, and I'm tired of trying to hold onto the umbrella when the wind is relentless, and my shoes slip through the mud at every turn.

FORTY-FOUR

COLSON

I FUCKING DID IT.

I took a dive, and Tommy was none the wiser. Eli and two other guys hauled me back over to the delivery dock after. When I finally opened my eyes, most of the crowd was gone, only a few guys lingering for their payout. Relief moved through me like a freight train barreling down a goddamn railway.

My face is almost unrecognizable, but as I lay in Mom's bed and look around, I know it was worth it. This is mine now. *All fucking mine.* I just have to go see Clyde and tie the deal up with a nice frilly bow. I can already see him signing off on the house, can imagine his chicken scratch signature at the bottom of the piece of paper that will make me the owner.

I'm already going through plans in my head of what I'll do to the place, and for the first time in what seems like months, this sense of relief ripples within me. Mom's grief isn't pulling me in every direction. The truth of who my father is doesn't trail behind me like a lost shadow. I haven't even thought about Finn. That could be because he hasn't shown his face like he once did, but I'm more than okay with knowing that he finally got the hint.

After I get tired of lounging, which doesn't take long with this new excitement coursing through me, I hop up and head for the bathroom. I catch a glimpse of my face in the mirror and am met with a swollen eye, busted lip, and bruising all over my face. It's like I went head-to-head with a UFC title champ.

I flick on the shower and step in before the water fully warms. It moves over my sore muscles. It isn't until I glance down to wash my body that my skin glares back at me in a washed-out combination of sunset clouds leading into nightfall.

Violet shapes in my mind at the sight of it. She's been doing that a lot lately. Her beautiful face materializes, and it's hard to push away. I've managed it for weeks now, but it's getting harder not seeing her. I convinced myself she didn't need this lifestyle, that she didn't need me, but more than ever, I think I need her. It's not just that, though.

Waking up in Mom's bed alone every morning has me thinking how much I miss what we had. The laughs, the smiles, the love. Love that I never got to know before her. Love that I buried deep beneath the surface because my grief didn't want to share me.

The outrageous words I said to her. The way I acted. I'm ashamed of it all, and I know she doesn't like me fighting, but we could come to some kind of compromise. *We could.* We could get back what we had.

This needy sensation overcomes me as hot water races down my back. I think of all the time we spent together. I recall how it was a blessing to run my palms over her perfect skin. The instances where she looked at me with adoration filling her eyes. Like she cared about every aspect of my being and thought I was always more than enough. And I fucking miss it. *Her.* Those intimate moments. Those eyes that hold a thousand stories. Her body rolling on top of mine while I caress her in all the sweetest spots.

It tugs at something carnal in me and before I know what's happening, a heaviness settles between my legs. I grip myself before I can count to three.

I feel good in my hand, but Violet...she feels even better in my mind.

MY CAR DOOR SLAMS, and there's a pep in my step as I climb the porch landing at Clyde's. There's this eagerness, filling my heart and pumping out through my extremities, reminding me of the pogo stick Mom got for me when I was a kid, and how elated I was to have a present to open on a birthday, but also that she was thoughtful in choosing it.

I wonder if Finn ever had that. Something tells me Clyde never thought about birthdays and holidays or simply tucking his kid into bed each night. Not that I got that with Mom, either, but when I think about the woman who answered the door the last time I was here, part of me hopes she was able to give him more than I got. Even if I do hate his guts.

I pound my fist on the door.

Finn's Mom isn't standing there when the door swings open. Instead, it's my half brother himself, his hand firmly gripping the edge of the door as he does a double take. His gaze travels back into the house before he walks onto the porch with me, pulling the door shut behind him.

He lowers his voice to ask, "What the fuck are you doing here?"

I smirk. "So, you can show up to my place whenever you damn well please, but I can't show up at yours?"

"Whatever the reason, you need to get the fuck out of here. You want to chat, I'll meet you at your place later."

But see, that's just the thing. He's as unimportant in my mind as he was the first time I told him I didn't want a thing to do with him.

"I'm not here for you." I glance back at the door. "Where's your dad?"

An odd expression takes over his face. For a split second, I wonder if he's bummed out over it—me wanting more to do with Clyde than him.

"The fuck you need him for?" he questions with a fine line between his brows.

"Afraid I'm stealing your golden light?" I ask with a quirked brow.

"Fuck if I care. You can have as much of it as you want."

"As much as I'd love it," I whip out sarcastically. "Not interested." I know it's eating him up inside, not knowing what's going on. This petty part of me high fives myself for it.

He narrows his gaze on me at the same time the door opens behind him. Clyde looms in the doorway.

"Look at that," Clyde quips with a devilish smirk. "My sons are bonding."

"He's here for you," is what Finn grits out before jogging down the steps toward his car. Too in my head, I don't realize his car is in the driveway until I glance over.

Finn doesn't spare either of us a second glance as he climbs into his SUV and backs straight out into the street without checking for traffic. He zooms off down the street, disappearing around the corner a second later.

"Kid always got a goddamn bug up his ass." He walks

back into the house, and I take it as my sign to follow. There are a few guys lingering in the living room, no sight of Finn's mom as I look around. Their attention follows me as Clyde guides me to the same room we spoke in last time.

It has the same moody vibes and stench of burning cigarettes clinging to the furniture. Clyde doesn't bother to sit, but he does light up a smoke.

"I'm here to collect on our deal," I tell him.

"Do I look like a pussy-whipped dumbass?" he asks, though I'm pretty sure it's rhetoric. "I know why you're here."

"So, then you're ready to sign off. Hold up your end of the bargain just like I did mine."

"Not so fast." He turns to look at me. Similar to last time, I watch my surroundings and never let my back face the door. I don't trust those guys out in the living room wouldn't storm in and try something. "Your loss pulled in quite the pretty penny, but not near enough to cover what that prick took from me."

What the hell is he talking about?

"We never discussed an exact amount," I say it to remind him, but it almost sounds like I'm reminding myself. He didn't give specifics before. Just said that he wanted to give Tommy a taste of his own medicine and that's what we did.

He bet on the other guy, and I lost the match so he could take the money and have the satisfaction that he got one over on a guy who he thinks betrayed him.

I take a demanding step forward. "You wanted me to lose the fight so you could win. That's exactly what I fucking did."

Clyde chuckles, but this isn't funny like he thinks it is. He's looking at me like I'm one big bonehead. He just wanted to walk away with a couple hundred dollars in his pocket and the gratification that he could pull a fast one on me. That's exactly what the fuck this is. He never planned on giving me the house.

I run a hand over my jaw and grip at the back of my neck.

"You were never going to give it to me," I mutter, even though he shook on it. I put my palm in his, and we *fucking shook*. I lift my chin to the man who has single-handedly taken from me while lurking in the shadows. First Mom, and now this? Why did I think he'd stay true to his word?

Clyde Lincoln is nothing but a snake. An incarnate of the devil himself. A man with not blood pumping through his veins but pure greed.

There's no doubt in my mind that he planned having those guys out there for a reason. Because he wasn't sure how I'd react, but if I blew a gasket, he'd have them to reel me in and do who the fuck knows what to me.

"You motherfucker," I growl, a snarl curving my lips. His dark eyes mimic mine as he stands there smoking his cigarette. Like it's no big deal that he took advantage of me. That he used my emotions to manipulate me. He dangled the house in front of me and now he's ripping it away. Again.

The last I have of her, he's taking, and he thinks it's a joke.

"If you ask me, I was surprised you actually thought I was serious. Part of me was hopeful I'd have one smart kid out there. Turns out you're no better than the other one." That's how he refers to Finn? As the other one? Jesus. "You stand there with your shoulders thrown back like you have a goddamn idea, but you're as fucking clueless as he is."

A cloud of smoke puffs out of his mouth. "You think I give two shits about you being sad over Janie caring more about being high than getting straight? You think I give a flying *fuck* that you want her house? Newsflash, boy, the only way to get to the top of the mountain is to step on the heads of everyone below you."

I swallow down the chaos of emotion climbing my throat. Not only did he manipulate my state of mind, but he screwed me where Tommy is concerned. My only saving grace is hoping Tommy never notices that I threw my fight for the hell of it.

Most of all, I hate how flawed Clyde's perception is, and as wrecked as I am over being stupid enough to believe him... "I feel sorry for you."

He chuckles as if he's heard worse insults. I'm sure he has. He's a giant fucking prick wrapped in shit-flavored bacon. But today, he's not going to get the best of me. I've been living as if the only thing that matters is what Mom left behind, including the grief she left me with. I've been out of control and pushing away the people who have made permanent residency in my heart and for what? To surround myself with people like this?

To have this realization fall over me as I stand in front of my biological piece-of-shit father is almost comical. He's a reflection of a man I could become but don't want to be. He's someone I will look at and always pity because he never found a way to pull himself out of the water. He has burned so many bridges that he has no choice but to choke on the sea that surrounds him.

But that's not me.

Fuck, *it's not me.*

I have buoys out there; lifeguards and lifejackets and an entire search and rescue team willing to reel me in and bring me back to life.

The expression on his face morphs into a man without a heart. I'm not sure why I ever thought a pulse existed inside of him. "You got a day to get your shit out before my men out there move in and make it theirs."

"Yes, Daddy," I snark, shaking my head at him like the pathetic waste I've always known him to be. I turn for the door, because it's not worth my energy to fight with him. I'm over it. *All* of it. If I'm going to put energy into anyone at this point, it isn't going to be for a Lincoln. What I want most is to find my way back to Violet. Back to a time in my life where I was trying to figure out who the hell it was I wanted to be. The kind of man I wanted to grow into and forge.

A replica of my father is not a version of me worthy of Violet's love.

A replica of my father is not who I *want* or *deserve* to be.

The anger that used to come over me at the thought of him vanishes as I make it out to my car. It catches on the breeze, riding it down the block as I start my engine and make the decision to never come back to this house or drive down the street it sits on again.

FORTY-FIVE

COLSON

I PARK my car outside of the twenty-four hour grocery store on the other side of Harrison Heights after driving around for the last few hours and make my way inside. My nerves heighten when another car pulls in behind me and parks a few spaces down. I didn't plan on stopping on the way home, but if I'm going to pack all my shit up in record timing, then I need fuel. I need something to eat and one of those natural energy drinks Sebastian got me hooked on. I toss a glance over my shoulder at the vehicle that trailed me for the last few blocks and head inside toward the deli where there are pre-portioned meals.

There's this itchiness that covers my body, this weird knowing I can't explain but can feel. Ever since Finn, I've been more aware of my surroundings than normal. Tonight is no different. My old paranoia hooks into me, trying to convince me that the other car out in the lot isn't just nothing.

I've learned to trust my gut and lean into my instincts. Now is no different as I grab myself a platter that looks a lot like meatloaf and mashed potatoes. Protein and carbs are exactly what I need after this shit with Clyde.

Clutching it in my hand, I go an aisle over and grab a blackberry flavored drink that will hopefully give me more energy than I currently have. Physically, I'm still wrecked from the fight I threw. Mentally, I'm completely drained from Clyde's mind games. My hand curls around the aluminum can that promises an energy high from all natural ingredients and some other shit I don't have half a mind to care about right now.

The only two thoughts in my mind are that car and the fact that I have to get back to the house and pack up, my biggest lesson of the last week knowing I can't trust the man whose DNA flows through my blood. I have no doubt that Clyde won't move himself in and rip through my shit if I'm not out by when he said. There are a couple things I'd like to grab, including the cookie jar I've stashed my fighting money in.

My issue is that I don't know where to go when I leave. I could stay in a hotel for a bit, but I'll run through my money fast. There's Aunt Bess and Uncle Thad. I could ask to stay with them until I figure out what it is I want to do with my life, but I'm not so sure that's a good idea.

Which points me back in the direction of Spring Meadows. I don't want to go back to the apartment, but it's starting to look like that's my last resort. It wasn't all bad there. It was quiet for the most part. Drama didn't wrap itself around me every chance it could get.

And Violet is there.

Along with the possibility that I'll bump into her.

And for the first time in a long time, I really, really want that.

God, I really fucking do. *She's* who I want to be around. A person that doesn't remind me of the pain of my past but the hope of my future. Violet is proof that I can have a lot more than I've been given. A promise that I'm more than what I was born into.

Hope flourishes inside of me, but still, it's not loud enough to drown out the gnawing sensation in the pit of my stomach. I hear a squeak at the other end of the aisle as I make it toward the registers. The sound matches that of wet rubber boots on tile, only when I scan the area, no one is there. It's just me, the quiet elevator-type music playing, and my own sneakers squeaking against the hard floor.

I stop in my tracks and listen intently, keeping my gaze in the direction where the sound came from and wait. Nothing comes.

I swivel toward the front of the store and make it to the one lone open register where a kid younger than me is scrolling through his phone. He sets it down when he sees me. "Hey, man. Would you like to add on a brownie?" He points to the end of the conveyor belt where there's a square container of baked goods individually wrapped. "Goes to a good cause," he adds in a tone that tells me he has no clue what the cause is.

"No, thanks," I mumble, twisting around and scanning the area once more. "Hey, did you see if anyone came in after me?"

He scans my food then looks over at the entrance about fifty feet away. He has a direct line of sight to it. He'd notice if someone came or went. "Uh..." His gaze drops to his phone sitting atop the register and uses a finger to keep the screen from dimming. "Not sure."

"Forget it." I shake it off, pulling a ten out of my wallet and grabbing my change.

"Need a bag?"

"No," I answer in a clipped tone, peeved the fuck out. I *heard* someone behind me. I know I did, damnit.

It seems darker when I make it back outside. I don't know how when it's close to midnight, and the sun has been gone for a long while. My eyes track the parking lot, noting a beat-up Chevy in the employee parking section and my Ford Focus in the same spot I left it. My gaze snags on the now-empty spot where the other car parked, and a shiver works down my spine. Not because I'm scared but because I'm relieved.

My life has been a circus for months, and now I'm at the point where my paranoia wants to win out and convince me I'm being followed? I blame it on wondering what Tommy might do if he ever finds out about me throwing my match.

Fuck.

"No one is following you," I mutter to myself as I get back into my car and toss my groceries on the passenger's seat. I'll eat as soon as I get back to the house, but first I rest back on the headrest and let out a sigh.

Finn's and my business has been over for weeks, and while Clyde showed his true colors earlier, the reality is that he doesn't want a thing to do with me. Once he gets Mom's house in his hands, he'll forget I even exist, having gotten the last thing he wanted from Janie Moore.

Which brings me right back to Tommy.

I threw his fight, but there's no possible way he could have found out. The only people who know about it are me and Clyde. And Clyde wouldn't go off and run his mouth when he hates the guy. *Would he?*

I run my tongue along my teeth and contemplate it for a minute.

For one fleeting second, this awful sensation trudges through my system. My neck breaks out in a sweat, and my hands turn clammy as I grip the steering wheel. I stretch my legs out and get comfortable enough to make the drive home.

"No," I convince myself out loud in the space of my car. "It's done and over with. He doesn't know." I scrub my hands over my face and try to relax my shoulders. "It's all in my head. It has to be. *Fuck.* Why am I talking to myself about this?"

I jab my key into the ignition and twist it over, but then my phone vibrates from my back pocket. I manage to wiggle it free, seeing a call from some spam number. I tap ignore, but then my eyes snag on Violet's name in my call log.

With a purple heart emoji before and after her name, I run my thumb over my screen. It's so simple yet causes a cacophony of emotion to swell in my chest.

Just fucking text her, the sorry-as-fuck version of myself taunts from inside my head. *Tell her how much she means to you. Tell her you* love *her.*

I balk at that four-letter word.

Do I *love* Violet?

How couldn't I, is the better question.

Wrapped up in one glorious package, she's everything I never thought I'd get in this lifetime. I don't deserve her, and she deserves a man more than what I'm worth, but when I think about who I want to be, it's her who I see standing beside me.

And if nothing else ever goes right in my life again, if I only had one wish left, I'd wish for her every goddamn time. Forever. Until the day I take my last waking breath.

I used to think I could get through this grief and all this bullshit on my own. That I'd be better for it. But I'm not. I'm nothing without her.

I spent weeks pushing her away, fighting, and ignoring the love I have in my heart and for what? To prove to myself that I can do something that most people can't do on their own? I remember her saying that once, telling me how it's normal to need support through the tough stuff. I didn't want to hear it then, and I almost feel like a fool for coming to the same conclusion now on my own. One that she *tried* telling me, and I was too closed-off to hear.

I'll never meet a girl as good as Violet. She's my saving grace, my daisy in a field of sludge, my entire heart.

I don't waste another second before tapping on her name and typing out a text. I need to make things right with her. I'll get down on my knees and grovel if that's what it takes to win her back. Because she's worth it, and fuck, so am I.

Colson: Need to see you. Can we meet up?

My phone ends up on the seat with my food as this newfangled eagerness taps in rhythm with my heartbeat. I glance over at the screen, willing it to light up with a response as I back out of my spot and make it back on the road.

I roll to a stop at an intersection and make my way through, noting the giddiness that seems to be taking over that previous paranoia. Damn. I've felt too many emotions in such a short span of time, but this feels good. Like I'm finally finding myself again.

I look at the time on the dash, the blurry red numbers staring back at me.

12:37.

That buzz fades when it hits me that Violet is probably sleeping. She has classes and her gig at the daycare, so unless she's up late studying, I won't hear from her until morning. It takes everything in me to stay on the street leading back to my mom's instead of making a right turn for the 401. Spring Meadows suddenly sounds like a better destination.

What would she do if I showed up, my fist knocking against her apartment door until she opened it for me? This overwhelming need to prove myself to her hits me. To prove that I'm not the asshole I've acted like. To prove that even if I'm not worthy of every ounce of her, I'll work every goddamn day to show her how grateful I am for her. To prove that I can be what she needs, if only she'll let me back into her life.

I come to a stop at a traffic light where the tri-colored lights sway in the cool midnight breeze.

I can't believe I fucked it up this much with her. I wouldn't be surprised if she never wanted to see me again, but no. I can't give her that. She *has* to give me a second chance. I'll show her I'll never need another one. At least not to the extent of this one.

I smack my palm on the steering wheel when the light takes forever to change back to green. "Come the fuck on." I got shit to do. Like pack up what I want at Mom's house and go win my girl back.

When it finally blinks green, I ease my foot off the brake and reach over for my energy drink. I press down on the gas slowly and flick my can open, tilting it to my lips to get a head start on my energy high, but then headlights come out of nowhere from my left.

I turn my head to get a better look at the car in the distance, noting that it's driving pretty fast for having a red light. My drink falls from my hand, the condensation making it slip and spill out over my lap. The cold liquid spanning out over my legs and groin steals my attention. I don't press harder on the gas like I should.

I turn my attention away from the headlights coming at me like a bat out of hell.

By the time I look back over at them, it's too late.

I'm too late.

FORTY-SIX

COLSON

BLACKNESS.

That's all I can seem to focus on.

And pain.

It's *everywhere.*

My legs, my head, my arm.

I try to open my eyelids, but they're too heavy, and I…I can't. They don't budge. Something is wrong, but I don't know what.

I attempt to move my arm, but it seems like the hardest thing in the world. It doesn't get the signal to shift like I want it to.

I try my eyes again.

Nothing.

It's too…dark.

Like the night sky after all the stars have fallen from it.

A weird smell encases me, briefly distracting me from my body failing to work. *It worked mere hours ago.* Fuck, why can't I lift my arm? Why does my head feel like someone took a hammer to it?

I choke out a cough that makes my ribcage throb.

The smell. It's so potent, reminding me of a gas station, that unforgettable smell of gasoline when you pump it into your car. But this is worse. Not something you want to stand there and sniff. It fills my lungs, preventing me from getting a deep enough breath of oxygen in.

I wheeze out another hack, my throat turning into the Sahara-fucking-Desert. I lick my lips, my tongue being the only part of my body that wants to listen to me. A funny taste moves over the tip of it.

Why do I taste blood?

Sirens wail in the distance. It's like they're next to me but also miles away.

Finally, after willing them to time and time again, my eyelids peel open, giving me a chance to see my surroundings. Except...I can't make sense of it.

My head is full of pressure, like when you hang upside down on the monkey bars as a kid. But this is so much more than that. More invading. More crippling. More dizzying.

And then I look down—or am I looking up?—and see red on my clothes.

There's so much of it. More than I've ever seen in my life.

My stomach heaves at the sight of it, acid and bile flowing into my mouth in a disgusting amount, then the blackness comes all over again because that red is blood and it all...

Belongs.

To.

Me.

FORTY-SEVEN

COLSON

I SUCK in a lungful of air when a gush of oxygen blasts through my body. A flaring pain shoots out over my hand, but it's nothing compared to the rest of my body.

It's almost not even there, but then it comes a second time, reminding me of the pricks of torment from when I got the roses and lion's face tattooed over my forearm. Somehow, this hurts both less and more at the same time. I blink again, bright lights pouring down on me like a rainstorm. I catch a glimpse of a person's head off to my left and try to turn my head, but of course it doesn't move when I tell it to. There's something strapped around it, holding it in place.

I'm getting tired of my body giving me a big "fuck you" every time I give it a command.

"Try to stay still," comes a feminine voice from above me. I wonder for a moment if it's God playing some weird ass trick on me, but then a head of hair slices into my vision. It's reddish brown and frizzy with the person's bangs clipped back. "My name is Sandy. You're in an ambulance being transported to Harrison General Hospital. You were in a car accident."

I blink repeatedly as if it'll clear up the confusion thrumming through my head. A car accident? That isn't right.

I wasn't…that didn't…

I squeeze my eyes shut, trying to pinpoint what Sandy is talking about. I was in the grocery store. I picked out a meatloaf and mashed potato combo. The cashier was watching stupid videos on his phone when I walked up to pay.

That pain that came over me before vibrates through me, intensifying when I try to move my leg from its uncomfortable position. When the nick at my hand happens a third time, I try to pull away because *what the fuck is that?*

"Stay still, dear. I'm trying to get an IV in so we can manage your pain, but your veins are being finicky."

"I—" I attempt words, but it's too hard to talk. *What is happening to me?*

"Ah, there we go," Sandy says, applying pressure on my hand before letting go.

"Wh—"

Her face comes into view when she says, "Your only job is to rest and trust that you're in good hands, Colson." She glances away, and a beeping ensues or maybe it's been there the entire time. But wait, how does she know my name?

I groan and even that hurts, which is a new development. A line of heat wraps around my arm. It's in my leg as well, and my head isn't far off from exploding.

All of this, it's too—

"You're in rough shape, Colson, but I just administered morphine into your IV line. You should have some comfort in a moment."

Solace sweeps over me as soon as she finishes her sentence, coursing through my body on a straight and narrow path, ending once it reaches my mouth. A bitterness ensues in my tongue. Not over it but *in* it. Also a new development.

Sandy says something else, but I can't focus. Too much impales me at once and then in a split second, it vanishes.

So does the light.

FORTY-EIGHT

COLSON

THERE ARE VOICES.

Lots of them.

Men and women.

They aren't shouting, but they're not whispering, either.

My head is as light as a feather. I'm moving through space, looking down on what's happening around me, but the trippiest part of all is that my eyes aren't even open.

I hear my name and a bunch of words that follow it.

I don't know what they mean, but they're there.

Floating in front of me in a galaxy of darkness.

FORTY-NINE

COLSON

IT'S SILENT.

Like when I plug my sound-canceling headphones into my ears and all I hear is nothing before the music streams through them.

My heartbeat, I think that's what it is, pitter patters in my head. *Tha-thump, tha-thump, tha-thump.*

That agonizing—*no*—crippling pain that made my body ache with mind-blowing intensity from before is gone.

I feel nothing.

I see nothing.

I hear nothing.

I'm surrounded by one giant black hole of nothingness.

And, fuck, do I like it here.

There's nothing at my back nagging me to do this or that. My stress levels are at an all-time low. Mom isn't giving me a hard time.

Wait...*Mom.*

It comes back to me in a flash that she's no longer alive. I expect a wave of grief to crash into me, but it doesn't come. I wait and wait and wait, but it never shows its ugly face.

Because here, I'm weightless.
And I never want to leave.

FIFTY

COLSON

THE VOICES ARE BACK AGAIN.

Only they're different from the last ones. Before they were very chaotic but also collected. To the point, maybe, is a better way to describe it.

I'm awake, my senses in a tizzy. Except for my sight. I haven't opened my eyes yet and have no plan in doing so anytime soon.

I like being in the black where my body is insignificant. Where I can hide. Where I don't have to face my demons and fuck-ups. But, shit, I want to see Violet. I want to open my eyes and have the brown-eyed-beauty I've fallen in love with staring back at me.

Only I can't find the familiarity of her voice in what I hear, so I reach for the darkness instead.

FIFTY-ONE

VIOLET

Olive: What's the likelihood that if I turn around and show up at your doorstep again, you'll let me in?

Violet: Please tell me you're not doing that.

Olive: I'm not. Not yet, anyway.

Violet: Not ever.

Olive: Never say ever.

Violet: That's not how the saying goes, Olive Garden.

CLOSING the apartment door behind me, I slip my shoes off and lower the strap of my yoga mat off my shoulder. It catches on my wrist until I prop it against the wall and head into the kitchen.

Everleigh sits on the island counter, legs folded into a pretzel, with a piece of paper in her hand. "You're never going to guess what this says," she tells me, lifting the paper between her fingers.

I grab a water bottle from the fridge and crack it open. I spent an hour downstairs in the gym, stretching into poses that typically give me relief. They only semi-worked, leaving me with this underlying anxiousness under my skin. I can't pinpoint what it's from, but I can make a good guess.

Some days I hate myself for creating boundaries until I remind myself how crucial it was. I've replayed the same mantra in my head for days now, telling myself that I deserve better no matter the feelings I have for Colson.

I pluck the piece of paper from Everleigh and scan the top. Both of our names are scrawled in Sylvia's perfect bubbly letters with hearts as dots over the i's. "Why did Sylvia write us a letter?" I ask her. "That's not like her at all."

"She left," Everleigh says point blank.

My eyes flick up to her. "What? Why?"

"Read the letter. It's all there."

I scan over Sylvia's short and to the point string of sentences. Shock sinks down in me when I get to the part that says she's moving back to Ireland to be with her family. However, there's not really a direct reason behind why she's going. It just says that by the time we read her letter, she'll have already boarded her plane back home. She mentions not worrying about the rent for her room for the rest of the semester, the last line confirming she won't be coming back.

Confusion swirls in my head, mingling with my post-workout endorphin rush. I step back and lean against the counter. "I'm not sure what to say." I look at Everleigh who's sporting a downcast expression. We've known for a while that something was going on with Sylvia, but I never thought she'd just…up and leave.

"Me either. I had to stay late for that T.A. gig I was telling you about." She huffs out a sigh. "That's a whole other story I'll have to tell you about later, but that was on the counter when I came in. She just left, Violet. Didn't even say good-bye. Did she text you at all?"

"No, nothing," I tell her.

"When was the last time you saw her? God, I feel like it's been weeks since I've actually seen her face to face."

I think back, remembering when I saw her in the kitchen that day she went straight for the alcohol cabinet. And again when she found me and my sister watching TV. "It's been days at the minimum. She was on a different schedule than me and must have stopped showing up for classes, because I haven't bumped into her on campus at all."

"I heard her come in late the other night," Ev says. "But that's it. I didn't think much of it because it seemed to be her new way of living. Sleeping in late, coming home late."

"Yeah, I don't know. Think her parents forced her back to their homeland?"

"That's one possibility. She was getting those letters. What do you think they said? She was always so hush-hush about them."

"I have no clue."

"Do you think we'll ever see her again? What if something was really wrong for her to leave under the radar? What if we've been so deep in our own lives that we ignored her?"

I look at the letter again then back at my friend. I love how thoughtful Everleigh is and how intensely she cares about the people in her life, but Sylvia was riding through life to her own tune. "We didn't ignore her, Ev. We *did* try to be there for her, but she pushed us away. You saw how she got when she was approached about certain topics. What were we supposed to do?"

She worries her lip. "Yeah. You're right. It just sucks. We

were friends, Vi, and now we're nothing but two people who live in different countries?" Her concern shifts. "What are we going to do about the rent? Her family paid a bigger portion. Fuck, we're going to be screwed next year."

Cutting through the space between us, I wrap my arms around her and squeeze. She's not wrong to worry. Sylvia's parents did pay a bigger portion because they're, to put it simply, loaded beyond what our imaginations can conjure. "We'll find someone to rent out Sylvia's room, and it'll be fine. Worse case, we'll both chip in more if we want to stay in the building. We can always downscale to a smaller apartment, too."

"Vi, my parents can't pick up more of my rent," she admits with a hint of embarrassment. "My stepdad has been out of work since October. He was helping a family friend move and sidestepped on the curb and fell. Apparently, he was walking around with a broken neck for weeks. The doctor's rushed him in for emergency surgery when they found it."

"Oh, my God. Why didn't you say anything?"

She shakes her head. "I didn't want to bother you when you're already going through so much with Colson. And, anyway, he's going to be okay, but their income took a hit from it, and they don't know when he'll be back to work full time. I don't want to put that kind of pressure on them when the most important thing is him healing and getting back on his feet."

She wraps her arms around me and sinks into my embrace. "I'm so sorry for not being here for you," I whisper. "If there's anything I can do, you'll let me know?"

"Ugh, stop," she groans. "You are here for me. It's on me for keeping it on the down low. Between that, Tristan, and dealing with the professor I T.A. for, my patience is dwindling quickly. I legit could fill up a bucket full of tears right now," she huffs out in a sad laugh.

I pull back, my brows furrowed in concern. "What's going on with your professor?"

"It's nothing." She sighs, but I can hear that it's definitely *something.*

"I don't believe that for one second."

"Let's just say he's a total ass. A broody, miserable, *growly* know-it-all."

"Aren't those the kind of guys you read about in your books?" I ponder aloud to help shift the mood. Last week she was swooning over the male main character in the romance book she was reading because he did this huge public display of affection and at the end of it growled the words, "you're mine," into the female character's ear.

"They're sexy when they're fictional. Not so much when they're six feet tall and every other word out of their mouth can be taken as an insult."

I wince, sort of glad I'm not the one having to deal with it but feeling every sympathetic bone in my body reach out to her. "Can you switch over and T.A. for a different professor?"

She shakes her head. "It was supposed to happen that way but the original professor had something come up and Chatham U had to bring in a fill-in. He's who I got, so sadly, I'm stuck with him."

"Brutal," I murmur.

"Mmm, you don't even know."

I look at Sylvia's letter again, feeling the strain in my muscles. Yoga always helps, but having this dropped on me while simultaneously worrying for Ev has the knots in my muscles tightening all over again. I need a bath pronto, the warm water dulling the ache in my body if only for a little while.

Ev hops off the counter and makes a quick coffee before retreating to her bedroom for the remainder of the night. She promises she's okay, and that if anything changes, she'll come find me. We decide to sort out the rent issue when we're both more clearheaded.

I find myself in the bathroom later that night, my body covered by warmth with my eyes closed and my head relaxed back. After the water starts to turn the slightest bit cooler, my phone pings from the floor. I'm half inclined to ignore it and continue soaking but it's late, and if it's Olive, I want to make sure her trip back to Florida went okay. That she's all unpacked and ready for the start of the new semester.

I grab a washcloth from beside me and dry my hands then reach down for it. I don't realize how long I've been in the tub until I find it's after midnight when I unlock the screen and swipe to access my unread message. Familiarity swoops in my belly when I see Colson's name at the top of my unread texts.

What could he possibly want? We ended what was between us. For real, this time. So why is he messaging me this late?

Nerves skitter through my bloodstream as I weigh out my decision to open it and read it versus just letting it go. I'm trying to be a new version of myself, one where I don't cave. I caved with Webber until I didn't. I don't want to keep doing it with Colson, not when it comes with this insurmountable affliction that clutches my heart every time after.

Against my better judgment, I open the message. A masochist, I am. At least for the moment.

Colson: Need to see you. Can we meet up?

I blink, rereading it numerous times before I drop the

phone to the floor, screen still lit, and rest back against the tub. A million different scenarios run free in my mind.

Now he wants to see me? After I spent weeks trying to be there for him? How many times do we have to play this game of cat and mouse with each other until it's enough?

I scrub my hands over my face and push the few flyaways back with the rest of my hair. I sink my hands into the now room temperature water, cup a handful, and splash it over my face. I let a little bit of water drain and top off the tub with more scalding water before sinking down until my ears are covered.

Am I supposed to respond?

Am I supposed to agree to meet up with him after we both know what happened the last time we saw one another? He doesn't want to change. He wants to be a broken, hurtful version of the man he is.

My heart clenches with the idea of being in the same room as him again. Between his mom dying and everything he found out afterward, I know he's reeling from the pressure and weight of it. But what about me? Am I supposed to constantly allow my feelings to be dragged through the mud?

No, my inner voice tells me. *You're not.*

If I put my foot down with Webber, it's only right that I put it down with Colson, too, isn't it? *God.* I wish there was a guide with answers telling me what to do. Nothing feels like it's the right response. Agreeing to see him makes my heart stumble over itself. Telling him no makes my stomach cramp with guilt.

Rather than doing either, I let the water lull me into a near meditative state and ignore his message altogether.

Colson and I are over, and it's time I move on.

FIFTY-TWO

COLSON

A SOFT WHOOSHING of water rams into my legs. Like a wave rolling onto shore, it wraps around me, wetting my shins and calves. When I look down, there's a bandage over my left leg from the knee down. It's submerged in the water but miraculously hasn't absorbed a drop of it. I reach down and smooth my hand over the scratchy material to see a hole in my hand healed over by marred, reddish skin. It's the size of a quarter and as much as I want to freak out over it, my body remains calm.

I take a step back. The water reaches for me all over again, stretching to claim my legs. My feet are bare below it, catching on a surface I can't make out until I look up and see myself in Mom's house.

Why is there water inside?

I glance around, my eyes climbing the walls and checking the ceiling for a leak. Perhaps a pipe burst, and it's letting out water. Only, I don't come across the culprit.

I don't come across anything.

The house is spotless. The yellow tinge to the wallpaper has even cleared. The futon in the living room is gone.

Outside of the cookie jar, there's no dishes or random trash on the kitchen counters. The sink shines back at me.

And yet there are two feet of water bypassing the floor and trim.

A hushed voice travels down the hallway, and I swivel toward it, calling out, "Hello?" My face scrunches in confusion as I try to pinpoint where it comes from. "Is someone here?"

A laugh comes next, and I dart in the direction of the rooms. I check my bedroom, the bathroom, and push open Mom's bedroom door last.

A silhouette of a person stands in the far corner. "Hello?" I pause. "Who are you, and why are you in my house?" I glance down to find that there's no water in the bedroom. An invisible barrier is set up at the door frame, keeping it confined to the hall and open living space. I swallow down the uncertainty suddenly coursing through me. "Do you know why the place is flooded?" I ask, needing answers.

The person spins, brown hair sweeping off their shoulder when a clear, beautiful face regards me. "I don't see any water," comments the silhouette, stepping away from the corner and closer to the middle of the room. The only piece of furniture inside is the bed, where this person sits down.

I look down to my feet again, not understanding how she doesn't see it. It's right fucking there, and by the looks of it, it's another inch or two higher than it was initially. Wherever the leak is, it's gotten worse in the small amount of time I've been standing here.

"How?" I question, pointing down. "It's right there. You couldn't miss it if you tried."

I catch the end of her shrugging when I glance back up. Her body is small, but she looks strong and healthy. I squint, trying to get a better look at her, but it's not as bright in the bedrooms as it was in the living room.

"The only thing I see is my son," she simply says, her lips twisting up into the most genuine smile. A rush of emotion works through my heart and body. I look closer, noting the color of her eyes, how the hazel is so much more vivid than I remember it. How her teeth are as white as the bandage on my leg. How her face is clear from wrinkles and blemishes. There are no bags under her eyes, and her clothes are clean.

It can't be.

"Mom? Is that you?"

She chuckles, and it takes me back to some of my first memories as a toddler. Before her sickness got in the driver's seat and took control of the direction of her life. It's airy and light. The chirp of a baby chick on a Spring day. The smidge of dew coating the grass early in the morning. A kite soaring in the wind with no possibilities of it freefalling to its death.

"Of course it's me," she says. "Who else would it be?"

"I don't know...I don't understand. You're...you're supposed to be dead."

She clicks her tongue on the roof of her mouth. "That did happen, didn't it?"

A surge of grief and anger clutches me by my throat, the water from the floor suddenly in my eyes. I have a hell of a time blinking through it. Half a sob works its way into my mouth before the water returns to my shins. "You left me."

"Oh, darling," she mewls around a sorrowful tone. "I'm so sorry."

"No, you're not," I accuse, burning up from the inside out. The water floods higher, sneaking past my kneecaps. "How can you be? You only ever cared about one thing." And it surely wasn't me.

Her face falls. Her beautiful fucking face. She's the same

person from the picture Aunt Bess gave me for Christmas. She's not sporting a pregnant belly, but there's life in all of her features.

"That's not true," she tells me, standing from the bed and stepping closer. She's still half a room away. I hate her and want her gone, but I also really want her to make the trek to the door so I can hug her. Just one last time. "I loved you deeply, Colson. I still do love you. I'll never stop."

An ugly tear seeps from my eye and drips down my cheek. "You say that, but I don't feel it."

"I made plenty of mistakes when I was with you," she agrees. "But buried beneath all of my shortcomings was my love for you. Perhaps it was hidden, but it never faded. I'm sorry I couldn't show that to you."

"You could've tried," I clip out. "You were too busy doing whatever the fuck you wanted. *Clyde Lincoln*, really Mom? You married him, *and* he's my father? Why didn't you ever tell me? I deserved to know the truth."

She gives me a sad smile. "He was one of many mistakes. I couldn't see that at the time because I was so deep in it that he felt like home to me. But now..." She averts her gaze, fumbling with her fingers. "I can see I've hurt you, and I really, truly am sorry for that. I never wanted to cause you pain. I wasn't good when it came to feelings. I can admit that now."

The sob that I swallowed down makes itself known again. My eyes fill with tears. I don't bother hiding them. I need her to see the truth of what she left behind. I need her to look at her son and understand how deeply she scarred him—and how that'll stay with him forever.

"There's a part of me that wants to hate you for what you've done. For all the bullshit you put me through, for never making me feel like I was enough to forget about all the other stuff. But then my heart wins out because…I still love you. I always fucking will, and that's the hardest part in all of this," I tell her.

I don't want to care, but it's etched into the marrow of my bones. I can't get away from it even if I tried.

"You're just like Bess in that sense," she tells me with a small smile, walking closer again. "She always had the biggest heart. Always put herself in other people's problems thinking she could fix them if she tried hard enough. That can be both a strength and a weakness, Colson."

"She paid Clyde off to stay out of my life," I mutter out of the blue. "I could've known my father, but she kept him from me. Did you know that?"

Mom gives me a rueful smile and shakes her head. "I told you, a strength and a weakness. She did the right thing, Colson. Don't be mad at her when she was only trying to protect you from something I wasn't strong enough to."

She cancels out the last few steps and stands in front of me. The water sloshes around my upper thighs now and she notices, reaching out until her palm rests against my ribcage. The water moves violently below me, bubbling into a wavy mess without the added heat.

Emotion like I've never felt surges through me like an electrical current. It renders me immobile. All I can do is blink at the woman in front of me who has put me through so much yet is telling me to let go of it all.

How can I possibly let go of all the pain she caused?

"Easy," she answers like she's in my head, hearing my thoughts as I'm thinking them. "You have to forgive."

"How can I do that when everyone has betrayed me?"

Her. Clyde. Bess.

She tilts her head, and her eyes glow a beautiful shade of green that draws me in. I blink and there's another person in the room. My eyes cut to the form standing behind her.

A ridge forms between my brows. "Violet?"

"She hasn't betrayed you," Mom points out.

Violet turns on her foot, looking around like she's trying to figure out where she is. Like a double-sided mirror, she can't see us, but we can see her.

"Did you bring her here?" I question my mom, frantically looking between the woman who raised me and the love of my life.

"I know she is," Mom says softly.

"What?"

The water rises higher, and I can't move my legs. Mom's hand remains on my chest, and it's like I can *feel* her heartbeat merging with mine, twisting into a double helix of emotion. The kind that encompasses me when I'm with Violet.

Pure love.

"I know she's the love of your life, but you pushed her away when you needed her most."

Embarrassment clutches me like I'm a football soaring over a field laden with hybrid greens. "Because I thought she didn't deserve the weight of what I carried. It doesn't matter if I want her when the fact is that she deserves someone who can give her more than I can."

"There is no one better suited for her than you, my love. Look at her."

I glance behind Mom, settling my gaze on Violet's wispy brown hair and curious eyes. They lock with mine, and it's like everything around us fades. The house disappears, the water draining and absorbing back into the dirt below. Mom vanishes, too, though her voice remains.

"Look around you, Colson."

"The water is gone but so is the house," I observe out loud.

"No more of the bad," she confirms. "She settles you, and you do the same for her."

"How can you know that?" I swallow, trying to push down the lump in my throat. "You're dead."

She huffs out a laugh as if that fact holds no merit. "I can feel the way she looks at you."

"How?"

"Because I'm everywhere and have clarity I never had before." She breathes out a soft breath, and then Violet is gone, and the house is back, including the water.

It catapults to my neck, little droplets jumping into my mouth. "What the fuck?"

I begin to panic, knowing it won't be long until the water moves high enough to cover my head. What will I do then?

"You'll reach for her," Mom says like it's the easiest thing in the world. "Don't force yourself into misery because you're afraid to feel what I couldn't give you. I kept you from love, but that doesn't mean you have to hold yourself from it, too. You deserve it, darling. You deserve to be loved and for it to come in a way that calms and lifts you."

My lower lip trembles, moving in sync with the sloshing water. "Mom, I can't...you have to get rid of this water."

"I can't, Colson. You're the only one with the power to do that."

"But how?"

Make it stop.

"I just told you. Now, go," she encourages with a film over her voice that mutes her words. "You have people waiting for you."

"I don't want to leave you yet."

The water covers my mouth and washes over my eyes, too. Mom turns into this blurry, watery image before me, and before I can figure out how to stay, my vision cuts out.

FIFTY-THREE

VIOLET

"VIOLET!"

My brain registers someone yelling my name, but because I'm stirred from sleep it takes a second for me to think of a response or understand what the hell is happening. The warmth cocooning my body gets yanked from me as my bedsheets are ripped away. I roll to find Sebastian pacing my bedside, his hair sticking up on the sides like he, too, was just sleeping while simultaneously running his hands over his head repeatedly.

"Sebastian?" I question, still half asleep. The only gleam filling my room is from the hall dome light by the open door where Everleigh stands. I reach for my bedside lamp and click it on. I try to wipe the sleep from my eyes. "What's going on?"

"That's what I'm trying to figure out," Everleigh tells me. "I heard pounding at the door, and this is what was on the other side when I opened it. He rushed in here without saying a word."

Heavy breaths work in and out of Sebastian's chest, and for the first time ever, I think he might be losing it. His casual, charming demeanor shifts and in its place is a man who is trying to gather his thoughts and feelings, but his physical symptoms are overriding all else.

Anguish roils in my stomach, clashing with every other part of me. I sit up at the edge of the bed, eyeing Sebastian cautiously as he frantically moves from one side of my room to the other. Something is terribly wrong. I can sense it in his untimed movements and the way he has yet to speak.

"Sebastian," I say cautiously as I slowly stand. I make it over to him and stop his continuous pacing. I grab hold of his arms and look him in his eyes. They're completely wrecked, bloodshot and watery like he was crying. "Why do you look like someone just ran over your dog?" I ask wearily.

His throat bobs with a swallow, and this time, tears do collect in his eyes. "Not my dog."

Confusion plops in my brain like an apple in a bucket of water. I give Everleigh a look like, *what the hell is going on,* before saying, "Okay, do you want to tell us what happened?"

"Fuck," he heaves out, resting his hands on his knees. "I think I'm going to be sick," he mumbles, holding the back of his hand to his mouth. Everleigh grabs my trashcan next to my desk. She shoves it into Sebastian's chest in time for him to spin and throw up into it. He gags and retches again, Everleigh and I at either side of him, rubbing soothing circles over his back.

He spits the remnants of saliva into the can then sighs a heavy breath. "Vi, we need to go."

Everleigh chimes in next because we still have no idea what is happening. "Sebastian, we don't know what's going on. You need to tell us why you're," she grimaces, "vomiting and can barely get two words out."

He turns back around and lifts his chin, his eyes filling with what look like more tears.

I've never seen Sebastian so worked up in my life. He's usually the calm one of the bunch. The one who always tries to mend what's broken. The guy who can use his charm to get the saddest person in the room to smile or laugh. But not tonight, tonight he is...a shell of our friend.

"It wasn't my dog that got hit by a car," he says seriously, eyes on me. "I don't even have a dog."

"Okaaay," Everleigh draws out. "Make it make sense for us, Seb. Spit out what needs to be said."

His throat rolls again as he swallows. He squeezes his eyes shut for one brief second then drops a nuclear-sized bomb neither of us expects. "It was Colson. *Colson* was in a car accident. They, uh, they called my mom. I got off the phone with her and came right here because you need to come with me. *Fuck.* We need to get to the hospital, like, yesterday, Vi. But, shit, I'm having a hard time even *seeing,* let alone driving."

I stumble back a step, replaying only one of Sebastian's sentences in my head. *Colson was in a car accident.* No. That can't be right. I shake my head, but my heart withers. *Is he okay?!* I don't know, but this tingly sensation moves over my body, anyway. Like it just knows the results aren't going to be good.

My calves bump into the bed, and I lower onto the mattress, my gaze dropping to the ground as I try to make sense of those six words. Colson was in a car that was hit. Or maybe he hit another car with his. Either way, he was in an accident, and if he's at the hospital then that can only mean one thing.

He's not okay.

He's hurt.

And, oh *God,* I think I might need that trash can, too.

"Holy shit," Everleigh blurts out. "Why didn't you start with that when you nearly broke down the front door!"

"I couldn't..." Sebastian pauses. "I couldn't get it out. My entire fucking body is seizing up on me."

My heart beats like a drum in my chest. I know exactly how Sebastian feels. Like nothing is touching you yet there are straps tying you down. Without looking up, I ask, "What did your mom say? Did they give details on his condition?"

"His left side was hit. He has broken bones they need to operate on to fix. That's all I know. I'm supposed to meet her there, but fuck, I didn't want to do it alone, and you should be there with us."

I stand abruptly, pushing down every bit of pain and emotion that's threatening to choke me as I stand before my friends. We need to get to the hospital pronto. Colson shouldn't be alone for even a minute. He needs his family and friends with him.

That, and I need to see him with my own eyes. I need to see he's okay.

I remind myself that a broken bone means he's still alive and breathing. That he might be hurt, but he's alive. I lift my hand for Sebastian's keys. My fingers tremble as they hover in the air, my entire hand shaking. "Which hospital?"

Sebastian drops them into my palm. Everleigh swipes them almost immediately. "Harrison General Hospital."

"Neither one of you are driving," she declares, wrapping her hand around mine and giving me a reassuring look. "Take a deep breath, both of you. He's going to be okay."

"He has to be okay, Ev. He's basically my fucking brother," Sebastian says in a quavering voice.

Tears prick the corner of my eyes when Sebastian's voice breaks. My heart shreds to ribbons from his heartache alone. My legs are wobbly, half of them numb.

A tremendous amount of guilt hits me when I think back to Colson's message from earlier. I don't know what time his accident happened, but what if I could have stopped it? What if one reply would have derailed him off course and kept him safe?

The need to throw up hits me all over again.

No, I tell myself, shoving away the regret that tries to grip me. *I was only trying to protect myself before. I wasn't the one who hit him. I wasn't the one who put him in the hospital.*

And yet, he's still there.

Everleigh gently shoves us both toward the door. She climbs behind the wheel of Sebastian's Aviator when we make it to the parking lot. None of us speak as we make it onto the 401 and cross the Sycamore River for Harrison General Hospital.

FIFTY-FOUR

VIOLET

MY LEG TAKES on the needle-like sensation of what it's like to have your arm fall asleep after laying on it for half the night. I uncross my other leg from it and shimmy my foot to encourage blood flow. The crick in my neck is the next thing my attention turns to. I roll my head from shoulder to shoulder, hoping it'll release the pressure.

Unfortunately, it only makes it worse.

Bess talks on her phone in a hushed tone across from me, relaying all we know so far to Thad. He flew out earlier in the week for business and isn't able to make it home until tomorrow evening.

I'm sandwiched between Everleigh and Sebastian, the unmistakable scent of hand sanitizer and freshly brewed coffee billowing into the waiting room. An hour ago, the doctors moved us from the emergency room to the orthopedic surgical wing where Colson is currently undergoing surgery for not one break but two.

We were told to be grateful he wasn't hurt worse. In these delicate moments, it all feels the same. Like every injury would hold a high magnitude. Even a scratch.

When the ambulance and first responders arrived at the scene of the accident, they quickly learned Colson was T-boned at an intersection on the far end of Harrison Heights. The car rolled multiple times until it stopped on its hood. Whoever crashed into him, their car was in decent enough shape for them to drive off. A classic hit-and-run the police assured they were on the lookout to solve but who knows if they actually will.

I can only seem to concentrate on Colson's body being cut open behind a set of doors we can't walk through. He couldn't have just walked away with a few cuts and bruises but was laden with a broken tibia—the break so bad his bone split through his skin—a fractured clavicle they're pinning while fixing his leg, and a fractured eye socket that the doctor explained would look far worse cosmetically than in actuality.

My gaze ricochets around the room as my leg bobs up and down in response to the anxious pinpricks. Sebastian's leg does the same, moving in perfect rhythm to my own. He's a lot calmer than he was when he showed up at the apartment, but I know he's worrying and wondering how much worse it could've been. Still, he hasn't said much, and I haven't prodded because I think we're all going through something we'd rather not discuss.

I look around the waiting room, noting the strangeness in knowing it wasn't long ago that we were in this same hospital where Colson had to claim his mother's overdosed body. And now we're back for him. My stomach churns with a trifecta of overwhelming emotions.

Terror.

Devastation.

Somberness.

Each one folds over the other until they're the perfect

mixture of premade dough ready to bake, only a pretty loaf of bread isn't what I'll get in return. I'm blessed with a queasiness that rivals the worst twenty-four hour stomach bug one can imagine, the constant adrenaline rush of what it's like to walk around the corner only for your sibling to jump out and scare you, and the caffeine hit that comes from downing one too many coffees in a row.

No one else is in the waiting room with us, which makes me both relieved and remorseful. Relieved because I wouldn't wish this kind of suffering on anyone. Remorseful because why does it have to be Colson who's here instead?

I try not to think about it too much, knowing it's not the mindset I should get stuck in while we're waiting to hear that he's out of surgery. There's a TV monitor on the wall with a screen that has each patient's name along with their status. In the last hour, I've looked at it no less than a thousand times. Each time I do, I'm saddened to see no change. Colson's status is perpetually stuck in the surgery zone, indicating that they're still repairing his broken body. They said it could take hours. More if they run into complications. I pretend like that's not even a possibility.

My eyes fixate on the time at the bottom of the monitor. It's approaching four in the morning, and because I've had only an hour of sleep, I shift and crowd Everleigh's space.

"I need to get up and move," I explain in a whisper. "Do you want a coffee? I'm wide awake, but I need to give my hands something to do even if it's just holding a cup for now."

Everleigh looks up from her phone where she's been lost in a book. Her attendance isn't required, but she's here because she cares about me and Sebastian. Colson, too, despite not being very close to him. For a second, I think about Sylvia, wondering if her plane touched down on Ireland soil or if she's already back at her family's palace. It was only a few hours ago that I read her departure letter. If she were still here, would she be sitting with the rest of us in this waiting room?

Probably not. Tristan nor Webber are here. I wonder if Sebastian even told them about his cousin. Then again, he could barely tell me and Everleigh. I hate that it's gotten to this point—that we don't know how to be there for one another. That there used to be six of us, and now we're down to three.

Everleigh breaks me out of my thoughts when she says, "I can go get us all coffee. Why don't you sit and wait in case there's an update?"

I shake my head. "I need to get up and move."

She frowns. "Okay. We'll both go then."

"I don't think it's very far. I saw one of those machines around the corner when we got off the elevator."

"Perfect." She looks between Bess and Sebastian. "Would either of you like a cup of coffee? We could all probably use a little pick me up."

Bess twists her phone to the side. "Yes, that would be lovely." She fishes a couple of bills out of her wallet and hands them to Everleigh. "Get one for each of us, please."

I look at Sebastian's forlorn expression. He doesn't look up from wherever his gaze is set on the floor in front of his feet. *God.* He looks ruined. Ever since Colson came around, it's been clear how much he cares about him, but tonight that notion hits hard. He wouldn't know what to do if something happened to him. Just like Colson didn't know what to do when his mother turned up without a pulse.

Everleigh and I walk past the surgical orthopedic receptionist desk where there's a *be back in fifteen* sign suctioned to the glass slider. We push out through a door that leads to a hallway. I guide us to where I saw the coffee machine until we hear a commotion coming from the other end of the corridor where the elevators are located.

Near them is a help desk for those who are trying to find different wings of the hospital on this level. I didn't pay much attention to it since a nurse from the E.R. brought us to where we needed to be.

We make small talk as we wait for the machine to brew four extra-strong coffees. It adds cream and sugar for us as well. All while that same commotion from the help desk travels down the hall.

"What do you think that's about?" Everleigh asks, eyes wide when the person's voice bellows louder and the woman's voice behind the desk threatens calling security.

"Who knows."

"Hardly the way to be this time of night or should I say morning? God, I can't believe we're even here to begin with." She reaches out and squeezes my elbow. "You holding up okay?"

I nod in response, even though I'm a mess.

When I notice the familiarity in the male's voice from down the hall, I blink at the same speed of the last few drops of coffee falling into the last cup. Everleigh collects a carrying tray from the station next to the machine.

My attention seeks out the voice of the person who I can't see around the corner, waiting for them to speak again. A grumbled, "Fuck," booms down the hall, ping-ponging off the walls until it lands at my feet.

Wait a second.

I tell Everleigh to head back to the others without me. I'm not keen on being away for longer than necessary, but I'm also incredibly interested in finding out if my instincts are correct.

I wait until she's gone to make it around the curve in the hall where I can get a better view. Down the corridor, a man dressed in black denim with a long-sleeved gray thermal paces back and forth. His equally dark boots smack against the tile with each step he takes. When the man's profile turns, and I get a side view of him, my gaze connecting with the inky black lines drawn over the skin of his neck, my hunches are confirmed.

Finn.

I don't know if I should be relieved or worried to see him. I know which Colson would be. He'd hate knowing he's in the same building as him. Still, I can't turn and walk away now, not when I know who he's here to see.

I'm quick to make it to him so he doesn't give the lady any more trouble. He hasn't noticed me yet, so I reach for his arm to gently let him know I'm behind him.

He swivels around as soon as he registers the pressure of my hand. "Don't fucking touch me," he snarls out, his eyes darker than ever. Long strands of his hair brush over his forehead like curtains and then recognition dawns. "Violet?"

"That'd be me." I smile at him sheepishly.

"Fuck, I didn't mean—"

"It's fine," I cut him off. "You heard about Colson, didn't you?"

"Word travels fast in Harrison Heights. Someone fucking hit him and ran?"

Worry traces the color in his eyes as I try to find the proper words for an answer. I just nod and murmur out, "Yeah."

"He's okay, though, right?" This is exactly how I know Finn cares, regardless of what he's connected to on a day-to-day basis or what he did in the past.

I shake my head at the same time a glassiness fills my

eyes. Aside from the shock and dread that came over me when Sebastian stormed into my bedroom, I've been doing a decent job holding it together. However, there's something about Finn standing in front of me, his face distraught from the idea of Colson *not* being okay, that tears my heart in two. It's quick and easy, like shredding a piece of paper down the middle, but no less painful.

My arms come around my middle and clutch my stomach. My fingers dig into my shirt, twisting the fabric in my palms when Finn spins and runs his hand through his hair. He fists it, pulling at his own locks as if there's no pain attached to the action.

"How bad is it?" he questions after he's able to swallow down his fear. For a moment, I think how incredibly strange it is to be in this hall with him when the first time I saw him outside of Spring Meadows I referred to him as Stranger Guy.

I remember judging him, thinking how mysterious and out of place he was. How he didn't look like he belonged in Chatham Hills. I think back on the times Colson warned me to stay away from him and the night I learned about all he did.

I push it all away as if it doesn't matter because it doesn't. Finn came for me when Colson was fighting and he was worried where he may end up. He was there for me and Olive the night we showed up at his strip club. And now he's here again, at the hospital where his half brother lies on an operating table for injuries he sustained in a motor vehicle accident.

Maybe that's what draws me to clutch the fabric at his wrist and yank him down the hall toward the waiting room where we've been for the last hour. I don't know how everyone will feel over him being present, but he deserves a chair in that waiting room. He deserves the updates and details. He deserves to know the man he's trying like hell to earn forgiveness from is going to be okay.

We make it so far before Finn stops me by the coffee machine and presses me. "You didn't answer me, Violet."

I squeeze my eyes shut and blow out a breath. "He's in surgery, Finn."

He grits his teeth. "Surgery for what? The lady at that desk wouldn't tell me a fucking thing.*"*

"He sustained breaks. One of them was what they consider an open fracture."

"I'm not a doctor," he retorts. "What does that mean?"

"When his bone broke, it tore through his skin. The only way to fix it was for him to get surgery right away. He has another break, too, that they're putting a plate and screws in to repair while he's under anesthesia. They said it could take up to a couple of hours until they're finished. More if there are complications or they find more damage that needs attention."

"Did you see him?" Finn asks, voice way lower than when he was dealing with the woman at the help desk.

I give him a pitiful shake of my head. "None of us have."

"I'm going to find the bastards that hit him," he mutters under his breath, face turning so he can look down the hall. He takes a step back like he needs to retreat from reality.

"Finn," I call out softly.

"And then I'm going to break every goddamn bone in *their* body."

"You can't do that," I tell him, reaching for his arm to calm him.

"See how fucking pleasant it is for them. I'm going to wreck them, Violet," he promises without a lick of shame. A scowl twists his lips. "Fucking *ruin* them."

"*Finn.*"

He walks over to the coffee vending machine and smacks his palm into the side of it. The rumble of his assault echoes down the hall. I close in on him, not entirely sure what to do or say to get him to calm down but knowing he needs to before that lady really does call security.

His eyes are wild when he spins on me. "Prick isn't going to know what's coming for him."

"Attacking someone over this isn't what's needed."

"The hell it isn't."

I roll my eyes, annoyance running through me. Agitation like no other fills me. How dare he come to the hospital to act like this. It isn't the time or place, nor has he been the one sitting here, patiently waiting to hear how the heck Colson is doing or if his surgery was a success.

"Is this why you came? To get off on your own ego? Do you think *any* of us need you having a tantrum while we're shitting our pants with anxiety?" I bite down so hard I'm afraid my teeth might splinter and then say, "You know what? Go home."

I turn to walk away, leaving him next to the coffee machine with my own restlessness rising in me like a forgotten bathtub so dangerously close to spilling over. That's me. Near the edge and ready to roll over it and drip, drip, drip to the floor in a wave of defeat.

A tear slips past my eyelashes as I curve around the wall. I swipe it away, making it twenty feet until Finn calls out. He grips my bicep and spins me around a second later.

"Goddamnit, I'm sorry, okay? I didn't mean to...I *did* mean what I said about finding the person, but I get that it isn't the time or place to get into that. I just..." He looks away, then back down at me. There's this uncanny similarity between him and Colson in this moment that my heart slows to an underwhelming pace, slowly pitter-pattering against my ribcage.

"I don't know how to handle this," he admits, all that hardness he usually exudes nowhere to be found. "I find out that I have a brother, one who I've physically put my hands on more than once. I try to make it right, be in his corner, but it's fucking useless because he'll never forgive me. Had I known..." His jaw clenches, rippling from the weight of his bite.

"If I knew who he was to me, it would've never happened. As heavy as my past with Colson is, it's like in the snap of a finger it doesn't matter anymore. The only thing that matters is that he's okay. I keep thinking about how I *just* found out I have this brother, and that goddamn quick, he could've been taken from me. And I...I would've lost my shot at getting to know him. Like...*really* getting to know him. Not that surface level bullshit. Fuck, I sound like a pussy."

"I'm sure what you're feeling is normal for someone in your shoes," I murmur. "And I'm sure he'd be happy to know you're here for him now."

"Yeah fucking right. He's going to be pissed when he sees me."

"Does that mean you're staying?"

He nods solemnly. "Until I see he's alright."

I take a step closer and wrap my arms around his torso. If Colson saw us, he'd flip, but Finn could use the comfort. Hell, I could, too.

Finn wraps one arm around my waist, barely hugging me back. I take it for what it's worth, figuring he isn't used to this kind of affection. If he were, he wouldn't be so rough around the edges.

I take a step back when it seems like he's had enough and tip my head in the direction of the waiting room. "Come on."

FIFTY-FIVE

VIOLET

JUST AFTER THE turn of the clock, when visiting hours begin, Colson's status changes from in surgery to recovering from the anesthesia. It isn't long after this that his surgeon meets with us to discuss his progress. They repaired the break in his leg and collarbone with plates and pins. However, his collarbone went as far as shattering into microscopic pieces which was what took them so long to operate. They had to irrigate the area and clean it thoroughly before suturing him closed.

Now he's back in his own room, recovering from what they gave him during surgery and taking his good ole time doing so.

I watch the lines rise and fall on the monitor he's hooked up to as I sit across from his hospital bed. There's a steady beep that comes and goes, and every so often his blood pressure cuff fills, hissing out a stream of air. My gaze bounces between the monitor screen, watching as his heart rate stays at a steady rhythm, and his beautiful, battered face.

My heart jackknifes with every glance. The doctor was right, his face is terrifyingly black-and-blue. I can barely stomach taking in his eye, the skin around it heavily swollen and tinged a deep berry shade. His entire left side is beat-up, reminding me too much of his torso when he came to me that one night. I expect he's most likely bruised all the way down, but as my eyes drop to his hospital gown and the thin white blanket that's pulled up past his hips, I push the thought as far away as it'll go.

It grips me by the throat, trapping the air in my lungs, making it impossible to get enough oxygen in my body. I wish I could take it from him. All the pain, all the hardship. Seeing him in this condition does odd things to my extremities, making them restless and feel as though they have anchors strapped to them. It's hard to swallow the intermittent sips of water I drink between finishing my coffee.

I want to reach out to him, skim my finger over the edge of his hand, but I'm keeping my distance for reasons linked to my own self-preservation. I haven't seen him awake yet. He was too sleepy when he was still in the recovery unit, and I happened to step out before he came to for a few minutes, allowing Sebastian and Bess to be with him since visitors were limited in that section of the hospital.

I'm afraid if I touch him, he'll wake up, which is stupid because I *want* him to wake up. I want to see life in his ocean-blue eyes and to watch the corner of his mouth tip up in that smirk I've always loved.

But I'm also terrified of what he might say, how he might look at me, and what my reaction will be to all of that. Guilt finagles its way in again when I think about his text I never responded to. I'm trying to hold myself up and give myself the boundaries I need. After Webber and the debacle with my own father, I need more stability. I need what we had before the teeter-tottering aftermath of his mom's death.

However, a relationship is the last thing he needs and

wants—something he has made very clear. Not to mention, he'll have months of healing and physical therapy to focus on to gain back his strength. His energy doesn't need to be tied up with me, even if I desperately want to push it all away and have just that.

His uninjured leg shifts and his head rolls to the other side of his pillow. He's propped up in a comfortable position that allows him to see most of the room.

There are bandages on the leg they fixed and what looks to be a splint there. A sling, looped around his left arm rests on his chest. An IV is set on the back side of his other hand. His fingers twitch when his groggy eyes peel open. My stomach flips. Hell, my heart and brain do, too. I'm a complete mess as I watch him come to, suddenly wishing I wasn't the only one in the room.

Finn and Everleigh are out in the waiting room, marking time until Sebastian and Bess return with breakfast. So far, Bess has allowed Finn to stick around, though I've seen the way she keeps an eye on him, assessing to see if he's here because he actually cares or for another reason. He saw Colson when he was still in recovery, when it was way more unlikely for him to wake up and notice him standing there. He has yet to step in this room. I don't think he will, too worried about what Colson might say or do.

Colson's eyes blink sleepily. I watch as his throat bobs with a swallow, his face twisting into a grimace when he has a hard time with it.

I'm quick to stand and move over to his side, because if there's one thing I've always struggled with when I'm around him, it's giving him space. I drag the chair that's next to the bed closer until my knees smoosh against the cool, hard plastic. My hand reaches out on its own, my internal conflicts fading into the space behind me.

"You're awake," I manage to get out without choking on my own sob-filled cry.

Colson tilts his head to face me, his lips perking up in the tiniest purse. "Vi," he breathes out hoarsely, like he's in more pain than just the physical kind. Like his heart is screaming from the hell it went through. "You're here."

I breathe out a sigh, tears threatening to blur my vision. I can't keep them away. My eyes fill with the unraveling burn of emotion. "Of course I am," I tell him, my voice cracking on those four short words. "Where else would I be?"

"Anywhere else," he murmurs, lifting his non-injured hand around mine before giving it a weak squeeze. "Fuck, you got prettier."

A soft chuckle moves up my throat, and a tear slides down my cheek. "I look the same as I always have."

"Mmm, don't cry," he whispers, letting go of my hand to wipe the wetness from my cheek. I have to lean closer so he can reach. "I hurt," he groans, still a little out of it. "My entire body hurts, Vi. Make it stop."

I glance over at the morphine drip they have him connected to and grab the self-administering handheld button they briefed us on. It'll allow for small doses intermittently when he needs it, rather than giving him copious amounts of the addictive substance without a limit.

"You can press this when it's too much, and it'll give you a dose of pain medication if you haven't had one in a while," I tell him. He jabs his thumb into the button almost right away. "Do you have any memory of what happened?" I'm not sure if it's the best question to ask, but I'm curious to know how much he remembers.

"I just remember being at the grocery store one minute and then feeling like I was hanging upside down the next. Everything else is a bit blurry."

I nod, curling my fingers back around his when he settles, and his eyes fall closed again. "You might remember more over time. They gave you a lot of different medicine so they could help you."

He starts to doze off but manages to open his eyes once. I know he's talking about the bandages and sling when he asks, "Is that what all this is?"

"Yeah, Colson, it is."

"I'm gonna be fine, though?" he seeks, his eyes falling shut again.

My heart wrenches from the way he asks it. It's so unlike him to be unsure of himself. The person that hit him stripped him of his confident ability in always believing he'll get through. His blue gaze is dull and full of uncertainty when his eyelashes flutter and he looks at me again.

I physically ache to extend my hand out and trace my fingers over his sharp jaw, but his left eye is so incredibly bruised from the eye socket fracture, I'm scared touching his blemished skin will result in a wave of suffering.

"It might be hard for a bit," I offer in return, willing my voice not to break. "But you'll be okay. You have a lot of people around who love you and will help take care of you, Colson."

His eyelids flicker shut. I wonder if it has to do with the indulgence of morphine overriding his system. He licks at his dry lips that lack a little bit of color and murmurs, "Yeah, baby, but do I have you?"

He falls back asleep after that.

FIFTY-SIX

COLSON

THE LEFT SIDE of my body is fucked.

I'm bandaged from my shoulder, my arm stuck in a goddamn sling, down to my ankle. I haven't had the chance to see what my face looks like, but I don't need a mirror to know my eye is swollen shut and worse for wear. Christ, it hurts to even blink my *good* eye.

I can't wiggle my toes without an ache popping up somewhere else in my body. And don't get me started on how it feels like someone took coarse sandpaper to my throat and didn't relent until it turned into a bloody mess. The cottonmouth has been steady, too, but the doctors assure me it's a normal side effect from all the meds they gave me. Along with the nausea that comes in surges from the anesthesia wearing off.

I'm looking at weeks of recovery and then physical therapy afterward. The docs say I'll make it back to a hundred percent as long as I take care of myself and follow their strict orders. For now, I'm supposed to rest, but I'm slowly starting to resent this room. Everywhere I look holds a reminder of my actions. A reminder that I pushed away people I loved, took up illegal fighting to soothe the war on grief, and the deal I made with Clyde. How I threw that fight. How I'm in a hospital bed, the damn room resembling the barrel of a shotgun I have no choice but to look down with shame.

The initial anger of Clyde backing out on our deal resurfaces, and I'm left stewing without having an outlet. I can't get out of this bed. I can't walk without someone close by to help. Hell, I haven't even been able to stand to take a piss.

There's no way around my dilemmas other than to *think* about them. And I hate thinking. It's what drove me to drink that Jack all those weeks ago and what forced me to approach Eli.

The incoming and outgoing thoughts make me think about Tommy. I can't help but wonder if he found out about me throwing the fight. Does it look suspicious that I lost and haven't been back since? I mean, my accident only happened yesterday, but I don't have a working phone. It got lost when the car rolled, and first responders couldn't find it in the cleanup.

I have no way for anyone to contact me. No way for me to get a hold of anyone. If Tommy is pissed, I won't know until I'm released, which only makes the anxiety worse.

I fucked him over, thinking it would get me what I wanted in the long run: Mom's house. But see, I made a deal with the devil and lost. I should've known better. I should've realized that Clyde was never going to give me the house.

How didn't I see that?

A soft knock sounds at the door before it swings open, and my nurse comes in. She checks my vitals, asks about my pain levels, and lets me know I have a visitor waiting. One she was waiting to send in until she finished checking in with me. I give her the go ahead to send them in when she leaves.

Sebastian has been in and out of my room since I've been here. Sometimes he sits in the corner and falls into silence with me. Much like he did back at Mom's house. Other times we'll shoot the shit about whatever is playing on the TV. This morning, he brought me cream-cheese filled bagels from one of the coffee shops close to Spring Meadows. I managed to get one down before the urge to throw up came over me, and I pushed it away, assuring him he could eat mine, too.

Minutes later, after I find a movie to watch on the mounted TV, I sense the door opening and say, "Grandma's Boy is on. Been ages since we've seen this movie."

When I don't get Sebastian's heartfelt chuckle along with his confirmation of how much he cracks up whenever Jonah Hill is on the screen, I glance over, and end up doing a double take.

Sebastian isn't looking back at me.

My mouth pinches into a sour expression and the revulsion from this morning returns. "Who the fuck let you in?"

Finn shoves his hands into the pockets of his jeans. "Didn't realize I needed a permission slip."

I turn my gaze back to the TV.

He huffs out a sigh. "I'm not allowed to visit my brother?"

My entire body vibrates with annoyance. "Didn't I tell you about that before? You know, how we're not even fucking close to being brothers?" I turn and stare into his dark eyes. "That we never will be?"

"So you keep saying." His eyes trail over my body, on the IV taped in place on my hand. On the oxygen tubes that dangle over one of my shoulders, because they force me to wear them when I sleep.

"Don't let the door hit you on the way out," I grit out.

"Or, actually, do let it hit you if it means it'll knock some sense into you and make you leave me alone."

"What the hell do you want from me?"

"I've told you time and time again what I want. For you to leave me be, but you can't seem to understand I want nothing to do with you, Finn."

A moment of silence passes between us, and when I look back over, I swear I catch the tail end of his face falling. "I was here the night of your accident, waiting just like your aunt and your friends were."

He was? I had no idea. Not that it matters.

"What? You want a prize? You want a watermelon sucker to make you feel like a good boy for showing up?" I quip.

"I'll take butterscotch if you got it."

My eyes squint in irritation. "What?"

"Not a fan of watermelon, but I'll take butterscotch." He takes a step closer to the bed, his hands leaving his pockets for him to cross his arms over his chest. I don't know what he's doing, why he's wasting time on a lost cause. "I know I'm not going to find forgiveness here, but..." He collects his hair in his hand and pulls at it. Pulls at the stainless-steel ring pierced into his lip, too.

"Just leave, Finn. We'll both be better off if you actually start listening."

"Thing is, I don't want to fucking listen to that, Moore."

A host of memories come when he refers to me by last name. So many times, that word has left his mouth only for me to have to endure his wrath over deals that had nothing to do with me.

"He didn't tell me," Finn says. "I had no idea who you were to me. And if I had known—"

"If you had known, what? You stand there and act like it would've changed things, but it wouldn't have. You run drugs, and who the fuck knows what else, with that piece of shit you call Dad. He would've forced your hand; we both know it. I can't wrap my mind around you not realizing that on your own."

"He's your dad, too," he interjects.

"No…he's not. I'm nothing like that man, and I never will be but you…you're a spitting image of him. You drain people of the little bit of life they have left in them. Then when you do, you toss their pruned bodies out like they never had a chance." I lick my lips and continue. "I may have turned to shit I should've left alone after my mom died, but that's not who I am. Isn't that why you showed up and brought Violet into it? To get me to snap out of it and stop throwing my life away? That's the difference between you and me. There's still hope where I'm concerned even if I have to work double time for it now but you? You ran out of potential a long fucking time ago, Finn."

"Watch what you're saying," he warns, his eyes flared with heat.

I laugh, swallowing down the raspiness that comes when I say, "Or what? You going to do what you did to me back then? In case you can't fucking see, Finn, I'm already laid up in a hospital bed. Not much more you can do to make me suffer. Unless you're willing to end me, and if that's the case," I hold my one good arm out, "then have at it. Put me out of my goddamn misery."

For what feels like the first time ever, he rolls his eyes. "Jesus, fuck. That's not what I want. You don't fucking get it. You will *never* understand what it was like growing up in a house with a man like him and being forced to look up to him."

My heart gallops in my chest. Fuck him for trying to make it sound like he suffered to the extent I did. At least he had two parents. Not only his father, even if he is a royal fucking prick, but a mother as well. No one fed *her* drugs until she wound up in jail then proceeded to sneak them in for her. He doesn't get to do this to me, goddamnit.

"I don't care what it was like for you, Finn. My free passes shriveled up a long time ago."

"A free pass isn't what I'm looking for. All I'm saying is…"

"Is what?" I press, because I'm getting fed up. Since he came into the room, my pain number has gone up no less than three digits.

The words must be hard for him to get out, because he mulls them over for a solid minute. He ducks his chin, his voice a decibel I can hardly hear. "I'm fucking *sorry*, okay?"

"You're sorry?"

"Yeah, I am." He raises his head, not backing down from the weight of the conversation. "We're family, and we're supposed to protect our own. I went against you every step of the way because I *had* to. I let him turn me into him, so he could get what he wanted. It was fucked up."

"You're just realizing this now?"

"Consider yourself the smarter one of the two of us," he half-jokes but there's not a smile in sight.

I look at him. Really look at him as he stands at the foot of my bed. For a fleeting moment, I see it. The scared little boy who would run around the playground during recess with a gigantic smile on his face until life caught up with him. The boy who went off on summer vacation and came back colder and meaner with two burly cousins who flanked his sides during our middle school years.

The playground games stopped, and the pocket picker and lunch money thief made his entrance. Back then, he thrived off the punishments and the cruelty he dished out. His older cousins would pat him on the back, and I'm sure that filled his eager little heart, knowing he'd get to go home to receive the affection he so desperately wanted from Clyde as well.

His expression flattens, the tiny smirk that was playing at his mouth vanishing. "I'm not him."

"You're a spitting image," I remind him again.

"I don't want to be," he admits sheepishly, which is fucking weird because I've never seen Finn wilt so easily. "I was born into that life, Colson. Same as you. Sure, I made some messed up choices along the way, but they weren't for my own enjoyment."

"Then walk away if you're so bent out of shape about it. Or don't. You're still not hearing that I don't fucking care."

He shakes his head. "You say that like you weren't at his beck and call a day ago trying to make a deal with the man." I look at him. "Yeah, I know about that. What the fuck were you thinking, anyway? Screwing over Tommy is the last thing you need. I told you what he'd do. The kind of man he is. You better hope he doesn't find out."

My stomach swoops with that same feeling of wanting to fucking puke. "The only way he'd know would be if your dad told him."

He narrows his eyes at me. "You still don't get it."

"Get what?"

"Clyde doesn't give a shit about anyone but himself. He wouldn't blink before throwing you under the bus."

"Is that what you're saying happened?" I challenge. If anyone would know, it'd be him.

"I don't know what he did. I don't want in on any more shit with him than I have to be. The older he gets, the less he gives a fuck about discretion."

If Clyde ran his mouth to Tommy after I threw that fight...

I'm fucked. Totally obliterated.

Like earlier, I sense the door opening, despite my full attention being on Finn. I'm not necessarily expecting company, but Aunt Bess and Sebastian have come and gone all throughout the day.

Violet was here once, too. The first time I woke up in this room, but I was still groggy as fuck from the surgery that I fell asleep after only being awake for a few minutes. She was gone by the time I woke up again. Understandable since I'm sure she has to keep up with her course schedule, but hell if I don't want her at my bedside. When I close my eyes and think about it hard enough, I can sense her hand curl over mine.

I don't get the chance to do that now, though, because three men I've never seen a day in my life waltz into my room like it's nothing. They all look alike in dark pants and leather jackets, each of them rocking a buzz cut.

Finn spins, following my gaze. His shoulders immediately stiffen. It's enough of an indicator for me to know they didn't make a mistake and walk into the wrong room. This was intentional. Them showing up here.

"Who the fuck are you?" Finn demands, his hands now at his sides, the vulnerability in his tone long gone. He's back to the stone-cold man Clyde Lincoln raised, puffing his chest out in a way that tells these guys how unafraid of them he is.

The last man to walk in the room dips his hand into his waistband hidden by his jacket and pulls out a 1911 pistol. With his large hand wrapped around the grip, he nudges it at Finn before one of the other men flanks his side with their own gun pressed to his temple.

"What the fuck is this?" Finn commands, insistent on wanting answers.

"You get boss's message loud and clear," the head man in charge says with a broken Russian accent.

My body sinks into the uncomfortable hospital mattress, my muscles rioting with enough trepidation to spike my pain yet again. The only way out of this is facing it head on, because it's clear these guys aren't fucking around.

"What boss?" I ask, keeping my voice even.

"Mr. Tommy. He sends us to make sure you understand."

"Understand what?"

My conversation with Finn replays in my mind. We were just talking about the possibility of Tommy knowing about me taking a dive in my fight. Did we fucking summon these guys? The probability that he's talking about anything else is low. I haven't been up to no good. Not really, anyway. I may be fighting, but outside of my deal with Clyde, nothing else exists.

"It was Tommy," Finn announces, the cool metal of a gun muzzle pressed into his skin. He acts as if he's not bothered. Like he deals with this kind of shit every day, having weapons with live rounds pointed at him. "He fucking ordered a hit on you."

The Russian chuckles. I feel his deep laugh in my own chest at the revelation.

That can't be. Sure, Tommy is serious about his money, but paying someone to perform a hit and run at my expense?

He won't spit you out, and if you're one of the lucky few he doesn't want, I promise you won't be whole by the end of it.

"Wouldn't exactly say hit," the man says nonchalantly, his accent curling around every word. "But message, yes."

I sink my teeth into my cheek before asking, "Message regarding what?"

"You give his hard-earned money to Harrison Heights sleazeball who likes to run mouth."

Fucking Clyde.

We had a deal, damnit.

When my gaze darts to Finn, I find his nostrils flaring, his tongue rolling against his teeth like he can barely contain himself. I envision him twisting that pistol out of the guy's hand behind him, lowering it to his gut, and emptying a round into it.

And then I'm back in my car, seeing the headlights flying toward me, wondering why the hell they aren't slowing down. I'm there for the collision, floundering in my seat when the force of it is so powerful it lifts my car on its side. I'm dangling from my seat belt as it rolls multiple times and skids to a stop on its roof.

I'm in the ambulance again.

In the emergency room under the blinding lights.

In this bed when I open my eyes for the first time and find Violet.

Violet.

What I wouldn't give to have her with me. To have her curled into my side with her beautiful eyes staring up at me.

I almost lost that. I wanted Mom's house so badly that I turned to Clyde and trusted him even after he fed Mom all those drugs and continued to sneak them into the county jail for her. He killed my own mother, and I sought him out, made a deal with him, and trusted that he would follow through without putting a big red X on my back.

A sickness like I've never felt roils in my guts, traveling throughout my body until it's everywhere. My lips flatten into a straight line. For the life of me, I can't get words out. Everything slows down as this sense of dread filters through me and tunnel vision consumes me.

Finn must notice because he speaks for me. "What is it he wants?"

The Russian turns to look at him. "You speak for him now, yes?" he questions, the words rolling off his tongue.

Finn ignores the question. "What does Tommy want?"

The Russian breathes out. "Replace what your thieving hands took from him."

"Okay, fine. He'll pay it back," Finn spits out, his chest rising and falling in quick succession. I imagine it isn't so easy for the roles to be reversed. For him to be cornered like he used to do to me all the damn time.

"How much?" I eventually ask, my heart dropping three flights because here I am again, needing to pay someone money I don't have. Only now it's worse because I'm stuck in this goddamn bed and can't do anything about it.

The Russian rattles off a number in the thousands. It's money I don't have, but then I remember all the fights I won and the stash of money I collected from them. Relief floods my veins, but that money is at Mom's house and who the hell knows if Clyde took it over by now.

Once again, I'm strung out on a line to dry.

Clyde will never let me back in to get it if I tell him there's something there I need, let alone it being money. Hell, I didn't even get the chance to pack any belongings because I ended up here instead.

"Mr. Tommy promises worse shape if money is not paid back." The man holding a gun to Finn's head lowers it. "Tomorrow."

"That's not enough time. If you haven't noticed, I'm strapped to this bed. I can't fucking walk without help."

"Your problem. Not Mr. Tommy's."

They tuck their guns back where they can't be seen and

file out of the room like they didn't just come in and flip tables.

Finn moves to the door as soon as they're gone. "These doors don't have fucking locks?"

There's no point in locking it. They'd find their way back in regardless. I don't know how I'm going to get out of this one. How I'm going to get them their money when all I have is under Clyde's roof, a man who had no issue letting Tommy, his enemy, in on what I did just so he could brag and feel like the bigger man for all of a minute.

Did he not understand that his braggy nonsense would be at *my* expense? That he was lining a firing squad up in front of me when he clued Tommy in on our plan?

"I think they're gone," Finn says in an agitated tone when he opens the door to presumably check the hallway just to close it again. "I should cut that fuckers hand off for pressing that gun to my head and feed him his fucking fingers."

I regard Finn with a look I can't quite pinpoint. My head spins along with the rest of my body. The room swirls and twirls like one of those mind games that fuck with your eyes.

Violet's face forms in the small space between all the movement, and I lock onto it. Onto her pretty features. Her curious brown eyes. Her full, sweet lips. The beauty mark on her cheek.

She's a figment of my imagination, but I want the real thing. For her to teleport into my space. Mom was right in that dream when she said she calms and grounds me.

Beeping ensues around me, but I can't tell where it's coming from. A weight rests on my chest I've felt one other time: when I was leaving Eli's. It's all-consuming, like what it would be like if the room filled with water, and I remained in this bed. Much like my dream. My lungs have the hardest time pulling in air, and fuck, I'm not sure if I even want them to. It doesn't matter, though, because no matter how hard I try, my breaths don't reach where they need to go.

The beeping comes quicker. Violet's beautiful face gets farther away. I reach for it, but I'm too weak.

Is it always going to be like this?

A deep voice is at my side uncharacteristically fast. It takes me a minute to process that it's Finn. That he's next to me, reassuring me that I'm okay, that I need to breathe, as he grabs the oxygen tubes and holds them to my nose.

FIFTY-SEVEN

VIOLET

Old text messages...

Colson: Gonna be late tonight.

Violet: Everything okay?

Colson: One of the other dudes never showed
for their shift. I don't want to leave Llewellyn
on his own for the rest of the night.

Violet: That's sweet of you.

Colson: The only sweet part about me is you,
baby.

I'M HALFWAY through the quad, walking home from my afternoon class when Finn falls into step with me.

"He needs you," comes from his mouth so effortlessly. Like he chanted it repeatedly on his drive to Chatham Hills.

I glance up at his dark hair and even darker eyes, swirls of black ink tatted down the sides of his neck. When my eyes move back to focus on where I'm walking, I also catch ink on the back of his hand. I don't realize he has a cigarette between his fingers until he pulls a lighter from his pocket, puts the cigarette between his lips, and lights it.

"This is a nicotine free campus, Finn. You have to put that out."

"I either smoke this or I grab the next prepped up fucker that walks by to let out the frustration inside of me. Which will it be, Violet?"

He takes a long draw from the cigarette while I skip over his rude remark. I fix the strap of my messenger bag on my arm, not in the mood to deal with him right now. "What are you doing here?"

"Already told you," he states, following me toward Main Street. I'm on my way back to Spring Meadows after a long morning of classes. "He needs you, so whatever you got planned, cancel it and get your ass to the hospital."

"You can't command me around."

I left the hospital after I had to get back to campus for class and daycare duty. I couldn't cancel or call off sick. Besides, it's better Colson's actual family is there for him as he recovers. I don't want to make it harder for him by ripping up the memories of the end of our relationship. We've already been through so much, and I don't want to make it worse. However, the way Finn's voice sounds all hurried makes me wonder if maybe I should've stayed. Or at least gone back to visit again.

"Just fucking go see him, will you?" Finn barks, half of his cigarette already smoked.

I roll my eyes. "Coming from the one who was too scared to step into his room when he was recovering."

There's a short pause before he confirms, "I went in to see him."

I snap my gaze to him, knowing he was worried about Colson knowing he was there. His earlier statement about him needing me gets pushed to the back burner. "And? How'd it go?"

"How do you think?" he quips, full of attitude.

God, what is his problem?

The last time I saw him he was practically on his knees, ready to beg for Colson's forgiveness, though that vulnerability is long gone, replaced by the man I first saw outside of Spring Meadows.

"It was shit. He doesn't want to forgive me, blah fucking blah," he informs me. "We're moving on to more important things now."

"Anyone ever tell you how unmistakably rude you can be?"

"One of my finer traits," he dryly jokes with a straight face, cigarette between his lips.

"I'm not just going to run to him because you say I need to. I can't do that anymore. You need to respect that."

He grabs my arm, plucking his cigarette out of his mouth. When the smoke from it billows between us, my face screws into a grimace. "He had a goddamn panic attack, Violet, so can you drop the prissy preppy act for one fucking minute and listen to what I have to say before you write him off?"

Unease flows through me. I choose to ignore his insult and land on Colson letting his anxiety get the best of him. "What caused it? Was it his injuries? Is he okay?"

"Physically, he's fine, but..." Two girls walk around us, and he pulls me closer to the side of the walkway. He lowers his voice and says, "A few of Tommy's guys showed up when

I was there. A bunch of Russian dudes who just strode right in and held us up with guns."

My eyes go wide. "Oh, my God."

"They didn't stick around, but long story short?"

I nod, eagerly wanting details. "Yes, what is going on?"

"Tommy put a hit out on Colson because he threw a fight and lost him a shit load of money."

"I don't understand." I shake my head. Colson wouldn't do something like that without a solid reason. "Why would he do that?"

"For our dad."

Where does he come into the fighting picture? I rattle my brain with the knowledge I have. It feels like there's something missing, something I don't know.

"Colson made a deal with him for his mom's house. Agreed to lose one of his fights so Clyde could bet and win a truckload. He has bad blood with Tommy and wanted revenge."

"So, he used Colson to get back at him."

"Essentially. No one thought Tommy would find out, except Colson didn't exactly know who he was making a deal with. Our dad turned around and went back on their deal but that's not all."

I motion for him to get on with it. "What else?"

"Clyde told Tommy about it. Probably bragged over getting his ass back after all these years. Tommy knew Colson betrayed him with the fight. The hit-and-run wasn't a coincidence."

All the air leaves my lungs. I feel my face go pale with shock. "The accident was intentional?"

"'Fraid so." He drops his cigarette on the ground and snuffs it out with his boot. "They want the money back that Colson lost them."

"How much is it?"

"More than either of us carries around."

My eyes glance between Finn's. "And if he doesn't have it? If he doesn't pay it back?"

"They're going to make right on that hit. Finish what the accident failed to do. They left and not a full minute later Colson got this glassy look in his eye and zoned the fuck out. The nurse had to come in and give him meds. His heart rate machine kept going off. Fuck, I can still hear the incessant beeping."

"He's going to be okay, though, right? Did he calm down?"

Finn shrugs. "I don't know. The nurse kicked me out, saying he needed rest. I think she thinks I'm the reason he freaked. But it was *them*. Those Russian fucking bastards. They waltzed in like they owned the goddamn place, Violet. And Tommy...he takes another go at Colson—"

"Just...calm down. When does he need the money? Did you tell his aunt?"

So many thoughts zip through my head it's hard to hold onto one for long.

"You saw the way she was sizing me up in the waiting room. I go and tell her, and she'll blame me. Who the hell knows if she even knows what Colson has been up to all this time."

"That's fair, so when do they want it by?" I ask again.

"Tomorrow," he answers grimly.

"Can't he go to the cops?"

"Sure," Finn shrugs. "If he wants to speed up getting one right between the eyes," he says sarcastically while tapping a knuckle between his eyebrows.

"Tommy wouldn't do that, would he?"

He gives me a look as if I'm dumb and haven't heard

anything he's said. "Is the grass green, Violet?" He looks away then back at me. "The fucker paid someone to crash into him to teach him a lesson. *Yes,* I fucking think he'd go that far. Not to mention he sent three of his douchebag bodyguards into a hospital fully strapped. I told you this was going to happen if he wasn't careful."

I mull over all possible outcomes.

Colson not paying him back because he's stuck in the hospital. Him answering to Tommy's wrath. Him ending up in far worse condition than he is now.

I can't see that.

I cannot walk into that hospital and see him with more injuries.

Finn is already looking at me when my gaze slides back to him. Colson can't leave the hospital to tie up these loose ends with Tommy, and we're the only ones who know about it.

"We need to get Tommy that money," I tell Finn.

"Fucking right we do."

My focus wanders to Chathum U's campus. It may be the middle of winter and the chilliest it'll be all year, but students still mill around, walking from one building to the next, finishing assignments on benches, and overlooking the quad from within the campus buildings. "You're going to tell me you have an idea now, right?"

Finn looks both ways then gets right into it. "You're not going to do anything but walk your ass back into that hospital and stay by his side."

My expression falls. Putting myself back into Colson's orbit is dangerous. As much as I want him to be okay, *I* want to be okay, too.

"What about the money?" I ask. I don't have thousands of

dollars to hand over, and if I ask my parents, they'll lose their minds.

"I'll handle that. I assume those guys are going to show back up at the hospital tomorrow to get it from him. I'll get what he needs and drop it off in a duffel bag. We can't leave it alone and no one else can know about it."

I nod. "Okay." I can do that.

He gives me a look. "I'm serious, Violet. No one can know what kind of shit Colson is in. That car accident is nothing compared to what guys like him will pull to make sure people know he's not one to fuck with."

"I won't say a word. I'll stay with him as much as my schedule allows. You'll have to fill in the gaps in between."

"You're going to have to skip a class or something. This situation is too sensitive, and I can't risk Colson throwing me out of his room before they get there. He likes you a whole lot more than me. Besides, if that nurse sees me, she might not let me back in."

I don't respond right away, and my name falls from his lips. "Violet?" The way he says it tells me he's not kidding. This is how it has to be if Colson is going to be safe. "Can you handle this?"

"Yes. I'll show up and stay with him."

He narrows his gaze, rolling his tongue over his lip ring. It gently tugs back and forth. "What's the deal between you two, anyway? Anyone with eyes can see how much you fucking care for each other. He'd sell a kidney to save you. You're willing to do this to save him, and yet you're holding him at arm's length. Why?"

He lights up another cigarette, ignoring a dirty look from a guy who walks by. I don't mention how he wasted half of his last one by stomping on it. I deduce that it's more of a nervous tick than anything.

"It's not that simple," I mutter. Nothing with Colson in the last month has been easy.

"The fuck it isn't. If you love each other, what the fuck else matters?" he questions, but then he walks off without letting me get an answer in.

I think he does it on purpose.

FIFTY-EIGHT

VIOLET

I WALK BACK to Spring Meadows with a quicker pace than when I left class. I toss my bookbag down in my room, pace for a couple minutes and decide I'll hold off on my assignments until I get back from Harrison Heights.

I can't believe I'm doing this, bulldozing straight through my boundaries for someone else again. I remind myself I'm not doing this for just anyone. It's for Colson, and if roles were reversed, I do think he'd do it for me, too.

Sorting through my closet and drawers, I slip on a pair of sweats, knowing Colson doesn't care about what I wear. He isn't petty and materialistic like that. I could wear a ripped shirt and stained pants that haven't been washed in a week and he'd still look at me with fire in his eyes.

Or well, that's how he used to look at me.

I push the thought out of my head, twist my hair into a sloppy braid that falls over my shoulder and make it down to my car. I blast the current top hits to keep my mind on merging onto the 401 and crossing the Sycamore Memorial Bridge. It almost feels like my trip is cut in half with how time speeds up. I drive up to Harrison General Hospital minutes later, the bright red E.R. signage taunting me as I find a parking spot. It's there as a reminder of what it was like to show up the other night. How my heart was in my throat and my stomach wasn't far behind.

I shove away the thought and make it up to his wing. Bypassing the nurse's station, I stand outside of his door, noticing it's cracked the tiniest bit. Not enough for me to peek inside to see if he has any other visitors but enough to notice voices and a television playing.

My heart seizes, and my brain overthinks walking in. They rage a war with each other right outside of his room like I'm not even present. A nurse walks by with an ice pack, giving me a friendly smile as I internally freak out.

I don't know why I'm acting like it's the first time I've spoken to Colson. We have history. We *know* each other.

A little bird tells me why I'm stuck from moving another step forward. It has nothing to do with the situations we've been through and everything to do with not wanting to be rejected again.

I don't want to put myself back out there, demolish my own boundary lines, and have him douse me with his frigid side and push me away.

Mentally, physically, emotionally…I can't withstand a storm that tumultuous.

I blow out a steady, though anxious, breath and tap my knuckle on the door. I have my messenger back strapped over my chest with my assignments due at the end of the week in case Colson sleeps and I'm able to get time to work on them.

A soft, "Come in," chimes from inside. It sounds like Bess. I toe a thin line between wanting to ditch this place and run straight into Colson's arms, nuzzling my face into his neck until he's miraculously healed.

The room is darker than the last time with the shades

drawn closed and the fluorescent lighting brightening the space in a soft white-glow. Bess is sitting on an armchair in the corner when I make it past the door, Thad sits next to her in an equally as comfortable chair, and Sebastian hovers next to Colson's bed, showing him something on his phone while he sits up, forking what I assume to be his dinner into his mouth.

"Oh, look who we have here," Bess croons, standing from her chair and crossing the room. She pulls me into a hug, squeezing me in that motherly way of hers as my attention darts around the room.

Still in her embrace, I raise my hand in a little wave. I've never felt so awkward in my life. "Hi, everyone."

"Nice to see you, Violet," Thad greets, giving me a chin nod.

Bess pulls away, scanning me head to toe. She's quiet when she says, "Thank you for coming." She looks at me like she was waiting for this moment. Or maybe, rather, her nephew was. "I think he could use cheering up."

I swallow at the sudden thickness in the back of my throat. I didn't consider Colson having visitors. This awkwardness blankets me from top to bottom, and I don't know why. Two days ago, I sat with Bess and Sebastian as we waited for Colson to get out of surgery. I was with them the night of the fundraiser when we all raced to this same hospital. But then my gaze wanders over to the bed sitting in the center of the room, and my eyes connect with the pool of blue already on me.

How is it possible he can look like *that* after enduring the trauma he did? He may be in a hospital gown, only one arm free due to his sling, but he's as gorgeous as ever. The physical memory of his accident curls up over his neck, the skin around it peppered in bruises, but he's still the Colson I met and am still so much in love with that it isn't even funny.

He sets his fork down on his tray, pushing back his half-eaten attempt at dinner. His eye still sports one hell of a shiner, the swelling still there, but I'd stare at him forever, pushing down the uneasy sensation it pulls into my stomach if it meant he'd always be okay.

A thin layer of stubble coats his chin and cheeks. I want to run my palm over the roughness of it before slipping the pads of my fingers over the smoothness of his beautiful, thick lips.

Bess returns to her seat. At least, I think she does. With Colson's attention focused solely on me, it's hard to pay attention to anyone else. He looks at me like I'm the only one in this room. Like he can't believe I'm here but also like he's been waiting for me for an eternity.

"Look what the cat dragged in," Sebastian teases, slipping his phone into his jeans pocket. I tiptoe farther into the room and his hand grasps my shoulder, squeezing it reassuringly before he slips past me in a silent offering of giving me his perch at Colson's bedside.

"We were just getting ready to head out for the evening," Bess informs me, gathering her belongings.

I twist back on my heel, catching Colson as he picks up a napkin and wipes his mouth from my peripheral. "Please stay. You don't have to leave because I'm here."

"We've been here for, like, three hours," Sebastian says, grabbing his coat hanging over the foot of Colson's bed. "Surprised he hasn't kicked us out yet."

"I was giving you five more minutes," Colson jokes back.

Sebastian chuckles—I'm relieved to see he's back to his regular self—and slips his arms into his coat while Bess comes to Colson's side and gives him the best hug he can manage. She kisses the side of his head then moves for the door. "Have a lovely visit, you two," she says before Thad gives Colson's leg a squeeze and pat. He follows her out to the hallway a second later.

Sebastian loiters with a content smile playing at his lips. He looks so much better than he did when he busted into my bedroom full of worry. "Be back in the morning with your bagels?"

"Only if they have the strawberry filled ones," replies Colson. "The regular cream cheese makes me want to gag."

I awkwardly keep quiet and glance at Colson's tray. There's still food on his plate; mashed potatoes, a lump of chicken, and mushy carrots. A cup of vanilla pudding sits off to the side, a spoon next to it.

Sebastian says his goodbyes. "See you later, Vi. Don't let this one out of your sight."

Colson rests his head on his propped pillow, not bothering to shove his table off to the side. It's one that hovers over the bed, and it makes it easy for him to reach for his can of ginger ale. He grabs it and sips through a straw.

Sebastian exits the room, and then it's just us. Two people who used to be more than awkward glances and uncomfortable words. And then he points out how I haven't been around. "Wasn't sure if I'd be lucky enough to see you again."

I drop to the chair next to his bed, the feet of it screeching across the floor when I tug it closer to the bed. "Surprise," I give him a cumbersome smile. "I'm here."

His gaze dances across my face. "You really are."

My stomach is laden with butterflies as he takes me in, the heat of his stare making me spark with anticipation. He used to look at me like that all the time. With this underlying affection begging to peek its way out and be seen.

I point to his food. "Not hungry?"

He shrugs his non-injured shoulder and blinks. "My stomach is still woozy from the pain meds. Doc says it's normal, but I have a hard time eating a lot in one sitting. That, and, the food around these parts isn't exactly Michelin star quality."

I grimace. "That bad?"

"Let's just say I'd rather drink that peanut butter and jelly smoothie you love so much."

My stomach swoops from the memory of sitting across from him and sharing drinks at Sweet Smoothies. "Careful what you wish for," I tell him with light humor. "Or you might find one materializing in front of you. *Poof.* Out of thin air."

"If you're the reason for it magically appearing, then by all means, I'll drink down every last drop."

I grin. "Sure you would."

"I'd endure a lot more than a smoothie to keep you around, Vi," he murmurs.

I drop my gaze, fumbling the sleeves of my sweatshirt as a warmth breaks out over my skin.

"I didn't mean to make you uncomfortable," Colson mumbles. "I'm just glad you're here."

"No, it's, uh…" I look up at him, pushing away the need to crawl onto his bed next to him. "It's okay." I change the subject, remembering why I'm here. *Because Finn said he had a panic attack.* Or something a hell of a lot like one.

"How are you feeling?" I ask. "You look tired but like you're getting stronger every minute."

"Well, I'm basically imprisoned in this goddamn bed. I piss through a tiny tube, and my entire left side feels like it fought a war my right side knew nothing about."

"And you had to be sedated earlier," I add for him,

watching his face for a reaction. "Might not want to leave that one out."

His gaze cuts to me as he thinks about how I'd know that. "I told you to stay away from Finn, Violet. He's bad news. When are you going to believe that?"

"I was walking home from class, and he came up to me," I explain. "I didn't seek him out."

"You should've told him to get lost."

"He's worried about you."

"He's worried about his own internal demons. He thinks suddenly being in my life is going to fix his past and make us the brothers he thinks we are. Besides," he adds with a brief pause. "I wasn't sedated. They just gave me anxiety meds to relax."

"You *are* brothers, Colson. Maybe it's in an unconventional way that inconveniences you, but you are."

"Drop it, Vi," he says coldly. "He's the last person I want to talk about, especially with you."

Annoyance flitters over my skin. *Of course he doesn't want to talk about it.*

This isn't what I want. I don't *want* to struggle through important conversations. I need him to talk to me. I need him to trust in me enough to share his buried wounds and personal tribulations.

I hate that I don't know how to make that happen. That we had something so incredibly special that was stripped away by the storm clouds that rolled in above us. They're a permanent fixture, dangling with the most conniving smirks on their emotionless faces just because they can.

I lean back in my seat, feeling resigned. "Fine, Colson. We don't have to talk at all."

I reach for my bag propped on the floor and dig out my notebook for class. I'm boiling with unadulterated irritation but trying like hell to shift my focus to something that will mellow me out.

Two minutes go by before he says, "Jesus, Violet, put your book away." It sounds like an order, but it's not a very demanding one.

"If you don't want to talk, then I'll keep myself busy," I retort.

"Why'd you come then? When it's clear you don't even want to fucking be here. You want to study for your bullshit classes then go do it at home."

I nibble on the corner of my lip because *how fucking dare he.*

I'm here for his own well-being, whether he knows it or not. I wonder if he knew, if he'd change his tune, if he'd treat me with a little more kindness. If he'd stop looking at me like he suddenly doesn't want me next to him.

Our eyes connect when I look up, my notebook resting on my lap. "You can be a real jerk sometimes, you know that? I'm here because I want to be."

"Fuck, I'm sorry," he breathes out, annoyed with himself, as his eyes fall closed. "It's the meds. They make everything feel like so much more than it is." His voice softens, and he opens his eyes to look at me. "Still, you don't need to be here, Vi. I'll be good on my own. Go home," he says in defeat with a gentleness he didn't have a minute ago.

When he turns his attention back to the movie on the TV, I get this urge to rip the screen off the wall and toss it out the window when he pretends like I'm not sitting in the chair next to him anymore.

All along, I've only ever wanted to be there for him. I wanted to stand by his side and help him through the hardships because I *love* him. I've tried communicating with him time and time again for him to repeatedly push me away and tell me he didn't want me anymore. *This is why I didn't want to come and put myself back out there.*

My tongue rolls over the fronts of my teeth, and I let out an exasperated breath. Emotion claws at my heart and clutches it in a fine grasp when I don't force it away. The heartbreak I've worked so hard to get over circles me.

I shove my notebook back into my bag and stand. I hoist the strap of my bag over my head and walk for the door. If he doesn't want me here, then fine, I'll leave. Finn can figure this out on his own.

My hand curls around the door handle, ready to yank it open and be free, except Colson's voice tackles me from behind. "Violet, wait." There's a sincerity in it but also this pleading undertone that voices how much he needs me to listen. "Please," he mutters. "I'm sorry I'm being an asshole. I don't want you to leave. I don't want to watch you walk out that door and be left with the guilt that'll consume me when I realize how much I've fucking ruined what was between us."

My hand pulses on the cool metal handle. I debate ignoring him and walking out, similar to the night of his accident when I received his text. Until I remember what followed; the horrific news of him being hurt.

I turn back around and ask him the one thing that has been prodding me in my sides ever since. I want to know why he sent that message. "Why did you want to meet up with me?"

Confusion slips over his features, taking some of the heartbreak that was present in his tone. "Meet up with you?"

Grabbing my phone out of my sweatpants pocket, I lift it and show it to him. "You sent me a message the night of your accident. Don't you remember?"

"Oh, shit," he sighs. "I forgot about that."

"You said you wanted to meet up and talk. Why? What

did you want to talk about? I need to know so I can gain clarity or closure. Something other than what I've been feeling."

His teeth scrape over his bottom lip and he asks, "What are you feeling?"

I shake my head, glancing away before settling back on him. There's a wide berth between me and his bed. One I don't plan on closing anytime soon. "Like what we had was nothing. Like you don't want me here. Like we're not worth fighting for. Like if I walk away now, it'll be the end of whatever is left of us."

"So, then don't walk away."

"Colson, I—"

"No, look at me."

"I am looking at you. A minute ago, you told me to go home. Now you're telling me to stay. It's so fucking confusing. I don't know what to think or feel when I'm in the same room as you because I don't…"

His capable hand fists the bed sheets below him. "Because you don't what?"

"Because I don't know if you want me. And not just in that way, but in any capacity. I've tried to be there, and you've shoved me to the side so many times I physically can't take it again."

He imprints a slash over his bottom lip when he bites into it again. "Will you please come over here? I don't want to have this conversation with you a million miles away."

I nod subtly, swinging my bag onto the chair I was sitting on and stand next to his bed.

"Sit down?"

Squeezing my butt on the sliver of space at the edge of his bed, he lifts his right hand over my legs, resting it on my outer thigh. My stomach erupts with a volcanic level of nerves when he grazes his hand over me and gently digs his fingers into my covered skin.

"Why is it you're always wearing sweats when I'm desperate to feel you?" he whispers, blue gaze set on mine.

"Colson," I murmur, because now isn't the time to comment on my outfit of choice or how thick the fabric might be.

"I know, I'm sorry." He rubs his palm up my leg again until it's high enough to hook his fingers into my pocket. "I do want you, Vi. There's not a day in my life since I've met you that I haven't wanted you. I thought we'd both be better off if I pushed you away. I couldn't fucking think straight after finding out about my mom. I wanted it all to fade to black, and I couldn't risk the same happening with you, so I let you go," he explains.

My chest caves with the intensity of his words and stare.

He's so freaking handsome, even in this bed, even with cuts and bruises smattering his face.

"I want you in *every* capacity, baby. My body aches every time I think about you just to be reminded that you're nowhere near. Everything good that exists inside of me is there because of you. I don't want to fight with you. For the first time in a long time, I have clarity. I texted you because I want you back. I want every goddamn piece of you. You're mine. You always will be in my head. And you're right, what we have—or had—*was* special. I was an idiot to ever throw it away, but I can see clearly now, and you're all I fucking want. You're all I've ever wanted."

I reach up and carefully cover his cheek with my hand. His hair is longer, and I run my fingers into it gently, making sure not to hurt him. "Colson," I choke out. "I've waited a long time to hear everything he just said, but…I don't know if it's too late.

"Don't say my name like that, Violet. Like you're already halfway out the door and can't get away fast enough. Please let me drag you back into my life. I want you in my orbit. For fucking ever, I swear."

He unhooks his fingers from my pocket and runs his hand up my extended arm. He goes up until his fingers smooth over the chunkiness of my sweatshirt and his palm fastens to the side of my neck, drawing me closer.

His gaze bounces around my face until his eyes drop to my lips and stay there. "You're so fucking pretty, Vi. It makes me insane, knowing you're so close but so goddamn far away." His thumb trails over my bottom lip. "Put your walls down. I know they're there because of me, but I need you to tell the army to stand down. Tell them I'm done hurting you. Tell them..." he swallows, and I commend his ability to stay focused because I'm barely hanging on myself.

My lungs are so close to giving out after not drawing in a breath for far too long. My heart thumps in my chest, pounding out a beat like the paws of a cheetah running at full speed.

"Tell them what, Colson?" I whisper, running my fingertips over a scattering of scratches under his lashes.

"Tell them I'm so fucking incredibly in love with the girl they guard. And that they'd be doing a disservice to mankind by not allowing me to love her the way she deserves."

Someone must tie a string to my heart because it's suddenly out of my chest and floating with the likes of the clouds. He pulls my face a smidge closer, and yes, I'm dying for him to kiss me, but the logical, fearful side of my brain has me pumping the brakes.

"You love me?" I question, because I need to hear it again.

"Like you wouldn't believe," he whispers in a brittle voice.

"I..."

"You don't have to say it back, Vi. That's not why I said it. I said it because it's how I feel. I am lost when it comes to you. I'm sorry it's taken me so damn long to get here."

I drown in the deep blue of his gaze. "No, that's not what I was going to say. I'm scared, Colson."

"I know, baby. But I promise, I'm going to be better. It's okay if you need time and proof to believe that. We don't have to write anything in stone. I won't force you to be here if you don't want to be, but I would fucking love it if you were."

I nod, unable to take my eyes off him. "It might take a little bit of time." Between Webber and everything with Colson, my heart needs time to catch up, and to be sure it's no longer in a danger zone.

"I understand." He applies pressure to my neck, a silent nudge for me to cut away more of the space between our mouths. I follow his lead because I'm helpless when it comes to him.

"Thank you," I mutter.

When we're centimeters from touching, he hums, "You're welcome, baby."

His lips smooth over mine in the slowest of ways a beat later. They're soft and sweet and exactly how I remember them. His stubble cuts into my chin, but in a way that is mind-blowingly delicious. A groan tumbles out of his mouth and into mine when I skim my tongue against his. His fingers tangle in the hair at the nape of my neck. The slight pull of them tugging at the strands ignites a flurry of arousal through every inch of me while simultaneously mending my cracked heart. It soars from the dark depths of deprivation.

My heart squeezes when he pulls away and nuzzles his nose against mine. He presses one more kiss to my lips then rests back, his eyes glazed over with an emotion I know all too well but haven't seen in forever—affection. "I fucking love your lips."

"These old things?" I tease, pointing at them.

"There's nothing old about them," he quips, staring at them. "They're the perfect combination of pink, wet, and plump. Enough to heal. See." He lifts his slinged arm and gives it a tiny jostle like it doesn't trigger excruciating pain in his collarbone.

"Colson!" I chide. "Don't do that."

"Ah, yeah," he winces, gently pulling his arm back close to his chest. "They're more of a five-to-seven day treatment plan than an instantaneous cure."

I shake my head at him, smiling. "So," I mull, running my fingers over the softness of his hospital gown. "Are you going to tell me what happened earlier?"

He stares at me. "I don't want to," he admits. My heart falls like a house of cards and a frown pulls at my lips. "But I will because I can't relive you walking away from me with that look of disappointment you had in your eyes earlier." Hope blossoms in my chest, because *finally*, we're making progress. "I've seen it too much and this look you're sporting now? Way fucking better."

FIFTY-NINE

COLSON

SHE'S BACK.

Violet is back in my arms. Well, not literally but she's within reach, sitting in the chair next to my hospital bed where she was last night and is again this morning. Her notebook is out on her lap, and she's scribbling something from the textbook that's propped up on my good leg. I can't help but stare at her every minute I can.

So much has happened, and once again, I can't believe I thought it'd be better for me to push her away than bring her in close and tuck her under my side. Last night when I told her how I felt, I half expected her to give me the middle finger and leave after what I put her through.

Some might say I'm downright undeserving of her, and normally I'd agree, but I can't live in that mindset when it nearly took her from me for good.

I *need* her, and I'll do every damn thing I can to hold onto her every single day of my life. I hope I proved that to her last night when I told her about my nurse coming in yesterday with anxiety meds to calm my ass down. Between that and a nap, it was enough to short-circuit the panic that loomed low in my gut.

All because of Tommy and Clyde.

Those fucking Lincolns. I'm convinced they'll always be at my neck, trying to take something from me. I'm hoping that fades with time. Violet is convinced that Finn means well. I don't know how she can believe that after telling her what he did to me. He hasn't been a topic of conversation since yesterday, and I'd like to keep it that way, but my luck gets cut short when he waltzes into the room.

With a duffel bag hanging from his shoulder, he pulls me away from gazing at my girl. "Morning, stud," he jests, though I don't want to hear it. He's back again after I told him to stay away. The voice of that Russian materializes as he stands at the foot of my bed, reminding me of those three men barging into my room yesterday.

With it comes the startling truth of Tommy putting a hit out on me. All because of my biological father's keen interest in running his mouth in efforts to come out on top.

I could sit here and beat myself up over knowing better than to trust a man like him, but the truth is, I was weak. I was in a bad place, and I wanted to hold onto Mom's memory by having something of hers.

I've come to realize that I don't need it to keep her close. Not when she's all I've ever known. She'll live on in my memories. Only the good ones, I've decided. All the others I've doused in gasoline and set fire to while I've laid in this bed. I only want to know her as the version that came to me in my dream. The version of her from the picture Aunt Bess gave me.

"Again?" I grit out. "Did they fail to check your ears as a kid?"

Finn's gaze cuts to the girl next to me. "Violet," he says, a too cheeky smile on his lips in greeting.

She lowers her pencil and gives him a smile I want for myself. "Hi, Finn."

"See, now, why can't you smile at me like that when I enter the room?"

Ah, so he's in that kind of mood today. He was barking up an entirely different tree yesterday. I'm not sure which annoys me more. Him, today or yesterday.

I decide I dislike both and cut to the chase. "Do I need to plaster a picture of you in the wing so the nurses know not to let you enter?"

"Can try," he comments, pulling the bag off his shoulder and unzipping it. "But you might want me to stick around." He tilts the bag in my direction. I have to squint to see it's filled with cash.

My gaze jerks back to his face. "What the hell is that for?"

A wary sickness clusters in my stomach, and I think, *not again.* I will not get swept into another deal with Finn Lincoln. I'd rather take my chances with Tommy, which says a fuckton.

"Oh, I don't know, how about the beefy motherfuckers who had guns pointed at us yesterday. Remember those?" He zips the pocket closed and hoists it onto his shoulder.

"No." I shake my head, my attention dropping to the tray propped in front of me. I reach for my ginger ale to soothe the nauseous fit that's starting. I say it again. "No. Absolutely not."

"That the only word you know these days?" He tips his chin at Vi. "Talk some sense into him before they come back and paint the wall with his goddamn brains."

"Colson—"

"No, Violet. I'm not taking money from him."

"He wants to help you," she tells me. I don't know what he did to manipulate her into thinking he's one of the good guys when, in reality, he's only a step down from Tommy.

"The hell he does." I look back at him when she stands and comes to my side, swinging her leg up onto the mattress. Like yesterday, my hand finds her thigh, and I knead my fingers into her, my frustrations slowly easing just from the touch. "He wants to rope me into another deal with the Lincolns, and I'm not doing it. I told him I was done with him." I turn my words on him. "Remember that? When I said I was finished doing business with you."

"I'm not sparking up a deal with you, idiot," Finn insults. "I'm getting those burly fucks off your back."

"Exactly, and then I'll owe you. Fuck that."

I'm not doing it.

Violet's hand comes up to my neck. She gently runs her fingers across the portion of my collarbone that isn't fucked. Her skin on mine calms the fiery tips burning a path through my body. It's soothing. *Tranquilizing.*

"I never said a word about you owing me shit. In case you haven't seen yourself lately, you're tied to that goddamn bed. There's no way you're going to get up and get them what they need by, let's see, *today*."

Yeah, well that's a given considering I can't walk without assistance. But he's the last person I want in my corner helping me.

"Let him do this for you," Violet murmurs, trying to get me to look into her eyes.

"Violet, I know you might think you know who Finn is, but I'm telling you, you don't. He's no better than Tommy and these guys." I pause for effect, slicing my eyes to Finn. "He broke my finger without blinking twice about it."

"How long is it going to take you to move on from the past?" Finn huffs out.

"An entire goddamn lifetime."

"I'm not taking no for an answer," Finn asserts. "Consider it a peace offering. A different way of saying sorry for all the shit you won't let go."

"I'm not taking a cent from you."

Finn growls, twisting the bag down his arm and flinging it into the wall on the opposite side of the room. "They're going to come back, Colson. Those fucking guys, did they seem like they were just chitchatting yesterday for the hell of wasting their breath?" He lifts his index finger to his temple. "They had a fucking gun pressed to my head just because I was in the same *room* as you. *You* screwed Tommy over, and they want blood, but they're giving you the chance to settle it with money. When are you going to learn to read between the words people say?"

"I did listen, but there's nothing for me to do about it. The money I do have is stuck in a house your father took from me. I wouldn't be surprised if it's long gone by now. I'm not a fucking idiot. Well aware that I'm a sitting duck, but I have no other option than to take my chances and hope Tommy steps off his high horse and forgets about it."

Finn spits out an obnoxious laugh. "You think he's going to *forget*?" He grasps his jaw and spins around, eyes right back on me in the next second. "Real shame for you, Violet. You're in love with a goddamn dumbass."

"We don't want to see you hurting more than you already are," my girl says, her brown eyes full of worry.

"He doesn't want me hurt so he can manipulate me into paying him back, and who the hell knows what else."

"This isn't then," Violet tries to assure me. I can't stop wondering if her care for me travels deeper than her sitting on the edge of my hospital bed looking at me like she is. She said before that she loves me, but would she be utterly wrecked if Tommy came back around and took more of me?

I try to think about what I'd do if I were her and she was me. If she made a series of bad choices that led to her being confined to a hospital bed with an underground fighting lord up her ass, would I tell her to take Finn's money?

My jaw clenches, and I look over at the man who's desperately trying to push his way into my life. "What do you want from me?"

"Fucking nothing," Finn says straightaway, conviction behind every word. "Not a penny. You want me to write that down and get it notarized?"

What's his angle? He has to have one.

But as I watch him, hands on his hips with a look of resignation on his face and like he might actually care, I wonder, for the first time, if maybe there isn't an underlying scheme planned.

What if Finn is being real with me?

What if Violet is right to trust him on this?

What if he wants to pay back Tommy for the simple notion of keeping me whole?

"If I go along with this…"

"I won't ask a fucking thing of you," Finn claims.

A knock sounds at the door and unlike yesterday, our hackles raise. I sit taller in my bed and silently motion for Violet to get into the attached bathroom. I don't want her near Tommy's guys if that's who's walking in.

I swallow the boulder at the back of my throat when I see the three of them, tall as fucking skyscrapers, walk into the small room. This time, they don't pull their guns out. Guess they got their point across yesterday.

The leader of the pack steps forward, eyeballing me. "You have Tommy's money, yes?"

His Russian accent would be cool if he weren't working for a total fucking asshole. I hope Eli knows what he's doing when it comes to his boss. He hasn't been in to see me once, not that I expected it, but I wonder if he even knows what happened.

"If I don't?" I question, toeing the line. I want to see if the same deal is on the table as yesterday because I really don't want to take Finn's money. I'm beginning to realize I might have to.

The Russian brings his thumb up to his neck and slices across it. "Just like we discussed."

"I'm in a fucking hospital bed that Tommy put me in. How does he expect me to get anything for him?"

The Russian shrugs. "Your problem. Not Tommy's."

Finn whips his duffel bag at the guy, but my stomach sinks for an entirely different reason—relief. It whooshes through my veins like the meds I've had every day since my accident.

"There's all of Tommy's goddamn money. This ends his ties with Colson."

"Funny man," Russian smirks as he unzips the bag. "Thinking you set rules." He pushes the cash around, indicating to the two men behind him to count it. They set up shop beside me, using my hovering table as a surface to put stacks of cash on.

I count a couple thousand before my eyes cut to Finn. There's a dark expression on his face, a look of disdain as he regards the Russians. *Is that what he looks like when he's doing deals for Clyde? Emotionless and raw?* I don't need the answer. I remember what his face looked like the day he broke my finger. He didn't have a warm drop of blood in his body that day.

Perhaps having Finn on my side isn't all bad.

The two cash counters nod at their leader.

"They assure all money is there," the man says.

"Just like I said it was," Finn snaps.

My eyes skit to the bathroom door where Violet hides. What would they do if they knew she was inside? Thankfully, I don't find out because they gather at the door, keeping Finn's bag and the cash inside.

The leader speaks, his broken English coming through tenfold. "You no longer step foot in Battleground. Tommy finds you disobey, and he will retaliate with no other option than sending me to break bony little legs."

"Fine," I chirp. Fighting is the last thing I need with Violet back at my side. I was foolish once before, but I'm not willing to risk losing her again over something I need less than her. "He won't see me around."

Just get the fuck out and stay gone.

"Not just yours," The Russian adds, turning to Finn. "I will find you also and wipe that scumbag look off face by breaking you into four. And if you're wondering how possible, trust I've done to many others on Tommy's behalf and will do again. To both of you if you do not understand message loud and clear, yes?" He makes a snapping sound with his mouth. "You will break like twig."

Finn tongues his cheek, glaring at the man threatening dismemberment. "We fucking understand."

"Wonderful," The Russian says and then he's out the door with his guys, leaving my body in a similar flurry of panic. Only this time it's mixed with so much alleviation that I could jump out of this bed and dance like Grandpa Joe from *Charlie and the Chocolate Factory.*

Violet peeks her head out of the bathroom. "All clear?"

"Yeah, baby," I breathe out. "I think we're finally goddamn solid."

Finn stands at the foot of my bed, expelling a tight breath. He scrubs his hand over his face then holds his arms wide. "Looks like we're both on the chopping block if you decide to take your dumbass back to the fighting scene." I glare at him because I have no plans on doing so. That was a lapse in judgment, a mistake I'll never make again now that I have Violet back in close quarters. "Still think I don't give a fuck about you?"

I just scowl at him, ignoring his presence when he sits in the corner and switches his attention to his phone. I don't tell him to leave, but I don't necessarily want him here, either. Then again, he did just spot me thousands of dollars to save my ass from Tommy Lescaro.

So, I let him stay.

SIXTY

COLSON
ONE MONTH LATER

Finn: How're things going?
Colson: Don't tell me you've been domesticated
     and are actually asking about my well-being.
Finn: Shut the fuck up and answer the question.
Colson: I'm fine, now get the hell out of my text
     inbox.
Finn: Whatever you say, Brother.

SEBASTIAN TOSSES the controller on the coffee table. It skips over the polished surface and lands on the carpeted floor. I chuckle over his ensuing tantrum.

"The fuck was that for?" he asks.

"You were camping," I tell him, clutching my chest in amusement.

"The hell I was. I was waiting until I figured out my next plan of attack."

That makes me laugh harder. "Yeah, that's the literal definition of camping."

He turns, pointing at me with a look of accusation. "You were looking at the map, weren't you? You only knew where I was because you cheated, you asshole."

I toss my head back on the couch, laugh after boisterous laugh coming out of me.

Since being released from the hospital a month ago, I've stayed with Aunt Bess and Uncle Thad. I needed twenty-four hour care since I'm in a wheelchair. As much as I wanted to burrow myself into Violet's pocket the day I was released and go home with her, I couldn't.

I didn't want to burden her with my injuries or having to help me to the bathroom in the middle of the night. Besides, it's been good for Aunt Bess and me to have time together. We're slowly working on mending our relationship.

I'm finding my forgiveness when it comes to her keeping Clyde from me. The deal I made with him that he rescinded on helped a lot, showing me the type of person he truly is, even if I did already somewhat know. It put me in close proximity with him for a short amount of time. Enough for me to realize that she did right by paying him off to stay the hell away.

Sebastian has been keeping me company in between Violet coming over to hang out. We took it slow the first two weeks, but our relationship has definitely progressed these last few days. I can't go more than an hour without talking to her. It annoys the hell out of me when she's in class and her texts are sporadic in timing. Worse, when she's at the daycare and can't respond at all. But I stay patient because it's who she is. Finishing college and doing something with her life is important to her. I haven't told her yet, but I secretly look up to her because of it. How she hasn't let everything that's happened derail her like it did me.

It's why I plan on registering at the closest community college as soon as I'm able to get around on my own. Gone are the days of succumbing to Harrison Heights and not being much more than a piece of gum stuck on the bottom of a shoe.

I want a life for myself that makes me proud when I look in the mirror. I want to be part of a bigger picture. One that doesn't involve crime, paying people money, or drug addictions.

"What's going on in here?" Aunt Bess asks, coming into the room with a plate of Sebastian's favorite: M&M's cookies. The fucker swipes the tower of them when they're within reach and walks away, shoving one in his mouth. "Those are for the three of you," Aunt Bess scolds.

"Three?" There's only two of us, unless she's counting Sebastian's sore loser side of his normally easy-going personality.

"Yes," she smiles down at me. "You have a visitor."

Violet walks in from the foyer then, trailing around Aunt Bess like she's done a million other times since I was released from the hospital. This moment is the best part of each of my days. Seeing her walk in after being separated all day, her mouth tipping up at the corners when she sees me. Her in those tight little leggings she wears all the time. She knows they drive me crazy, that I can't do anything about it for another few weeks because I've been prohibited by my doctor.

My collarbone is almost in the green and fully healed. My leg still has a bit to go and remains casted. The second the doc gives me the go ahead with my shoulder, I plan on dragging her onto my lap, regardless of the status of my leg, and letting her straddle me for a solid hour. Maybe more.

Yeah, that's exactly what I want—the real thing.

Violet in my bed, her wrapped around me, my hand smacking and kneading that juicy, delicious ass.

"Don't trust him, Violet!" Sebastian shouts with a mouthful of cookie, crumbs flying out of his mouth. "He's a traitor."

"Ignore him," I tell Violet, giving Seb my middle finger when his mom shakes her head and leaves the room. I think she likes having a full house again, Sebastian and me screwing around like we used to all the time as kids.

I grab Violet's hand from my perch on the couch and steer her toward me. Sebastian grumbles and leaves the living room, too. Situating her between my legs, I gently pull her down on my lap and kiss her.

"Colson," she says in warning, holding up half her weight. "I don't want to hurt you."

"You're not," I murmur, sprinkling kisses down the side of her neck and under her chin. "You're perfect right where you are."

"Where am I supposed to put my hands? Your collarbone isn't healed yet."

"It practically is," I muse, running my tongue over the sweet spot behind her ear she melts over.

"It's not. Oh, God," she moans, my dick twitching from the breathy little moan she lets out. "Why are you doing this to me?"

This.

She means torturing her with my mouth. The same thing she's done to me since she kissed me that first time in my hospital room.

"What's the matter, Violet?" I rumble, willing her to tell me just how badly she wants me.

She pulls on my ear, but only because she's afraid she'll hurt me if she slaps my chest. I rear back, grinning up at her like a damn fool. Because I am one. I am completely smitten with this girl. Head over heels in love with her.

"You're doing it on purpose. Trying to get me turned on in your aunt's house. What is wrong with you?" she asks, a playful undertone in her words.

"A lot is wrong with me," I comment. "But lucky for us, I know exactly what'll fix it."

She runs her hand down my neck and toys with the neckline of my T-shirt. My arm is still in a sling, so I use my other hand to grip her hip and drag her center over exactly where I need her.

Her eyes turn heady and her pretty lips part. "Well," she lets out. "Are you going to tell me?"

I knead her waist. "Patience is a virtue, Vi."

"Colson."

"I was going to say…" I pause, drawing it out. "That my cure would be you on your knees, those gorgeous brown eyes looking up at me while you give me those lovely lips."

She tilts her head to the side. I take it as an opportunity to lick my way up her throat. We haven't gotten physical outside of her grinding on me once or twice since we made up. Every time I convince her to sit on my lap, she stays for all of a minute before she's up, too afraid she'll hurt me.

Yesterday, we made out for an hour and a half until my blue balls couldn't take it anymore. She helped me into my wheelchair, and I rolled into the bathroom so I could finish myself off. It took all of two minutes.

"You'd like that, wouldn't you?" she muses in that flirty tone of hers.

"No, baby. I'd fucking *love* it. I fucking love *you.*"

She smiles against my lips when she comes in close to kiss me. My chest soars with the promise of a lifetime with her. I wouldn't mind that. Spending the rest of my days with my heart in a similar shaped box, hers for safekeeping.

"It never gets old hearing you tell me that," she whispers, running her tongue along the seam of my lips before flicking it against mine.

A fiery pressure builds in my groin.

I pull away. "You have me rock hard."

She swivels her hips over me. "I know. I can feel you."

"Ah, fuck, baby," I groan, imaging what it'll be like when I finally get inside of her.

She brings her mouth close to my ear, and my stomach rolls with the anticipation of what she's going to say. I hope it's something dirty. I hope she's gearing up to tell me how goddamn drenched her pussy is or maybe that she can't wait to be on all fours taking me.

My breaths turn shallow and my dick throbs in my sweat-pants. She drags her weight over me again, and I nearly come in my pants from the contact—that's how much I need her.

Her breath fans over my ear and she says, "I'm going to go see if Bess needs help in the kitchen."

Damn it.

She's up and off of me before I have the chance to grab on and keep her on top of me. "Why the hell would you go and do that?"

"Because she cooks for us every night," Violet tells me, bending to give me one last kiss before sauntering away. I stare at her ass until she disappears into the kitchen. I don't bother wiping the smile off my face once she's gone.

"I CAN'T BELIEVE I'm doing this for you. Remind me again why I agreed to bring you here," Sebastian grumbles from beside the car. I opened the passenger door as soon as he parked. I'm currently watching him struggle setting up my wheelchair. When he finally secures it, he rolls it over to me. It's been a hassle getting in and out of vehicles since I'm down a leg and arm, which is why he was the one I asked to bring me to Gulliver's. Aunt Bess can't hold my weight as well as he can.

"Stop bitching and moaning and help me," I tell him as I reach for the door handle. He comes over to my side and lets me lean into him. He holds my good side as I swivel down into the wheelchair. He pushes the passenger door shut and toes off the wheelchair brakes.

"I should make you wheel yourself in just for the hell of it. Getting kind of tired of you bossing me around." His tone drops as if he's mimicking me. "Sebastian, do this for me. Sebastian, do that for me. Sebastian, take me to Gulliver's."

I grin at his antics, knowing for a fact it hasn't been like that. If anything, he's the one that pesters me. He's just like Aunt Bess in that way. Always making sure I'm okay. I fucking love him for it, but still, I quip back, "Trash talking doesn't look good on you, Seb, and it'd be an awful shame to lose a modicum of that charm you carry around. What would all the females do without it?"

"Shut the fuck up," he jests. I've been getting on his case a lot lately when it comes to dating. Mostly because it's been forever since the guy has had any female attention. He's a ten out of ten, so I'm just wondering why he's not more adamant about it like every other guy his age.

I guess, in the grand scheme of things, what I'm wondering most is when the time will come that he'll meet *his* Violet. Someone who's there to take care of him while he's so busy trying to be there for everyone else.

Just to get on his nerves, I put my good foot on the ground, skimming my shoe on the pavement as he pushes me toward the entrance. It's my newest favorite pastime since I've been in the thing for the simple fact that it bugs the hell out of him. My foot snags and slows us down.

The wheelchair skids, pulling to one side. My shoulders hunch in preparation for what I know is coming next—a slap to my head, aka Sebastian's go to reaction when I pull this stunt on him.

"Ouch, what the fuck?" I chuckle even though it doesn't hurt one bit. He always smacks me soft enough to get his annoyance across but never enough to harm me or my injuries.

"Don't start with me or I'll leave you here. Let Llewellyn deal with your ass."

My brow arches as he gets me past the entrance door. "Then who would put up with your sore loser attitude at all times of the day and night?"

I can hear the smirk on his face when he replies, "Hmm, Violet wouldn't be too hard to teach."

"Fuck you." I don't really mean it but only because I know he doesn't really mean it.

Once inside, Kelsie greets us from the other side of the front desk. She leans on the countertop, looking down over the edge with a wave. "Hi. Welcome to Gu—oh, it's just you."

"It's just you," Sebastian repeats with amusement. "What the hell did you do to her to get that kind of reaction?"

I ignore my cousin and nod my chin at Llewellyn's niece. I admit that I could've been nicer to her in the past, but there's no rewinding time now. "Hey, Kelsie."

"Ah, so he does know how to say hello." I don't get to reply because in the next breath she informs me, "If you're looking for my uncle, he's back in the locker rooms putting a load of wash in because someone hasn't shown his face in weeks."

Damn. She almost strikes me speechless. I was expecting a shy, reserved Kelsie. The girl who waves as people come and go. Not this version with a sharp tongue and quips strong enough to riddle a guy with guilt and knock him on his ass. Maybe I was all wrong about her. Maybe she's not as quiet as I thought.

Sebastian steps around the wheelchair. "Kelsie, is it?"

She nods, and I'm hoping like hell Sebastian gives it straight back to her. Instead, he grins at her. "What do you say we take you home with us just to help keep this one in line?"

Her forehead rolls with an emotion I can't place since I don't know her that well. "Um...no thank you?"

I roll my eyes. "Ignore him," I tell her. "He's not usually so..."

"Charming?" Sebastian supplies.

"No, obnoxious. We're going to go talk to Llewellyn now. Let's go, Seb."

"See what I mean," he whispers at my back, surely for Kelsie. "Bossy. All the fucking time."

I glance over my shoulder to see a small smile appear on her lips as he pushes me away. Pointing in the direction of the locker rooms, Sebastian deposits me inside when we catch sight of the man I'm here to see. Llewellyn knows I haven't been medically cleared to work again, but I wanted to come see him, anyway. A lot has happened, and I want him to know how much I appreciate him trying to help me all those weeks ago. I also need to apologize for going MIA on him and not letting him know sooner about my accident.

Sebastian pats my shoulder, leaving me next to a bench, then walks back out to the gym area. I wouldn't be surprised if he found his way back to the pretty redhead at the front counter.

"Colson, my boy," Llewellyn greets, extending a palm to shake mine. He drops down into my space and gives me the best hug he can with the hunk of metal under me. "Wasn't sure when I'd see you again."

I drop my chin. "I know, I'm sorry I didn't call you sooner." After my accident, I waited a full two weeks before I called with the news. So, to him, it appeared like I just stopped showing up.

He sinks down onto the bench nearby. "Don't fret. Your aunt called to let me know what was going on."

I just stare at him because I had no idea she did that. Then again, it's not that hard to believe. Aunt Bess has always had my best interests at heart. Now is no different, I guess. But also… "You didn't mention that during our phone call."

"I didn't?"

"No." I let out a laugh.

"Wanted to keep ya on your toes a bit." I shake my head at him. "Ya know, help you learn from your mistakes and all that."

I hum in response.

"Have you?"

"Have I what?"

"Learned from your mistakes."

I suck my bottom lip into my mouth and make sure I'm

looking him in the eye when I say, "Yeah, I have. Turns out rock bottom wasn't what I thought it was. All those weeks ago when we talked about it...I thought I was there, but there was still room to fall."

He crosses his arms across his chest. "And? Did it hurt when you finally landed?"

I motion to my body. The very one that's still healing. "What do you think?"

"I think you never go through stuff unless you're meant to learn some kind of lesson from it. It's those experiences where you gain wisdom, Colson."

I understand that now. I sacrificed my own happiness for a long time because of it. But I'm done doing that now. I'm ready for a new beginning. One that includes healing, Violet, and everything in my life that feels good.

Curiosity gets the best of me. "How long did it take you to pick yourself back up when you hit?"

"It's not about the time it takes to get back up," he explains with a contemplative gleam in his eye. "It's about what you make of yourself in those moments and what comes after the resurrection. It's about what it *gives* you."

"Yeah? What did your resurrection provide for you?"

He looks at me for a long moment then stands. I almost don't even think he's going to give me an answer until his hand falls on my shoulder and he gives it a reassuring squeeze. One that I only ever thought I'd get from a father growing up yet comes from the man who has always given me his kindness and time.

I don't recall ever really choosing Llewellyn that first time we talked. Not that it matters because he chose me. He chooses every person who steps foot in this place. And for the first time in my life, my mom's struggles feel like a blessing. In some odd way, despite all the heartache and grief it caused, it gave me this man. A person I would've never known otherwise. A person who has helped me understand that I don't have to be what I came from, that I can rise from the hardships a brand new person and do it in a way that brings peace.

I glance up when he doesn't immediately answer. I'm met with his cauliflower ear and the side of his meaty neck. It isn't until he shifts his chin down that I notice the mistiness in his gaze. "My resurrection gave me Gulliver's. It gave me every single person who has stepped foot inside since I opened its doors. And…it gave me you."

His words simmer in the form of a rolling boil inside of me when he heads back out into the main gym area. Not because I'm angry or anything. Outside of the little family I have and Violet, I've never had a person admit how much of a blessing it is to have me in their life.

My heart staggers, nearly face planting in my chest from the impact of his admission. I sit there and take it, allowing the love from his words to consume me in a way I normally push away. I relent, surrender, and accept it for what it is while telling myself it's okay. I'm deserving enough to have people out there who care about me. People outside of Aunt Bess, Sebastian, and Uncle Thad.

When the door swings open a minute later, I expect to see Sebastian ready to wheel me back out to the car. But it's Eli who does a double take, ignores me, and makes his way over to one of the lockers.

After my accident, I never did get a text or call from him asking how I was doing. It was radio silent where Eli was concerned, and I'm beginning to see how okay I am with that. Because I don't want people in my life who turn their back on me as soon as life gets a little fucking hard. And I certainly don't want someone who has ties to Tommy Lescaro in my corner. Not after the dude put a hit out on me and burned my trust to the ground.

"I don't even get a hello?" I ask, resting my good hand on the wheel of my chair. "Or a, wow, glad to see you're alive?"

He pops a locker door open, his tone emotionless when he repeats back, "Glad to see you're alive."

I lick my lips and drop my head. "I thought you were better than this."

His back stiffens at my barb, his movement halting for a split second before he toys with something inside the locker. It's hard to see what it is when the door and most of his body blocks my view.

"You don't want to talk, fine," I reply. I can't force him to have a conversation with me nor can I expect him to show up for me in ways others have. Eli was always a means to an end for me. A way to get out the emotions that took over every ounce of my being. But I'd be lying if I said it doesn't mildly sting that he doesn't look me in the eyes as he dismisses me.

It's on the tip of my tongue to warn him the same way Finn did me about Tommy. I have no doubt he'd step on his other fighters if the opportunity arose, but...Eli is a big guy. If he can write me off without the decency of acknowledging me as more than a simple glance, then so be it.

Sebastian pushes into the back room with the remnants of a cheeky grin on his face. He notices Eli in the room with me. He doesn't have the pleasure of knowing the role he played in my life. That he was the one who got me into The Battleground. I sure as shit don't clue him in now.

He walks behind me and grabs the handles of the wheelchair, pulling me back toward the door. "Ready to go?"

"Yeah," I tell him, my eyes still glued to Eli's back. "Get me the hell out of here."

SIXTY-ONE

VIOLET
THREE MONTHS LATER

I FLICK my turn signal on, pulling into Spring Meadows. Spring is finally taking effect, the trees regrowing their leaves. The flowers in the beds around the entrance of the apartment building are beginning to blossom, too. I imagine Mom's garden is starting to come to life as well with the warmer weather and longer days.

I make an internal note to call her sometime this week and pull into a space next to Sebastian's Aviator. He slips out of it when I turn off my ignition, and then I see him.

Colson.

My boyfriend.

The man I don't just love but am in love with.

Putting into words how grateful I am over how well he's doing has been hard for me. Every time I see him walking around, without that pesky sling on his arm, I think about how happy I am to have him in my life.

We took it slow those first few weeks, but our relationship has gotten increasingly better as each week passes. He wouldn't be moving into my apartment with me if things weren't looking up, and my trust in him wasn't restored.

He's done a complete one-eighty since Janie passed away. I know it still bothers him. He has times where grief grabs hold of him, and he's quiet for the better part of the day, but so long as he's not running away or pushing me out of his life, I'm okay with that.

I give him space on those days and pray for the ache in his heart to hurt a little less as each one passes. Sometimes I think it works. Other times I wonder if the effort is futile, if he'll still always feel exactly what he's meant to.

His family has been more than supportive, his aunt having been the one to take care of him post-release from the hospital. Aside from weekly physical therapy visits for his leg, he's all healed up, the terrible bruising that painted his face also gone.

Tommy, those Russian bodyguards he sent, and Clyde haven't come around at all. The cops never did find the vehicle that hit him that night, but I think we're all just thankful that Colson is happy and healthy and finally letting himself live his life.

Finn even went MIA for a bit, only popping his head around again in the last two weeks or so. Colson is still getting used to having him around, but I think it was reassuring seeing Finn put himself and his own money on the line to get him out of trouble. They have a long way to go, but creating a foundation as brothers has to start somewhere.

Climbing out of the driver's seat, I wave to Sebastian and find Colson at the other side of Sebastian's vehicle. He wraps me in his arms when I walk up and nuzzle my face in the crook of his neck; one of my favorite places.

"Hey, baby," he murmurs, squeezing me with all the love in his body. "Missed you."

"How was therapy?" Sebastian took him this afternoon

because my morning schedule was overridden with classes followed by an afternoon at the daycare.

"Gave them a run for their money."

I pull back and grin. "Just what I like to hear."

He spins me and backs me against the car door.

"Ah man, can't you two wait until we get upstairs?" Sebastian complains.

I grin because Colson and I are very affectionate. If we're near each other, we're constantly touching, kissing, grazing our hands over one another.

"Tell me how much you missed me," he says to me, and I know it's only because of his own internal struggles; the need to hear that I want him and love him daily.

"I'd rather not tell you," I mewl. "Showing you would be way more fun."

He cocks a brow at me and brings his lips to my ear. "Are you wet for me, Violet?" He drops his hand down between my legs like we're not in public. The cars on either side of us give us all the privacy we need. "If I slipped my hand in your panties, what would I find?"

"You'd find what's yours," I breathlessly whisper back.

"Mmm, mine. Now, that, I like the sound of."

I suck my bottom lip into my mouth and bite down. "We can christen my room after we get your stuff moved over," I suggest, wanting nothing more than to get wrapped up in my sheets with him.

Colson chuckles. "You mean like what we've done every night this past week?"

"Exactly that."

He pulls back and gives me his handsome smile. "I tell you today how fucking beautiful you are?" he asks, tugging at my braids over my shoulders.

"You told me this morning," I remind him. His daily

compliments are almost too much for me to handle, especially when he looks at me as if he never wants to spend a day with anyone else.

"Yo!" comes a voice from the front of the car. "Fuck, are they sucking face again?"

"Yep," Sebastian confirms, his back to us. He gives Finn a fist pound, and I can't help but turn back to Colson to ask what's going on.

"You invited Finn?"

He shrugs a shoulder. "Needed more arm power to lift the heavy stuff."

I smolder a laugh, giving him an amused expression. "You barely have anything to bring down to my apartment. In fact, I think the heaviest thing you own is a trash bag full of clothing."

"Can't lift heavy items," Colson says to me. "Doctor's orders, baby."

He says that but really Colson Moore is finally warming to the idea of having Finn around. "Could it be that you're just looking for quality brotherly bonding time?" I accuse, lifting my brow at him this time.

"I've told you both a million times, he's not my brother."

I roll my eyes. He's been stuck on that line for months, but we all know it's only because it's easier to say that than admit he might actually like having another person around.

"Hi, Finn!" I shout from where we're hidden between cars. "Colson was just telling me how excited he is to see you."

Colson shakes his head at me and promises punishment later. "I hope you're wearing that red thong I like because your ass is going to match it by the time I'm done with you."

"Come on, guys!" yells Sebastian. "We got shit to do."

My phone buzzes in my pocket, and I slip it out as Colson

rounds the front of the car and bumps Finn's fist the same way Sebastian did. I find a missed text from Olive that I plan to answer later and a new one from Everleigh, who messages to say she won't be able to make our pizza outing as a group later after we get Colson's belongings moved.

Since Sylvia left and we haven't heard a word from her, we figured it'd be best to move forward with plans to rent out her room. Colson agreed to move into mine to help with the expensive rent bill as well as our commutes back and forth from his aunt's house. But even with him living with us, we'll have to find a roommate to fill Sylvia's room come September.

A worry for another day, I decide, as I lift my gaze and catch sight of Webber on an adjacent sidewalk heading in the opposite direction of Spring Meadows. He's with a group of girls and guys, Tristan included, and raises a single finger in greeting when our eyes meet. Outside of a waved hello at Sebastian's New Year's Eve party and our conversation at the gym, it's been quiet between us, and I can appreciate that. What we had is in the past, the two of us finally moving on to bigger and better things.

As for Tristan, it's as if he's a stranger. More so when he follows Webber's gaze and doesn't offer a nod in acknowledgement. Like he never even dated one of my best friends and ruined her hopes of what love could be by choosing everything besides her.

I choose to ignore his audacity and pocket my phone to join the guys, relaying how Everleigh isn't coming. Finn pulls me under his arm when I fall in step between him and Colson. He gives me a quick side hug, ruffling my hair like a big brother would, before Colson tugs me over to him, and tucks his hand into the back pocket of my jeans.

And I just smile to myself.

Because there's no place else I'd rather be.

ALSO BY SARA TALLARY

QUAINT SERIES

I Choose You (friends to lovers)

I Still Love You (second chance)

CHATHAM HILLS SERIES

Beneath the Lies (Book 1, Complicated Truths Duet)

Above the Truths (Book 2, Complicated Truths Duet)

TBA (Book 3)

TBA (Book 4)

ACKNOWLEDGMENTS

To Joshua, the one who will always be first on my acknowledgments page. Your love is unlike anything I've ever experienced. It is selfless, unconditional, and stretches to the lengths of the universe. I feel like the luckiest person in the world to be at the receiving end of it. Even on days when it seems like it's taken for granted and my flaws make themselves known, know that I feel you to the center of my soul and beyond.

To my beta readers, who have not only been there to help me give Colson & Violet the HEA they deserved but for also giving me their friendship. Thank you for your continuous support and giving me a safe place to share these characters.

And lastly, a BIG shout out to everyone who has read Colson & Violet's story and shared it on social media or otherwise. It lights me up to know that I'm not the only one who has fallen in love with this duet. Thank you for being patient with me while finishing this book. Thank you for reminding me that these characters are loved and have a home in your hearts and on your bookshelves. Let's give them the love they need to stay alive for years to come.

Xoxo,

Sara

ABOUT THE AUTHOR

Sara Tallary lives in eastern Pennsylvania with her husband, two kids, and dog. When she isn't spending her days writing or brainstorming new ideas for stories, she's homeschooling her kids, cuddling up with her gorgeous Malinois pups, and binge-watching TV shows with her husband or playing Mario Kart (and winning, hah!). Though she tries to stay on a healthy diet, she has a love for sweets, is constantly adding books to her TBR, and loves a good laugh.

Follow me on social media (@saratallaryauthor) and sign-up for my newsletter for book updates, special offers, and exclusives at: bit.ly/saratallaryauthornewsletter